Endorsen

D1097139

"Deanna Fugett's writing is gritty, fast-paced, and absorbing. Once falling into her stories you'll be pleasantly lost in a well-crafted world where characters explore hard questions and truth resonates deep."

~Brandy Vallance, Award-Winning Author of *The Covered Deep*

"Deanna Fugett seeks to create more than memorable characters. She truly desires for her readers to dig deep within themselves to expose the sort of moral questions that ultimately a faith in God can answer. She hopes that through her writing the audience will not only unearth their own bravery, but know that while evil exists in our world, good will conquer in the end. Her passion for her readers is evident in each sentence she crafts."

~Lauren Brandenburg, Author of the Boone Series,
MG Fantasy

"Fear's struggle to triumph over her broken past is told with honesty and hope in a refreshingly innovative dystopian setting. Her moving journey is one readers won't soon forget!"

~Laurie Lucking, Author of *Common*

"Deanna Fugett has penned a remarkable story of a world in despair and God's steadfast, unfailing love. *Ending Fear* is an excellent tale of grace and grit colliding."

~Lucette Nel, Author of *The Widow's Captive*

"*Ending Fear* is an engrossing, thrilling read! From the first sentence, the reader is plunged into Fear's world. Add this dystopian novel to your library because Deanna Fugett is a bold new voice in speculative fiction."

~J.M. Hackman, Author of *Spark*

"Some stories are meant to lull us to sleep with fantasies in which no one ever sins and nothing bad really happens. Some stories are meant to wake us up to the darkness of sin in a broken world. *Ending Fear* is a riveting, futuristic tale that brings us to our knees in sorrow for the lost and vulnerable, yet still offers hope that no matter how dark our world becomes, God is still active and working through the most unlikely of heroes."

~Robin Scobee, Writer and Blogger at www.quillandinkblotts.wordpress.com

"Deanna Fugett explores how a young girl copes with crippling fear. I loved her sensitive characterization, the fast-paced action, and the redemptive message woven throughout this gritty and realistic tale. Do yourself a favor and pick up a copy of this moving story. Young adult dystopian at its most hopeful!"

~Jebraun Clifford, Winner of ACFW's 2016 Genesis and 2015 First Impressions Contests, Young Adult Category

ENDING
FEAR

Coming Soon:

Living Brave

Book Two of the Gliding Lands

ENDING FEAR

Book One of the Gliding Lands

Deanna Fugett

Love2ReadLove2Write Publishing, LLC
Indianapolis, Indiana

© 2017 Deanna Fugett

Published by Love2ReadLove2Write Publishing, LLC
Indianapolis, Indiana
www.love2readlove2writepublishing.com

Library of Congress Cataloging-in-Publication Data is on file at the Library of Congress, Washington, DC.

ISBN: 1-943788-16-2
ISBN-13: 978-1-943788-16-3
Library of Congress Control Number: 2017946565

Cover Design by Sara Helwe (www.sara-helwe.com)

To Chad,
the one who believes in me the most

Future Earth. The now poverty-stricken western hemisphere.
Farming County. Downer Territory.

Chapter 1

Crouching down in our hovel, I shiver. Hard, cold dirt digs under my fingernails. I can't get away from the dirt. Not out in the fields, not even in my own home. It's everywhere, ingrained in our very existence.

I grip my mat and my nasty, stained pillow. It's the kind no person, if given a choice, would keep around. It would be thrown away in another family. Not ours. If I ever asked for a new pillow, they'd probably set mine on fire and tell me I should've been grateful for the old one. He'd probably be the first to light the flame.

He's out there. The clomping boots are undeniably his. Something in the air stirs as if Pa's very presence agitates the environment around me. Pulling strings of tension through my small room — if you could even call it that — urging me to stay still.

Must stay quiet.

A match flicks on the wall. I cringe as cigar smoke wafts its ugly scent into my small corner. I will never, ever get used to that blasted smell. But if I dare mention it, I'll get a whipping. Nothing I care about matters. It never has.

A door slams. I hold my breath as my mother's footsteps enter our hovel.

"Where have you been?" asks Papa.

Mother's voice quivers. "I was outside, talking with Pernicious."

The clank of something metal hits the wall. "Did I give you permission to talk to Pernicious?"

The nighttime ritual has begun. I swallow hard and slink into the shadows, letting the nook that serves as my sleeping space take me further into its grip. *Become invisible. He'll forget all about you.*

Mother whimpers and gasps in pain. The nauseating stench of burnt flesh meets my nose. Then the hitting starts. More whimpers. My intestines twist into knots with each blow, and I cover my ears. Mother's pain stings my heart. I can't block it. Each *thump*, each *clang* provokes my stomach to empty its contents—which isn't saying much—onto the cold floor. I swallow the vile substance back down.

Make it stop! My neck muscles knot. His rage is never satisfied. Why can't I go to sleep faster so I don't have to endure this torture?

More yelling. More hitting.

Then silence.

Papa trudges off to bed. He lowers himself to the thin mattress on the floor and pulls up the dirty sheet. Mother will probably join him after he's snoring. Why can't I have a mattress too? Selfish jerks.

Hinges squeak as mother opens the liquor cabinet and pulls out her favorite hard drink. Here we go again. Her bony behind hits the kitchen chair with a *thump* as she sits for a night of stupor and wallowing in her own misery. How can they afford that stuff when my brother and I go hungry all the time?

A manic sleep grips me as I drift in and out of nightmares. I'm afraid. I'm always afraid. It's not that strange. My name, after all, is Fear.

Something disturbs me.

I open my eyes. Sunbeams streak through windows and reveal swirling dust. What's going on, and why's it so sunny? Did I sleep in? That's not possible. I'd be beaten if I had.

Where the scraping of pots and pans should be, silence creeps through the thin walls instead. No heavy tread from my papa's and brother's boots. Nothing but my own breathing. Where are they?

I shove my hand through tangled clumps of mud-colored grease some might call hair. If I owned a brush, maybe I could get this mess under control. No such luck. I tug my stained, muddy dress over my hips as a wail of despair reaches my ears.

Running to the door, I spot my brother, papa, and mother standing next to a burly man. Curly chest hair peeks from the top of his shirt. Gross. They stand in a cluster in the middle of the dirt pathway between battered, loosely boarded hovels. Mother sinks to her knees and clings to my brother's pant leg. Wish she'd care a smidge about me too. Hate sneers down at her. He has no respect for the woman. Papa crosses his arms nearby, the same look on his face. Hate learned from the best. Jagged black hair hangs in Hate's face, covering half of it, but there's no denying his disdain.

I step away from the front door. I know better than to speak up. Clouds whisk through sunny blue skies in sharp contrast to the gloomy atmosphere around me. The group shouts and flings their arms around. Maybe I should turn back before they notice me?

The distant city that floats in the sky captures my attention. The Gliding Lands city darkens every blade of grass brave enough to grow beneath it and blackens the rusty soil. What would it be like to live up there? Free from dirt and grime. Free from Papa's fists. To be an Upper? Voices pervade my reoccurring daydream, and my thoughts snap back to earth.

I want to know what they're saying. I have to. Having visitors is usually a bad sign. Especially ones this angry. I sneak closer and pause.

"You can't do this," Mother pleads. "He's only fifteen years old."

"It's too late. It's already done. You don't steal from me and get away with it. This isn't the first time, and I'm not putting up with it anymore." The gruff man snorts. Ah. The local grocer. Beast of a man. "It's set for four o'clock. Sentinels will pick him up at noon. You have until then to say yer goodbyes." The grocer whirls around and stomps off.

My mother lurches forward and grabs his arm. "Please," she begs. "Don't do this to us."

He slaps her, and she falls to the ground, holding her face. My fists clench. As if she isn't beaten enough at home. Papa watches without a word, without action. Of course he does. He's no better.

Papa's glare strikes Hate like lightning bolts. Papa turns and stalks into our hovel. We shuffle forward, following the wolf into his den.

I know what's happened now. Sentinels only pick someone up if they've been Challenged. The grocer Challenged Hate. He's going to the Pen, and he doesn't have a choice.

From the looks of things, he'll never return.

I can't hold back my smile.

Mother spirals into hysterics. "Why is this happening to us?"

Papa brushes past me and shakes his head. "Maybe you should ask your fool of a boy over there."

Hate's slim body fades into the shadows of the wall behind him, his black clothing a camouflage of darkness.

Mother amps up her volume. "He didn't do anything wrong."

She's got to be kidding. He does wrong things all the time.

"He's a thief, and you know it!" Papa roars.

Sweat itches my forehead. I scamper to the sink and reach for the spigot on the container that holds our water supply. Mother paces between the cabinets and the kitchen table. Papa hates when she does that.

"Knock it off!" He grabs her arm. She tries to free herself, but he refuses to let go. "When are you ever going to learn, woman?" He raises his fist, and her body flies to the ground.

Mother!

Hate lets the darkness of the corner swallow him further. I scrub dishes to a sparkly shimmer.

Just work hard, and he'll ignore you.

One swing of his leg, and instead of silencing Mother, Papa furthers her hysteria. She rants and whines in a high pitch so horrid I wish I had cotton to stuff to my eardrums.

Papa redirects his rage toward the shadows. He lunges into the darkness and pulls back, Hate clutched within his sausage-like fingers. "You think you're so smart, boy? You can't even get away with stealing!" He jabs Hate's stomach. "When I was a boy, I never got caught."

His fist collides with Hate's temple. It fails to move me. Boys in the hovels have died that way. Besides, he deserves it. He should've never touched me.

Smack. I hope he dies.

Thud. He drops to the ground.

Maybe Papa will finish him off before he reaches the Pen. Won't the grocer be mad then? I smirk. Pa glances at me. My face goes blank. If he's done with Hate, he'll come after me next. I scrub dishes with so much gusto, I nearly break a plate in two.

I stop myself. *Breathe deep. He's getting out all his anger on Hate. He won't have any left for me. Just breathe.* I pick up a blue-checkered towel and begin drying.

Papa whips my brother from the floor to standing. Hate's lip and eyebrow piercings glimmer as sunlight shines through the acrylic-glass window. Mother retreats to an opposite corner to continue her whining.

Papa turns to her. "Shut up, stupid." He grabs a kitchen chair, raises it over his head, and sends it soaring in her direction.

Stop! My shoulders tense as the object finds its mark. *Don't hurt her!* I flinch as though the blow hit me. *I hate you.*

He turns to my brother. "Go pick up cow crap. You might

as well do something useful before you leave for good."

My brother hangs his head as he plods out the crooked door. Even then, his head almost skims the top of the doorframe.

A smirk works its way to the corner of my mouth. It's a shame he has to die today.

When Sentinels show up at noon, Mother is as pallid as if someone threw a bottle of bleach on her. I can almost see her soul shrivel up as she wraps her arms around Hate one last time. Why won't she ever do that to me?

Hate and Papa nod to each other. Hate turns to me. His ivory skin reminds me of the milk that swirls around the bottom of the milking bucket. The contrast between his light skin and his dark, semi-spiked hair is stunning. No one can deny he's a striking human. Too bad his darkness outweighs his beauty. The glint of pure evil in his eyes never fades.

He grins his perverted smile, gives me a once-over, then climbs into the back of the Sentinel's truck. I don't care. He's never been kind to me. Won't miss him. Won't ever think of him again.

The bodyshield the Sentinel wears is lightweight but can deflect a bullet or even an axe, were someone to swing one at him. The same hyper-advanced material encompasses the man's helmet. If Downers ever get their hands on that technology, there'd be no stopping us from wreaking all sorts of havoc.

Like we'd ever get that chance.

The engine springs to life. Good riddance. The awful truck roars off, stirring up dirt until large puffs float straight in our faces. I cough. Grit sticks in my eyes. I turn to walk into the hovel.

"Where do you think you're going?"

Papa's voice freezes me. I face him. "I have dirt in my eyes. Is it okay if I wash it out real quick?"

"Get to crying like your mother over here." He pushes Mother's shoulder, and she stumbles forward. "That grit'll wash right out."

How can I shed tears for a brother who destroyed me? "I have nothing to cry about."

He looks at me as if I've grown an eyeball on the tip of my nose, then stares me down until I'm a pile of quivering gelatin. He curls his lip, shakes his head, and brushes past me. "You and your mama better get to work. Those Uppers will want their food this harvest." Just like Papa not to care about the blistering heat and mother's already-weakened state.

Mother staggers to my side and wipes her tears on her torn cotton sleeve. "You just lost your brother. Isn't that reason to cry?"

"Yes, Mother, I suppose it is," I lie.

She grunts and turns away. Why does she care about that wretched boy more than me? All I ever wanted from her was a hug or something to show there's a glimmer of love in her heart for me. I've been good to her, yet all she's ever done is treat me like a grubby slug someone would kick from their shoe.

We reach the fields. "Sit." I fetch her water from the well. My grumbling stomach reminds me we haven't eaten all day. The heat sure isn't helping. She's going to faint soon if she doesn't get some liquid. I hold out the water. "Drink."

Her shaking hand stretches toward the cup, but she grabs my shoulder instead, her grip painful. "You!" she hisses. "This is all your fault."

My chest hurts. How could my brother's stealing have anything to do with me? I wince as she tightens her grip.

"You always made your brother crazy with your curvy little hips. You seduced him to the point of madness until he couldn't resist you anymore!"

My eyes turn wild. How did she know about that? And how dare she accuse me of being in the wrong? "No! It didn't happen like that. He hurt me." My voice shakes. "Wait…you knew all this time…what…what was going on?"

"Hate always loved you more than me." Her eyes narrow to slits.

You know nothing of love, Mother.

"You drove him to insanity," she continues. "He couldn't think clearly. This is entirely your fault. You…you little tramp."

I freeze. Every part of me wants to scream. How could my own mother accuse me of something so wretched? *He* violated *me.*

"Get away from me. I never want to see you again." She stands and towers over my cowering figure. "Go on." She pushes me, hard.

"Mother…"

"I'm not your mother. I never was. You were one of the parachute babies the Uppers dropped from the sky. I was forced to take care of you."

My shoulders tense. Is she serious? "Mother?" I stare at her, mouth open, heart bleeding. "Are you saying I came from the Gliding Lands?" My hands tremble. Wait. That would mean…she's not really my mother.

"Your papa told me never to say a word to you or anyone else. But now…now I don't care. You drove off my boy. I never loved you, and I never will. Now leave, and if I ever see you again, so help me, I will find a way to send *you* to the Pen."

I can't wrap my mind around it. They're not my family. Any of them.

I stumble to my feet, turn, and run straight into the fields, tears hot on my face. Running too fast, I trip over rows of clumped dirt ready for planting. My head spins, and a wildfire burns in my chest. I race like prey aware of a predator fast approaching. Then again, a Wildie could attack any moment.

I take a hard tumble, and the dirt road rises to meet me. My feet throb. I look down to see why. A bundle of raw, blistering thorns has replaced my pain-filled feet. The sunny sky above me looms like an uninvited guest. I force myself to get up. I have to keep going. I pick up my pace. Fast, urgent. But where will I go? Time melds with agony, and I ramble without direction.

A Wildie roars in the distance, and prickles dart up my spine, snapping me to my senses. I need to find somewhere to stop. Can't keep on like this forever.

I cross the road, pass the lake, and find a thick patch of trees close to a pond. A million shimmering lights settle on the pond in front of me. Savage foliage behind. I collapse to the ground and curl up, hidden in the bushes. Then I rock myself until my mind goes blank. A Wildie could come and eat me right now. Nothing matters anymore. Did it ever? I stare at the sky and the floating land drifting afar.

I'm from there. But instead of living in luxury like them, I'm stuck down here to do their bidding. To be their slave. Figures. I always get the short end of the stick. Story of my life.

Looking at my feet, I cringe. This won't be pleasant. I pluck out the first goathead thorn. Okay, maybe it will feel good to be rid of them. I flick them out, one by one. Dots of red sprinkle the bottoms of my feet by the time I'm done. Good thing I've built up calluses or I would've never made it this far. I dip my toes in the water, testing the temperature. Not bad. I plunge my feet in up to my calves. Instant relief. Now I'm probably going to get a parasite or something. Pulling my legs out, I shake them like a freshly bathed dog.

Now what do I do?

The sun hovers over the horizon, sending shoots of rainbow beauty through the sky. I stretch my aching body and admire the colorful display.

Beauty that doesn't belong on such a dreadful day.

My hand lands on something smooth. The prettiest stone I've ever seen. Too bad it's going straight into the pond. Ripples circle out from the sunken rock. I sigh. Like a soothing balm to my soul, each stone I toss somehow makes the day less horrible.

I've been sitting here doing nothing for far too long. Only an hour, at best, of daylight left before Wildies come out to hunt in packs. I need to find somewhere safe to spend the night and fast.

I struggle to my feet. Where am I? Need a better view. I curve around the trees and bushes. Each step reminds me of my long and thorny trek earlier today, distancing myself from the hovels. The flat farming horizon never ends. More fields. More trees. There, in the distance. Either a small barn or a large shed. I need to get closer.

The sun is setting fast. Might as well kick myself for waiting this long when I've had hours to find something before dark. Idiot. I hobble on my aching feet as fast as I can manage toward my goal. I'm closer now. It's a barn for sure. I scan the area, looking for signs someone might be using it. Nothing. I reach it and slink around the side, looking for the door. On the other side of a large grassy area, a house nestles within a patch of trees.

My heart sinks. They must own this barn. I turn to the wilderness behind me. What are my chances of surviving the night? Not good. I stare at the house, wasting precious sunlight. No movement. Maybe I can be out before they wake up?

My decision made, I slide open the unwieldy door enough to slip through. I wait, letting my eyes adjust to the dim interior, making sure I wasn't followed. A rusty tractor, falling apart, captures my attention. Along with...hay. I stagger toward it and fling myself into the pile, burrowing deep within the scratchy loveliness. A smile twitches the corners of my mouth. This will do. Rank mildew fills my nostrils, but the hay is thick and will bring warmth during a chilly night.

The last of the sunlight slips away, and dusk shrouds the barn. Stars blink to life one by one.

It may have been a hot day, but it's early enough in the season the nights can get downright cold. Gazing up through the open door to the sky above, I thank whoever...whatever... is responsible for this newfound luck.

Danger signals flair in my skull. I jump up, hay flying everywhere, and close the door tight to ward off any night predators. The hay engulfs me once more in a golden pile of snuggles.

This is even better than my thin mat at home.

Home.

The thought brings a wave of tears. I can't stop the flow. I hated it, but it's still my home. It's messed up and terrible, but they're still my family. At least I thought they were. No idea what I'm going to do now. No friends, no extended family, nowhere to go. Might as well let the Wildies get me.

My stomach rouses an all-too-familiar grumble. Ah…the ol' hunger pains. I drift off to sleep with the comfort of knowing some things never change.

Chapter 2

I bolt upright and clutch at my shirt. No blood. It's morning, and a Wildie hasn't gorged itself on me. Not bad for the first night on my own. I sink into the hay and eyeball the sheet-metal roof above me. My breathing steadies until I remember I'm homeless.

What am I going to do?

I could wander aimlessly, waiting for death to come. Which it will if I don't have a home. Maybe it'll be a quick demise by a random fly-by shooting. Yeah, that'd be nice. Nicer than being torn to shreds by a Wildie. Just *bam!* and you're gone. I'll hope for that one.

My parents' faces come to mind out of nowhere…I guess they aren't really my parents. They raised me for fourteen years. That should count for something…but, no. My real mother dropped me from the sky.

An *Upper* dropped me from the sky.

What does that mean? Am I an Upper? I guess so. That's crazy ridiculous. I'm as Downer as they come.

But an Upper *did* give birth to me. What does that mean? Thoughts and questions rush through my brain all at once like cars on a multiple-lane highway, looping, curving, and intertwining above and below one another.

The door rattles. My shoulders tense, and I hold my breath as sunlight streams through the opening door. A mop of messy brown hair and a pair of curious eyes appear around the doorframe. My eyes widen. A little boy. He's probably about seven years old. No big threat. No big deal. Except, they've found me.

My throat goes dry. I'm trespassing. People have been sent to the Pen for less. My senses heighten as I prepare for flight.

"Hello there." The little boy's voice resonates like the fast-paced song of a fiddle, full of life.

I don't know about this kid. "Hello." I narrow my eyes, my jaw tense.

"Who are you?"

I stare at him. Not sure if I should respond.

"My name is Justice," he continues, oblivious to the fact I haven't answered. Then again, he is only a child.

"Would you like breakfast?"

My heart beats faster. Well, if that just isn't pathetic. I'm afraid of a *child*.

"My Granny's waiting for you."

My forehead scrunches. We examine each other. Him— standing in the doorway. Me—still lying in the hay, propped up on my elbows. Still, I refuse to speak. In my experience, no one is this cheerful, especially when the sun is just peeking over the horizon.

"Well?" Justice circles the tip of his shoe on the dirt floor. I catch sight of his feet. I snap my teeth shut and brush a clump of hair out of my vision. His shoes are nicer than anything I've worn in my life.

I force myself to meet his gaze again. I don't trust him. Why would his Granny want me in for breakfast anyway? She should be chasing me off her land, not offering me food. My stomach grumbles. I can't take his staring anymore.

"How does your Granny know about me?"

He tilts his head to the side and scratches it. "I looked out my window and saw you go in our barn before I went to bed. I told Granny this morning. I would've told her last night, but I was supposed to be sleeping. Didn't want to make the old lady mad. She could have a heart attack, you know."

I stifle a grin. What an odd boy. He isn't afraid to talk to strangers, and he's friendlier than all the people I've ever known. I squirm under his direct stare.

"I bet you're pretty under all that dirt."

My temper flashes. How rude! Little brat.

I start to say something but glance down. Okay. He's right. Grime covers my navy-blue dress, and my copper-brown arms aren't my actual pigment. I'm sure my face isn't much better. Disgusting. I take a deep breath. "I am pretty hungry."

"Good." Justice darts toward me and grabs my hand. I wrench away, but he latches on again and tugs me to my feet. Strong kid. He drags me out of the barn and runs toward the house. I stumble behind him, each step a throbbing reminder of yesterday.

"Gotta run," he yells. "Don't want the Wildies to get ya."

I pick up my pace to match his. The boy runs like a Hoverpod. We reach the house in no time.

I glance at the porch and halt. A gray-haired woman stands there. Her pleasant smile screams honesty and erases most of the age from her face. I don't trust her.

"Good morning. Please come in. You look like you could

use a bite to eat."

My feet ache. As though a weight prevents me from walking forward, I can't move.

"We don't bite, but the Wildies sure do. I'd say your chances are better in here."

I have nowhere else to go. I start to object anyway. A slight breeze drifts past me, and the words fall away. The aching pit inside churns. The smell of bacon and syrup is so intoxicating, I lose myself and step inside.

My feet walk forward, but I pay no attention to the pain as I near the lavish fragrance. In the kitchen, I stare like the imbecile I am, soaking up the savory deliciousness as I imagine the aroma seeping into my pores without a single taste. If only it worked that way.

I glance around, and my eyes widen. Wow. They have lots of furniture! And stairs to a second floor. Even a separate kitchen from the living room. I've never been in a nice house before. The farmers on my block had their homes smashed by Uppers about twenty years ago. Living in hovels and shanties is the norm for us. But this…*this* is fantastic. It's better than anything I've ever imagined! Never thought people lived like this anymore.

Granny ushers me to the table and urges me to sit. My throat catches. A real table that looks like it was bought in a store! Matching chairs surround it. So pretty. I run my fingers down the smooth wood. So perfect.

Granny sets a plate in front of me. I can't stop the bit of drool that escapes my mouth and ends up on my chin. I pick up the fork beside the plate, and the food swirls around my tongue. Oh, my goodness. Who knew such flavors existed? Another bite. Then another. This must be a dreamland I've drifted into. Soon my plate holds only crumbs. I lift the most beautiful tableware I've ever seen and lick it. Every last morsel needs to go in my mouth. My reverie breaks. Oh, no! I don't have any money to pay for the food I just devoured. And—did I really lick my plate? Might as well slap a stamp on my forehead that reads "Wildie."

"Who is she?"

I freeze. That's right. Other people are in this room, aren't they? And I had to plop down and start stuffing my face like a dummy. And lick my blipping plate. Stupid, stupid, stupid. I follow the voice to a guy just gracing manhood. His broad shoulders are muscular enough to lift me and possibly one other person without much effort. And he's definitely not hard to look at. I'd even say staring at him all day might not be such a bad thing. If I stuck around for a while. My eyes narrow. But can I trust him? Probably not. Not any guy. Especially not the good-looking ones. Still, my gaze is reluctant to leave his face.

Granny steps forward. "Honey, this is Manly."

He smiles, and all rational thought flees.

"Isn't that the perfect name for him." He startles. Oh my gosh. Did I really just say that?

Granny stifles a laugh a moment too late. I glare at her, but she ignores it. "Faithful's over there."

She points to a girl in the back of the room. Beautiful. Tall. Redheaded. She must be older than me, but not by much. Her bright eyes warm my insides, and my smile peeks out at her. Not a threat. Maybe.

"And this here"—she points to a middle-aged man—"we call him Daddy."

Ice clamps around my heart. Does he beat them too? I haven't seen bruises, but still. I square my shoulders. I won't be weak around him. He's closest to me, so I thrust out my hand and shake his. My fingers graze calluses embedded on his palm. He must be a hard worker.

Granny faces me. "Now it only seems fair that since you know our names, we should know yours."

I gulp. This is it. They're going to kick me out. I can tell. "Fear." My voice carries no farther than a whisper.

Granny swallows hard.

My parents named us after negative attributes, a popular practice nowadays. I'm guessing Granny doesn't approve by the look in her eyes. She smiles a second later and gestures for everyone to join me at the table.

"Food's getting cold. Eat up."

Granny dumps a second helping on my plate. My eyes widen as I stare at the mound. How in the Gliding Lands will I ever pay this off?

I cradle my fork in my hands, determined to worry about that later. Even a beating is worth tasting such loveliness once more.

Daddy settles next to me. He smiles at me, then at each person seated. I stare at him, mouth open. Where's the roughness? A brute must be inside him somewhere. He is the father, after all.

Granny makes eye contact with me. "Do you have a home?"

"No." My mouth belts out an answer before my brain can connect.

She puts her napkin beside her plate and looks Daddy in the eye. "She should stay the day with us, and we'll discuss our options tomorrow."

Static speeds down my spine. Are they going to make me their servant?

Inspecting their faces for manipulation, I discover only peace and…happiness?

What? Why are they so happy? Are they on drugs? Must be. No one is this content without assistance. I shrug, eyeing my plate. Even if they make me their servant, it won't be so bad as long as I get to eat food like this. Anything is better than going back to those monsters. I swallow the lump in my throat and dig into the second plate, savoring each bite. Beyond amazing.

They finish eating before me and start putting their dishes beside the sink. I stuff the last few bites in my mouth. I'm not letting one morsel go to waste.

Granny squeezes my shoulder. I freeze and hold my breath. I should've paid attention. What kind of pain will she inflict once she figures out I don't have money to pay for the food? My exhale is painful and slow.

She calls over her shoulder. "Faithful, please take her upstairs to your room and get out fresh clothing."

Inhale. Exhale. Just breathe. I bet Granny can tell my clothes haven't been washed in quite a while. Or maybe it's the smell.

I stand. Pricking pain sends jolts up my legs. It's nothing compared to some of the pain I've felt before. I follow Faithful and her gorgeous trail of red hair up the stairs and into a back room. I walk in and gasp. "You have a bed?"

She looks at me as if I'm the goofiest person she's ever seen. "Yes, I do. Didn't you have one?"

I drop my gaze and don't say a word. I've never met anyone who has.

"I see. How old are you?"

I freeze, my eyes glued to her face. "Why are you asking me that?"

She tilts her head. "Just curious. I'm seventeen if you care."

I shrug and reach for the quilt on her bed, sliding my hand

across the cotton material. Who made this? It's not store bought. My fingers thrill to touch such richness. Not a hole in sight. I can hardly believe it.

Faithful stares. "Were you living in the hovels not far from here?"

I nod before I can think. Gambits. Why do I always have to answer people right away? Oh, that's right. I'm used to a fist flying my way if I didn't. My throat constricts. "Please don't tell anyone."

"I don't know what it's going to hurt if anyone knows." She lays out a cute top with thin pull-strings at the throat and jeans that are way too long for me. She's so tall, and I'm—not. Not at all. "Besides, we don't keep secrets in this house."

My face scrunches. "You don't?"

"Nope, Granny and Daddy expect total honesty. It's the only right way to be," she says as though I ought to know and fully agree with her. I'm not so sure about that. "And speaking of honesty"—she wrinkles her nose—"you need a bath." She throws a towel at me.

A water faucet squeaks on from down the hall. Water gushes and fills my ears with the sound of luxury. Running water too? I step forward, then hesitate.

"Go on, Granny's getting you set. Bathroom's to your left."

I leave the room, stop, then poke my head back in. "Fourteen."

She stares, face blank. "What?"

"You asked my age. Fourteen."

A half-grin heightens her beauty, and she nods. A smile blooms on my own face as I rush to discover the wonders of a real bathroom.

Will it be as fantastic as the rumors I've heard?

After I've been scrubbed pink as a spring pig, I wrap myself in a fluffy towel. How did they find towels this soft? Granny pops her head into the room.

"Let's see those feet of yours, my dear."

She guides me to a wooden chair and places a small bucket of medical supplies next to my feet. My eyes widen. Where did she get those? How can she afford them? She kneels beside me and nestles my foot in her hands, turning it over so she can see the underside.

"Oh, you poor dear."

She rubs balm on the wounds, then wraps them tightly. Tears gather in the corners of my eyes. No one's ever bandaged me up before.

"There. All better. They should be like new in no time."

I stand. My bound feet throb only slightly now. A grin stretches my mouth like a hammock from tree to tree. Is this what it feels like to have a family who actually cares?

Faithful and I trample down the stairs, my feet positively singing. Whatever was in that balm works. Justice trails behind. My skin, warm and smooth, is now free from dirt.

Lemon verbena body wash permeates me with the odor of royalty. I run my hand over my outfit. This is that sun-resistant clothing only the fancy people in town wear. And today, I get to be one of them.

Manly meets us in the foyer and throws a rifle over his shoulder. "It's time to weed the fields." He smiles.

My eyes stray first to his firm jawline dotted with the beginnings of a five o'clock shadow, then to the muscles straining his shirt. Goodness but he fits his name.

"We've got quite a bit of land left to weed."

Air releases from my lungs. Oh good. Payment time. I can handle hard labor. We head out the door single file. Glad I didn't let Granny talk me into staying inside and resting my feet. The sooner I can pay off my debt the better.

When we get to the field, Daddy's already there. A large rifle drapes across his back.

Leaning close to Faithful's ear, I ask, "Isn't it illegal to have guns?"

She kneels in the dirt, tugs on a pair of tattered gloves, and glances at me out of the corner of her eye. "Technically it's illegal to kill a Wildie. The Uppers never actually made it illegal to own a gun. But they did eradicate them. Or at least they thought they did. They missed some."

Manly stares at me, long and hard. "Don't go telling other people about these here guns, you hear me?" When I fail to respond, he folds his arms. His eyes pierce mine. "We aren't supposed to have them, but we need them for protection."

I continue my silence. He fidgets with the cuff of his sleeve. *Go on, say something. I've got all day.*

He squarely plants his sparkly sea blues in my direction. "A Wildie could attack at any moment. We have to be prepared."

I almost laugh. He won't convince me, but he sure is cute. "But you're not supposed to shoot them."

"Humans are more important than animals. Don't you ever forget that." He kneels and starts yanking weeds from the ground.

Um, huh? My brow crinkles. "That's not what they tell us."

"You're right, that's not what they tell us. But they're wrong."

I raise my eyebrows. *No, you're the one who's mistaken.* "The Uppers are never wrong. They're in charge, aren't they? We're supposed to listen to them and do what they say."

Faithful and Manly exchange a slight grin as if they know something I don't. I'm not sure why he thinks it's all right to go against the Uppers, but they all seem fine with it. What about Faithful's raving about how they were so honest? Breaking the law sure doesn't seem honest.

"Didn't you go to the Teachings when you were younger?" I eye them both. It's illegal not to go for at least one year. Everyone must.

Manly squares his jaw. "Yeah, we went to the Teachings. Just like every other kid in this town. Doesn't mean we believe all that propaganda junk."

My eyes dart to the sky. "You'd better be glad spy drones aren't recording your voice right now." I rub my arms and shiver. I *hate* when they come around. Sentinels haul people off if spy drones catch someone doing or saying something they aren't allowed to. It could happen to anyone. "Speaking of spy drones. Won't they see your guns?" I scan the skies, half-expecting one to appear.

"That's the nice thing about the Uppers." Manly shakes a clump of dirt out of his sun-bleached hair. "They're lazy. They've kept those spy drones on the same schedule for years now. We've figured out their pattern, and we never have our guns out on those days. However, that could change at any time, so it's always good to be on the lookout."

He winks. Butterflies swamp my stomach. Man, he's cute. My hands want to fidget, so I press them to my sides. I try my best to smile, but I don't smile often, and the idiot in me shows.

What a smart bunch of people. But that still doesn't mean I can trust them.

My parents never bothered to figure out when the drones would show up, making sure we Downers are doing our jobs and aren't getting into trouble.

I grab some gloves off the ground. Better get started on the weeds. I plop to my knees and settle into a smooth pace alongside the others.

"Where are you from?"

I peek at Justice and open my mouth.

"I bet you're from around here," he interrupts. His crooked teeth stand out against his ruddy, sun-soaked skin. "Why don't you live with your family?"

Not answering that one.

"Do you have any brothers or sisters? Do you have a pet? I've always wanted a pet. Granny says no."

Pain cuts into my temples.

"Are you wearing Faithful's clothes?"

I give him a *duh* look.

"You know, those pants are too big on you." He points to my cuffs, which drape over my feet.

Oh my gosh! Will he shut up?

"Why was your dress so dirty? Did your mom ever wash it?"

My eyes bug out, and my face turns hot. I can't imagine it's flattering.

"Do you have a mom?"

I push air out of my mouth and respond through clenched teeth. "You already asked me that."

He tilts his head, his messy locks falling over his eyes. "No, I didn't. Why are you so quiet? Most girls talk a lot more than you."

I dig my hands into the soil. Maybe I don't feel like talking.

"Do you have any toys? My Daddy makes me toys. He's really good at it."

I'm seriously considering slapping that stupid grin off his face.

"Hello?" He waves a hand in front of my face. "Earth to quiet girl."

I plop on my heels and shove his hand away. "Stop! I can't take it anymore. Don't ask me so many questions! You're driving me crazy. I've never met anyone as obnoxious as you." My sharp words chase away his smile. His eyes lose their shine, but I don't care. He opens his mouth. "I don't want to hear it. Just go away and leave me alone!"

Faithful stops her work, her glare full of fire. "There's no need for that."

I stand and brush the dirt from my borrowed shirt. "He's obnoxious."

"He's just a child."

I roll my eyes. *A very annoying child.* His tiny shoulders slump as he turns and trudges across the field. An unexpected rip in the seams of my heart threatens to topple me. I clutch my chest. That was me trudging off. Did I just act like Papa? My head throbs as I try to comprehend what I just did. "I know. I just…" I don't have time to finish. The whir of a motor whizzes overhead.

Faithful's eyes grow wide. Her pale face grows even paler.

Manly yells at us. "Run!"

The world spins as I bolt for the edge of the field, Faithful next to me and Daddy trailing us. I run for the nearest bush and throw myself under it, lurching forward as a *thud* hits my back. Someone shields me with their body.

The motor gets louder as they hover down on our area. Young men laugh the cruelest laughter, followed by the *pop, pop, pop* of bullets hurled our way.

Over and over.

All we can do is stay still and hope they don't hit us. The figure behind me flinches and groans. Silence descends as the Hoverpod flies away. Weight lifts from my back. I turn and find it's Daddy who protected me. It's Daddy who got shot instead of me.

Sickness wreaks havoc on my stomach. It should've been me.

I shuffle back as oozing blood seeps from his shoulder. "You're hurt."

"I'll be okay." He teeters and lifts a shaking hand to shade his eyes from the glaring sun. I scan the area to see if anyone's alive. I spot gray hair behind a tree.

"Granny!" I yell. "Daddy's been shot."

She runs over as quickly as her worn-out body can manage. She stares at him, her brow creasing.

"I'm fine, Mama. Don't worry about me. They only got my shoulder. I'm not gonna die." His knees buckle, and he attempts to steady himself. If he faints, no way will we be able to lug him to the house.

"Not if I have anything to do with it." Granny wraps one arm around his lower back, careful to avoid his shoulder.

We both support him, our slight frames straining against his man-sized body. A few more paces. We're halfway there.

Where are the others? I squint against the sunlight, and a figure emerges. Manly's tawny arms carry a limp body. I still. My world spins in slow motion.

Justice.

Granny falters and cries out. I grit my teeth. She bolsters herself so I won't bear Daddy's weight alone.

I grunt as Daddy slumps against us. Just a few more steps.

Chapter 3

Manly rushes to move Justice inside. When Granny and I hobble in, we help Daddy to the family room. My arms strain as he leans against us. We settle him in a threadbare recliner. I can't believe he took a bullet for me.

"Thank you," is all he can manage.

Granny waves me to her side. "Go to the kitchen, get a clean cloth, and put pressure on the wound. They're in the drawer by the oven."

Rushing to the kitchen, I stop short as the unanimated body of Justice splays across the table. Manly's at his side, busy undressing the boy to check for wounds. Uppers did this. I'm from a land in the sky where they just randomly shoot people. For fun. I rush to the drawer, rip it open, scoop out a cloth, and slam it shut, rattling the pans beneath it. Maybe it's a good thing I didn't end up staying there.

I glance at Justice again. My heart pounds at the sight of skin and blood. Grabbing the cloth, I dash to the family room. I still haven't seen Faithful.

"Where is…?"

Granny stops me. "She's outside, trying to get it together before she comes in. Stay with Daddy a minute. I'm going to talk to her." Granny treads out the door.

Beads of sweat emerge on Daddy's brow as he takes deep breaths, fighting the pain. I hold the cloth against his wound, then sit still for a while, waiting. My life has been filled with one too many tension-filled silences. I can't stand the quiet between us anymore.

"So…you're Granny's son?"

What a stupid question. I visualize my foot kicking myself in the derrière.

"Yes, I am." He manages a halfhearted grin, followed by a grimace. I gasp and jerk back. I pressed the cloth too hard against his open wound.

"Sorry." My forehead wrinkles as I hold my breath. Now I'm gonna get it.

"It's all right, dear. I'm just glad I'm alive."

My eyes widen. He means me no harm? I remember how to breathe again. He's so different from Papa. Such a teddy bear. My eyes drift to his shoulder. I've never seen a bullet wound before. "Infection could still set in, decreasing your chance of survival."

His face turns a shade paler while mine bursts into flames. Wish I hadn't said that.

"I'm so sorry. I'm so dumb. I always say the wrong thing."

He pats my arm and smiles.

"You saved me, you know," I blurt.

He stares forward, then up at me with shining eyes. "Guess I'm a hero then."

He sure is. "Thanks for saving my life. That bullet was meant for me."

"No, don't be telling yourself that. That's not fair. They aimed at all of us."

I ball my hands tight. "Those stupid Uppers. Sometimes I just hate them so much." *And I'm one of them.* My stomach lurches.

His face changes. "Hate is a mighty strong word."

I shrug. "It seems a perfect word to describe my feelings for them."

"They're self-absorbed and downright wicked. They force us to work to feed and clothe them yet take no responsibility. But it's not right to hate anyone."

My brain can't wrap around this statement. Where'd he come up with such weird notions?

"Sorry, but anyone who could hurt a little boy like that deserves to be hated." *I'm not like the Uppers. I refuse to be. Maybe Mother was wrong?*

"How's Justice?" His love for the boy is clear in his cracking voice.

I can only shake my head. "Uh, I…I don't know. I'm not sure."

"Would you check? Please?" His eyes plead with me.

"I shouldn't leave you." I don't want to view Justice's limp body again. It's an image I don't care to have ingrained in my soul.

He brushes me off. "I'm not a big baby. I want to know how my boy is. Please go talk to Manly."

Used to doing as I'm told, I nod and head for the kitchen. When I reach it, Justice still lies on the table, his skin clinging to his little ribs. They're not moving.

My neck stiffens. *Breathe, Justice, breathe!*

I inch closer and stare. His ribs move up and down. Slightly. I press my palms against my stomach and take a step back. Good. He's alive.

I notice Manly watching me. I meet his gaze.

"He's not doing so great." He drops his head to his chest, and his eyes sear into Justice. "He lost a lot of blood. Got shot twice. Once in the gut, the other in his shin. Thank the Good Lord he's still with us, but he's weak."

Good Lord? Who is this Good Lord? Is this a saying around here, or is there an Upper I should thank as well? "What should I tell Daddy?"

Manly straightens. "I'll go have a few words with him. Stay with Justice, please?"

"Of course."

I move toward the boy. The boy who, minutes ago, drilled me with questions. The boy who took notice of me and cared enough to bring me into his home for breakfast. The boy who, just before getting shot, I'd lost my temper with.

I feel rotten.

What if he dies and I can never take it back? What if his precious life ends? I was so mean. A shudder grips my body. Nauseated, I grab my mouth, putting a stopper on the inevitable flow as Faithful and Granny walk in.

"How could they do this to one of their own?" Faithful says, but my mind barely registers the words.

I rush out the door, down the steps, and onto the dirt. I bend over and dry heave. The waves of nausea cease. Standing, I wipe my forehead.

Justice has to wake up. He just has to! I need to tell him I'm sorry.

Faithful's words re-enter my head. *How could they do this to one of their own?*

My breath catches. Justice isn't a Downer. He must've been a baby the Uppers dropped too. I'm not the only one.

How many others were thrown overboard like a piece of trash, only to end up on this miserable earth?

I spend the rest of the morning fixing up the wounded the best I can. I boil water, sterilize needles, and bring out thread and tweezers. Alcohol is poured into wounds to heal and mouths to comfort. The morning goes by in a blur of bloody rags and doctoring.

I overhear bits and pieces of conversation, but my head stays fuzzy for most of it.

"If only they knew Abba, things like this wouldn't happen."

Someone else: "Bitterness will only lead to our destruction."

Then, "The Good Lord will heal them."

None of it makes any sense. Who's this Abba or this Good Lord they keep mentioning? If they're friends with an Upper, I want to know about it. But that would be impossible since it's illegal for Uppers and Downers to associate for reasons other than business. We can't go up to them, so whoever this Good Lord person is, he must be coming down here to interact with these new friends of mine. How did they meet? Who is he? How can he heal anyone? So many questions, so many things to think about, and I've just met these people.

After Daddy and Justice settle in their beds, Granny gathers the rest of us. "Fear, you and I will take turns at Daddy and Justice's bedsides. Manly, Faithful—you're done. Just stay inside and help out here. We can always weed tomorrow.

No more working the rest of the day, okay? Everyone needs to take a break and calm their nerves. I know I sure do."

Manly's jaw tightens as a glint leaps into Faithful's eyes.

"I'm going back out," Manly says.

Faithful jumps in. "Me too."

Wow. They're not stubborn at all.

Granny stares them down. "I don't think that's a good idea. What if they come back? I can't worry about you guys, too."

They're both shaking their heads before Granny can even finish. I shrink back and try to stay out of it. Will Granny hit them for talking back?

"Granny, they're not coming back today." Manly's so much bigger than Granny, I'm not sure what kind of damage a hit from her would do anyway.

"Yeah," Faithful pipes up. "Besides, we've got to do something other than sit here and worry."

I'm sure not brave enough to venture into a field where I was just shot at. They're a little nutty in the head.

Granny glares at them, but she doesn't yell, and she definitely doesn't hit either one. Incredible.

Manly plunks a wide-brimmed hat on his head. "They've already done their damage. We'd be safer going out now than we would tomorrow morning."

"Fine. But take your gun, Manly. And don't leave Faithful's side."

"Yes, ma'am," they both chorus.

His jaw tightens as Faithful jaunts past him and out the door. He slings the rifle across his back and follows his little sister.

Granny sighs and turns to me. "Come on, then."

I nod and follow her as she trudges up the stairs. I pause at Daddy's door. An old chair snuggles up to the edge of his bed.

Granny sits, folds her hands, and closes her eyes. That's odd. Is
she going to sleep? I don't blame her. I could use a good nap
right about now, too.

I enter the room next to Daddy's and approach Justice. A
deep sleep has overtaken him. Just hope it isn't a coma.
Following Granny's example, I grab a battered wicker chair
and bring it close to the bed. With each rise and fall of his
chest, my spirit rides an emotional tide. Will he make it?

In the silence, I fill the passing minutes with my thoughts.
My parents—my chest tightens with the pain. My life—what it
was until yesterday. The same day in and day out, never
changing until now. I have no idea what tomorrow will look
like, not even an hour from now. I should be terrified. But
something about this place, something about these people,
brings this…peace. This almost instant camaraderie. It's
unexplainable. They're different from everyone else I've ever
met.

My thoughts shift to the body in front of me. Why was I so
mean? The truth smacks me in my face. I'm just like Papa.

I groan, dropping my head in my hands. I'm such an idiot.

Self-control was forced when it came to my parents. If I
didn't want to get smacked, I kept my mouth shut. That must
be why I let loose on the little boy. I felt *safe* around him.
Lashing out at him wouldn't result in a whipping.

I want—no—I *need* Justice to get better. It will torment me
for the rest of my days if he doesn't heal…*if he dies*.

My thoughts travel to Daddy. I can't let him die either. Not
that I have much choice in the matter. Who am I kidding? I
have no choice whatsoever. Who chooses who lives and who
dies? I really don't know.

There are rumors of people who believe in an Abba who
controls everything, even life and death, but I know nothing

about this weird god in the sky.

The Uppers forbid belief in any gods except theirs. They especially don't like this Abba for some reason. Most Downers think religion is stupid. I haven't given it much thought.

All I can do is hope for this boy and the man in the next room. Hope they heal, hope their wounds aren't life threatening, hope they won't get an infection.

Hope they live.

A couple of hours into it, I'm about all hoped out and woozy. A gentle hand touches my shoulder. I turn. Granny stares at Justice, her eyes shimmering with unshed tears. I can't comprehend her compassion. No one's ever looked at me that way before. If I ever got hurt, all I heard was a gruff, "Get back to work, you're fine," or "Quit your whining," or some other mean-spirited comment.

Granny takes my hand and stands me up. "It's time to eat, my dear."

I glance at Justice. "Is it safe to leave him?"

"He'll be fine. There's nothing more we can do for him at the moment. You need to keep up your strength if you're going to help me get them better."

She walks out the door, and I stop her before she reaches the stairs. "Do you mean…" I struggle to find the words. "You're going to let me stay here longer than just tonight?"

Granny leads me down the stairs. "Why yes, dear. I can't let you go out on your own again, now can I? You could get mangled by one of the Wildies. It's best to stay here for now."

Warmth spreads through me as we head into the kitchen. I'm not sure what to make of that last comment, but I'm grateful I have a place to stay, at least for now. "Thank you so much, Granny." I squeeze her hand. "It means the world to me!"

She waves me away but grins. "It's the right thing to do."

Something lights up in my brain. It's so bright it almost hurts my head. I must do something nice. That way I won't owe them. "How's Daddy?"

Granny opens a cupboard and doesn't respond right away, so I hold my breath. It must be bad. Granny hands me a stack of plates. "Abba will do what he thinks is best."

My brow furrows as I move toward the table. Abba? So does that mean they believe in this so-called god the Uppers are so against? I've never met anyone before who did. Or if I had, they'd kept quiet about it. I set down the last plate. Granny hands me forks and napkins next. Wow. Napkins. They're so proper. She heads for the stove and reaches for a simmering pot.

"Granny?"

She continues stirring. "Yes, dear?"

I fidget with the table settings. "Why do you think the Uppers are so cruel?"

Granny lets the long wooden spoon go, and it spins in the pot. "Everyone has the ability to be cruel, Fear. It's up to us to learn to control our actions. They never learn self-control up there." She sighs. "They never learn kindness."

"Kindness?" I've heard this word before, but I haven't experienced much of it in my measly fourteen years. "Like you guys?"

Granny's face breaks into a grin. "Have we been kind to you?"

"Uh…" I rearrange all the forks. "I thought it was obvious."

Granny chuckles and wipes at the corners of her mouth.

My mind wanders. I can't believe I'm going to get to eat another amazing meal with them. Saliva pools under my tongue. The hours have sped by. Must've missed lunch earlier. Yet, it's a little too early for dinner. She walks to the back door and presses a button on a square box. A bell comes to life, and I jump. Within minutes, both Manly and Faithful race to the table.

"Wash up," Granny reminds the two. They respond to her command with a jolt.

Lunch or dinner—still not sure which to call it—fills with a weary silence of a family who struggles to keep it together. I reminisce about the meals with my old family and how this one resembles them with its quiet stillness. The difference is, they thank Abba, this god of theirs, before they allow themselves to eat. Heaviness thickens the air.

It feels just like home.

Chapter 4

After a quick visit to the wounded, Manly clomps down the stairs. "I'm going to weed for another couple of hours. Still have some daylight left." He leaves without giving me a second look.

Faithful and Granny stand in the kitchen. Their spirited conversation whirls into a tornado of wild hand gestures and jerky movements, but their subdued voices stay constant. From the way they point and throw glances my way, it must be about me. Granny plants her hands on her hips. Clearly the conversation is over. Faithful sulks past me and out the front door. She fails to say why she's in such a lousy mood. I slump into a lumpy chair.

Granny propels herself toward me. "You and Faithful will share a bed."

I nod. Ah. So that's why Faithful has a thumbtack on her bottom. I wouldn't want to share my comfy bed with a stranger either. Hopefully she won't kill me in my sleep.

"You two can take turns sleeping while the other watches

over Justice and Daddy. Manly and I will take over in the morning."

"Yes, ma'am."

I'm ready and willing to accept anything this family throws at me. There's a roof over my head and food in my belly. This is more than I've come to expect out of life. A smile works its way to my lips. These people aren't half bad.

Days later, Daddy is stronger, and color returns to his face. He strolls through the house as though he got a mosquito bite rather than shot with a bullet. Justice, on the other hand, fades fast. He reminds me of death every time I check on him.

"Fear." His voice croaks like a frog calling its mate.

"You're awake!" I jump off the edge of the bed. "I need to tell Granny."

"Wait." A pathetic cough erupts from his cracked lips. "Stay with me."

Gray half-moons shadow beneath his eyes. It's obvious he's not well. Air gushes from my mouth like a deflated balloon.

"I'm so sorry for yelling at you." I resettle next to him.

Justice crinkles his forehead. "Huh?"

I clutch his hand. "In the field before you were shot, I yelled at you."

His forehead uncrinkles, and he attempts to sit up but quickly scraps that idea. "Oh yeah. I forgot all about it."

The lump in my gut dissipates. He forgot? "Well, you've kind of been in a coma for a while."

"True." He hauls his blanket to his chin. I clear my throat and scan the old paintings of landscapes scattered on the walls of his room. "I overheard something about you."

His eyelids lift.

I lean toward him. "You were a parachute baby, just like me."

"Yeah, I already knew that."

"Oh." Of course he did. Honesty is the best policy in this family. "Does it bother you? To know the people who tried to kill you could possibly be your family?"

He shakes his head. "My family is right here."

I tilt my head. "Aren't you curious to know what they're like?"

"Not really. I do wish they'd learn about Abba and change their ways, though."

What's with this Abba junk? What does that have to do with anything anyway? "I just wish I knew what it's like up there. Maybe, you know, find my mom. Ask her why she did it."

"Did what?"

What do you mean, did what? "Threw me over. Don't you want to know why you were thrown over?"

Justice lifts his chin toward the ceiling. "I forgive her."

"Forgive who?" What's he talking about?

"My mom."

I freeze. Is he crazy? I lean closer. "You do? What in the Gliding Lands makes you do that?"

"If she hadn't thrown me over, then I never would've ended up in this family of Downers. They're much better, don't you think?"

I remain silent. He's nuts. True, this family is amazing, but to forgive your mother for something so horrendous?

It makes no sense.

Justice starts coughing. He twists and turns, clenching his stomach, groaning. I stand and back away. What should I do? Someone pounds up the stairs.

Granny rushes in. "Justice? Honey? Drink this." She cradles his head and helps pour the liquid down his throat. He coughs a few more times, then relaxes. The worst of it's over. She fluffs his pillow, settles him on the bed, then turns to me. "Let's let him rest. You two will have plenty of time to talk later." She forces a fake smile and guides me out of the room.

She's not fooling me. She's worried about him. He's not getting better, and we all know it.

This doesn't stop me from visiting. Each time I do, he looks worse, but he chats away as much as his frail body will allow. Somehow, the kid can *still* outtalk me. He's so positive, even on his deathbed. He's like my little brother now. To lose him...I can't even think about it. My chest squeezes as I try to block the billions of hornets threatening to sting my soul the second he leaves this earth.

"Fear?"

"What?" I bet he needs some broth.

"Just want to thank you."

"Thank me?" What's with all this thankfulness stuff? "For what?"

"For being my friend." His weakened muscles do their best to perk up his face.

I give him the warmest smile I can muster. "I've never had a friend before. Thank you for being mine."

"I guess we're a good team."

I clasp his small hand. So cold. "The best team ever."

I don't want to know this kid or feel this kind of pain. To care for someone so deeply only to realize I can't keep him.

He'll be gone before I can blink. I can tell it's coming soon with his sunken eyes and the sallow color enveloping his entire being. I can't stand it. He struggles with each breath. It isn't fair, watching this precious kid fade before my eyes. It isn't right. I get up to leave. I can't handle this pain, but I don't want to hurt him. Don't want him to see my tears, either. He clutches my finger and tugs. I turn.

"Before you leave, you need to know something."

I can't speak or I might lose it. I nod instead.

"Abba is real. Don't be afraid for me. When I pass on, I'll be able to hug him. He'll be right there, taking care of me."

I nod as if I understand what he's talking about. He makes his god sound so kind, like a good father. But I can't buy it. It's too hard to wrap my brain around. I go on as though I'm listening, as though I'm taking it all in, just so Justice knows I care.

"One more thing. Don't forget, Fear. Abba loves you too."

My throat constricts. I nod. "Okay." Letting go of his hand, I turn and dash out of the room. My tears run fast down my cheeks. He can't know I don't believe him. Abba can't love me. No one can. No one ever has.

When Justice slips away, the earth falls from beneath my feet. Peace implodes as the entire house shatters around me. Faithful and Granny won't stop crying. Manly stands, staring at the lifeless body for hours. No words. No tears. Just a face full of agony. Daddy wails for his boy from the front lawn.

I cram my negative emotions into a box. It's how I deal with pain.

He's gone. Justice is gone. I'll never be able to talk with him again. Those crooked teeth will never shine from his smile again. His pale body will never feel the warmth of the sun again. Why is life so unfair? If there is a god, he's a cruel one.

In the morning, Granny pulls out a large book covered with beautiful lettering.

My eyes widen. I can't believe they have that. If the Uppers find out, they'll get in so much trouble.

When she opens the book, she starts in the middle, not the beginning. The words don't make much sense, or maybe I'm not really listening, but the words are medicine for their weary souls. Their eyes twinkle, mouths smile, and Daddy even laughs. What gives?

"How can you be over his death already?" I ask, interrupting.

Granny gives me a half-grin. "Far from it, honey. We're still aching for our loss. However, we can't help but be excited for Justice since we know where he is." She places the book on a shelf.

Huh? I thought he was dead? How can he be somewhere? Just as I'm about to question her, she speaks up again.

"Today I need to go into town to make arrangements for the burial." Granny wipes her hands on her apron. "Would you like to come with me, Fear?"

Going to town has been the only entertainment of my miserable life. I nod.

"Granny, I'd rather stay here and clean up. Is that okay? I just…can't…go into town today," Faithful admits.

"That's fine. No weeding today. It's Sunday, after all." Granny grins at me. "We rest on Sundays. Days off are scarce, so we make it a priority."

Wow. That's pretty awesome. My family never took days off. I like this resting idea.

Granny goes to Manly's side and peers into his face. "We could use help carrying bags."

Who can resist those soft gray eyes that match her soft gray hair? Obviously Manly can't. He melts like butter. "Okay, Granny, let me get my nicer shoes." The muscles in his back flex against his shirt as he walks up the stairs. I can't help but stare.

Tearing my eyes away, I turn to Granny. "Will I need to bring a pig?" Her mouth drops open. Manly stops his ascent. Faithful stifles a giggle. *How rude.* "My family always brings pigs or chickens to barter with."

"That would be awfully hard for us, dear, considering we only have two pigs, and they have yet to make piglets." She winks, grabs her light jacket, and walks out to the truck. Manly's footsteps creak up the stairs. Did he just chuckle under his breath?

I wait for Manly to come back down. When he does, I gape at his feet. Those sure are nice shoes. I wish I owned a pair like that. I stare down at my dirty feet. Last pair of shoes I owned was a few years ago. I wore those suckers till the soles fell off.

He opens the screen door for me and squints into the sun as I walk past. I tread the cobblestone path to the truck, then eye the small front seat. Apparently the three of us will have to squeeze in there together. Great. Granny scoots into the driver's seat, and I slip in next to her, while Manly flanks me on the other side.

"These silly trucks have the smallest cabs."

Granny eyeballs my stiff limbs as I try to avoid contact on

either side of me.

"How do you all fit in here?" I ask.

Manly points behind us. "Some of us ride in the back."

"Oh." Makes sense.

We start down the road, and I struggle to untangle the seatbelt, which clearly hasn't been used in a while. I drop the belt. Forget it, stupid thing won't untangle.

Granny hits a large pothole, and I fly in Manly's direction. My hand lands on his chest, and intense heat barrels through me. I reel back from his touch. Fire soars through my arms up to my face and explodes out the top of my head. "I'm so sorry!"

"It's okay." The corner of his mouth lifts. "Are you sure you're all right?"

"I'm fine." Heat still dances through me. What the fritz was that?

For the remainder of the ride, warmth passes back and forth between his leg and mine as they press much too close together for comfort. I can't think of anything to say. My mind drifts on the breeze, uncatchable. Intense heat sears me, stifling the air. I catch my breath in short spurts as though my air supply's being cut off, bit by bit.

What's wrong with me?

Scooting as close to Granny as I can possibly manage, I ignore Manly and the strange feelings creeping up inside.

He keeps his face glued to the window. I guess small talk isn't his forté, and that's cool with me. Town seems so ridiculously far away. I know it's not, but for some reason, this car ride takes forever. When we finally arrive, I get out, stretch my short legs, and gaze around me. Nothing has changed in this town for years. The stores are the same. The people are the same. Plain, old, boring everything.

A shadow rests on half of the stores. I look up. A Gliding

Land's merchant town floats directly above ours, a few
thousand feet in the air. It always amazes me how entire towns,
entire cities, some small countries even, just float up there.
Although I've seen it my whole life, it still shocks me every
time.

Is that the specific city I was thrown from? Probably not.
Mother said I was found in a field. Maybe my parents were
wrong. Maybe I was just abandoned. Not a parachute baby
after all. It's not like I'll ever know the truth.

Goosebumps springs to life on my arms. What if my
family's here? Oh my gosh, why didn't I think of that earlier?
My eyes dart around the dusty streets, watching people's faces
as they pass. Sweat forms on my brow. What day is it? Sunday,
right? My shoulders relax. Oh, thank goodness. Mother likes
to do her shopping on Thursday.

Granny swings her ragged purse. "Normally we wouldn't
shop on our rest day, but today's an exception. We have to get
burial arrangements underway."

I nod. Shopping on a Sunday doesn't bother me, but I
understand.

She hands Manly a list of needed supplies and a coin sack.

"We pay with real money. Not pigs." He winks as he passes
me.

He was listening at the house! Warmth floods my face as I
follow him down the street to the market. He keeps one step
ahead of me. Maybe I should go faster. Stupid short legs.

We step inside, and Manly slips his hands into his pockets.
"I'm not sure where everything is. Usually this is Granny's and
Faithful's department." He rubs his head, fingertips sliding
through sunny locks.

I answer before the movement can distract me. He's *very*
distracting. "I've been to this store so many times, I know it

backwards and forwards." I pluck the list from his hand.

"Thanks." For a few minutes, he follows me through the store, acting like a man caught in the lingerie section by accident. He carries random items for me, and soon his arms overflow. He leaves to fetch the cart we should've gotten in the first place. I continue to scour the store for items we need.

As I compare pricing, a dark feeling hits me in the gut, and a shadow passes behind me. I whirl as chills dash up my neck.

Nothing. No one's there. *Calm down, Fear.*

What am I so worried about, anyway? I go back to my shopping when a hand whips me around. Cruel fingers dig into my arm, and I stare into the eyes of a ghost.

Hate.

He stands before me, a dark eye peering into my own as black hair covers half of his face. I drop the bag of millet I hold, and it bursts open at our feet.

"You stupid girl. Look what you've done." He gestures to the ground, not taking his evil eye from mine for a second.

"How?" I flinch. "H-how…are you…"

"How am I alive?"

I'm too scared to nod. "You went to the Pen." My stomach lurches. "How did you defeat that huge man?"

"The Grocer? Easy. He was old and fat. I was younger and stronger than him." His hand clamps down on my other arm, his fingers digging until my muscles ache. He hauls me to his chest. "How are *you* still alive?" His foul breath spews venom. "Who have you been shacking up with? We thought for sure you would've been shredded to pieces by now."

A wicked grin spreads across his face. I start to shake. He yanks on my arm.

"Stop…"

He leans forward and shuffles my hair back as he takes a

whiff. "I've missed you, Fear," he whispers. "Come back to me." He pulls my arm again.

My entire body freezes. "Stop!" I try again, louder, through gritted teeth.

"Get ready for some fun, girl, 'cause I'm taking you home."

A shudder runs through me. *No, no, no. Please, no!* That's the last thing I want.

He drags me through the store, digging his painted black nails deep into my arm. I shut down and can't even speak. I glance behind me. A prick stabs my neck, and I wince. Ouch! What the—? My head whips around, but Hate still drags me toward the storefront.

Oh, please, somebody help me!

A figure emerges, and a massive fist collides with Hate's face. Blood splatters everywhere, and I jerk as crimson sprinkles me. Hate releases me and grabs his nose. Red covers him. Manly towers over the cowering boy who clutches his now-disfigured face. If looks could kill, they'd both lie dead in the aisles.

Manly grabs my hand and hurries us out of the store. I spot my parents across the street on the corner store's porch. Mother clings to Papa's arm, waving frantically in my direction, trying to get the man's attention. She sends a scowl straight at me. Papa finally heeds his wife and turns his head. His eyes lock with mine, and he crosses his arms. I know that look.

No going back. It would only result in being broken and bruised, helpless to defend myself against such brute strength. Wretched, toxic pain courses through my body, pushing me to my knees. What's wrong with me? I go limp. No! I have to stay awake!

Something…something awful is happening. If only I could

remember what…

Manly's warm arms wrap around me. I smile at him. He's so handsome. So nice. My head droops. The truck fades in and out of view. Darkness descends.

Fluttering in and out of consciousness, bits and pieces of conversation breeze through my ears. My body responds like death. Nothing makes sense. I'm back at the house. In Faithful's bedroom, or maybe Justice's old room. I peek. Granny stoops over me, a washcloth pressed to my forehead. Faithful and Daddy hover near me too. My unclear eyes distort their faces.

But most of all, Manly's presence warms my soul.

He sits by my bed. He's always there when I open my eyes. Through my fluttering lids, I glimpse him sitting in the old wicker chair, just waiting. For what? For me? I fall into the darkness. I pry my eyes open again. The pretty book lies open in someone's hands. The beautiful words caress my soul. What does it all mean?

Granny bows, hands clasped, just as she did when Daddy was hurt. "Good Lord" and "Abba." She says these familiar words again and again.

Time passes like soup through a sieve. I begin to hear and understand more. The words from the book are so beautiful. The only thing I can focus on is those sweet words full of love, joy, and peace. Granny reads some, but mostly Manly reads to me. I hope he never stops. My eyes drift shut once more.

Chapter 5

Strength trickles into my body. Consciousness ripples through me. Granny whispers the word poison.

Poison. What? How was I poisoned?

The sharp prick at the store. Did Hate stick me with something? Is he so evil he thinks if he can't have me, no one can? I clench my fists and wish I had enough strength to strangle him. He's evil. No denying it. Anyone can tell the instant they meet him.

I'm too tired to think right now. My body melts into lead, and my head lolls on my pillow.

I wake to singing and an empty room. My first night of peaceful sleep has restored my body to normal.

I'm going to beat this.

The whole family must be singing on the floor below. Music drifts up to me where I lie staring at the peeling paint on the ceiling. I sigh. The open window lets in a light breeze, and the old curtains flutter. The sun simmers on my skin.

Hotness and icy chills no longer accompany the wretched sickness that wracked my body. Poison. How did this small body of mine beat that?

I am well.

I should be dead.

This is the second time in just a short period I should be dead. A new record for me, I think.

The music swells and ebbs. Sometimes loud and fast, sometimes soft and slow. I revel in their glorious voices as I lie in total comfort and peace. Something about these people, this family stirs me. Something I've never felt before. They're so... compassionate. So loving.

First watching it with Justice, now myself. I can't fathom it. Why would they care about me? They barely know me, yet it seems I've been here a lifetime. They could've thrown me to the Wildies rather than be burdened by taking care of a girl they hardly know. But they didn't.

I have no idea what day it is. I also have no idea how long it takes for poison to run its way out of someone's system, or even if it can. If that's what happened, then being here—alive —is nothing short of a miracle. I want to thank someone, anyone, for this amazing gift, but I don't know whom to thank.

The beautiful voices stop singing. A musky stink rises from the bed. Oh wait, that's me. Yuck. If I don't get a bath soon, flies are going to start congregating and use me as their own personal maggot farm. I lift my frail body to a sitting position on the bed. I teeter on the edge, gathering my wits, when

Granny and Faithful walk in.

Granny gasps. "Oh! The darling girl is awake."

Faithful rushes to my side, eases onto the bed, and holds my hands. "Are you feeling all right?" Her eyes shine.

Granny hurries to the hallway. "Manly! Daddy! Get your heinies up here right now."

Boots clomp upward in a fast, steady rhythm. Manly pokes his head in first, followed by Daddy. Grins spread across their faces.

"Ain't she a sight for sore eyes!" Daddy comes over and musses my greasy hair, his callused hand dwarfing my head.

"We're glad you're better. Praise the Good Lord," Granny chimes in.

There's that Good Lord again.

I smile at these wonderful people surrounding me. This love stuff? It's a good feeling. One I'd like to keep forever.

"Thank you all." My voice scratches like scraping a stick against bark. "I think I need a bath."

Faithful stifles a giggle. I'm such a dork. Why do I even open my big mouth? Manly catches my eye before he leaves the room, and I swear his eyes sparkle. I sigh. Granny and Faithful exchange a glance before they get to work helping me with towels, soap, and the tub.

Once again, I smell my best. I'm about to slip on my old dress when Faithful stops me. She nods at Granny, who exits briefly and reenters. My heart stills at the pile of blue cradled in Granny's arms. Material cascades like a waterfall from her fingers, and a bright blue dress with short sleeves and a wide-pleated skirt that falls to mid-calf reveals itself.

I can only stand there gaping like an idiot.

Granny slips it over my head and turns me to look in the cracked vanity mirror. A little red bow graces the waist, sitting just above my left hip. I've never in my wildest dreams imagined owning anything this nice. The fabric is even kind of stiff. All of my old clothes were so worn out. It even smells good. I take a few whiffs for good measure.

Granny squeezes my shoulders and heads for the door.

Faithful chuckles and pushes me into the vanity chair, soon tugging and yanking on my hair. Could she be any less gentle? "Well? What do you think?"

She opens a drawer and hands me a small mirror—is there no end to their money?—then spins my chair around and urges me to look at the back of my hair. I gasp. Beautiful fishtail braids slide over my shoulders. Small red bows that match the one on my dress tease me from the ends. I scrutinize myself in the mirror. I look amazing! Did I really teeter on the verge of death? Maybe I wasn't as sick as I thought.

"Why would Granny buy me a dress if she thought I was dying?" I fiddle with one of the braids.

"She had faith you wouldn't." Faithful grabs a makeup brush off the vanity and dabs it in a jar of ivory powder. She swipes it across my cheekbones.

I touch my cheek. That feels odd. I'm actually kind of pretty. Who would've thought? I choke back tears and try to pretend it's not a big deal. Justice's face flashes through my mind. Where did that come from? I don't want to think about him. But…I have to know. "Justice?"

Faithful's eyes deaden. "We buried him the day after you fell sick."

"Oh." I can't manage anything more. Faithful's gaze holds mine in the vanity mirror. Our eyes hold rivers of tears.

Faithful clutches my shoulders. "He's in a better place."

"Where?" Granny still hasn't let me in on that part of the story. "How can he be in a better place when he's dead?"

Faithful stands me up and cocks her head. "It's a wonderful place full of light where people who believe in Abba get to go when they die." She searches for something in the room, scavenging through drawers and the closet. "I'll explain more later, I promise."

"Thanks. That would be great, because I have no idea what you're talking about."

She pauses, her eyes capturing mine. "You don't, do you?"

I shrug and look away.

Faithful returns to her digging. A squeal emanates from the recesses of the closet. "I found it!" Her head pops out, and she shoves a vintage hair pin into one of my braids. A silver-plated crown of thorns. Interesting, and sort of strange. Why not something girly like a rose or a butterfly? I finger the cold metal. Despite the oddity of it, it's still beautiful.

"One more thing." Faithful opens her closet and retrieves something off the floor. She whips around and hands me a pair of shoes.

Weightlessness lifts my spirits to an unfathomable level. I clutch the shoes to my chest. "How?" My weak voice barely pricks the room.

"We measured your feet while you were out. Granny wanted you to have something nice to wear when you woke up."

I don't deserve this. A tear falls from the corner of my eye. Why are they so nice? Faithful kneels and shoves my feet into the shoes, much like a mommy would for a toddler. She stands, spots my red eyes, and fidgets with her hands. I can't help it. I've never had new shoes. Or a new dress. I've never owned *anything* this nice in my life. She nudges me out the bedroom door.

When I descend the stairs, all eyes shift to me. I squirm.

I'm not used to this kind of attention. I don't understand why they care about me, this homeless wretch, sucked into their lives without warning. I meet everyone's eyes and smile my awkward little smile.

My eyes drift to Manly. Our eyes lock and, for a moment, there's *this look*. It awakens all sorts of stirrings. Usually when I'm around guys, I feel like entertainment. Manly's different. Maybe my head's not screwed on straight. Guys are all nasty. Aren't they? He can't possibly be any different. But…he is. I can't help but admit it. I glance at him again, and he's still looking at me.

Stop staring. Seriously. I can't think straight.

Casting my gaze down, my face burns as I hurry to take a seat. How can I like any guy who can crush my soul? Hurt me? They're all the same. I ball up my confusion and kick it out the door. At least for now. Maybe I'll entertain those feelings later. Once I know he's safe. As far as I'm concerned, safe guys don't exist.

Dinner that night prompts my mouth to water. It's Sunday again. A whole week has gone by. I survived on water and broth and am now hungry. Starving, in fact. The smell of Granny's cooking overwhelms my shrunken stomach. I breathe deep and imagine it melting in my mouth.

"Who wants to say the blessing?"

I'm still not sure how I feel about this praying business. Everyone looks to Daddy, but Manly speaks up without hesitation.

"Dear Abba, thank you so much for the food you've blessed us with. Thank you for always providing for us. You are an amazing God. I also want to thank you for bringing our new friend into our lives. She's gone through so much in the short time she's stayed here. It's only because of your healing,

Abba, that she's with us today. Thank you for sparing her. And thank you for the wonderful addition to our family. Amen."

I stare at him, my eyes wide through his entire prayer. He means me! How did they accept me so fast?

Saliva fills my mouth as I devour the scrumptious meal. Wave after wave of deliciousness crashes over my taste buds. I swear my head will explode if I experience any more of this. Is this really my new family? Will they let me stay here, living as one of them? My mind swirls with unanswered questions.

After dinner, I follow my new family onto the front porch. I bask in the sunset and the light breeze cooling the heat of the day. I settle on the porch swing next to Faithful.

"I'm going to try to be a better friend," she says.

I glance at her, and my brow wrinkles. What in the Gliding Lands is she talking about? My eyes dart to the others surrounding me.

Granny sits in a whitewashed rocker next to us, and Manly leans against the railing while Daddy sits on the steps.

"Thanks." I guess. I don't really need a friend. Never really had one before. Except Justice. But whatever, if Faithful thinks she can be mine, I won't stop her.

Granny reaches over and squeezes my hand. "We want you to have Justice's old room."

The question burning inside my chest explodes. "You mean, I can stay? Like, forever?"

Everyone laughs but me.

"Of course we want you to stay." Granny squeezes my hand once more and lets go. "We're your new family now. Consider yourself adopted."

My face beams. I couldn't wipe away my smile if all the stars came crashing down right now. A side hug from Faithful startles me. Why's she touching me? They're so weird. But nice. I kind of like their weirdness. I'm going to have to figure out a way to repay them for their kindness.

Daddy slaps the porch. "Time for singing. My new daughter needs to learn some songs."

His daughter? I'm going to have to pinch myself if this night gets any better. It's true, I don't know any songs. It was a foreign concept in my previous home, but I've heard enough music—bits and pieces picked up in town—to know I love it. I adore music.

The others stare at Manly, who waltzes inside. He steps out a moment later, and the screen door swings shut with a *bang*. But I can't take my eyes off what he holds. He holds a guitar. A real guitar. My eyes widen. I've always wanted to see one up close! New strings contrast with the beat-up instrument. He strums the strings, tunes it, then plays a song I'll never forget. Everyone except me joins in the glorious melody.

Manly's muscular arms strum the guitar for all they're worth. His voice carries clear and strong as he leads the others. The entire experience mesmerizes me as if a hypnotist sways his pendulum. His beautiful lips sing in the moonlight while the stars shine in the sky.

Daddy swings his shoulders and hips while waving his arms, as he tries to imitate the most popular dance of the season. A shrieking chorus bursts from the rest of us. He doesn't seem to mind we're laughing at his expense. Best night of my entire life, hands down.

For a week after that, I weed, water, and do anything they ask of me. I help Granny cook. I shine Daddy's shoes and mend his clothing. Faithful hates to sew, so she hands that responsibility over with relish. She shows me how to make soap. I spend every night on the porch with Manly as he attempts to teach me the songs my soul longs to learn.

He's patient with me, instructing me as a good older brother would. Not like my brother, who hurt, harassed, and abused me with his twisted idea of love.

Everything about Manly exudes safety. When I'm near him, my breathing calms, and my heartaches cease. He won't hurt me, only protect me. Trust blossoms between us, and I no longer cringe when his hand brushes mine. In fact, I like it. Every song, every word, every note, he instructs until I master it. He never gives up on me. And though I swore I'd never do it, my guard dissipates into nearly nothing the more time I spend with him.

A song ends on my lips. Why can't I make the words sound as pretty as he can? "You're so much better at this than I am." Slouching, I try to rein in my whining as a moth enters my vision. I swat at it.

His nose tilts to the sky, his blond locks sweeping back from his face. "I grew up around music. You didn't. It'll take time, but don't worry. You'll get it eventually."

Warmth floods me, and I can't stop my smile. My family never believed in me as he does. My smile fades. Why did I have to land on their farm? I gnaw the insides of my cheeks. All they ever did was discourage me. Hurt me. I turn to Manly. "How do you do it?"

He points to his throat. "Vocal chords are muscles. They build over time."

"No. Not the singing." Laughter tinges my voice. "Although, your singing is pretty amazing." I draw my knees close to my chest and twiddle them back and forth. "I mean, how do you always manage to make me feel so special? To be so kind?"

His eyes spark. "I dunno. I guess because Abba wants me

to be kind. I've grown up this way."

My heart sinks. Oh. So it's not me. It's just something he thinks he should do because his god tells him to. I was wrong. He *can* cause me pain. I curl my lip and stay quiet.

After a minute, he pokes my side. "What's going on in that head of yours?"

You should know. "Nothing that concerns you." I shove off the porch, march up the stairs, and grab the handle of the screen door.

"Girls," Manly mutters before I can make it inside.

I make sure to slam the door just a little harder than necessary.

Friday comes, and Manly decides to try something new. "I've watched you eyeing my guitar," he states after we finish the last notes of a duet.

My voice resembles a squawking parrot. His, on the other hand, reminds me of an ethereal creature not of this world.

"Yeah, maybe I've looked at it a couple of times."

"Would you like to try it?"

I nod as butterflies swirl in my belly. Oh, I'm going to make such a fool of myself. He launches into an impromptu lesson on notes and finger placement, then shoves the guitar in my hands. It shines as the moonlight strikes its sides, and he instructs me on what to do.

Why does he think I can do this so quickly? This isn't going to be pretty. I give it my best attempt, and a horrible racket breaks the evening. I cringe.

"You're doing really good." Yeah right. He chuckles at my feeble attempt. "Next time, maybe you should try it like this." He snuggles closer and puts his arm around me, resting his giant hand over my small one.

Thumping pounds my chest. I stiffen as my protective wall goes up.

"See, you put your fingers like this," he whispers in my ear.

My brain goes fuzzy, and I can't concentrate on what he's telling me. These feelings are not the feelings a sister should have for her brother. His soft breath tickles my hair, and weakness flows through my bones.

What's wrong with me? Why does he make me feel like this? All squishy and weird inside. The complete opposite of how Hate made me feel. I eye the man encircling me, though he doesn't seem to realize it. Manly won't hurt me. He's nothing like Hate.

The protective wall comes crashing down.

My eyes lock with his. That look he gave me in the kitchen, when I walked down in my new blue dress, lurks on his face. I don't know what to make of it, but I like it. My cheeks flame hot as I stare too long. I hang my head, and not a second later, the warmth of his lips touches my forehead. I jump back as fast as he does. My breathing intensifies.

"Uh, I'm...I'm sorry," he stutters and bolts up as if someone holds a cattle prod to his rear. He stumbles back and catches himself before he tumbles to the porch. He bangs his wrist on the screen door and clamors for the handle. He grasps it, glances at me, and rushes inside.

I catch my breath. "I'm not."

Staring into the night sky, I touch the spot his sweet lips brushed.

Now I'll never know if that kiss was meant for my mouth.

That night I go to bed with warm fuzzies streaming through me.

Does Manly think I'm pretty? He wouldn't have tried to kiss me if he didn't. Right? Maybe he was just being nice. They're always so nice. Sometimes I want to yell at them to stop with the nice stuff. I look worse when they do all that.

Faithful and I have been sharing a bed until she can quit crying all night for Justice. Even though it's been a couple of weeks, and even though they've given me Justice's old room, she asks me to stay with her. We stay up late and talk when we should be sleeping. I can't forget Granny's face when she's had to shush us a few times. We laugh so hard. I never really wanted a sister, but now that I have one, I wouldn't give her up for the world. But what's even better? We're actually friends. How many sisters can say that?

No talking tonight. Faithful lies next to me, already in a deep sleep, her light snoring muffled by her pillow. Tonight I wouldn't be a good conversationalist anyway. It's better this way. I almost drift off until sharp voices rouse me, incomprehensible through closed windows and doors. Granny isn't happy with someone. Then *his* voice strains through the walls. Shooting upright, I palm the sheets within my fists, and my heart rate quickens.

Oh no, Granny's upset with Manly!

It's not because of the kiss, is it? I nearly choke.

Do they want me to leave?

I shake my head. I have no clue what Granny and Manly are arguing about. I'm just being paranoid. Might as well try to rest.

I struggle to sleep, and eventually, I coast into a fitful dreamland.

Chapter 6

I wake up and remember. The porch. The guitar in my hands. Stern voices. I hope Granny won't be cross with me too.

The kiss.

My stomach flutters. Cheap kisses are a thing of the past. No more. Why is this so different? He didn't even kiss my lips! Just a simple forehead kiss, yet my heart won't stop melting. My first kiss that wasn't repulsive. It was beautiful. And he apologized for it.

I don't get Manly. He shows affection, then apologizes? The guy makes no sense.

The other side of the bed sits empty, devoid of Faithful, who must already be downstairs working hard. I adorn myself again in the blue dress and run my fingers across the new material. No holes, no tears, no stains. An outfit fit for a queen. I hardly seem worthy to don such luxury. I throw water on my face, rub it dry with a towel, and run my fingers through my thick, unruly hair. I flip it into a quick ponytail and rush downstairs to find eggs and bacon burning in the skillet. The kitchen is barren.

Where is everyone?

I turn off the burners. Don't need my first real home burning down. A darkness creeps through me again, the same one I had when Hate tried to kidnap me. Something's not right.

I run into the living room. Faithful's nose is glued to the window.

"Hey. What's—?"

"Fear. Get down!" She shoos me away.

I crouch as fast as possible. "What is it?" I scoot closer to her.

"Don't let them see you. I'm not sure who they are"—she moves to the side so I can peek out the window—"but they look like trouble."

Two guys are surrounded by Daddy, Granny, and Manly. My spirit falls to the pit of my stomach.

Faithful grabs my shoulder. "Who are they?"

Jagged breath puffs from my lips, and I can't speak. Everything's ruined now. They came to destroy any happiness I found. They will rip it from me, smash it to pieces, and pull me back into a living hell.

"Fear." She shakes me. "Snap out of it."

My gaze finds hers, and her eyes widen. I might as well tell her. "It's my papa and brother. And they're here to get me."

"I thought so," she mutters.

I've told Faithful enough stories at night for her to know this is one of the worst things that could happen to me.

"Is he the one who poisoned you?" She points to Hate.

Goosebumps run from my shoulders up my neck. "Yes, and he'll do it again without hesitation." I peer closer at Hate's nose and sneer. Crooked. Must be from Manly punching him in the store. He isn't a pretty boy anymore. My heart leaps at the thrill of vengeance.

"What I don't understand—if what you tell me about your brother is true—his sick obsession with you...why would he want to kill you?"

Heat simmers under the surface. My fists clench. "He wants me back so he can have me again." My eyes lock with Faithful's. "But he'd rather kill me than let someone else claim me. Papa just wants me back to work the fields and clean his kitchen, not to mention, be his personal punching bag. 'Course he has Mother and Hate for that." My dead voice doesn't match the turmoil raging within.

I can't go back. My stomach sickens into a pit of tar.

Faithful's face pales. "We need to hide you. Right now."

Hide? It won't do any good. They'll just find me. They always find me.

Granny, Daddy, and Manly have their hands on their hips as they form a protective barrier between the intruders and our front door.

A wave of bravery washes over me. "No, I can't leave them. They have no idea how brutal Hate and Papa are."

"They can take care of themselves, Fear." She tugs me away from the window.

I push back. "Faithful, stop! I can't let them get hurt." And they will if I don't stop it.

She grabs my arm and drags me across the room. No matter how much I thrash, I can't escape her grasp. I can't win this battle, so I give up.

"A secret room lies below the stairs. We'll hide you there."

They'll still find me. Once they want something bad enough, there's no stopping them.

She moves a bench out of the way, opens a slanted door,

and shoves me inside, throwing in an old afghan for comfort, I suppose. "Now be quiet," she orders. The door slams.

Darkness. I won't panic. I won't.

She moves the screeching bench in place. Her feet patter over the floorboards as she moves to the kitchen. Things stay quiet except for clanking dishes and running water.

A ruckus clamors at the front door. Yelling. The screen door bursts open, and bodies tumble to the floor. Grunting and angry voices seep through the cracks. Hate and Manly raise their voices as they struggle from the floor. More yelling. *Thud. Bang.* Two more *thuds*. Knuckles crunch into flesh. Bodies crash into walls. I wince with each blow.

What's going on out there? I wish I could see what's happening.

Granny screams, then Faithful. Something slams into the bench right outside my hidden door. Scuffling and banging reverberate through my claustrophobic haven. Hate's voice breaks through the door, mere inches from my hiding spot. I jump and stiffen.

"You can't keep her from me. I'll get her back."

Manly groans. "Wanna bet?"

I scramble away from the door. *Don't let him find me!*

More *thuds*. The front door slams. All goes silent, and I hold my breath.

It's all I can do to restrain myself from bursting out of my hiding spot. Shuffling feet and quiet reassurances fill my ears until I want to scream, "Is everyone okay?" A shaft of light filters in as the door creaks open. Faithful stands in the opening. I search her face, her arms, everything. She trembles, her face pale, but no blood, no wounds.

"Thank the Good Lord!" Look at me, copying these people. Guess they're rubbing off.

I hug her, and she clings to me. My eyes shift to Daddy and Manly who crouch by a figure splayed on the ground near the front door.

"Granny!" I push past the men. Blood gushes over Granny's face. I gasp as weakness rushes through my legs. I drop to the ground, grabbing Faithful's arm on the way.

"Calm down," Daddy says. "Head wounds bleed a lot, but they usually seem much worse than they actually are."

My mind believes him, but my body doesn't. So much blood!

Manly grabs my arms and guides me to stand. He holds my arms and tilts his head toward mine. "He's right. She'll be okay."

I hug him tight, pressing my cheek to his chest, and he cries out. I'm hurting him!

I rip my arms away. "They injured you, too."

"Just a couple of bruised ribs." His strained voice says more than he's willing to.

He's in pain, and it's all my fault. "Manly, I'm so sorry. None of this would've happened if I hadn't come here." I break down and sob into my hands.

"Calm down, kiddo." He smooths my hair away from my face. "It's not that bad."

I meet his eyes just as he grabs his ribs. My eyes narrow. *Liar.* If he weren't hurt, I'd hit him myself.

Daddy helps Granny to her feet and moves her to the kitchen. Angling Manly into the living room, I lug a chair to him, suppressing my sobs.

"Not that bad?" I take his arm to settle him in the chair.

"I need to rest." He clutches his chest. "Go check on Granny."

I glue myself to the side of his chair. No way.

"Please go check on her."

I'm not budging. He needs me. "Daddy and Faithful are with her. Someone should be with you." I place my hand over his.

"I'm not a big baby." He echoes the words Daddy used the first day I met them, when I tended to his wounds.

"You sound like your dad."

His eyes widen. "And you sound nothing like yours."

The compliment both warms and chills me. I nod. "He's a horrid man."

Manly's eyes soften and gaze into mine with an intensity I've never seen before. He blinks, and the sturdy young man returns. "Go check on Granny." His stern words weaken my resolve.

Fine. I'll do what you ask. I sulk into the kitchen and scrutinize Granny's face. They were right. The cut above her eye bleeds no more. She may only need a few stitches.

Like a Wildie with its tail on fire, Faithful storms through the kitchen. She slams the table with her fist. "What cowards!" She yells at no one in particular. "To hurt an innocent old lady."

"Hey now, I'm not *that* old."

My tension eases, and I take a deep breath. If Granny's joking, she'll be all right. Faithful continues her ranting and stomps around the kitchen, while Daddy, who seems to have the only level head, tends to his mother.

He peers up at me. "She'll be as good as new in a week or so."

"Daddy!" I screech. I point to the purple circle encompassing his eye. In the hustle to fix Granny's wound, no one thought to check Daddy.

Granny gasps. "What happened to you? I couldn't see your

black eye through all the blood. Are you all right, honey?"

"It doesn't feel real good, I'll admit."

Granny waves at Faithful, who continues to stomp about. "Please go to the outside freezer and get him one of those soft ice packs." Faithful whirls and storms out of the room.

"An ice pack on my eye, Mama? That won't be comfortable." Daddy grimaces.

"Do you want your eye to swell shut?" Before he can even shake his head, she continues. "So do what I say and use an ice pack. Got it?"

Daddy puts up his hands. "Whatever the queen says," he jokes.

I falter. Uppers reserve the title of "queen" for themselves. Downers can't call themselves that. Apparently, no one gives a fruity fig but me.

Faithful hurtles in with the ice pack. She tosses it to me, flings herself on a kitchen chair, and sobs. Oh brother. She didn't even get hurt. Granny takes the ice pack from my hands and gives it to Daddy.

"Now, who's going to stitch me up?" She extracts a tiny wooden box from a drawer and plops it on the table.

"I'll do it." Everyone turns my way, faces blank. I rush to explain. "My papa was kind of the violent type." Daddy coughs. I know, I know. I couldn't have said anything more obvious, but still. "I've mended many wounds in my day. I'm pretty good at stitches. Even done it on myself once or twice."

Granny rests her soft hand on my arm. Her eyes pool with liquid. "I would be honored if you would do my stitches."

Before long, I have her patched up good as new. Daddy and Manly seem impressed. Guess I'm not completely useless. Consumed with her blubbers, Faithful doesn't even notice. Granny cups my chin, and a glow emanates from her smile full of aged and yellowed teeth.

"Would you be a darling and help clean up the mess?" She heads over to the sink and fills a bucket with water. She nods in Faithful's direction. "This one here isn't much help when it comes to blood. Lord give me strength."

I chuckle. That wasn't hard to tell.

She waves her hand at the mop and blood on the floor.

"Sure. I can take care of that. No problem."

Her worn-out eyes crinkle.

I lug the bucket to the fight scene, sloshing water on their wooden floor as I go. The mop scrubs up the smeared crimson markings in no time.

Weary, though the day has barely begun, I grab a towel from the kitchen and sop up my liquid mess. I glance up to find Manly staring at me with a forlorn look in his eyes. I stop, towel dangling in my fingers.

"It's not safe for you here. They know where you are."

My face flushes hot, and I duck my head. *What do you want me to do, leave?* I grit my teeth and continue cleaning up blood and water. His boots don't move from my line of vision. He's probably expecting me to say something. "How did they find me, anyway?"

"I'm guessing your parents saw our truck after your brother stuck you with poison. It's the only truck like it in town. I guess they asked around, put two and two together, then figured out where you live. It's a small town. People talk. I can't believe I was so stupid I didn't think of that."

"You're not stupid, Manly. I didn't think of it either till we got there." I get up. My legs teeter, but I steady myself. "But—what does that mean?"

He looks down. "I don't know. We need to talk it over after everyone rests."

He leaves without another word and trudges up the stairs, Granny and Daddy trailing after him.

Faithful nudges me. "We should probably clean up."

Done sobbing then? "You all right?"

She barely nods.

She isn't fooling me. There's still a tornado going on inside of her. She's just chosen to ignore it for the moment.

Faithful and I tidy up the disheveled house, then sink into living room chairs. A puff of dust ascends from Faithful's. She blows a piece of hair off her forehead. "We ought to take these chairs out and beat them with the dust stick."

Neither of us moves. I'm defeated. Worn out. We sit in silence and, within a few minutes, Faithful dozes off. Sun hits her right in the eyes. I go to the curtain to close it. The yard stands empty. Thank the Good Lord Hate and Papa are long gone.

Ha! I'm starting to sound like them more and more. My new family. My better family.

I bite my lip, refusing to give in to the tears. Why did Hate and Papa have to find me? It's not fair.

I'm too riled up to nap. Might as well figure out a meal. When they come out of their rooms, they'll be famished. Granny shouldn't be cooking in her condition, and Faithful only knows how to burn things. I glance into the adjoining room, where her snores rattle the silence. Aw, so sweet. Except when she does it in the middle of the night. Maybe she'll be okay with me sleeping in Justice's room tonight?

After searching the kitchen, I choose a midday meal and get to work. It takes me about three hours on my own, but in the end, I've accomplished a little miracle.

I brush the flour off my dress and set the table. A shadow approaches down the stairs.

"Ooh! What's that scrumptious smell?" Daddy descends and does his little happy dance that makes me giggle.

"You are the silliest man I've ever met," I tease.

"And don't you forget it," he says with a turn and a wiggle. He takes off his hat and gives a grand bow. I return the bow, and a veggie peel falls out of my hair. I can't stop my giggles. When I straighten, I spot Manly at the top of the stairs.

"Did I just hear an angel laugh?" He meets my eyes, and a giant butterfly flicks its wings inside my gut.

Daddy's eyes widen, and he chuckles. "No. That was just me."

I burst into laughter.

Manly takes a rigid step down the stairs, and my laugh lodges in my throat. Daddy and I frown as we watch our loved one in pain. Manly tries to hide he's hurting, but his stiff body and the way he holds his arm over his ribs says otherwise. He seems determined to ignore it.

"I was talking about the little lady." Manly points at me.

Daddy feigns hurt. "You mean my laughter isn't angelic?"

"Hardly."

Granny teeters into the room. She spots the food on the table, and her eyes light up. She grabs my face and kisses me. "No one's made dinner for me in so long." It's all she can manage. She clears her throat and brushes past me to inspect the meal. I glow with each little grunt of approval.

"It wasn't that big of a deal. It was fun," I insist. I'm not lying.

"Fun? You call cooking fun?" Faithful walks in behind me. "I call it torture."

She grabs food off the counter and places it on the table. I rush to help her as everyone else sits. As soon as Faithful and I join them, Daddy says the blessing. My lower back tightens and aches. Are they going to enjoy this meal? What if it makes them sick? I hope I did everything correctly.

They scarf it down and request seconds. My shoulders relax. A slow grin spreads across my face. I must've done something right.

Then the compliments start. Everyone showers me with kind words and thanks. Everyone but Manly. He sits and stares hard at his plate. His forehead wrinkles like a little old lady who spent too many years in the sun and too few years applying moisturizer.

"What is it?" Faithful pipes up.

"Huh?" His dreamland disappears in a poof. "Oh, I was just thinking. This is the first time in nine years someone other than Granny has cooked for me. Since I was ten." He glances at a digital image of a woman on the wall. "When Mama died." His words fade as his mouth creases into a frown.

That explains why there's no mother around. His frown digs at my heart. I don't like seeing him like this. Wait. Did he say nine years from the time he was ten?

I beam in an absurd manner as I calculate how old Manly is. *Nineteen.*

Faithful frowns. "I miss mom, too." She shakes her head and tosses a roll at him, hitting his chest. "But Fear didn't just cook for you, dummy. She cooked for all of us."

He blinks a couple of times, snatches the roll, and throws it back and forth between his fingers before chomping down on it. He catches me staring and stops chewing.

Oh, gambits! Look away, look away. I jerk my gaze to my plate. Heat envelops me. Will I ever stop embarrassing myself around him?

After everyone eats their fill and I help put dishes away, Daddy waltzes over to the south wall and pulls out an out-of-date Electro-Screen.

"Wow! You guys have an Electro-Screen? I've only seen a couple, ever."

Faithful squints. "You don't get out much, do you?"

Manly glares at his sister. "Neither do we."

Faithful turns her nose to the sky.

Ooh. Burn.

Daddy messes with the buttons. "It's not much. It's pretty ancient, but it does its job. All the houses were equipped with these a while ago. After the war ended and tensions were still high, they ripped out most of them. They somehow missed ours."

"The Uppers missed your guns *and* your Electro-Screen?" I peer around the tidy house. Did I miss anything else about this place? "You guys are sure lucky."

Granny shakes her head. "More like blessed, I'd say. Abba always watches out for those who love him."

Abba again. Geesh. Abba this, Abba that. For crying out loud, just shut it. I turn my attention to Daddy. What's he up to?

After what feels like an eternity, Daddy's button pushing produces a slow melody. A sad, sweet song so ancient, I only dreamed such music existed. Daddy grabs Faithful's hand and spins her around, trying to improve her sullen mood. It does the trick. Soon she's all smiles. I sneak a look at Manly. *Please, please ask me to dance.* He coughs, winces, and grabs his ribs. Oh yeah, that would be impossible right now.

Daddy takes my hand before I can react and drags me out to dance. A shudder runs through me. What if I mess up? Will he hit me? He palms my waist and gently clasps my hand in his, whirling me around. He spins me and dips me until I'm laughing. This is fun! He doesn't even seem to care that I keep stepping on his toes. My stomach aches. I can't stop giggling! Daddy spins me once more.

In the middle of a spin, I meet Manly's eyes planted firmly on me, which sends sparks up my neck and into my temples. Daddy bends in a dramatic bow, concluding our dance. He grabs Faithful next as I retreat next to Manly. Invisible rubber bands encircle my chest, pinching and squeezing the air out of me. Don't care. I would do it over and over again. I beam at Manly. He's still staring at me. Awkward.

Faithful and I take turns dancing with Daddy, enjoying the love of a father who knows how to treat his daughters well. A faster song comes on, and Faithful grabs my hands, scoots me forward, and moves to the beat. I copy her moves and pick up the rhythm. I'm not nearly as talented as she is. We twirl and spin. Manly's eyes sparkle as he grins. Daddy continues to slow dance.

"Change your rhythm!" Faithful yells at her dad. He keeps dancing at the same steady pace. Stubborn, silly man. I adore him so much.

The song cuts short. Silence fills the room, followed by Faithful's and my groans. Granny stands near the Electro-Screen, her finger hovering over the emerging holographic image of a strange glowing symbol.

"I hate to be a spoilsport and ruin this"—she waves her hand, indicating the dancing—"but we need to figure out what's best for Fear. I'm afraid if we keep her here much longer, those two knuckleheads will return. Fear needs to move, and it's got to be tonight."

Staring at Granny, my mouth hangs open. She doesn't want me anymore?

She stares back, the love on her face surpassed only by her determination.

"We could keep her safe." Manly takes his hands out of his pockets.

Faithful turns on him. "Yeah, y'all did such a great job keeping yourselves safe, didn't you?"

Manly's neck reddens. "We're not dead, are we? And Fear is safe. We did our jobs."

Faithful whips her fiery hair behind her shoulder. "Those monsters are still out there. And now they know she's here. You don't think they'll be back?"

Manly's jaw clenches. "*I* can keep her safe."

Faithful's eyes shed their fire and fill with tears. "But who's going to keep *you* safe?"

My heart thumps harder with each passing word. They're going to kick me out. I have nowhere to go. I grind my teeth and rub my arm until the friction sends prickles to my shoulder.

Granny eyes me, her smile gentle. "Your family is out to get you back, and when they do, no telling what kind of pain they'll put you through. They may very well kill you. Your brother already tried."

Yeah, about that. "I'm still confused how I survived the poison anyway?"

They glance at each other, and Daddy clears his throat. "Abba healed you. You should've died, Fear, but Abba kept you safe. He gave you another chance."

Granny nods. "Apparently Abba has some mighty big plans for you, Fear. If he kept you alive, we'd better try just as hard. You have to hide. You need to get away tonight."

My stomach lurches. *No! I'm not going anywhere.* The conversation flows around me, and I hold my breath and will my lunch to stay where it belongs.

"Where will she go?" Faithful asks.

Granny turns to the Electro-Screen and pulls up the Communicator. Now I understand why she interrupted our music. Not that I'm any happier about it. She punches in a variety of patterns, turns to us, and puts her finger in the air.

"I have an idea." She shoos us out of the room.

I wait in the living room with everyone else. The others must be able to tell I'm none too pleased about the idea of leaving them. I'm on edge as I wait for Granny to finish her conversation. A lifetime passes as I wait—and wait. And wait.

Granny enters the room. "Good news."

Her voice is much too perky. I'm not buying it. Leaving will never be "good news."

"My aunt owns a ranch called the Fallen. They harbor orphans. Mainly parachute babies like yourself."

My eyebrows shoot up. A whole ranch of kids like me? My interest dies a sullen death. Oh, goody.

She hurries on. "She has plenty of room and would love if you stayed with her. And plenty of horses, campfires, songs. Not to mention lots and lots of friends."

She smiles as though this should make me happy or something. It doesn't. Not even close.

I cross my arms and scowl. "I don't want more friends. I just got a new family. I'm not leaving." She can't make me. I stomp my foot.

Manly swallows hard. How can he keep quiet? Doesn't he care? I clench my fists.

Granny quiets for a moment, then lets out a deep breath. "You know we love you, Fear. You know you are, and always will be, a part of our family. That's the reason you can't stay. It's not safe. And I will always do whatever it takes to protect my family." She comes up and touches my shoulders. "You must go. And you must leave tonight."

Chapter 7

I throw myself on the bed. My head spins in all directions.
I don't even know what to think. Faithful peeks in. I won't talk
to her. I won't. I sit on the bed with my arms pretzeled tight.
She tiptoes in and packs a bag with my meager belongings. It
doesn't matter. I won't be using it, 'cause I'm not going.

She sneaks in a few of her own things. She's way too nice,
giving me her stuff. My head throbs. This isn't happening.
How can I leave this family I've grown to love? I can't. I just
can't do it. Why did my old family ruin everything? Their faces
spiral through my vision: Mama, Papa, Hate. My brain boils,
and I envision smoldering hot lava engulfing their feet,
creeping up their bodies, inch by inch as if alive, finally
devouring them whole.

Faithful finishes packing my bag. She sits beside me and
hugs me. I'm too angry to push her away.

"Abba, be with Fear right now. Please take away her pain.
Help her know you're taking care of her, whether she's here or
thousands of miles away. Thank you for loving Fear. Comfort

her. In your name, amen."

Tears stream down my cheeks, and for some reason, the hatred toward my old family dissipates. Peace fills the room. Where's it coming from?

"Thank you," I blubber as I grab tissues for my runny nose. "That does make me feel better."

"You can thank him," she replies.

Does she mean Abba? Voices come from below, and this time, Daddy and Manly are in the middle of a disagreement. Faithful grabs a hand towel and dries my tears. She grins, and we both rush to the banister and lean over to listen.

"Come on, you gotta let me. I can get Fear to the Fallen just as well as you can."

"I know that, son."

They're arguing over who gets to take me to the ranch? My legs weaken, and I weave into Faithful, bumping shoulders with her. She wiggles her eyebrows at me. I hope Manly wins.

"I don't think it's wise with your injured ribs and all." Daddy presses his fingers to his forehead. Oh, yeah. Manly's wearing him down.

"They're only bruised." Manly places his palms on the table and leans forward.

"How do we know that?"

"I just know." Manly's more stubborn than I am. "Besides, you know me—I can't slow down. If I stay here, I'll hurt myself further. You know I can't stay out of the fields. At least I'll be sitting for three days in the truck. I can't make it any worse by sitting, can I?"

"Six days," Daddy retorts. "You still have to drive home after dropping her off, remember?"

Manly gives his dad big doe eyes.

My heart melts just a little. Okay. Make that a lot. Oh my

word, he's adorable.

"Your Granny won't like it one bit. Did you forget the conversation you two had the other night?"

Manly's shoulders droop. Ooh, what's this all about?

Manly paces back and forth, almost running into a misplaced kitchen chair. "Yeah, I remember. I would never let anything happen." Daddy raises his eyebrows. Manly flinches. "I swear. Please. You have to trust me." Daddy rubs his forehead again. "Have I ever been untrustworthy?"

Daddy stalls. He's weakening. I send up a silent cheer. "No, son. I'm just worried about you is all. And the girl."

Manly swats a fly away from his face. "Come on, I never get to go anywhere! This is my chance to do something exciting for once. Something new." A puppy begging for food has nothing on him. "Plus, you know you're a better shot than me. If those guys come back, you'd do a much better job of keeping Gran and Faithful safe."

"I wouldn't exactly call this exciting, son."

"Isn't that sad, though? That riding in a truck for three days is exciting for me?" Manly huffs.

Daddy stuffs his hands into his pockets and putzes around in a circle before returning to the conversation. "Fine. Have it your way. But when you come home and your ribs are killing you, don't blame me. I'll figure out a way to explain this to Granny."

"Yeah!" Manly pops a fist on the table, then rubs Daddy's shoulders as he sucks down a grimace. Must have jostled his tender ribs. "Thank you! You won't regret this. I'll—"

They notice their eavesdroppers at the same time.

"What are you two beauties doing standing up there?" Daddy waves us down.

The four of us gather in a huddle, and Daddy begins

another blessing. He asks for protection on our trip and that Manly won't further hurt himself while being a "knight in shining armor." Whatever that means. I just hope this knight won't get us lost in the wilderness somewhere.

Granny comes in from the garden and hands me a net of six tiny apples. "They're not even close to ready yet, but at least it's something to eat. These are the biggest I could find." She goes to the cupboards and empties whatever won't spoil over the next few days into a basket. "I wish I had more to send with you. There's no time to bake bread or go into town."

She's so worried. Poor Granny. I've got to say something. "This is wonderful, Granny. It's plenty. Please don't worry. You said it's only a three-day drive. This should do fine. Thank you." I hug the gray-haired woman, and her softness envelopes me.

"I'm sure Aunt Joy will give Manly something for the drive home. I'm such a worrywart sometimes." Granny pulls back from the hug with tears in her eyes. "I'll miss you, girl. I was just getting used to having you around."

"I'll be back, won't I? When the threat is gone?"

Everyone looks everywhere but at me. I glare at them, daring one of them to answer me. Do they think I won't come home? Ever? I push back tears, and my glare intensifies.

Granny gives in and meets my eyes. "Of course, honey. But don't get your hopes up it'll be soon. Your pa was mighty angry, and I doubt he's going anywhere."

Wish he'd take a permanent dunk in the outhouse.

"What if they come back? How will you defend yourselves?" A vision of this beautiful family lying in their own blood flashes before my eyes. I wipe it away with a hard blink.

Daddy reassures me with one tap on the rifle. "Got it covered, sweetie. Don't you worry about nothin'." He hugs me. "I love you, sweet girl."

I go completely still in his embrace. Papa never told me that, not ever. Does Daddy mean it? I pull away and look into his eyes. Wow. He does. He really, truly does. "Thank you for being a great dad. I've never had one before."

His eyes well up with tears. I turn away. I can't bear someone watching me cry. I can't imagine he feels any different.

Faithful attacks me before I can take a breath and blabbers on about a quilt we talked about making. "I'll still make it even though you won't be here to help and even though I hate sewing. That way, when you come back, you can have the quilt. I'll sew half of it, and you sew the other half. When we meet again, we'll sew it together as one giant quilt."

"I love that idea." My heart swells. Maybe I *will* see them all again. "If I can find quilting supplies where I'm going, I'll do it for sure."

She fastens her vintage hair pin to my braid. "A parting gift," she chokes out.

I yank a homemade bracelet off my wrist and shove it into her hands. She taught me how to weave this bracelet, and more importantly, she taught me what it means to have a friend. I can't say a blasted word. She throws her arms around me, and we can't stop hugging. Manly comes down from packing his bag. Good. I need to get out of here before the ocean falls from my eyes. I give everyone one last hug, then head to the truck.

The sun sits low in the sky. Not too many hours before nightfall.

Daddy gets in first.

My forehead wrinkles. "You're going?" Wasn't expecting that. I really wanted to spend time with Manly. Preferably alone.

"No, but Manly's never been there. I'll program the old GPS. I'm pretty sure it still works." He punches a couple of buttons, and a glowing holographic map shows up near the dash. He winks. "Works."

Manly throws our bags in the bed, and Granny gasps. "You'll need bedding."

As Daddy fiddles with the ancient programming, Granny and Faithful hurry inside. I occupy myself by filling our water jugs at the well a few yards from the truck.

A few minutes later, they come out with arms full of pillows and blankets and dump them in the pickup bed. Granny rushes into the house one more time and emerges with a rolled-up pad, thick enough to ease the discomfort of an unforgiving surface. I grab it from her and hoist it over the side of the truck, my lack of height not helping. Granny places her silky old-lady hand, complete with mocha-colored spots and prominent veins, on my shoulder.

"I still feel lousy sending you two off without making dinner first."

"That's sweet, Gran, but I'm still full from the late lunch."

"It was a great lunch, too. I'll never forget that, sweetheart." She smiles, then gets down to business. "Best you two leave before it gets too late. The pad can be laid out in the truck bed. Maybe I should send more blankets and pillows."

Granny lurches toward the house, but Manly and I put up our hands to stop her.

"Granny, I think twenty pillows is enough," I tease.

She bats my arm and blushes. "I will continue asking Abba to keep you safe."

Daddy reemerges from the house. I didn't even realize he left the truck. A rifle is slung across his back, and he clasps a box of ammo. He gives them to Manly. "Just in case."

They nod to each other, and I hurry to get in the cab before any more hugs or words of encouragement can stop us. Manly joins me.

He looks at me and raises his eyebrows. "Time to get outta here."

The highway zooms past. Have we already been on the road a full half-hour? Time speeds by when I'm with Manly. I breathe in deep. The scent of fresh shampoo and earthiness fills my nose. Oh man, he smells good. I won't get moments like these much longer. A hot iron stabs me in the chest.

I'm going to miss them all so much!

The thought bursts out in the form of one of those ugly cries. The kind only a person who cares can witness without the other person feeling like a complete idiot. Wracking sobs consume me. I can't stop. Leaving them will take away any shred of happiness. I must not be meant for happiness. Always lemons, never lemonade.

Manly pulls over. "Are you all right?"

Some guys would panic right about now. Not him. He must've seen this before from Faithful. I'm a ginormous baby.

My nose plugs as my cheeks stream.

"I'm fine." Can he even hear me through my sobs? I'm such a liar. A liar and a baby. Good grief.

"No, you're not." He scoots toward me and holds me close.

I stiffen. Why is he touching me? *It's okay. He's safe, remember? He's not Hate. He's Manly.*

I allow myself to relax in his embrace. My breathing evens, and my sobs decrease. I glance down, afraid I dripped more than just tears on his arms. I detach myself from him, pull out a tissue, and attempt to wipe his arm.

Manly points to my face. "You should use that on your nose."

I punch his arm with the strength of a toddler and wipe my nose until it stops running. He revs the engine and eases back onto the road.

"That was embarrassing." I stare out the window so I don't have to face him.

"Why? I thought it was sweet."

You did? I snort, making him laugh. My cheeks burn hot. I fidget with the red bow on my dress. "You're seeing all the ugly sides of me today, aren't you?"

"If we're going to spend three full days together in a truck, I'm assuming we'll see the ugly side to both of us. Don't worry, my turn is coming."

Grinning, I turn my attention out the window. I love how he always tries to comfort me. I guess this is what it's like to have a best friend.

Out the windshield, the world flies by in glorious shades of greens, blues, and yellows. I've never left our town. Same goes for Manly. Adrenaline fills the cab as I examine everything I see. It's nothing unusual—the normal fields, trees, shanties, and an actual house thrown in every so often.

"I never realized how blessed I was to grow up living in an actual house. It seems like they're few and far between." His wide eyes take in everything.

Holographic images pop up, shifting and changing each time we need to switch direction. Thank Abba or we'd never get there. Manly seems to know even less of the world outside our town than I do.

"I didn't grow up in a house."

His jaw ticks, and he wipes his mouth, not saying anything. Peaceful silence permeates the cab for most of the ride.

I wake up. Pitch blackness enshrouds the truck, which sits unmoving, engine off. An eerie, tendril-like tingle crawls up my spine. Where's Manly? I take shallow breaths as my mind races. What happened, and why is it so dark? I'm not awake enough to get out of the truck and find out. My temple throbs since I've spent the last few hours hugging the passenger door.

My door flies open. I scream and fall backward, but strong arms catch me. The person grunts as I whip my head back to catch a glimpse of the responsible party. Manly's hair cascades over his face as he peers down at me.

"You don't want to sleep in there all night, do you?" He asks through gritted teeth. He heaves me to my feet and leads me to the back of the truck, holding his ribs. "Sorry for scaring you."

Wild eyes bug out of my head, and I will my heartbeat to still as I trail him. "You sure did."

He ignores that. "I made up a bed." Manly shines a light at the pickup, and sure enough, a comfy little bed waits for us. Who knew the pad would be a perfect fit?

Good. Now maybe he'll let me thank him the proper way. "Thank you. This looks great."

Unsteady from waking, I let him help me up. That all-familiar burning when we touch scorches me as he lifts me over the side of the truck. As I lie down, a tremor courses through me. The bed's not as comfortable as it looks, but it'll do. And soon he'll be lying here. Beside me. Sweat breaks out on my brow. Gambits. What have I gotten myself into? I take a deep breath. It's okay. I can work with this.

A grimace shakes Manly's voice as he peers over the side. "Do you need anything?"

"Water would be amazing." *And so are you.*

He shuffles through the tall grass, only to gasp and groan.

I sit up. "Are you hurting?" I could slap myself. Of course he's hurting.

"Just a bit," he admits. "That's the main reason I decided to stop for the night. I could've driven for another couple of hours if not for these ribs. I'll be okay after I rest." He hands me the water jug.

"Thank you." *Now come to bed.*

He nods and walks toward the cab.

"Wait!" What's he doing?

He stops.

"Where are you going?"

"I'm going to get some sleep?" Confusion rings through his voice.

No! I have to thank him. He's been too good not to. "Why don't you sleep back here with me?" I pat the fluffy pillow beside me.

He's quiet for a moment. "I'm not so sure that's the best idea."

"Why not?" I retort. "If your ribs are hurting, you should lie flat, not scrunched up in a tiny cab." What's his problem?

"That's true. But…I mean, are you sure you're okay with that? I don't want…I mean, I just…"

"Quit your stuttering and climb in." Seriously, he needs to get a grip. I'm not going to bite him. "It'll be best for both of us. Your ribs will heal better. We can share body heat. And if a Wildie attacks, you can blow its head off."

He grabs a pillow, blanket, and rifle from the cab, walks back, and lifts himself over the side, careful not to bump his ribs. "When you put it that way, it does make sense, doesn't it?"

The night covers him in darkness, but a smile laces his voice. Glad he got some sense in his head. He rearranges the bedding in the pitch black—not doing much good—and elbows me in the side a couple of times. He even pulls my hair.

"This is working out great, isn't it?" Sarcasm drips from his voice.

"It's all right. I'm sure you didn't mean to beat me up."

"No, I did not." His flurry of movement dissipates. Turning away from me, he groans and rolls to his back. Lying on his side apparently isn't an option with injured ribs.

Time to make my move.

"Thank you for coming back here with me. This will help me sleep better." I scoot closer to him and rest my hand on his thigh. He stiffens.

"What…what are you doing?" His voice shakes.

Playing dumb, are we? Surely he knows what I'm doing.

"I'm showing you my thanks." I run my hand up his thigh to his belt loop and wrap my finger under it.

He sucks in a breath and grabs my hand. "Stop! You—you don't need to do that."

My face burns. "I'm only trying to repay you for your kindness." Is he rejecting me? Seriously?

"Please." He gently places my hand at my side. "Just being around you is thanks enough."

Wait. He tried to kiss me. Surely he's attracted to me? Maybe I'm wrong. Maybe he just sees me as his kid sister. "Sorry." I turn away. "I won't do it again."

"See that you don't." His gruff voice doesn't disguise the tremor running through it.

I sigh. Schnitzel fritz. I thought there was something between us. At least I can still enjoy being around him, even if my feelings aren't returned. My heart aches. I frown. I've never felt this way before. I've also never been rejected by a guy. This kind of sucks.

The warmth between us radiates like the steamy motor of the old truck after a long day on the road. I don't know if it's the fact I've already taken a long nap or that I can't stop the heat from our close contact, but my eyes won't shut. Even in the darkness, I sense his presence in such a powerful way. My thoughts won't calm. Lucky for me, he'll never know because he falls asleep within minutes.

Looking at the stars, I shiver as the night air wafts over my exposed face. I breathe in his intoxicating scent and sigh. Nothing could be better than this.

Chapter 8

The Fallen breaches the horizon. Good, almost there. Manly's been awfully quiet these last few hours. Is that sweat on his forehead? His normally tan skin has paled. Why, he's almost as pale as Faithful. He pulls into the drive. A flowing willow tree sits to our left. Row upon row of mud-brown cabins fill the landscape. Well, isn't this place quaint?

Manly falls to the seat of the truck with a *thud*. No, no, *no*! Screams fill the air. Screams coming from my mouth. I bounce out of the truck, jump up and down, and wave my arms. Someone has to hear me. Someone has to be there! I continue screaming to no one in particular. Should I run to that cabin? No. Have to stay with Manly.

It's hard to breathe. Where is everyone? What if this isn't the right place? What if these people aren't nice and won't help? Maybe I should try to pull him out? No, that's just stupid. What am I thinking?

Please Abba—this is my first attempt at a prayer—*please help Manly. Send someone to help him!*

I don't even finish my pleading before someone rushes into view. An old but muscular man, followed by another younger man in overalls and a lady in an apron, run over to me.

I wave my hands toward the truck. "He collapsed as soon as we got here. Please help him."

The men go to the driver's side and ease him out. A groan escapes Manly's lips as one of the men wraps his arm around him.

"Careful!" I shout. "His ribs are injured."

They heave him up, and his head falls to his chest. He groans, and I swallow hard.

The woman takes my hand. "Everything will be okay."

I disagree. Manly's hurting. Nothing's okay. Nothing will be okay until he's better. She slides her arm around my shoulders.

"My name is Joy, but everyone here calls me Aunt Joy."

She escorts me to a large cabin, connected on one side to an even larger brick building. I follow the men who carry Manly. Slow and purposeful steps. We venture inside, trailing the men. This cabin looks like an office and meeting area. A small Medical Room stands to the side, door wide open, with two hospital beds in it. Despite the gentleness the men display, more groans seize my heart as they lay him down. A moment of clarity snaps Manly's eyes open. I take the opportunity to let him know what I think.

"Why didn't you tell me you were in so much pain?" Stubborn mule of a man.

He shifts a sideways grin, then points to himself. "Manly? Remember?"

I want to strangle the guy, but instead I reach out and stroke his soft hair as he passes out again.

Aunt Joy takes my arm. "We should go," she whispers.

I leave the room and squeeze my watery eyes shut. I wipe at the corners. The last three days went by so fast. Why didn't I see how bad he was? How did he hide his increasing pain? I look behind me and try to catch one last glimpse of Manly, but the men block my view.

The men glance at each other, frown, and approach the old lady and me. The one in the overalls rubs his unshaved jaw. "You were saying his ribs are injured?"

"Yes," I reply. "They got bruised the morning we left."

The two men exchange a look. I hate when people do that! Can't they just say what they're thinking? I cross my arms.

The older of the two clears a scratchy throat. "It seems to be a bit more than bruising. I can almost bet he's got a fracture of some kind." His voice is gruff.

Aunt Joy clasps her hands. "There are no X-Ray MediPods around here. We do the best we can, but we have no way to know if his ribs are broken. For now, we'll treat them like they are. Let's let him rest." She walks to the room, dims the lights, pulls a lightweight blanket — much too small for his large frame — over his body, and clicks the door shut behind her.

"The best thing for him is rest," she repeats.

She guides me to a couple of couches on the other side of the cabin. We sit, and she gives me a sympathetic glance. Aunt Joy resembles Granny. I have no doubt she and Granny are related. The same sweet gray eyes, but Aunt Joy's hair is more blonde-white than gray. They have the same stature except Aunt Joy's frame is smaller and appears weaker. For an older woman, Granny's fairly strong. From her life as a farmer, no doubt.

I try my best to smile, but I'm too distracted.

"You must be Fear." Aunt Joy leans toward me. A

slingshot sticks out of her apron pocket. What old woman carries a slingshot? Weird.

"Yes." I wrap my fingers around my neck and wince as sandpaper scrapes the back of my throat.

"Honey, you must've worked up a pretty good sore throat with all that screaming. Tell you what. Some tea with honey will help soothe your throat. Does that sound good?"

I nod and lean against the sofa as she hurries from the room. My body and mind react to the softness. I haven't gotten a decent night's sleep in a couple of days. Weariness overtakes me. My mind goes blank, and my eyes shut.

I'm safe.

Someone shakes me. I open my eyes. Aunt Joy holds a steaming mug of tea. I sit up, groggy, and find we aren't alone. Four teenagers—two boys, two girls—and one little girl sit on the other couch, staring at me. I jump. I wasn't expecting an audience while I took my nap. How long was I out? Taking a sip of tea, my sandpaper throat burns. I wince. By the third sip, the discomfort lessens.

"Thank you."

Aunt Joy takes the mug from me and places it on a side table. I sit up a little more and stare at the group before me.

"These are your new friends." Aunt Joy motions to them. "They will introduce themselves and help you learn about the place. This is your new home; we hope you enjoy it." Aunt Joy gives my hand one last squeeze. "I have business to attend to."

I sit before my new "friends," tugging on my bow and twisting it. Three are alike in looks and age and have ivory skin and red hair, though the shades differ. The boy next to them looks my age. Straight, black hair shines as it falls to both sides of his head. Olive-tan skin covers his thin frame, and beautifully shaped deep-brown eyes grace his face. He's a friendly soul.

The dark-skinned little girl next to him smiles. "Your name is Fear?"

"Yes." My voice comes out in a raspy garble. I grab my mug and swallow a few more sips of tea.

"That's a funny name." Malice never enters her voice. I like this girl. Tells it as it is.

The dark-haired boy frowns at her. "That's not nice, Happy."

Give her a break. She's just a kid. I crouch to the girl's level. "Your name is Happy?" She nods. "I love it." She smiles wide. "You're right about my name. It *is* a funny name. That's because my parents weren't nice people."

Her smile disappears. "I never had any parents."

I'm not sure which is worse, having parents who hurt you or none at all. My heart goes out to this precious girl with pretty brown eyes. "I'm sorry. I wish you did."

"Me too." She drops her chin to her chest.

I tilt my head to catch her eye. Maybe I can cheer her up. "Let me guess. You're ten?"

Her chin shoots up, and her eyes shine. "Eight. But everyone always says I look older."

I pat her back and stand to face the others.

The boy with the dark hair introduces himself. "My name is Courage. And these are the triplets." He points to the redheaded bunch.

The girls introduce themselves.

"Melody."

"Harmony."

I nod. "Nice to meet you."

Melody's dark-auburn hair scrunches in a wild bun while Harmony's strawberry-blonde hair flows in flat, even layers across her slender shoulders.

Melody waves. "Hi! We're fifteen."

One year older than me. Why are they telling me this?

"We need to know how old you are so you can be sorted into the correct cabin. We room people based on age."

Oh. Makes sense. "Fourteen."

Melody tilts her head. "Really? I thought you were older."

Huh. That's a first. "Nope. Just fourteen."

She breaks into a grin. "Well, that's great. You'll be in our cabin."

Yay me.

Their brother puffs out his chest and straightens his shoulders, forcing me to notice him. Oh, his hair! The exact same color as Faithful's flops on his freckled head. It's only been three days, but I miss her so much. Our conversations at night when we were supposed to be sleeping, the teasing, even the annoyed glances she threw my way when I wasn't doing something to her liking—I can't believe I miss that, but I do.

"We call him Trouble. You'll see why," Courage says.

"Treble-Clef is kind of hard to say." He blushes.

I nod. "At least I'm not the only one with a strange name." Trouble grimaces. *Oops. Be more careful of what you say.*

Courage approaches me. "Would you like to explore the ranch with us?"

Not really. But do I have a choice? "Do you mind if I check on my friend before I go?" I glance toward the Medical Room.

"You mean the man you came with? Go ahead. We'll be right here."

Putting distance between us, I walk to the door and open it. Manly's chest rises and falls with his even breathing. I sneak to the side of his bed, careful not to wake him.

At least he can't feel pain when he's sleeping.

I stare at his gorgeous face. How can I bear being apart from him? Maybe he can just stay here forever. With me. Like a giant, male, sleeping beauty. I giggle at myself. I know I'm being ridiculous, but I can't help it.

The others must be getting curious. Better leave before they come snooping.

I exit the room and scan the large cabin. I frown. This doesn't feel like home. My home is where Granny and Daddy sit at the kitchen table taking turns reading from the book full of Abba's words. I sigh. But for now, I must bear it.

Melody calls to me, and I join them, my heart staying behind with Manly.

I follow the others around and try to listen, despite the washed-out feeling of having no control over my circumstances. I hate this all so much. I'm losing the only family who ever cared about me. I'm losing the people who love me. Will I ever have that again? Pressure jabs my temples.

Courage's voice cuts into my thoughts. "The main meeting place is here, in this cabin."

A large open room made of simple bricks and wood

paneling invites the entire camp to meet within its walls. Rugs, wooden benches, and a sporadic sofa litter the room. An enormous, old-fashioned fireplace sits at one end, and plain tables are set up at the other. A large modern building adjoins the cabin.

"That's the Dining Hall, where everyone eats." Courage points.

They take me outside and show me around. The short grass is a perfect area to play. Leafy trees plant their giant roots in the soil, and branches engulf the edges of the entire play area, creating a wonderful canopy of shade for hot summer days.

Large outdoor Electro-Screens stand on opposite sides of the play area. How'd they get their hands on those? Blessed. I'm sure that's what they'd say. I smirk. Weird, law-breaking people. If only the Uppers knew.

"They can program them into football nets or a myriad of other games at the push of a button," Melody tells me.

I've never seen such luxury on planet Earth before. Although, I admit my experiences on Earth thus far are rather...meager...to say the least.

They take me through the Fallen, cabin by cabin. A row of cabins for girls line the grass, mere yards from the forest. The opposite side mirrors multiple cabins for boys. At the end of these cabins, one stands out.

"And that's the Special Cabin." Courage's voice drones on and on.

I don't ask. Honestly, I don't care.

Cabins for the ranch hands appear farther down the property as well as a few tiny cabins scattered here and there. Probably for the grownups. They point out Aunt Joy's cabin, the smallest one of all.

The sun hits me in the eyes as I spot the tiny building. Putting my hand to my forehead, I shield my vision from the harsh rays. "Doesn't she run this place?"

They nod.

"Why doesn't she get the biggest cabin?"

Harmony lifts her eyebrows and tilts her head, her styled hair falling to her forearm. "Clearly you don't know her yet. She sacrifices everything for everyone else."

Melody sweeps her hand to the surrounding camp. "She always puts others before herself."

My eyes light up. She sure sounds like Granny. I'm going to like Aunt Joy. It puts my mind at ease a bit…but just a bit. I'm not willing to give in. I don't want to be here, and I want everyone to know it.

A sparkling lake shines ahead of us. I follow the group nearer. The light bouncing off the lapping waves is breathtaking. Too bad it's so small. I'd love if it stretched out for miles. Neverending. It's much too beautiful to end so abruptly. Happy grabs my hand and scoots me toward it. We walk along the edge as the girls list off a bunch of rules and expectations. Courage and Trouble interrupt intermittently to point out this interesting fact or that person over there. I don't listen to most of it because I don't care. This will not be my home. Ever.

Courage bumps my arm and doesn't apologize. "You'll be given a list of chores for each day. We're expected to complete them without grumbling."

That won't be hard since I was never given the opportunity to grumble growing up, not with my father's temper.

"We ranch buffalo here." Harmony points to the fields beyond, encircled by a thick metal fence.

I take a few whiffs. My nose wrinkles. Oh man, that's

awful. Hope the stench isn't permanent. "What is that?"

Courage peers at me. "You mean the smell?"

I nod and breathe shallow. The pigs and cows back in the hovels were stinky, but this smell is altogether different.

Courage grins. "It's the buffalo. You can't see them from here, but you sure can smell them."

Melody whirls past us with a skip in her steps. "You'll get used to it. The rest of us had to. Just like these slingshots." She extracts one from her back pocket. I glance around. They're each carrying one. "Aunt Joy makes us carry them for protection."

Ah, makes sense. Wildies are always on the prowl.

Courage continues his tour. Instead of buying high-tech robotic ranchers, they still do things the old-fashioned way with people and horses. The horses spark my interest.

The stables seem clean, but the horse manure still reeks. My nose wrinkles. Guess I'll be forced to get used to horse poo as well. Within minutes of standing around the gorgeous creatures, I forget all about the stink. I'm hooked. The guys want to continue on after we've spent a few minutes in the stables, but Harmony, Melody, and I whine.

Melody clasps her hands and jumps in front of Courage and Trouble. "We need just a few more minutes to appreciate the horses' beauty."

Harmony and I nod and mumble agreement.

The guys groan. Trouble rolls his eyes and stalks off. Courage tilts his head at Melody. "Fine. Just don't take too long."

We return to our horse admiring. I find an enormous one with a dark-brown mane. Muscles ripple through his body.

"His hooves look big enough to kill me!" I point to the horse's impressive feet.

Courage leans against the fence surrounding the arena. "Well, they could." He folds his arms. "Never, ever walk behind any of the horses. It's dangerous. One kick could end your life."

The hair on my arms stands at attention. "Good to know." I reach out to beckon the beast closer. "What's his name?"

Courage cranes his neck, searching the area. "Um...I think it's Pumpkin."

I arch my eyebrow. "Pumpkin? Really?"

"Hey, I didn't name them." Courage rakes his hand through his silky hair. "Stay away from the hooves until the horse learns to trust you." Arrogance skitters around the edges of his tone.

I'm not sure how to gain a horse's trust, but I'm determined to find out. I can picture myself enjoying this place.

I glance at Happy. The giant creatures dwarf her, and she stays a few yards away. She's so unsure of herself around these gorgeous creatures. It's sort of cute. Maybe she's not a horse person.

I think they're amazing.

Chapter 9

We head to the Main Cabin where Manly's staying. I rush inside while the others go eat lunch in the Dining Hall. I've worked up quite an appetite, but I've got to see Manly first. Leaping through the front door, I rush to the Medical Room. Forcing myself to slow down, I knock instead of barging in.

A weak voice behind the door beckons me. "Come in."

Yay! He's awake. "Hey, I got to go to the stables today! The horses are really cool. Some of them are so big, and there're even some tiny ones too. The whole place reeks like horse poo, but after a while, it's almost like my nose forgets. And there's this one horse named Pumpkin —"

Manly grabs his head and winces.

Oops, better shut my mouth. It's almost like I can't help but talk too much when I'm around him. I'm sure not like that with other people. "I'm sorry, I didn't even ask how you're doing. Am I giving you a headache?"

He laughs. "My head hurts from lack of water. Would you grab me a glass, please?"

He's just being polite. I know I gave him a headache. "Of course."

I open the cupboard, seize one of the few cups available, and fill it in the adjoining bathroom. He drains the cup.

"You really were thirsty." I refill the cup. "I should stay with you from now on to make sure you're taken care of. I can't let you get dehydrated again." I hand him water for the second time.

Manly takes the cup and wrinkles his forehead. "You know I don't need a babysitter, right?"

I roll my eyes. "Who's going to make sure you get well?" *Me, me! Pick me!*

"Aunt Joy poked her head in a few times. She's already offered me pain medicine. She's my great-great Aunt, you know. I doubt she'd let her own nephew suffer." He holds his hand over his bandaged ribs as he shifts. "From the stories I've heard about her, she has a heart of gold."

"I'm sure she does." Rumbling emerges from deep within my gut. I jump up. "Oh, lunch. I forgot." Before I exit, I whirl around. He's probably hungry too. "Would you like me to bring you something?"

He smiles. "That would be much appreciated. Thanks." I rush off without even a bye and run all the way to the Dining Hall. Lunch is halfway over by the time I reach the front of the line.

"I need two servings of everything."

The plump cook grunts. "Everyone gets one serving."

"But…"

She plops the food on my tray. "Next!" she hollers at the girl behind me.

Schnitzel fritz. That didn't go as planned. Oh well, we can share, I guess.

My new "friends" try to wave me over to their table. I act as if I don't notice them and head out the door. A pang hits me in the gut, but I push it aside.

Soon I'm at Manly's side, handing him the plate of food. He hoists himself up as much as possible, trying not to strain his ribs. He must be as famished as I am. I open my mouth to speak as Manly gobbles down half the plate. Seriously, this man would win any eating contest he entered. I can't help but watch with longing as he shovels more into his mouth, and… there goes my food. Thought we might split it. Sigh. It's all right. I'm not that hungry anyway. He needs it more than I do. He is, after all, injured and trying to heal.

"So." Manly wipes his chin with a napkin. "I'm glad you're enjoying the place so much already."

A prickle blasts through my skull. Um…wrong. "I'm not *enjoying* it. I just like horses. I'm not excited about being here." A frown settles on my face. "I'll have something to look forward to, that's all."

He smirks. Not cool. "Come on, it's not that bad."

Fine. Make me admit it. "No." I sigh. "It's a lot better than the hovel I grew up in, I'll give you that. But there are so many *children* here." Distaste spills from my mouth. "I'm not sure I'll be able to get along with them."

He snickers. My lips pinch as I narrow my eyes. He sure is smug today.

"I'm sure you'll find friends."

"I don't want friends." Shooting him a blank stare, I seal my point.

"Well then, you'll need to change your mind on that, Miss Stubborn."

Yeah. Fat chance of that happening.

Aunt Joy swoops through the door with a clang, covered

dish in hand. Steam emanates from the sides, and the scent of chicken, broccoli, and cheese casserole fills the room. She hands it to Manly.

"Lunchtime."

She winks at both of us and leaves.

"Seconds!" Manly takes off the lid to reveal the same meal I brought him. He digs in yet again. I gaze at his plate, and my mouth hangs open. He stops shoveling. "You hungry or something?"

"I'm fine," I lie. It's not like this is the first time I've gone without a meal. My eyes drift toward his plate again.

"You *are* hungry," he accuses.

The truth might not hurt. "I kind of gave you my lunch."

He closes his eyes and winces. "Why didn't you tell me?"

"It's not that big of a deal. Besides, you're a lot bigger than me. I thought you might need the food more than I do."

"Never do that again, okay?" He sets his fork on the plate. "You shouldn't sacrifice for me. Promise me you won't?"

I shrug. "Okay. I promise."

He attempts to sit up straighter and extends the food dish to me, only to reel back. The dish clangs to the ground, and food splatters everywhere. He shudders and lies on his back again, holding his ribs. I lose my ability to speak as I rush to his side. Grabbing his hand, I stand there like a dork and stare into his grimacing face. It looks excruciating.

"What can I do? Should I get someone?"

His face returns to normal. "No. I'll be fine. I just can't move for a while. I need to stay still and let these things heal."

He closes his eyes as I grip his hand. Sleep is more important to him right now than anything. I will myself to leave his side so he can rest. I don't bother to clean up the mess.

That night, after scarfing down my entire dinner within seconds, I go to bed mentally and physically exhausted. Why do I have to be stuck in this stuffy room with all these other girls? I long to be back at Granny's. Tears pour down my cheeks. I battle the downpour as my weary heart aches for the home I so quickly gained, then so quickly lost. Deep sleep engulfs me and eases my pain...for the moment.

They call the next day "Chapel." Every Wednesday and Sunday, it's a tradition. I'm not sure what this is all about, but we're supposed to wash and dress our best. I put on my blue dress and search through my meager belongings for the two red bows Faithful used on my braids. I only find one of them.

I survey the other girls and cross my arms. Someone stole it. My eyes sear into their skulls until they refuse to meet my gaze. A bunch of thieves, every last one of them. After all, that's what people do. They steal, cheat, use and abuse. Smack others down until they're a useless pile of mush.

One braid will have to suffice. I fix my remaining bow to the bedraggled braid. I will never do this as well as Faithful. She has skill when it comes to hair. I do not. The silver crown of thorns hairpin stares back at me from the bottom of my bag. I snatch it up and shove it in my braid. At least they didn't steal that. Must've not seen it. I peer into each face. They're the enemy, and I don't trust a single one of them. Not even Harmony and Melody, who walk on either side of me to the Dining Hall.

It's breakfast time. The food line stretches a mile long. Good thing I got here faster than most of them. The cook singles me out to receive less than my fair share. Probably trying to get me back for asking for two meals yesterday. What a witch. She's making me pay. I know it. Everyone's out to get me today. Well, I'll get them right back.

I reach the large meeting room and seethe venom. Most of the girls steer clear of me. Good. *Stay away, all of you.* I'm in no mood to be near anyone. I plant myself in the middle of a wooden bench, daring anyone to sit beside me. No one does. Not even little Happy.

Until the guys walk in.

Trouble spots me and plops his white, freckled body right next to me. What gave him the impression that was a brilliant idea? I turn and stare at him. He seems not to notice. Moron.

"Good morning," he says much too cheerfully.

I want to punch him. I turn away.

"Hope you slept well last night."

Really, Trouble? You're asking how I slept? He obviously isn't getting the hint. I can take care of that.

"Get over yourself and go sit somewhere else."

His jaw drops. "Ooo-kay." He does a double take.

I'm not bluffing. Get away. Move. His brows arch as he raises himself off the bench. *Good. Be gone with you, stupid boy. And don't come back.* Trouble sulks toward Courage, who has the good sense not to approach me. No one dares sit by me now.

A man stands and introduces himself as Shepherd Sam, probably for my benefit since I'm the only new one around. He pulls out a book, and my eyes widen.

A jolt of recognition zips through my brain. My face softens. It's the same book Granny read at home. Courage's eyes connect with mine. I harden my face so he'll know I still don't want to be here. This will never be my home.

The rest of the time Shepherd Sam talks about this Abba, who he is, what he's like, what he expects from us, and goobers and gambits, the fact that he loves us. How can a god love us? The thought seems absurd. I ignore the rest of his speech, and they end with singing one of the songs Manly taught me. My ears perk up.

My heart aches for home. The music draws me in its flowing melody as if a soft breeze flutters through my body and lifts me off my feet. I move my mouth as the words come back to me. I sing one line out loud, and the song ends. It lightens my mood, but only a little.

After a blessing, Aunt Joy dismisses everyone to go about their various tasks. I sit still. I have no idea what I'm supposed to do. Harmony and Melody draw near like kittens approach a fearsome dog. I make a rushed decision whether I will treat them brusquely or not. I choose not.

Melody hands me a piece of paper. "If you finish these chores, we've been given permission to take you horseback riding this afternoon." Melody smiles as Harmony flips her perfect hair over her shoulder.

My mood improves, and I get to work. Before I realize it, lunchtime arrives, and I have almost everything completed. I'm slower than the others, but they let me know it'll get easier. Others mill about, tasks long completed. Someday I'll be as quick as them. Not today. Apparently, tonight we're supposed to get together for "Study" after dinner. What's that all about? Sounds horribly boring. Maybe I'll just play hooky. It's not as if they'll notice I'm gone anyway.

Chapter 10

As I eat my lunch, Manly comes to mind. I relax a little. Aunt Joy brought him food yesterday. She'll take care of him.

I better check on him before finishing my chores, though. I miss him. This time I open his door without asking. He stares at the ceiling. Yesterday's food mess is gone. I attempt to break his trance. "Hi."

He turns his head but doesn't try to sit up this time. "There you are. I was wondering when you were going to visit me."

Oh no. He's upset. My face falls. He gives me that impish grin.

"I'm kidding," Manly reassures me. "Please don't take everything I say so seriously."

I lift my head and try to grin back. "I'm sorry. I was doing my chores. They assign everyone here a list of things to do every day. I would've visited you earlier, but they expect it to be done before lunch. You did get lunch, didn't you?"

He reaches for me, and I take his hand. "I love that you care about me so much." His voice falters, and he stares at the ceiling. "Yes, I did get lunch." He turns his head my way. "I wish you cared about everyone else as much as you do me."

My ears perk. "What do you mean?"

"I heard about your little attitude this morning. Everyone noticed, Fear."

I drop his hand. *Excuse me?* I jump to my feet. "I didn't have an attitude. Someone stole my hair bow. All those stupid girls. They're thieves, and they hate me. I know it. Then to top it off, that stupid cook only gave me a small portion for breakfast."

"Calm down, Fear. I didn't mean to make you upset. But you have to realize no one's out to get you."

Gambits! How do you know me so well?

"You will have to trust these people at some point. I'll be leaving, and this will be your new home." He stares. "At least for now," he adds.

Schnitzel fritz, he knows I'm mad. "But I don't want it to be." I glare at him.

"I understand that, Fear."

Don't say my name like that. It's hard to stay angry with you.

"But," he continues, "remember this is for the best."

I thump against the chair, cross my arms, and stare at the medical supplies on the counter. After a couple of minutes, I cave. I hate awkward silence. Scooting to the edge of the chair, I jerk my head up. "I'm going to get to ride a horse after I finish my last chore."

"That's great. It sounds like you'll have a wonderful time. You'd better get to those chores so you make it to the stables in time."

He's right. I'd better hurry. I may have taken too long as it is. I pull out my list. *Take out trash in Special Cabin.* Hmm.

"I'll come by later and let you know how the horseback

riding went." I rush out the door. Which direction am I
supposed to go? I need to find the Special Cabin quick.

My eyes dart around as I run back and forth, trying to find
the stupid cabin. Maybe I should ask someone for directions. I
run to the other side of the cabin area. Where in the Gliding
Lands—oh there! Smaller than the rest, it's nestled near the
end of the long row. I approach it, and my mind speeds like an
Upper's racer. What could possibly lie behind the doors? What
makes it so special? I put my hand on the door handle just as
someone pulls from the other side.

A petite woman in an apron presses her palm to her chest
and chuckles. "Oh, you surprised me! You must be Fear. We
expected you this morning. I hope you found us all right?" She
smiles so sweetly I can't help but like her.

"Yes, I found it fine," I lie. No need to let her know I'm
directionally challenged. "Trying to get used to this new
schedule."

"Of course." She pats her delicate hands on her apron. "I'm
Lithe. Follow me."

She guides me past the narrow office in the front and takes
me to the back room. I stop dead in my tracks. Toddlers, kids,
and teens sprawl out everywhere in beds or wheelchairs, or
using walkers and canes. Those lying on cots stare at the
ceiling, non-responsive to the environment around them. What
have I gotten myself into?

I follow the smiling lady as she meanders toward the back
of the room. Curious eyes follow me. I can't help but stare.
Severely crippled kids with legs jutting out in awkward
positions settle on cots throughout the room. Some aren't bad.
A few even look like they shouldn't be here. One girl, about
seven, seems totally normal. She turns her face, and the other
side of her skull is missing, creating a whopping indent. I gasp.

What happened to her? There must be more than twenty boys and girls crammed into this small cabin. They must be miserable.

We reach the back. Lithe shows me a drawer full of trash bags. "I want you to go through the whole cabin and collect all the trash." She points behind me. "Starting with that room. You must be quiet when you enter. No loud noises please." What does she have back there, a pack of sleeping Wildies? "Bring the trash cans out here to empty them so you don't wake them."

Who is "them"?

Like a spy on a quest for information, I crack open the door and sneak in. Drawn curtains block the windows and muffle sound. It takes my eyes a moment to adjust. Eight cribs line the walls. What will I discover inside?

My curiosity trumps my fear. I inch closer to the nearest crib. Inside, a precious little face pokes out of a full body cast. I jump back. I've never seen an injured baby before. My heart aches. I squint into the next one. Same thing. Next one over. At least this baby is only in leg casts. Injuries abound on every single one. I can't take it anymore. I grab the trashcan and bolt from the room.

Tears overflow as Lithe approaches. "Your response is normal." She clasps my shoulders and squeezes. "It gets easier."

Liar. How could this get easier? How can she work around this every day and maintain that smile?

I have no answers, so I stuff the trash into the bag and leave it by the door. I don't dare go back in. My sniffling would wake them for sure. I rush to the bathroom and grab tissues for my nose. I leave the stall and approach the mirror by the sinks. Staring at my own reflection, my puffy, red eyes gape back at me. Tears streak down my curved cheeks. This is all just a nightmare.

During the daytime.

While I'm awake.

A toilet flushes. Blippets and bagpipes! I turn around as a boy comes out of a stall in a walker. He must be about eleven or twelve.

"Um, this is the boys' restroom."

We stare at one another. My face flushes hot, and I leave without saying a word. Scrambling around the big room collecting trash, I avert my eyes as much as possible. My senses crawl. The odor, the machines, the kids. I can't stand it.

A boy with a misshapen head makes eye contact as a long string of drool falls to his lap. I cringe and turn away. I finish much quicker than I probably should, and misplaced trash strews across my path. I'm almost certain I've missed a trashcan or two. But I don't care. The walls are shutting in on me, suffocating me. I need to get out.

I burst past Lithe, dragging my bag on the ground. Hope there isn't a giant hole. Might as well flush my efforts down the toilet. I pick it up, find the nearest trash receptacle, and stuff it in without bothering to tie the bag. Wind scatters litter through the air like dirty autumn leaves.

The faint scent of horse manure drifts on the breeze. I jog to the stables. That'll get these images out of my head. I trample through grass and dirt as quickly as my stumpy legs will carry me. After two tumbles, I slow down. Don't need to taste dirt again anytime soon. The stables draw near. My chest tightens. I lean over and pant until I can breathe again. I peek up. Well, lookie here. Who's already on their horses? Harmony trots along, hair flipping as she bounces in her seat. Melody spots me from astride her steed. She pulls on the horse's reigns,

slowing it. Electrical currents pulse through my skull and burst
from me in angry spurts. Why'd they start riding without me?
I jump on the fence.

Harmony spots me too and comes closer, her white horse's
mane flicking in the wind. That's just great. She *and* her horse
have perfect hair. I'd laugh if I weren't so mad. Harmony
brings her horse to the fence.

"Where have you been? We're almost done."

"What?" I frown, and my eye twitches. "I thought you'd
wait for me."

Harmony shrugs. "Sorry. Maybe tomorrow."

She waves a fake-friendly goodbye, and I'm left stewing.
Today is not going the way I'd hoped. At all. I stare at the pair,
willing them to feel my glare like laser beams burning holes
through their backs, but to no avail. Ugh. At least I can visit
Pumpkin, even if I can't ride him. Might as well do something
while I'm here.

I head for the stable door when a small hand grabs my
arm. I turn and face the lady I just met, only this time she's not
smiling. In fact, her face looks rather comical as she twists it in
an attempt to look angry. Lithe must not have a lot of
experience with angry faces.

"You did not do your job well," Lithe lectures in a voice no
one would ever be afraid of. "Listen, I know it's"—she pauses
—"shocking, the first time you go in there. I would've talked
you through it, but instead of asking questions, you flew out of
there as fast as you could, leaving a trail of trash in your wake.
That can't happen next time, you understand?" I nod.
"Everyone must do their jobs well, or this place will fall apart,
then you and everyone else here will lose their homes. We
cannot let that happen, you hear?"

I nod again as my face flushes hot. I messed up big time.

She huffs and marches away.

I sulk to my cabin. I really wanted to visit Pumpkin. But I shouldn't have responded to the disabled kids like that. There's nothing scary about them. I guess it was such a shock, all of them together in the same place. I've never seen people like that before. Still not an excuse for the way I behaved.

Abba would expect better of me.

Now where in the Gliding Lands did that come from? Since when did I start caring about what this god thought of me?

I must be tired. My eyelids weigh a ton.

I *am* tired.

I know I promised Manly I'd visit him after horseback riding, but I never did that, so technically I'm not breaking my promise. Reaching my cabin, I enter the empty darkness.

I need a nap. My heavy head plunges me into a deep sleep.

I'm shaken awake by Melody.

"What?" Fuzziness clouds my brain.

"You're going to miss dinner if you don't hurry. When I got to the Dining Hall and saw you weren't there, I thought I might find you here."

I rub my eyes, then roll over to go back to sleep. She shakes me once more. I wrap the blankets tight around me. "Can't be dinner already." *Go away.*

"Well it is. And you'll be super hungry if you don't get in there quick. Come on, Fear." Melody grabs my blanket and pulls, unraveling me so hard I fall off the cot. I land smack on my rear end.

"Hey!"

"Hay is for horses. Now come on, let's go."

I ought to slug her a good one, but I restrain myself. No need to make too many enemies. Besides, she *is* trying to help. The thought flows through my mind before I can smother it. I shake my head. Whatever. I do want food, and I'd better get to the Dining Hall before it's too late. I hurl myself after the red-haired girl.

Melody grabs my arm and squeezes. "We meet for Study after dinner. Do you want to be in my session?"

A monotone syllable slips from my mouth. "Sure."

"You'll love it. There's so much to learn about the Word."

You're kidding me. Them too? "The Word? You mean Abba's Word?"

She nods.

"*That's* what we're going to study?" She nods again. "First off, unauthorized religion isn't permitted, and neither are topics that aren't pre-approved by the Uppers. This whole thing is crazy. My family and now you guys? How can you all go along with it? I don't get it."

Melody gives me a sideways glance. "You're kind of weird."

Gee, thanks.

We reach the Dining Hall, walk through the swinging doors, and head for the dinner line. My eyes stare past the glass sneeze barrier and land on the stocky lady with a crème uniform and turquoise apron scooping mounds onto plates.

"Actually, I'm the only normal person here, it seems."

"Whatever you say." She smiles and lets me go first. Sweet girl, even if she does think I'm weird.

I glare at the cook. I will get my fair share this time. "Pile on as much as you can."

Her mouth tightens as she plops enormous quantities of food on my plate. Making up for this morning, I guess.

I lift my hand. "Okay, you can stop now."

She rolls her eyes and moves on to Melody.

I keep to myself during dinner, though the triplets sit near me. They know better than to ask questions. Courage sits with another group a few tables away. We glance at each other, and he smiles and waves. I suppose he can be my friend. At least that way I can tell Manly I have one. Maybe then he'll quit pestering me about making friends.

After dinner, we all trickle into the Main Cabin. I find Courage and walk toward him.

"Whoa, better get out of the way. It's attitude girl coming fast!" He bobs his head as if I'm going to punch him.

Dork. I smile instead of getting angry. He has a disarming way about him. "All right. I can take a joke."

His lips turn up, but his forehead crinkles. "Really? Because I wasn't so sure."

I'll ignore that. "What are we doing here anyway? What's this Study all about?"

He holds up a book. It's another copy of the Word.

"How did you get one of those?" I snatch it away from him before he can respond. The leathery texture of the cover urges me to read the text within. I flip through the pages, enamored with the beauty of the script and the sleek pages.

"I'm my Study's team leader. All the sessions have one."

"Can I be in your session?" I respond without thinking. Gambits. I forgot Melody wants me in hers. She takes that moment to saunter in and plop down in the middle of Courage's session. That fixes that problem. A grin twitches the corners of my mouth as I sit next to her and wait for it to start.

Shepherd Sam steps to the front of the room again. He says another blessing, then explains what we're going to discuss in the Word tonight. He leaves it at that, and everyone in our session turns to Courage.

He reads a simple passage. "When my flesh weakens and my heart stutters and fails, Abba will lift me up with his mighty strength. Like an everlasting drink of water from an overflowing well, neverending." He puts down the book. "What does this mean to you?" He glances around.

A small girl, even shorter than me, raises a chubby hand. "Abba will always be our strength, even if we have none?"

Courage gives her a smile. "Yes, isn't that good news? What else?"

I listen to all their thoughts and ideas. They talk about this Abba in such high regard. Most of what they say doesn't make much sense; however, I understand the girl with a pierced nose.

She stands awkwardly before our session of gawkers, plucks one hand out of her pocket, and shrugs. "Abba's done so much in my life. You guys have no idea. There's no way I could've gotten through any of it without him helping me and giving me strength. I seriously wouldn't be standing here today if it weren't for him." She plops down to a pitter patter of clapping.

Sometimes I feel so weak. I could use that strength, too. For so many years, I've gone through hard times alone, never relying on anyone but myself. It's exhausting.

Those around me discuss how they daily trust Abba and how he's so intricately woven into their existence. They make him sound so real. My curiosity sparks, but I don't want to be the only one asking dumb questions. I keep my mouth shut.

Courage isn't asking me any questions anyway. My breathing evens. I think he's trying not to embarrass me. My soul rests on a river of peace I've never known before.

That night, as I tuck myself into my little cot, I once again don't bother to pay attention to the commotion around me. My mind is like a high-speed chase, and I can't catch up. So many questions. Will I ever know the answers to all of them?

Soon the lights snap off.

What does it all mean? Can any of it be true? Great. I won't be getting much sleep tonight.

Chapter 11

The next morning I wake up early, jump into the shower, and get ready before most of the other girls. I kind of like being on a schedule. I walk to the Dining Hall and grab breakfast. I'm determined to get all my chores done this morning. Maybe I won't get to ride horses today, but I want to get done by lunchtime like everyone else. I work harder, quicker, and more efficiently while watching the other kids, copying their methods. I ask questions and get answers. It turns out the work isn't too hard or exhausting. It gives me a sense of accomplishment as if I belong.

My jaw tightens. Nope. Not happening.

I don't want to belong here.

I scan my chore list. Instead of emptying trash in the Special Cabin, I'll be scooping manure in the stables. I don't mind this switch at all. At least I'll get to be around the horses, even if poo's involved. I head for the stables. A ranch hand rides my favorite horse, Pumpkin. I stride forward to get the man's attention. It's the same overalls-wearing guy who helped

Manly out of the truck that first day.

"You there!" He notices me and walks Pumpkin over. I stroke Pumpkin's soft nose. "This is my favorite horse."

The man looks down from the high beast. "He's quite stubborn. You can look at him all you want, but you won't be able to ride him. He's not suited for children."

There they go calling me a child again. I scowl. I'm not a child.

He trots over to the stalls and points to a small, older horse with dark-gray freckles and gray hair.

"This one's perfect for you. Just your size." He winks and trots away.

I take a good hard look at the horse. She's so small, she borders on pony status. I sigh. Nothing ever goes my way. She's not impressive like Pumpkin, but in her own way, she's still just as beautiful.

"Wait!" The man is long gone by now. I don't even know her name.

Movement catches my attention, and I swing around. Courage stands beside me. I jump.

"You're kind of nervous today."

I grind my teeth. Flaming darts fly out of my eyes. Of course I'm jumpy when a person appears out of nowhere. "What're you doing here?"

"It's my job to change their water and food. I told you that the first day." He holds a bucket full of horse feed.

Oops. "I wasn't really listening." Hey, at least I'm honest.

He tilts his head. "Why aren't you doing your job yet?"

Schnitzel fritz! I promised myself I'd hurry today. I'm such an idiot sometimes.

"I wanted to get this done before lunch. Do I have time?"

Courage chuckles and points to the holographic timing

device on the stable wall. We only have twenty-two minutes to get done and head back. My eyes widen. It won't be enough.

"Relax," he says. "That should be plenty of time as long as you work hard." He grabs a shovel and hands it to me. "Scoop and toss in there." He points to an old-fashioned wheelbarrow that requires the push of a button to move it, unlike the new voice-activated ones.

I push the button to get the wheelbarrow where I want it to go. I stop at the first stall and begin. Taking out the trash in the Special Cabin is a piece of cake compared to this. My stomach lurches at the overturned manure. I deserve this for screwing up yesterday.

"I was supposed to work in the Special Cabin." I breathe heavy. I'm too young to feel like this. Ugh. So tired. Sweat tickles my back as it rolls down. Gross. Now I'm going to be all sticky. "I guess they decided to switch me to this."

Courage's eyes twitch, and he screws his mouth to the side. He knows something I don't.

"What?" I set my shovel upright and lean on it.

His cheeks flush red. "I had them do that. I heard about the problem you had around the disabled kids. I thought you'd like it if I requested you switch to the stables. I saw how much you admired the horses the other day. Hope you don't mind."

I wipe sweat from my brow and stare hard at him. He isn't kidding. Does everyone have to know my business? He needs to stop trying to be so helpful. Suspicion slithers like a pointy-fanged fiend, ready for the kill.

"I don't have anything to give you, so quit being nice to me."

He stills, his eyes flying wide, but he keeps his mouth shut. I do one last cleanup of the place, then run to get food for my growling stomach. Courage follows. I slow down to let him keep up. A mess surges in the pit of my stomach. I shouldn't have been rude to Courage. Whatever, he shouldn't have made me work with horse poo. Can't believe he thought that would be a good idea.

I enter the Dining Hall, Courage at my side, and get in line. It's super short today. Soon, I'll get to hang out with Manly. A thrill sparks inside. I'm so looking forward to that. I plop on the hard cafeteria seat and eat my salad. I narrow my eyes and glance at the door. Let's get this over with. Manly's waiting.

Sitting at Manly's bedside, I stare at the sleeping man. His jawline and the perfect arch of his nose…just wow. Even asleep he mesmerizes me. He stirs as if he knows I'm watching, and his eyes flicker open. When he sees me sitting beside him, his face breaks into a grin.

"Hey there. I was beginning to miss you."

"Hi. I got…distracted. Sorry." He missed me? Warm fuzzies wrap me in their embrace.

He attempts to sit up but winces.

Good grief, man! "No, Manly, stop."

He lies back down.

"Aunt Joy says you need to rest."

"Does Aunt Joy also say I can't use the restroom?"

Awkward. I blush. "Sorry. Let me see if I can find someone to help you so you don't hurt yourself."

I rush out of the room and spot Courage and Trouble

hanging out nearby. They might be scrawny, but it's better than nothing. I wave at them.

"Please, my friend needs help getting to the...the..."

"The what?" asks Trouble.

"Could you just get him to the bathroom, please?" I spit out.

They jump forward and rush to his aid. I enter the room behind them. Manly sits up. He eyes the guys and lifts his eyebrows in a way that says, "*Why* did you bring these two weaklings in here?"

The guys let him rest his arms on their shoulders and help him stand with a heaving motion. Manly bites his lip. One... two steps. If he weren't in pain, this would almost be comical. Trouble and Courage look like a couple of gawky penguins next to Manly's lion-sized frame. One more step. The guys struggle.

"I can manage from here." Manly slips his arms off their shoulders and slides into the adjoining restroom with a grunt. Courage and Trouble turn toward me, shoulders slumped and eyes downcast.

"Thanks for helping." Don't want to damage their delicate male egos.

Trouble straightens and rakes his hand through his head of flames. "No problem."

Courage hops up on the bed, wrinkling the already too wrinkled sheets and blankets.

My blood boils. Who does he think he is, taking Manly's bed like that? "Don't sit there. That's not your bed."

Courage rolls his eyes. "It's not his either. He's only borrowing it until he gets better and goes home." He jumps off anyway. "Why do you hang out with him so much? Who is he?"

"He's my family." Why do they care?

"If he's your family, then why are you here? Kids who don't have family come here."

I mull over how much I should reveal. I still don't know them well enough. I'm not sure what kind of information I should trust them with.

"People are trying to hurt me. This is the safest place for me."

Trouble steps closer. "But you're planning on staying, right?"

I know that grin. I've seen it on many a boy, and I'm not interested. I shrug him off. "Only as long as I have to."

"Everyone here is like a big family," says Courage. "Maybe you'll learn to like it."

We hear a flush, and the bathroom door flings open. "He's right, you know." Manly shuffles to his bed. "It's not so bad here, is it, boys?"

They shake their heads in unison. His focus shifts to me. "You should get to know these people. Look around. Get used to the place."

Please don't make me. "I don't want to right now. I want to talk with you."

"Sleep is the best medicine for me. At least that's what Aunt Joy thinks. I have to agree with her."

I purse my lips at the obvious dismissal and leave the room with the guys. I brush past them, slump in a chair, and stare out the window.

Courage and Trouble teeter over to me. "Do you want to walk around?"

"Why? Is there something I haven't seen yet?"

They look at each other, pause, and exchange covered whispers.

"Actually, there is. Come with us."

"Um…no thank you." Not happening.

"Come on." Both guys grab my wrists and lug me to my feet.

Seriously? I brush them away.

Trouble lets go of me first. "You'll want to see this. I promise."

I have no choice as they drag me out of the cabin. Truth is, I don't care about any of this. I just want to spend time with Manly. He's the only person who means something to me — with the exception of little Happy. But whatever. Doing anything is better than moping around and staring out the window, since Manly's apparently too busy sleeping to hang out with me.

They lead me past the office, the long rows of residential cabins, the outhouses, and even Aunt Joy's small cabin. I drag my clammy hands down my pants. The guys are strangers. Sure they *seem* safe, but anyone is capable of inhumane things. I can't trust them. I can't trust *anyone.*

"Wait!" I stop short. "Where are we going?"

"Don't worry, you'll see." Courage grabs my hand once more.

I dig in my feet and stand as still as stone. "I only recently met you two. I want to know where we're going. If you don't tell me right now, I won't step one foot farther."

Courage lets go of my hand. "Sorry, I didn't realize." He stays silent for a moment. "The truth of the matter is, we don't know you either. The place we're taking you is a big secret. How do we know we can trust you?"

That's hilarious. "You don't."

He shakes his head. "Never mind." They both turn away and continue walking.

Ha! You really think I'm going to fall for that? "Well then, I guess I'll head for the cabins." I turn in the opposite direction. The guys' footsteps stop dead in their tracks.

Trouble spills the beans. "Okay, already. It's an underground library."

An underground what?

Courage hits him hard in the stomach and scans the forest as if someone's listening. Trouble flinches and grabs his belly.

I look at them blankly. "That means nothing to me."

Trouble spreads his arms wide. "Books. Lots and lots of books. You'll see when we get there."

Yeah right, as if huge piles of books are just sitting around underground somewhere. Gimme a break. "Books are illegal."

"*Most* books," Courage retorts.

"Isn't this a bad idea?"

Trouble snickers. "Only if we get caught."

Ah. Now I know where he got his nickname.

Shivers creep over my skin. I push down the adrenaline that comes with it. Must remain levelheaded.

Trouble extends his hand to me. "Please? I promise you won't get hurt."

I believe him…I think…and it's better than sitting around bored.

"All right. But one wrong move, and I'm outta here."

Both nod like eager puppies and drag me behind them once more.

Chapter 12

Following the guys through the field and into the forest, I make turns and zigzags, ending up where we were before. I recognize that twisted, moss-covered root. Sticky perspiration forms under my arms. Are they trying to trick me?

"We were here already. What's the point?" I ask.

Courage grabs a tree root. "To throw off anyone following us. Everyone's curious about you. Couldn't have any fans tracing us to this spot." He lifts the root. It's attached to a trapdoor covered in moss and weeds. The door reveals a hole big enough for an adult.

"That was unexpected." I peek in. Darkness. Yeah…that's not happening.

Trouble extends his hand. "Ladies first."

I peer into the blackness, and a tremor runs through my spine. I turn and look at the guys. "It's dark." *Plus, I still don't trust you two.*

Trouble kneels and reaches past me. He lowers half of his body into the hole, flicks on a faint light that travels as far as the bottom of the ladder, and pulls back. "The electricity still works. We're not quite sure how."

"It's one of the mysteries of this place," Courage adds.

"Isn't that peachy." Crossing my arms, I eye the hole. It's not too scary, I guess. If the guys were going to hurt me, they would've already.

Here goes nothing.

I head down the ladder. A damp, earthy scent meets my nose. When I reach the bottom, darkness envelopes me, and my outstretched hand remains invisible. I search for another switch. A smooth hand slides across mine. I flinch but don't pull away.

"Oh, sorry." Courage bumps into me in the dark. "The light is right here."

He guides my hand a few inches to the left, the cold wall lumpy under our fingertips. A bright light fills the room, and I wince. My eyes adjust. Wow. This place is fantastic.

Two walls still stand intact. The other two consist of packed dirt secured by diagonally placed boards and dilapidated bricks pressed against the sides. Courage points to the dirt walls.

"A few decades ago, a sinkhole swallowed the library. That's why the Uppers never suspect it still exists. They thought it was wiped out before they outlawed books. If they only knew what a treasure trove we have down here, a wealth of information at our fingertips. So much history they never want us to know."

"Whoa. We could get in so much trouble." I twine my fingers together and glance around the room that could ultimately lead three scrawny teenagers to our deaths.

"We won't. We're the only ones who know about it." Trouble's eyes spark as the light above us flickers.

Only ones? Creepiness chills my insides. How did I let myself get in a dark hole in the middle of the forest with two guys I barely know? I'm an idiot, that's why.

Courage grabs a book off the shelf and tosses it to me. I grab it, almost missing. My arms strain as I draw the book to my chest. Trouble stands before me, and I rip my eyes from the book to stare into his emerald greens. He seems safe, like Manly. Why am I so uptight?

A vision of Hate crouching over me rushes through my brain. I suck in a breath. Can't trust boys. They look at you and think only one thing. Gotta play it cool. They can't know I'm nervous. I've learned all too well monsters can sense fear.

"What about your sisters? Surely they know it's here?"

Trouble turns his back on me and rifles through a shelf, shuffling through the titles as if looking for a particular book. After a moment, he pauses and studies me. "My sisters are not quite what you would call trustworthy. They're also kind of irrational and emotional. We thought it might be better if they stayed out of it for their own good."

"Oh. So you meet me and immediately think I'm trustworthy?"

He grins, his freckles standing out the wider he grins. "Something like that."

Just like boys. They're all the same. Even this freckled-faced boy is rotten.

Courage stacks a pile of books, faded and worn around the edges. He brings them over and plops them on a dusty table. I cough as the dust coats the inside of my nose.

"How did you manage to find this place?" I run my finger over the spines.

Trouble rolls his eyes and sighs as Courage smirks. I smell a story.

"Dumb-dumb over here tried to impress a girl and went into the woods to hunt and kill a Wildie. I figured it was a good idea to follow him to make sure he kept out of trouble, no pun intended."

Trouble's face turns scarlet. Bet he wishes Courage would shut up. Courage doesn't seem to care.

At least they're funny. I give him a halfway smile. "Continue, please."

"I found him all right, stuck in a hole. If I hadn't, a Wildie might've had *him* for dinner."

Trouble butts in. "And that's how we came across the library. When Courage pulled me out of the hole, the earth gave way. We looked down with a flashlight and saw a bunch of books. We came the next day with a ladder to explore."

"Yep. The two of us fixed it up. It was a mess when we found it." Courage punches Trouble in the gut. "And we've been best friends ever since."

Trouble gives Courage the stink eye and flares his nostrils while holding his belly. "Yeah, more like brothers."

They're kind of adorable in a dorky way.

"Did you guys make the hatch door?" I glance at the opening above.

Courage wipes dust off the table with his fingers. "Yes, we did. That way no one could ever discover it. It would be a tragedy if they took this away from us. There's so much to learn down here."

I pick up one of the books and open it. Reading the words out loud, I stutter and struggle with each syllable. I catch the guys staring. Warmth creeps up my neck.

"What?" I jerk up, straight as a broom handle. As if they can read any better.

Courage clears his throat. "I could, uh, teach you how to

read faster if you like."

Great. Apparently they can.

I slam the book shut. My ears burn. I'm not an idiot. "I read just fine."

I'm done with this stupid place. They can take their stupid books and shove 'em. I take to the ladder and climb. I almost reach the top when I feel a slight tremor. I glance down.

Courage grips the rungs with his slender fingers. "I didn't mean anything by it. I understand you come from the farming community, and there's not much need to learn how to read. I get it."

My ears burn hotter. I don't care what he says. My reading doesn't need any help.

I throw open the hatch door and jump out. I'm paces ahead of them. Tromping over leaves, mud, and branches, I reach the cabins long before they do. My long, hard days as a farmer's daughter have done me good. I hurry for the door and rush through it.

"Ouch!"

"I'm so sorry. I didn't mean to—"

Aunt Joy stands there nursing her wounded arm I smashed with the door. "Oh my child, are you well? You're in such a hurry." She examines me closer. "And with such an angry face." She cups my cheek.

Stop with the touching! I avert my eyes, reign in the fire inside, and breathe deep. "I'm fine. Just frustrated with life." With boys, with books, with being stupid. Everything.

She lets go. "We all get like that from time to time. Here, I was about to deliver these papers to the office cabin. Walk with me, please? We can chat as we go."

That's more of a command than a question, isn't it? I sulk after her. *Fine. You're in charge.*

She gazes at me with eyes surrounded by crows feet. "I know being here hasn't been easy for you. But what's really going on?"

I shrug. Why should I tell her? I don't even know her.

She sighs. "It may not feel like you fit in — it usually doesn't, at least not at first — but I wish you'd give us a chance. We're like a big, happy family."

"That's what I keep hearing." I whack a branch out of my way as we near the office cabin.

"Maybe if you open your eyes and look outward instead of inward, you might find it to be true."

Ouch.

Aunt Joy gives me a little hug and enters the office cabin. I sit on the steps. Maybe she's right. Maybe I have been focusing on myself too much.

Someone slinks from the shadows.

Courage scooches next to me before I can protest. He nudges me with his knee. "I didn't mean to make you mad."

I sigh and pick at a large splinter splitting off the railing. "I'm not mad at you, Courage. I'm mad because I have to be here and I don't want to be. Maybe that sounds immature, but that's the way I feel." *Please tell me you understand.* I can't bear any more condescending words.

Courage pushes his black locks out of his eyes. "No, I get it. I didn't want to be here either when I first arrived."

Whew. Glad he understands. Wait, what did he say? "You weren't brought here as a baby?"

"No. I was adopted into a family of factory workers. They started having babies and ended up with so many kids, they couldn't afford to feed all of us. Since I wasn't *theirs*, I was the first to go."

Poor Courage. Unfair and rotten.

"That doesn't sound right."

"Well, it happened, and there's nothing I can do to change the past."

Where's the resentment? The pain? He's sure better at getting on with his life than I am.

My tense body relaxes.

He grins. "Did you notice how our names are the exact opposites?"

"The irony's not lost on me." I'll play along with this conversation change. "So do you live up to your name?"

"Many people tell me I do." Arrogance rings through his voice. "What about you?"

I nod fast. "Oh, yes. I'm afraid of everything."

If only he knew how true this statement is. We both break into a round of laughter.

"Is that why you're so mad?"

I freeze. "What?" My face hardens.

Courage winces. "Anger is usually just another form of fear."

My nostrils flair, and I force myself not to react. Humor. That's what they do. I'll give it a try. "They should've named me Anger."

He breaks into a wide grin, grabs my braid, and twirls it. "Why, hello Miss Anger. How are you today?"

My face warms, and I whack his arm away. "Ooh, I'll show you anger!"

The cabin door jerks open and slams behind us. We whirl around, and who stands there but the injured man himself. I jump to my feet like lightning. Courage follows. My stomach twists in unexpected knots.

The look on Manly's face is a new one. What is it? Jealousy? I smirk. Ha! He does really like me. Stubborn man just won't admit it.

"Hello." Manly's eyes bore into Courage.

Someone's angry. "Manly, I thought you were supposed to rest."

He takes a couple of steps forward. A grimace sneaks onto his handsome features, and he struggles to suppress it. "I'm going stir-crazy in there. Can't take one more minute staring at those off-white walls."

Manly ambles closer, and Courage backs up. "I need to find my friend." He runs away before I even get the chance to say goodbye.

"Good grief. You scared him off."

Manly chuckles and lowers himself to the steps, grunting. "So, do anything interesting today?"

I scoot closer, bumping legs, eager to spend quality time with him.

Aunt Joy appears. "Fear, you're on kitchen duty. Sorry I forgot to remind you earlier."

My heart plummets. Totally forgot all about that. So much for quality time. I pout to Manly, then turn back to Aunt Joy. "Be right there." I glance back at him. "Sorry, Manly. Duty calls."

A forgiving nod eases my frustration. I spring up and sprint down the stairs. I grind to a halt at the bottom. "Will you be able to join us in the Dining Hall today?"

"I could barely make it out here." He clutches his ribs.

"Then I'll make sure to bring you food when my shift is done."

His eyes gleam. I'm melting. Positively melting.

"You know Aunt Joy brings me food."

Why does he always have to be the voice of reason? "I know, but I'm sure I can score seconds tonight since I'll be working in the kitchen." I flash my teeth at him.

"Thanks." He waves.

I run around the cabin to the Dining Hall, aching with each step that separates us.

Chapter 13

The cook introduces herself. She's actually pretty nice. I may have misjudged her. Cooking is something I enjoy, so this is kind of fun. It's hot, sweaty, hard work, cooking for over one hundred people, but worth it when I hand them their food and they nod and smile.

When kitchen duty's done, I'm able to scrounge up a little extra food—a leftover muffin from that morning and a piece of grilled chicken. A weird combination, but Manly likes to eat *a lot*. I doubt he'll care what I bring him as long as it's edible.

Only ninety minutes of free time left before I have to report to the cabin to get ready for bed. I rush toward the office cabin. Oops, almost spilled the plate. I slow down. Don't want Manly to miss out on eating these extra yummies.

I arrive at his door. Why's it cracked open? Weird. I push it open. My neck muscles tighten. Aunt Joy and an older gentleman wearing a white uniform sit with Manly. A black bag sits next to the gentleman, and he examines Manly's bare chest with a strange-looking medical device. They notice me, and I stop in my tracks. Schnitzel fritz. Am I going to get in trouble?

Aunt Joy approaches me. "I called for the doctor the first day you got here. He arrived as soon as he could."

My lips turn up. "Thank you." Good. Now Manly can finally feel better. My gut sinks. Wait. If he gets better, that means he leaves. I don't want him to go! "I should probably leave."

I place the plate on the counter and turn to the door. Why did I barge in in the first place?

"Fear."

Tingles whiz through my core. I love it when he says my name. I turn around.

"You can stay. It's all right."

My face brightens, and Manly extends his hand. He wants me to stay. I reach for him, and his grasp engulfs my slender hand.

He looks at the doctor and Aunt Joy. "She's my pain relief."

The doctor gives him a knowing grin. "Sometimes a person's kindness is better than any medicine."

Aunt Joy fiddles with the strings of her apron, tying and retying. She shoots me a frown.

What am I doing wrong?

"Speaking of medicine," the doctor continues. "What have you administered to him?"

Aunt Joy grabs a bottle off the counter and hands it to the doctor. He scans the label.

"Oh my, you need something much stronger than this."

He rummages through his bag and extracts a few medicinal containers. He squints as he reads each bottle. The doctor chooses one, pops out two pills, and hands the bottle to

Aunt Joy. He then gives the pills to Manly, and they vanish in his mouth.

His face softens, and he sighs. Bet that helps. Poor guy. He's been so miserable.

"You'll need to lie here for about two more weeks, but it could take up to seven to heal."

Manly's jaw drops. "I can't stay that long. I have to get back to my family."

Flinching, I clutch my stomach. *Aren't I a part of your family?*

The doctor packs his belongings into the black bag. "You got hurt about a week ago?"

Manly nods.

"The minimum time for ribs to heal is three weeks. You have at least two weeks of resting left. If you leave any sooner, you risk re-injury. Wouldn't it be a tragedy if you were in the middle of nowhere and you passed out? With no one to help you? Please follow my orders. Two weeks will go by fast, then you can travel. But *only* if most of the pain is gone."

Manly's forehead wrinkles, and his breathing quickens. Why does he want to leave me so badly?

Aunt Joy stands and squares her shoulders. "I'll notify Granny immediately."

Manly grimaces and nods.

The doctor gives instructions about the medicine and bids farewell. Aunt Joy turns to us, opens her mouth, but says nothing. With a shake of her head, she exits.

"I'm not sure she approves of your spending so much time with me." Manly lets go of my hand and eases back on the hospital bed.

"Why? Is she afraid I'm going to hurt you or something?"

He closes his eyes. "I think she's afraid we're going to hurt each other."

"I'm not following." I glimpse his shirtless chest. My stomach flips like a pancake on a sizzling skillet, and I gulp. Well, this isn't awkward in the slightest. Can't. Stop. Staring. My cheeks warm. Can he tell I'm blushing?

"Listen, don't worry about it. I won't let that happen." He grabs his shirt and covers his torso. Not helping. I can still see his arm muscles. "Do anything interesting today?"

I place my hands in my lap. "Yesterday evening was interesting."

"Yeah?" He raises his eyebrows and peers intently into my eyes.

Hmm…I seem to have sparked his curiosity. "We did a session on the Word."

He breaks into a smile. "And did you enjoy it?"

Enjoy might not be the right word. "I'm trying to understand it." I twirl a strand of hair around my pinkie finger. "But it's hard." *Really* hard.

"I'm glad you're at least listening. I didn't think you heard a word I said when I taught you the songs."

How rude. I cross my arms. "I *was* listening. I think I was…" I slump into a chair and reassess that week. "Okay, maybe not as well as I could've."

He rolls his eyes. "You think?" He pauses then clears his throat. "Do you want to talk about it? I can answer some of your questions."

Ha! He thinks he can answer all the burning questions I've been harboring for weeks? He has no idea.

I take a deep breath. "What does Abba mean anyway? Why are the followers of Abba so nice all the time? Who wrote the Word? Why are there so many weird stories in there? And what's up with that story of sacrifice near the end? Isn't that a little dramatic?"

He raises his hand to stop me. "Okay. One at a time, please."

Okie dokie. I nod, eager to hear what he has to say.

"First off, I just want you to know, above all else, Abba loves you."

I restrain from rolling my eyes. I've heard that before. "That's exactly what Justice told me."

"Well, it's true." He leans forward, and his shirt slides off his midsection. He grumbles something and sits up, attempting to put the shirt over his head. He cries out.

I jump up and grab the shirt still halfway over his arms. "You're just hurting yourself. Let me help."

I yank the shirt down, and his head pops out the top. My fingers graze his skin. Scorching flames lick my fingertips. I pause, and electric currents flow between us. What's the point of breathing again? I pull the shirt down the rest of the way.

"I just hate feeling so useless." He rips his eyes from mine. "Can't even get my own shirt on."

The currents lessen until I can look at him again. I stumble back to my seat, and he readjusts himself on the bed. *Say something.* "So, um…you really think this Abba is real and he loves me?"

I may have thought it absurd before, but coming from Manly, maybe I can believe it. Maybe. A big maybe.

He nods. "Yep. And I'd love to answer all your questions. Just not all at the same time." He winks.

I melt. Perfect bliss.

I'll start with my most burning question. "Why would a god create us and put us here on earth anyway?" See if he can answer that one.

"He wanted someone to love and someone to love him back. We all have that desire within us, don't we?"

He didn't miss a beat, did he? I nod and look at the floor. So it's all about love, is that right? *I wish you would love me.*

"What's wrong?" he asks.

That longing happens again for Granny, Daddy, and Faithful back home. "Until a few weeks ago, before I met your family, I didn't even know what love was. I never felt it before." Painful to admit, but true.

Waves shimmer in Manly's eyes, and he turns his head away. Wiping his sandy locks from his forehead, his gaze veers to mine. I don't think he knows what to say.

"That's why I didn't want to come here. I finally felt love with your family. I haven't ever felt it, even from my own mother." The word "mother" comes out with a strain, and I guess I've underestimated how wounded I am by her.

"You know all believers—those who trust in Abba—we're commanded to love one another." It seems he found his voice again. "This camp is full of people like my family. You can find it with any believer. Trust me, Fear. That same love exists here."

My face hardens. I refuse to accept that. "I'm not buying it."

He sighs. "Well, I hope in time you'll see it's true. Just compare us with the rest of the world. You'll see the difference."

I pause. He's right. But I'm not going to let him know that.

"I don't get it." I shift in my chair. "Why would believers be any different from everybody else? I mean, I get that you guys are all so nice and stuff. But isn't that all relative? Who decides what's right and wrong anyway? To suppose that something's worse than something else is kind of arrogant, isn't it?"

Manly shakes his head. "Wow. The Teachings must've affected you pretty badly. You don't buy all that stuff, do you?"

I squirm. What's he getting at? "Sure I do. They're the Teachers, the ones who tell us stuff we need to know." Why is he so suspicious about what they teach? Surely he knows it's truth. "They teach us there are no such things as moral absolutes."

"Don't buy into their lies."

He really believes they're a bunch of liars.

"There's a difference between right and wrong, opposed to what the Uppers lead us to believe."

I scratch the side of my head. "Right and wrong are a made-up thing of the past. We aren't supposed to believe in evil. Aren't the Uppers the wise ones? I don't like them one bit, but we're supposed to trust them, aren't we?" I'm such a hypocrite. I've called my brother evil many times.

He shakes his blond mane again. "No, we can't. Everything that comes out of the Teachings is in complete contrast to the Word. I trust Abba and his Word. Not some man-made teachings."

"But we're here to serve the Uppers, period. It doesn't seem right, but that's what I've been taught. Surely not everything I learned as a kid was a lie?"

The Teachings had been one of the only positive experiences of my entire childhood. I've clung to those memories for years. Why is Manly trying to take that from me?

"Why would it be okay for one group to make themselves better than another group? As you just said, it doesn't seem right, does it?"

Not really. Again. Not telling him that.

"The Uppers have placed themselves in a position of authority, and they've completely ruined the Downers' lives by brainwashing them at these stupid Teachings. It's wrong.

Everything about them is wrong."

He's hurting my head. *Make it stop.* I rub my forehead.

Manly taps his fingers on the metal bed, interrupting my thoughts. "Fear, I don't mean to hurt you by bringing this up, but I want to give you a vivid example that will help you understand." He rolls on his side and grimaces. "When Hate was"—he gulps—"abusing you...was that right or wrong?"

"I...I don't know," I stutter. How could he bring that up?

"Yes, you do." His eyes dart back and forth, searching mine. "It was wrong because you knew it was. It felt wrong. It caused you pain. Abba never wants us to cause pain to anyone. Physical or emotional. He commands us to treat others with love, kindness, respect. There *are* moral absolutes, and I think you know that in your heart."

Why is he doing this to me? I clutch my chest as his words stir hurtful memories. Hate leaning over me. The nights of torture. Papa beating me. The days of agony. My mind spins as my temperature rises.

I'm angry.

Very angry.

"Well, if it was so wrong, and Abba is so loving, then why didn't he stop my brother? Why did he allow me to get hurt?" My voice climbs, and my body trembles. "If he loved me, he wouldn't have let that happen. What kind of loving god lets people feel so much pain?" I burst into angry sobs. Manly reaches for me. I pull back. *Don't touch me.* "No! I don't want your pity. I want answers."

His eyebrows scrunch.

Tell me something, for crying out loud!

Silence. That's all he's going to give me. No answers, just pure, unadulterated silence.

"That's what I thought."

I rush out the door and slam it behind me. In an instant, I distance myself from the cabin. Running deep into the forest, I collapse, flat on the ground. It's getting dark, but I don't care. I smash my forehead against a rock.

Nothing matters right now but the fire inside. I sit up and run my fingers across the rock, rubbing in my tears. I stand, look heavenward, and scream at a god who has forgotten me. A god who may love all of *them*, but never me. I scream at him until sandpaper replaces the inside of my throat.

When I fall again to the ground, I press my forehead against the rock as hard as I can.

I want to feel pain. Anything to take away this torment.

The pressure against my skull blocks the heartache. I hate my life. I hate everyone. God isn't real, and if he is, he'd stop this anger boiling inside. He would've stopped my family from hurting me. From using me. From killing every last shred of innocence.

A growl, low and fierce, tears through the brush. A lightening sensation blasts down my back. I freeze. The growl again, this time louder and closer. It's a Wildie, and I, because of my stupidity, am about to be mauled to death.

I lift my head. Not more than two yards away, the guttural growling and squawking of a Wildie shatter the darkness. I have two choices: stay or run. No question there. Grass whips against my bare legs as the creature chases me.

My muscles strain. *I'm going to die!* Thumping explodes in my chest. I clench my fists as I swing them, urging my body to go faster and faster.

The Wildie's hooves pound the dirt behind me, intensifying. Looking back is not an option. I keep up my pace but can sense it gaining. *Oh God!* Collapsing lungs are in my near future. I dodge trees. Clomping continues behind me. My neck prickles. I burst through the edge of the forest into the clearing. It's close enough that hot breath blasts my ankle. A *bang* rings through the night air. I shudder. Was that a gunshot?

I continue my escape, and the pursuit ceases. I slow and stop, turning to find out why. A large lump lies on the ground. Darkness shrouds the creature. I fall to my knees and bend over, clutching the grass. It's over. Abba saved me again. Then why won't my heart stop seething? The tightening in my chest loosens as I pant. I'm alive. Maybe I should've just let it eat me. Then my misery would be over.

The man in overalls approaches with a shotgun in hand. He comes near and whisks me to my feet. "What're you doing out here this late?"

I step back. My brain shuts down. I have no clue how to respond. His fists-on-hips posture tells me he's in no mood for insolence.

"If it weren't for your friend back there, you'd be dead. He told me you went into the woods. I wouldn't have known where you were if it wasn't for all your bellowing."

He grabs my arm and marches me to the cabins. Aunt Joy meets us. He turns and stalks off, leaving me to face the bewildered old woman.

"Where are you going, Lanky?" she calls out. The man keeps putting distance between the crazy screaming girl—yes, that would be me—and himself. "I heard a gunshot. What in the Gliding Lands is going on?"

I can't focus. Nothing matters. "A Wildie tried to attack me in the woods. Lanky shot it." He should've let me die.

"Why in the world were you in the woods, child?"

I don't say a word.

"Do you have any idea—"

I brush past her while she's mid-sentence. A noise of disbelief cuts off as I shut the door in her face. Now she can't lecture me anymore. The lights are out, and snores permeate the cabin. No chatter from these numbskulls tonight. Thank Abba. No, scratch that. He doesn't exist.

He saved you, Fear.

Shut up, brain. Lanky saved me. A tornado trashes my brain cells as a stupor of despondence and murk descends. I fall asleep before my head hits the pillow.

Chapter 14

The next day, I wake up in quite a mood. Darkness consumes me to my core and eats away at my insides. I like it and hate it at the same time. It plunges me into the depths of despair and clings to my skin, seething into my pores, not letting go. Wallowing in this darkness, my mind teeters on some sort of psychotic break. The monster inside me, the one lurking in the corner, breaks free from its chains and erupts in a fit of rebellion.

I refuse to do my chores. They think they can force me to work? Ain't gonna happen. When they find me, I ignore them and walk away. I'm not about to talk to these stupid people. Why won't they leave me alone? I don't even care if Manly's upset with me. I want nothing to do with any of them. Abba hates me. Let everyone else hate me too.

Meals are no longer important. I've gone hungry before. Many, *many* times. Aunt Joy seems worried about me. Serves her right for trying to make me do chores.

This lasts for days.

Bitterness swirls around me, whispering its cruelty into my ears. Abba doesn't care about me. Why should I give a scat about him? Sure, the Wildie didn't get me, but that was just because Manly alerted Lanky to my whereabouts. Abba didn't hear my plea. How could he when he doesn't exist?

Except he does. Truth breaks through and ignites the bitter root imbedded in my chest, plunging my depths with its breath, filling me. I will fight it to the death.

Shut up! Shut up! My mind aches from the constant battle. The murky darkness envelopes me once more. A false safety wraps me in its grip. Pain can't touch me if pain is all I am. If I become pain.

Aunt Joy forces me to attend Chapel, but she can't force me to wear my pretty dress. I have a feeling she doesn't care as long as I stay in the room. I skip out on Study and sit by the lake. Maybe I'll simply walk out into the waters and let it take me under. No one would notice. No one would care.

Happy approaches fast. I wish she'd leave me alone. I try to stay away from her so I can hide inside my darkness. But the girl is quick. She follows me as I dash away from the shore and scamper to the residential area. She corners me by one of the cabins. Light emanates from her like a ray of sunshine. If only I had a fire hose to blast that sunshine to Timbuktu. She's ruining my mood.

"Go away, Happy."

"I don't want to." What a typical response from an eight-year-old. "I want to know why you've been so grouchy."

Rude little girl. "And I don't want to tell you."

She stomps her foot. "Why not?"

I shove my fists on my hips. "Because I don't want to talk about it." *Just go away.*

"Well, I do." She's relentless. She softens her voice, batting her big, pretty eyes at me. "Please, Fear? Something's wrong, and I want to know what it is. I thought we were friends."

Ouch. Such a big guilt trip from such a little girl. Her words chip away at the iciness freezing my heart.

"I want to be your friend. I hope you want to be mine."

I sigh. "Of course I want to be your friend, Happy." This should get her off my back.

"Good, then let's talk."

I was wrong.

"Are you okay?"

"No, I'm not okay. And I won't be until you leave me alone!" She cringes. Schnitzel fritz! Why do I have to be the bad guy here?

A vision of messy brown hair and ruddy skin runs through my mind. Justice. The tone I just used on Happy was the same I used with Justice. Heaviness weighs on my chest. I circle my temples with my middle fingers. Maybe I can try to be kinder.

I calm my voice and repeat myself in a softer tone. "I'm not okay, Happy. I'm angry."

"Why?"

Seriously? Has she not been paying attention? "For a million reasons." *Duh.*

"That's sure a lot of reasons."

No kidding. I squint at her. "I told you I didn't want to talk about this."

Happy's eyes bug out, and she purses her lips. What a goof. I let down my guard, but not for long. I cross my arms.

"You know, Fear, you've been kind of a jerk lately."

My eyes widen. A jerk? I turn away.

"I thought you were so nice the first day I met you, but now…now I don't think you're nice at all. I think you're a big meanie." Her small frame doesn't intimidate me one bit, but her words sting. "You're not the only one who's been hurt, Fear. You're not the only one who's had a difficult life. You act like everything's so awful, but really, *you're* the one being awful. People around here want to help you. They care about you, and all you do is treat people like...like crap!" she yells. "They should've named you Jerk Face."

Warmth rises to my cheeks. The ice melts faster, and my heart aches from the pain. This time, not pain others have caused me, but pain I've caused others. She's right. I'm a jerk. A major jerk. The most massive jerk ever.

Happy's face softens. "You've had a crappy life, I get that. But guess what? There's this great thing Abba invented for us. It's called forgiveness. I think you could use some of that."

My past hurts surge to the surface and spill over. "How can I forgive what's been done to me?"

"I don't know, Fear. How can Abba forgive all the mean things you've done lately?"

Tears spring to my eyes. She's right. I don't want to admit it, but she's right. Justice easily forgave me after I'd been horrible to him. He taught me what it means to forgive. And I've been horrible...again...to everyone. Why can't I just be nice like most of the people around here? From what I've heard during Study, Abba will forgive me if I simply ask him. But it can't be that easy.

Happy sits next to me and pats my knee. "Remember there are two powers in this world. Light and dark. You don't want to be stuck in the darkness forever, do you, Fear?"

Of course I don't.

I shake my head, and more tears pop into my eyes, pushing the old ones out and down my cheeks. Justice wanted this for me so badly. So does Manly. To find what I'm missing. What makes them complete. But I don't know if I can ever be different. Is Abba the missing piece I need? Does he really see me for who I am?

Whimpering, I attempt to control my voice. "I've lived in darkness for so long, Happy. I only recently experienced light. It's what I want, but...I just don't know if Abba cares about me."

Happy tilts her head. "Didn't Abba just save you from a Wildie?"

I circle the dirt with the tip of my toe. "Well...yes. He did."

"What about the poison needle? Didn't he save you from that too?"

My jaw hangs open. "How did you know about that?"

"I've been hanging out with Manly." She grabs my shoulders. "Back to the conversation!"

This little girl is strong for her age. Geesh!

"Did he save you from the poison or not?"

I shrug out of her grasp and stare at the ground. "Yes." The thought of Hate stabbing the needle in my neck brings a fresh wave of pain.

"Didn't he save your life when those Uppers shot at you?"

"What have you and Manly *not* talked about?"

"That's not the point! Abba saved your life *three* times, Fear." She holds up three fingers. "Wait. Make that four. Let's not forget that as a baby you were pushed over the side of the Gliding Lands to fall thousands of feet, only to survive with no disabilities. Although I do wonder about your brain sometimes."

I scoff at this, but heat blankets my cheeks.

"How many more times will he have to save you before you realize he loves you?"

This girl is too smart for her own good. If she were older, I might punch her.

"And didn't he take you from that wretched home and give you a great family who loves you?"

My eyes burn with unshed tears. I have no words. I can only nod. They do love me. The only ones who ever have. Great, now my nose is running. More tears threaten to spill. I miss my family and those sweet few weeks together.

"I'd call that love," she says.

Tears slide down my face. I can't stop it. I wipe my nose with the back of my hand.

"You're right. I hate it, but you're right." I smile and thank Happy with a hug. If only I hadn't been so stubborn. If only I'd clung to the light sooner. I can't deny it. Abba loves me. "When did you get so smart?"

"I've always been this smart. You were being such a jerk you didn't notice."

I pinch her nose at this, and we laugh.

Her eyes turn serious. "Are you ready to stop feeling sorry for yourself and live your life for Abba?"

I'm tired of being angry. It takes so much energy. With Abba at my side, I won't need to be angry anymore. I've been such a horrible idiot.

"I think I am." The darkness binding me with icy tentacles releases me. Warmth spreads over me, murdering the last of the icy coldness.

"Well then, welcome to the family." Her words bounce through the air. She shakes my hand. "I'm going to give you alone time with Abba. Talk to him." She leaves without another word.

A bunny bounds past as I squirm. It's time. This is the piece to fill the hole inside my heart. I fold my hands and lift my eyes to the sky. "Abba, hey, it's me. I know a lot of people talk to you, so hopefully you know who I am. I guess you do, according to some of my friends. I just wanted to say…I'm sorry. I'm so sorry for everything I've done. So many bad things. So many people I've hurt." My soul splits open, spilling my life before him. Tears pour down my face onto my folded hands. "I'm so thankful for you, for your love. I feel it now. It's real. Everyone says you care. I'm sorry for not believing them. For not believing you. But I do now. I know you're real. And I know you care." Thankfulness for my new family and for all the people he put in my path, pointing me to him, spills from my soul to heaven. "I want to follow you. I'm yours."

His forgiveness rushes through me, and a weight lifts from my shoulders. Abba's loving arms surround me in a fatherly embrace. Blasts of sunlight blaze through me, sizzling my insides, filling me. It's the best feeling in the world.

The beginning of a deep change stirs within me. I only hope others will forgive me and see I've become a new person. See with Abba's help, I choose to be different. I choose to cast off my old self and be made new. Made whole. Complete.

My tranquil silence breaks when a Hoverpod appears in the sky. The whirr of the motor sends a manic wind pressing into the ground, strewing leaves and debris. My solitude breaks as people rush past. Everyone takes cover. I should, but curiosity has me inching forward, especially since I was born an Upper. What are they like?

The noise beckons me nearer. This is probably a bad idea, but I don't care. This is my chance! Getting to see Uppers up close may lead me one step closer to understanding who my biological parents are. Why they dumped me over the edge. The wind picks up as the Hoverpod nears the ground. I stop short and hide in the shadows of the cabins to spy on whoever comes near.

Happy runs up behind me, grabs my arm, and pulls. She

must've not strayed too far when she gave me alone time with Abba.

"We can't be out here. We need to go inside."

I ignore her and walk toward the whir. Nothing will stop me from seeing what this Upper looks like. I burst out from behind a cabin right as a Hoverpod lands. Curiosity draws me closer. Happy grabs for my arm again, but this time she misses. I move nearer.

My eyes are glued to the Hoverpod. An extremely large man attempts to get out. A robot sets up a Hover-Scooter for the spherical Upper, and the scooter shifts and rocks as he settles onto the seat.

Shiny, almost crêpe-like clothing wraps around this strange person. Half of his body is covered in forest green, the other half, royal purple. The outfit hugs his body, revealing every curve and clinging to every roll of fat. Arrogance drips from his person. I've never seen a man so big before. None of us Downers would be able to do our jobs if we got that fat.

Carefully sculpted hair clings to his round head. His triple chin creates a look of neckless-ness. Is this what my parents look like? Looking down, I glance at my frame. Short and curvy, but far from fat. Hmm…

We send most of our food up there—to the Gliding Lands where the Uppers live—to supply them with enough to fill their gigantic bellies. Although, I don't believe all Uppers are as morbidly thickset as this one. Are they?

His little robot goes up to the office and knocks. A minute later Aunt Joy comes to the door.

Her flat voice reaches my ears. "Count Cerberus. How nice to see you."

They begin what sounds like a business conversation, something about the Fallen, buffalo, current pricing. Happy slinks down behind me. She looks none-too-pleased.

Happy grabs my arm and tugs again. "Let's get out of here."

"Who said that?"

We freeze, Happy's hand stalling on my arm.

The large man and Aunt Joy turn their heads our way. Aunt Joy's face stills. The giant man steers his Hoverscooter forward to get a better look at us.

"Step out here," Count Cerberus commands.

I slither out from behind the tree as Happy cowers and clutches the back of my shirt. If I were as large as he is, she could stay hidden, but I'm not.

"Who's hiding behind you?"

No! Stay behind me! My skull pounds.

Happy pokes her head out and reveals her quaking self.

We stand side by side, shaking in our shoes as this stranger examines us. Aunt Joy's face darkens. My shoulders hunch. What kind of trouble did I just land us in?

He continues to eye us. Icicles plunge into my backbone.

He turns to Aunt Joy. "How much do you want for that one?" He points our way.

My eyes widen, and I hide Happy behind me. Now I understand why she wanted me to stay out of sight. Why didn't I listen?

Aunt Joy shifts. "Which one?"

Really, Aunt Joy? Maybe she's just playing along. He points to me again, and I step forward.

He waves me away. "No, the small brown one behind her. How much?"

Happy? *No, take me instead.* I will the man to change his mind.

"She's not for sale."

Aunt Joy is braver than I am. How can she talk back to him like that?

The man sneers at her. "You realize I don't need to pay you, right? I could take her without your permission."

I flinch.

Aunt Joy sighs, bordering dramatic. "You don't want her. She's filthy, full of diseases."

I brighten. He'll never want her now.

The man frowns but quickly regains his composure. He shrugs. "Oh well, I have a trip planned soon to Pleasure County. They're bred much better out there. None of these backwood hicks you have around here."

Aunt Joy nods. "You're perfectly right."

I never in my wildest dreams imagined Aunt Joy could lie. She's only trying to protect us. Oh Abba, please help it work!

He glares at her. "You will fix that little matter we discussed?"

Aunt Joy nods. "Everything will be set right. Your money will not be wasted buying our buffalo meat. We guarantee it."

She reaches into a basket on the porch and produces sticky buns wrapped in plastic wrap. "Would you like these?"

He yanks them from her hand without so much as a *thank you*. Rude. Loading himself into his Hoverpod is an ordeal. That's got to be a massive pain. But he's mean, so I don't really care. Finally he manages to plop into the Hoverpod and fly off.

Aunt Joy breathes down my neck within seconds. "Do you know what kind of trouble you're in?"

Chapter 15

I cringe and slink back from Aunt Joy's seething frame.
Knew she couldn't be sunshine and roses all the time. She's an
inch shorter than me, but with the amount of energy she
throws my way, I shrink in her presence.

"I'm sorry?" It comes out more like a question than an
actual apology. Oops.

"Do you know what you could've done by bringing Happy
out here? She could be gone right now, and the only one to
blame would be you."

Her words sting like a million bees tearing into me at once.

"Were you even listening when the others told you the
rules of this place?"

I hesitate. Should I lie? Faithful's little mantra "Honesty is
the best policy" runs through my mind. Nope. My lying days
are over. I shake my head. "I promise to pay more attention to
rules and follow them from now on." She doesn't know I've
changed. She won't believe me.

Aunt Joy glares at me. Nope. Definitely doesn't believe

me. "When any Upper comes to visit, you must run and hide. Never, *ever* show your face. You've seen what can happen. You've been irresponsible and uncooperative for over a week. It ends today!"

I totally agree.

She ushers me inside and produces a long list of chores I've shirked these last few days. She scratches a few more at the bottom, then hands me the list. I think she expects me to throw it at her face and sulk off, but I pluck it from her hand, catching her off guard.

"I'm different now. Let me prove it to you." Walking out the door, I commit to my tasks.

I glance at the list. I'll complete the entire job—no matter how long it takes—before I eat another morsel of food. By the time I'm done with all these chores, hopefully she'll understand I've changed.

The whole day flies by, my hands busy. The next morning, my stomach gurgles. I'm determined to stick it out. I can do this. I scrub shower stalls and toilets. I sweep and mop floors. I pick up litter along the length of the boy cabins, muck out the horse stalls, learn how to brush the horses' hair, and do many other random things assigned to me.

My stomach is empty, I've managed to push away anyone who may have even remotely been interested in being my friend, I miss Manly something fierce, and I've been an idiot and a jerk. This sucks.

How many people have I hurt around here? How can I possibly apologize to them all? I try to make note of who looks upset with me, but no one throws me angry glances. They're sure polite. I've never seen people who don't hold a grudge.

I talk to Abba. I might as well get used to the fact I have a Father who listens to me and watches my back. The air around me stills, filling me with calm. I can only hope and pray the people around me see the change in my attitude and give me another undeserved chance.

At lunchtime, everyone heads toward the Dining Hall. My stomach grumbles, but I made a promise, and I'm going to keep it. I have only one chore left, one I've saved for last because it's the hardest.

I approach the Special Cabin, one of the added chores Aunt Joy scribbled down for me. I gulp. She's trying to teach me a lesson, I know it. I steel myself. She didn't realize I'm ready to be taught—I only hope it won't be too painful.

Regret like desert sand covers the inside of my mouth. I push open the door to the narrow office. Again, the sweet smiling lady meets me. I screwed up so badly last time, I don't deserve this second chance.

"There you are."

I flinch, but she smiles. Why's she smiling? She should hate my guts.

"I'm glad you've chosen to return."

Wasn't much of a choice. I clutch the chore list.

"Let me explain about these kids before we head back."

I nod.

"A lot of these children are the babies who were dropped from the Gliding Lands without parachutes. That, or their parachutes failed to work properly. Most babies dropped this way are killed on impact, but there are those who survive... with obvious damage. These children had no control over what happened to them. We must have compassion when dealing with them."

This time I understand. This time I'm not scared, and I know what to expect. I sneak into the room with a smile on my face. I'm not going to be an idiot this time. They'll see a different side of me. The new me. I head to the back room where the trash bags are. The same curious eyes stare at me as I go, only this time I offer smiles in return. I see these disfigured and disabled kids in a different light now, through the light of Abba. He shines so brightly here.

With each passing face, warmth fills me. My soul could bathe in this light and love forever. These blessed kids, their precious faces, show me more kindness than I'll ever deserve. They should condemn me for the way I acted last time, running out of here like I did, but they're not.

My breathing slows, and my pulse steadies as I enter the baby room first. One previously occupied crib sits vacant, taunting me. I tear my gaze away and move on. I dare myself to stare into their plump little faces. My heart shatters into a thousand irreparable pieces. Gulping down tears, I reach for the next trash can.

I could've been one of these babies.

But I'm not.

I must've had a working parachute, which means maybe, just maybe, someone cared about me when they dropped me. Not like most of these poor creatures. Tossed over like trash. It's unthinkable.

Leaving the babies, I close the door. My shoulders draw tight, and I wipe my clammy hands down my sides. I survey the room and count the trashcans so I won't miss any this time. A figure startles me, appearing at my side. The boy, the one who informed me I was in the wrong bathroom, stands there. Oh joy. Now I can embarrass myself in front of him all over again.

He grabs the bag out of my hands. "Here, let me help you."

I blink at his walker. How's he going to manage that? I keep my mouth shut. We walk to the first trashcan. He opens the bag, and I dump in the trash.

"Thank you." He's not so bad.

He nods as we walk to the next one, working his walker through the aisles with proficiency. I peer at him. Poor kid. Using that walker has to stink.

He stares hard. "Don't look at me like that. There's no reason to pity me. My legs might not work right, but I have a smart brain." He taps his head.

Got it. No pity party here.

"I'm sure you do." I dump another trashcan. "I wouldn't think otherwise."

"I'm glad I landed on my feet, not my head." He gestures to the boy with the misshapen head I saw last time. He's not drooling this time, but he holds a stuffed rabbit and bounces it on his legs. He looks older than me but acts like a two-year-old.

Might as well tell him. "I was dropped too, you know."

His eyes widen. "And you're okay?" He inspects me as if I'm hiding some sort of disability.

"I was one of the lucky ones." Seems so unfair. Why should I be whole while these other kids suffer?

"Must've had a good parachute. And landed somewhere soft." He slumps on the side of someone's bed. "And there's no such thing as luck. Didn't you know that?"

I shake my head.

"Abba only sends blessings, not luck."

"I only just yesterday accepted Abba. I don't know much about anything. But I'm eager to learn."

"That's awesome you believe in him. I've been one of his for years."

I wrinkle my nose. That's hard to believe. He can't be more than eleven years old. Twelve, tops.

"No, really. I accepted Abba when I was five. My whole life I've tried to live for him."

Wow. He must know so much more than I do. "Maybe you can help me if I ever have questions."

Which I do. Lots of them. And I doubt Manly's going to answer any of them after the way I treated him.

His eyes brighten. "I would love to! It gets so boring around here. It'd be nice to have something to look forward to." He sticks out his hand. "I'm Tenacious."

A small smile lifts my lips as I pump his hand. "Fear."

I scan the cramped quarters. A screen on the wall runs old movies. Most of the kids stare at the wall or bicker with one another. Yuck. Not a stellar way to live.

"I wonder why they have you all squished into this small cabin?" It's so claustrophobic. I couldn't stand it.

"I've been wondering that for a long time now." His unfocused stare aims at the floor.

There's got to be something I can do. "I'm going to talk to Aunt Joy about it."

Lithe walks up to us at that moment, her shadow falling across us. "Talk to Aunt Joy about what?"

I clear my throat. "Why all these kids are crammed into this small cabin."

She gives a pinched smile. "We've wanted to utilize a larger cabin for the Specials for quite some time. Aunt Joy thinks it's too dangerous."

"Too dangerous?"

Lithe nods and joins Tenacious on the bed, smoothing the sheets with her delicate but strong hands. "You see, most of these kids are bedridden or can only get around on walkers or wheelchairs. So, to move them, we'd need major manpower. Aunt Joy is concerned if we bring all the Specials out into the open at the same time, the Wildies could attack. And there's always the threat of a flyby shooting. It's not like they can run or get away. I'm afraid Aunt Joy's been so busy running this place with just me, Shepherd Sam, and a few Room Moms to help her, she hasn't had time or energy to formulate a plan."

I pace the small aisle between the beds. "What about the Ranch Hands? Couldn't they help?"

"We tried that a few years ago. They flat-out refused because they said it wasn't their job. I think they didn't know how to act around disabled children."

Ugh. Just like I'd acted last time. "That's stupid. These kids shouldn't have to live like this."

"I agree, but there's not much we can do without help." Lithe squeezes my arm, then gets back to her job, which is endless and mostly thankless.

Someday I hope to be selfless like her.

It's late. Everyone in this whole camp probably hates me now. I've got to find a way to apologize. I'm not sure how, but I'm going to figure it out. Manly has every right to hate me. He probably thinks I'm psycho. Well, that might be a fair assumption with the way I acted. My face falls at the thought of approaching him. I can't wait to be with him again, but I doubt he feels the same way after I screamed at him.

Abba, please help me make this right.

Continuing to ignore my stomach, I head to the Medical Room. I reach it, but the bed is empty, and the bathroom door stands ajar. Did he leave without saying goodbye?

I hurry out of the room. Tell me he hasn't left. He wouldn't do that to me, would he? Rushing through the cabin, my chest squeezes. People know how erratically I've acted the last few days, so no one questions my behavior. He's not here! I search the whole cabin, then dart outside. In my frenzy, I run past all the cabins and stop at the edge of the woods. No! He can't be gone.

He left me. I was so awful to him. Now I won't get to say I'm sorry, and he'll hate me forever.

Pain like broken glass scrapes my bleeding heart. His last memory of me is yelling then ignoring him for days.

Walking aimlessly, my chest chokes me in a full-blown panic attack. *Breathe. Stop freaking out and just breathe. You're not going to die without him.* I will myself to believe it. I pause and scan the lake.

A guy perches on a large rock. I heave a sigh. Oh, thank Abba. He's so far away, I hope it isn't my imagination. I jog closer until I can make out his features. It *is* the man who makes my heart skip beats. A lump settles in my throat.

Manly faces me, and I stop short. I cannot form words. He lifts off the rock and takes a step toward me. "How are you doing? I've been worried about you."

Worried about me? My insides shred. I've been nothing but selfish these last few days, not caring about anyone else's feelings but my own. Putting my head down, I sense his approach. His shadow towers over me. I drop my chin and rub my nose. What am I doing out here? He doesn't want to talk to me. A finger lifts my chin. My eyes shift away.

"Are you all right?"

"Manly, I'm so sorry!" I blurt as my eyes fill with tears. How can he still care after how I treated him?

He forces me to stare into his gorgeous eyes. My legs weaken.

"It's all right. I forgive you."

What? I don't think anyone's ever forgiven me before, or at least they never bothered to tell me. No, wait. Justice had, right before he died. "You do? But why?"

He breaks into that sideways grin I love so much. "Because I should, so I do."

He's more awesome than I ever imagined. I wrap my arms around his waist. "But I don't deserve it."

"I know. None of us deserves forgiveness, yet Abba forgives all who ask. Why should I do any less?"

I glance up at him. "You're pretty amazing, Manly."

"Not really."

What about his ribs? I lessen my grip. How could I forget? I'm so stupid; I'm probably hurting him. "How did you get out of the Medical Room?"

"It's been almost three weeks since my injury. The doctor said I could be better by now, and I am." He gives me a squeeze, then releases me. "I heard you started doing chores again?"

I nod. "Yeah. I kind of had an attitude change."

He squints and twists his lips to the side, inspecting my face.

Don't believe me, do ya? I better tell him what happened.

I scuffle the dirt with the tip of my shoe. "I'm going to trust in Abba from now on."

His face lights up, and I can't help but give him a goofy grin. "Happy helped me see the light. I'm a believer now."

"That's fantastic, Fear!" He grabs my waist and whirls me around.

Weightless and free, sunbeams blast their rays through

every fiber of my being. *Never stop!* He plops me down, takes a step back, and holds his chest.

"I'm so excited to hear that! You don't know how happy that makes me."

Why's he holding his chest? The man said he was healed. Is he lying? My steps falter.

He lunges forward and grips my arm. "I also hear you haven't been eating." His tone reeks of disapproval.

"I'm all right." I stumble again. He grips both of my arms. "I'm just dizzy." With love or hunger, I'm not sure.

"Do I need to carry you to the Dining Hall and make you eat?"

I shake my head, which sends my dizziness careening out of control. I squeeze my temples until I'm steady. "I was going to eat right after I found you and apologized."

"Well, now you have, so let's go."

Okay, Mr. Bossy-pants.

He helps me to the Dining Hall and finds a seat. Everyone stares as though I might bite their heads off. *Great.* Living here's gonna be *just great* with a bunch of people who hate me.

"Hi." I offer a quiet voice as I stare at the table and tuck a strand of hair behind my ear. Those sitting nearby relax. They must be able to tell I'm not in my recent rampaging mood. Good, maybe I can earn their trust back.

Soon Manly brings me a steaming plate of food. My mouth salivates as he sets it down. I haven't eaten anything in over twenty-four hours. I use my fork to slice off bits and bring it to my mouth bite by bite. Forget this. I'm starving. I only hope I won't look like a fool as I launch food to the back of my throat, barely bothering to chew. Yes, I'm that hungry. And no. I don't really care. I glance at Manly, and he looks away.

Well, maybe I care a little.

Chapter 16

I eat every last bite on my plate and have to restrain myself from picking it up and licking it. After my binging ends, strength returns to my body. My mind clears. I gulp down two glasses of water to finish off the meal. Manly sits next to me, and Happy walks up and puts her hands on my shoulders.

She whispers not so quietly in my ear, "So are you and your boyfriend back together?"

My chin drops. "Happy!" Heat fills my face.

Manly turns away and fidgets with his food. He must've heard. Well, at least now he knows others think we're a couple. I wish he felt the same.

Happy rolls her eyes and aims herself in Manly's direction. "I hope our little talks won't end just because your *friend* is back in the picture."

My goodness, she has sass.

Manly shakes his head as the little girl swaggers away. He turns to me and grins. "Man, she's something else."

I wrinkle my nose. "She sure is, the little stinker."

We end our meal in laughter. After dinner, we go to the lake and stroll the rocky shore.

"Fear, I'm glad you came to see me today, because I'm leaving for home tomorrow."

My face falls. A vice clamps on my heart and squeezes tight. Why now? Why just as I finally get my head screwed back on?

"In the morning," he adds.

I bite my lip. "You weren't going to leave without saying goodbye, were you?" *Please say no.*

"I thought about it, Fear. I didn't think you wanted to see me anymore. But I knew you were hurting, and honestly, I don't think I could've left without seeing you one last time."

This warms me, but the sudden news puts an immense damper on my spirits. I can't accept the thought of him leaving.

"Hey! There's still free time left. Want to try horseback riding?"

My face perks up. Now he's speaking my language. "Do you think the stables are still open?"

"There's only one way to find out." He grabs my hand, and we jog toward the stables together.

My core sings at his touch. He clasps his free hand over his chest.

I pull back, slowing him down. "Knock it off, Manly. You're going to make your ribs start hurting again." He says nothing but slows. Maybe he does have some sense.

When we arrive, only one Ranch Hand mills about. He's on top of none other than my beautiful Pumpkin. It's Lanky, the overalls guy. Is that the only outfit he owns?

Manly clears his throat, and Lanky glances our way. "Is there any way we can ride a couple of horses until free time is over?"

Lanky shakes his head. "Sorry, Manly. I'm closing the stable for the night. All the horses have been put away. I have one more chore to do, then I'm calling it a night. Sorry."

Manly slaps his thigh and tightens his lips. He turns and walks away only to come back a moment later. "Does that chore involve riding your horse?"

"Well, no." Lanky wipes a boney hand down his face. "I was going to put him in for the night too. This big guy takes a skilled rider, if you're thinking what I think you're thinking." He inspects us as he pats the horse's neck.

"I believe you are, my good sir," Manly quips. "I happen to be a skilled rider since my childhood. We used to own horses. We'll only ride while you finish your last chore, even if it's only a couple of minutes. Besides, I'm leaving tomorrow. This is my last chance to show Fear my horse-riding skills."

Lanky scratches his head. "If you feel the need to show off so much, sure, go ahead."

He slides off the horse and hands Manly the reins. Manly guides me to the gorgeous beast I've made friends with.

I caress Pumpkin's nose and whisper, "See, I promised I'd be back for you."

The horse whinnies and nuzzles my face with his giant head. I breathe in his horsey scent, and my soul fills with longing to ride this magnificent creature. Manly checks the saddle. When he seems satisfied, he clasps his hands and holds them low so I can step into them.

I hesitate. "Your ribs."

"I'm fine."

Sure you are. "You're stubborn is what you are."

"No more than you."

True.

I step into his cupped hands, and he lifts me as though I'm

made of air. I swing my leg over the beast and plop down with ease. The beautifully crafted leather delights my palms.

It's like I'm meant to be here, at this time, this moment. The wind picks up and whips leaves around Pumpkin's legs. Even the air stirs with anticipation.

Manly leads the horse to the fence and uses it as a ladder. He settles behind me. My skin prickles. He leans against me and grabs the reins, placing them in one hand and encircling my waist with his other.

So many wasted days. Why was I so stupid? I missed out on this.

I'd continue to kick myself, but I want to enjoy the moment. We don't have much time before Lanky comes back.

Manly nudges the horse, but Pumpkin refuses to budge. He tries again. Nothing. Manly clears his throat.

"It's been a few years since I rode."

He nudges him once more, and the stubborn horse remains a statue. Manly takes a deep breath. The man's got patience. Can't deny that.

"We had horses when my mother was alive. She loved them with a passion. After Abba, Daddy, Faithful, and me, there was nothing she loved more."

Manly finally gets him moving, and we amble around the arena. Manly's quiet voice reaches my ear. "That's how she died, you know."

Leaning against his chest, I tilt my chin up. "No, I didn't."

"She fell one day, off her horse, and her head hit a rock. Daddy was so angry, he shot that horse."

I gasp. Daddy has a temper?

"It wasn't the horse's fault. My mom could be quite bullheaded and sometimes reckless with the horses. She trusted them so much...I guess..." His voice falters. "She never expected anything to go wrong."

"I'm so sorry to hear that. That must've been awful."

I picture Manly as a boy crying for his mom. Maybe that's why he never cried for Justice. He'd already run out of tears long before.

"It was awful. Daddy got rid of all the horses after that and refused to let us on one since. He wouldn't be too pleased if he knew about this."

Uh-oh. I lean forward and look back at him. "Should we stop?"

"What he doesn't know won't hurt him." Manly squeezes me a little tighter. I fall back, and his lips brush the tip of my ear. Tingles rage from my forehead down to my neck. My lungs burn, and I forget how to breathe. "Besides, no way would I let you get hurt. Mom taught me well. Faithful didn't get to ride much; she was young when the accident happened."

A few weeks ago, I didn't know I could feel both sadness and joy at the same time. This happens so often now, it's hard for me to figure out.

We ride faster. I let go of all worries for a few minutes and enjoy the time with Manly as the wind whips through my hair. He eventually slows Pumpkin and utters a grunt through clenched teeth. Oh great, he's hurting. I knew it.

Lanky stands by the gate. Bet he's itching for us to be done. Manly slows the horse, and we meander to the overalls man.

Manly nods at him. "Thank you."

He slips down and helps me down too. It went by so fast. I wish it didn't have to end. I gnaw the inside of my cheek.

After helping Lanky bed down the horse, we meet by the barn's gate. Manly swipes his hands down his pants. "Will you meet me before I leave?"

How can I ache and thrill at the same time? "Of course. Where?"

"By the front, um…I dunno…by the willow trees, maybe? Is that okay?" He rubs the back of his neck.

My pulse races. I don't want to say goodbye! His blue eyes glisten, and my breath catches. "Yeah, that's fine. Before breakfast or after?"

He does his little sideways grin. "You know me, gotta eat. How about right after?"

"Sounds good." I'm a big fat liar. No, it doesn't sound good. *Don't ever leave. Please.* I'm afraid my heart is going to burst. This sucks so much.

He turns to leave.

"Wait!" He circles back, shoulders tense. "You can't leave without saying goodbye to Happy."

His shoulders sag, but he grins again. "Don't worry. I'll make sure it happens."

My grin answers his. "Thanks."

We part ways. My throbbing pulse refuses to calm. Why does he have to go? I can't stand it.

Melody and Harmony greet me when I walk into our cabin. At least they don't hate me. I've been so terrible to everyone. I thought no one would talk to me again.

Harmony scrutinizes me. "You smell like a horse."

I sniff the air. She's right.

Melody shoves her sister. "That was rude."

Harmony puts her hand on her hip. "Well, she does. And she hasn't exactly been nice to us lately." She arches her eyebrow.

"I'm sorry for that. I'm really trying to change." She's never going to forgive me, is she?

Skepticism splashes across Harmony's face. "I'll believe it

when I see it."

Yup. Thought so. She flips around and marches off, strawberry-blonde waves bouncing as she goes.

"Sorry. Harmony sometimes struggles with forgiving." Melody touches my shoulder.

"No, I understand. I wouldn't want to be my friend right now either, especially after the way I've treated everyone."

Melody leans closer and sniffs my clothes. "You actually do smell like a horse. Were you riding this late?"

Should I lie? A small voice inside says no. "Yeah," I admit. "Lanky let me for a few minutes."

A slight frown touches her face. "He never lets us ride this late."

I can only shrug.

"Hmm…" She walks to her cot.

I watch her go, then glance at Harmony. I hope they can both forgive me soon.

The next morning comes. Manly and I meet bright and early before chores start so it won't interrupt my day. Who are we kidding? We both know his leaving will interrupt my day and every day to come. We sit beneath the willow trees. My heart rips open, exposed, in one bloody mess. I can't do this.

"Do you really have to leave?"

"I've stayed here two and a half weeks longer than I was supposed to. I only intended to drop you off and go back home, remember?"

"I know, I know. I just..." My words fade.

"I *do* know." His voice is low and husky. "I know it's painful for you, Fear. I feel it too."

He can't even face me. He must be struggling with this separation as much as I am. I take his strong hand in my own. He entwines his fingers with mine, still unable to look at me.

"Manly, I—"

"Just don't."

It's as though our thoughts are one, and he knows I'm about to declare my love for him.

"It will just make it that much harder."

His constant avoidance of his feelings brings me to a boiling point. "Why won't you admit what we both already know and feel?" The dam has been breached. There's no going back.

"Granny says you're too young for me."

"What?" Too young? My face fills with heat. Who cares about age? That shouldn't even be an issue.

"And I agree with her." He puts his head down.

You do? But why? I take my fingers out of his grasp. "It's not true." I jump to my feet. "People much younger than me have been with others much older. They even go through the Commitment Ceremony. Even Granny became a spouse at my age."

He stands and turns toward me. Pain intensifies in his eyes. "Don't you think I know that, Fear? But just because others have done it doesn't make it right or smart."

Why is he being so stubborn? He flicks the blond locks out of his face with one sharp turn of his neck.

"Besides, you're supposed to be my sister."

What a wretched excuse! How dare he pull the sister card.

"Not by blood. Only through adoption." My voice swells.

"That's not fair. So the brother I grew up with gets to use me for years for his own pleasure. But now that I've found a real man, a man who treats me with respect and kindness, a man I love…"

He yanks his head to the side as if the word "love" burns him.

"I can't have him because his family accepted me as their own? That's not right. Not at all." I find myself crying into his shirt. Why does this hurt so badly?

He nuzzles my head with his chin and envelopes me with his muscular arms. I savor this feeling, his love, and his protection. So close, so comforting. I cling to him, willing us to meld into one, never ever to separate.

"You've lived a hard life. You've never had a chance to just be a kid."

I frown. I'm not a kid. Is that all he sees me as? I loosen my grip.

"You need a chance to experience life as a kid."

It *is* all he sees me as. I push hard against his chest. "I'm *not* a kid."

"That's the problem. You need to be. You need to have the experience of a happy childhood. Please, just try for me? Have a little fun. Be the girl Abba wants you to be. We can't be in a relationship yet. If we were both older, maybe in our twenties, this wouldn't be a problem, but we're not."

Why is this such an issue for him? I don't get it.

He slips his finger under my chin, as he's done so many times before, and lifts my face to meet his. "Trust me, Fear, I do care for you." His eyes flood with unsaid words.

"Then stay with me, Manly, please," I beg him. "I'm sure we could find a job for you around here. You're young and strong; they'd be happy to have you."

I lean closer and offer a smile.

"I…can't. You know that. Granny and Daddy need my help. Faithful isn't strong, and Daddy's not getting any younger. I'm needed there."

I cling to his arm. "But I need you, too." Can't he see this?

A scratchy grunt emanates from his throat, and he abruptly turns from me. "Don't you think you're acting a little selfish?"

How dare he! Is it selfish to love someone? He shuffles away, practically tripping over rocks.

"Manly …"

"Well, don't you?"

I guess they *do* need him at home. It's not fair because I need him even more, but…whatever. He's right. "Fine. I guess I am. But I thought you might understand." I stalk off.

Footsteps intensify, and he whirls me around. I spot Courage in the distance, watching us. What's he doing? This is supposed to be *our* private moment. Stinking eavesdropper. I turn my attention back to Manly. "I don't want to stay here, Manly. You're my home now."

He plants his hands firmly on my shoulders and gives me a little shake. "Don't you understand? We're protecting you! You can't go back. Your family will find a way to hurt you. To make you pay for some crime they've made up. I'm leaving you here because I want you to be safe. Please understand."

He brings me close, and I collapse in his arms while tears surge down my cheeks. I do understand. But I don't care. I'd rather be with him and face the risks than left here where I barely know anyone. My fingers crush his shirt as though the world will end if I let go.

He places one final, sweet kiss on my forehead right as the clouds cover the sky. My skin throbs, and a quiver of arrows slam through my chest.

"I will wait for you, Fear, and I'll come back for you when it's safe."

But when? When will he be back? What does that even mean?

He detaches from my grip and staggers away from me, tucking himself into his waiting truck. *No! You can't leave me here!*

His truck pulls out of the driveway and heads down the long dirt road. The coldness on my skin matches the coldness of his heart. How could he do this to me? Rain pelts my skin. Drenched clothes cling to me.

All I see is him.

Chapter 17

That was a long, hard day. One I never want to experience again. I enter my cabin after dinner. Who needs free time while depressed? The rain hasn't stopped, so I couldn't do much outside anyway. The words echoing through my head all day fill my brain.

Wait for me?

I ponder the meaning of Manly's words as I sit on my cot in the cabin filled with nine other girls. The noise and commotion around me fade.

Does he mean wait for me to get older? If only age were just a number.

I know it's not.

I despise his responsible side. Why can't he just live a little and quit trying to act like such an adult? Life drains from my body, and the memory of Manly chokes me until I shake. Nothing but pain. My world is completely over.

The ocean swallows me whole, and I spiral into a whirlpool.

The next day comes, and Abba speaks to me. The sorrow lessens. It's still there, but it no longer chokes me. I need to change my attitude and live how Abba intends me to—with joy. No more of this despairing stuff. Healing balm soothes my wounded heart. Life will move on. Things will get better. I feel it in my gut. I hold tight to the promise of Manly's return, but I must move forward.

At breakfast I survey the Dining Hall full of people and see them in a different light. No longer are they out to get me. They enjoy one another's company. The room sparkles. My eyes stay off myself for once, and I'm able to see it. Tittering giggles fill my ears. None of these people deserve my anger.

I cup my hands over my mouth and nose and lean on the table with my elbows propped. What can I do?

Courage stares intently at me. "You okay?"

"How am I going to apologize to everyone here?" I wave my hand at the crowd. "I've been such a jerk. How can I ever fix this mess I've made?"

Knuckles to his chin, Courage strikes a thinking pose. Seconds later, he jumps to his feet and climbs on his chair. The entire room quiets as all eyes turn toward him.

"What are you doing?" I screech, muffling my voice with my hand.

He gestures to me that everything's okay, then gives a melodramatic bow to the crowd.

"Attention everyone!" He points to a group of littles in the back who continue to whisper. "You, listen up! My friend here, whose name is Fear, has something to say to you."

My face turns volcanic as he gestures toward me. Deafening silence swallows the room. I scoot my noisy chair back and stand. My face flames hotter.

"Hi." My voice shakes.

A round of "hellos" echo throughout the room. This eases my tension…a bit.

"My name is Fear. I've only recently come to live here, and so far I've been kind of a jerk to you all. I wanted to let you know Abba changed me, and I'm planning to be different from now on."

The entire room bursts into applause and cheering. Wow. Flashing my teeth to the crowd, I continue to stand, and they quiet down.

"I'm sorry if I hurt any of you. I hope you can forgive me."

"We forgive you, Fear!" resounds from the group.

A couple of happy tears fall down my cheeks, and I refuse to stop smiling. I mouth the words "thank you" as the roaring increases. Wow. What a rush. I sit and mouth a "thank you" to Courage as well, who claps for me along with the others. He embarrassed me to the highest degree, but he's also freed me. Any icicles that still cling to my heart detach and smash to tiny pieces.

I leave the room, bouncing on airy tuffs of cotton candy. This smile ain't going nowhere.

The guys and I huddle in the library with our noses in books, enjoying our secret place. It feels like a clubhouse.

I'm so glad I listened to Manly all those weeks ago. This having fun stuff isn't so bad. My childhood was void of it. Trying to cram an entire childhood of missed fun into the last few months has been exciting. I won't lie. I've been having the time of my life.

Courage sits next to me. Thank Abba I got over myself and let him tutor me. If I'm going to have hundreds of illegal books at my disposal, I should probably know how to read properly.

Courage nudges me with his knee and shows me the page he's reading. "It used to be called 'marriage' instead of a 'Commitment Ceremony.' Way back then, it was only legal for one man and one woman to become spouses."

"That wouldn't fly with so many people in the hovels." One of my neighbors had a husband *and* two wives.

The hovels are so dark. So full of confused and lost people. The screaming, the violence, the constant nightmares. Beyond horrible is the only way to describe it. If I stayed in the hovels and never met my family, never met these new friends, where would I be? Miserable and alone, that's where. I won't ever have to feel that way again.

"You two are the best, you know that?"

I stand, pull Courage to his feet, and yank him to Trouble's side. I give them both a big hug, and they squeeze me in a tight friendship circle. We come out laughing. Tears well up in my eyes. My life has changed for the better in so many ways. They even gave me my own copy of the Word. Tears drip from the tip of my nose, and my throat constricts. A spring of life fills my chest, threatening to burst.

"I want to thank you guys for all you've done for me and for being such good friends. I wish I could show you how grateful I am." I stop and think hard. I *could* show them in the same way girls show their appreciation to boys back in the hovels. Maybe that would work. "Wait, I think I know a way."

Unbuttoning my skirt, I start tugging it off my hips. Trouble's mouth gapes, and he blinks, grabbing Courage's arm. Courage immediately steps back, turning his head to the side.

"Stop! Fear, what are you doing?" Trouble's fingers dig into Courage's arm, and Courage's eyes stay averted.

My face flushes hot. Well, that was a bad idea. I hurry and button back up, turning away. First Manly rejects me, and now them? Horribly atrocious. That must be what I am.

"That's just great. I screwed up again." I sit on a cold metal chair to avoid their stares. "I'm not very pretty, am I? No wonder you guys don't want me."

Courage crouches beside me. "That's not true at all, Fear."

"Like I believe that," I mumble.

He takes a deep breath. "You honestly don't know how irresistible you are, do you?"

I glance at him. He's trembling. "What does that mean?" Never heard that word before.

Trouble chimes in, "It means every guy who lays eyes on you...thinks you're pretty."

"Yeah, right." I roll my eyes and slouch in my chair. "Then why are you two rejecting me?"

Boys in the hovels never treated me this way. I'm glad they're different, but rejection stings.

Courage touches my arm. "Trust me." He exchanges a look with Trouble. "We're not rejecting you. It just isn't something we should do."

But why? "I know it's wrong to just...take it from someone...but I was freely offering. Why is that wrong?"

I would never force myself on someone. The thought

disgusts me.

"Haven't you listened during Study?" Courage squints at me as though I'm a puzzle to be solved.

I look around, fidgeting with my skirt. "Not always. I don't always pay attention."

Trouble snorts. "Yeah, we've noticed."

Rude! I shove him.

"Hey!" He almost falls into the shelf behind him. "*That* was ladylike of you."

I stick out my tongue at him. "Whatever, Treble-Clef."

His face reddens at the mention of his gawd-awful name. I'm so mean.

Courage stands and gets my attention. "Abba wants us to wait to be with someone until we commit to that one special person for the rest of our lives. It's a gift not to be given away to just anyone."

"But you two are special to me."

Their eyes bug out. Why are they so stubborn? I don't get it. All guys are after one thing, right? Maybe they don't like girls. Well, that's not true. *Everyone* knows Trouble likes girls. And I'm pretty sure Courage has a crush on me. He hasn't exactly been subtle about it. The way he stares at me. Yeah. Any girl would be able to figure that out real fast.

Courage scratches his head while Trouble shifts, shoving his hands in his pockets. I must not be grasping the immensity of this conversation.

Trouble breaks the silence. "Yeah, we're all best friends. But does that mean you want to spend the rest of your life as a *spouse* to either of us?"

I glance down as Manly's face rushes into view. My stomach clenches. I miss him so much. There's barely been a night I haven't dreamed about his soft forehead kisses. I stay quiet. I don't want to hurt either of their feelings. But I don't get it. Why would having sex mean I'm bonded to someone for life? If that was the case…Hate's face drifts through my mind. I shudder.

Courage touches my arm again. "We know your heart belongs to someone else, and that person doesn't live here, does he?"

I *wish* Manly lived here. Gazing at Courage out of the corner of my eye, I shake my head.

"I didn't think so."

Silence fills the room as Courage turns his back on me. Did I hurt him? I loathe the awkwardness. He turns back around, composed, but his stoic face is pale. I did hurt him. My eyes veer to the bookshelves.

"And that's why we can never be with you, Fear. It's not what we want that matters. It's what's right in the eyes of Abba that matters most."

Wow. That's deep. Do they really feel that way? I mean, I guess they must, or the whole sex thing wouldn't bother them so much.

"I do want to please Abba. He's done so much for me. I guess I understand." The books on the shelves blend into fuzzy slashes of color as I focus on the meaning of his words. Stupid guys have to get all high and mighty on me. Enough of this seriousness. "I also understand you two are liars." Maybe I can lighten the mood. "I'm not even close to being irre…ireesi… whatever that word was you said." I sock them both in the arm for good measure.

They grab their sore arms but keep their serious looks. It seems my joking isn't getting me out of this discussion.

Trouble looks at Courage. "She doesn't get it, does she?"

"Get what?" I huff. Now they're just frustrating me.

Trouble walks away, toward the other side of the bookshelves. "What you do to guys."

I roll my eyes. Oh, brother. I haven't done anything.

Courage takes a hard look at me. "What we're trying to say is…sometimes it's almost painful to stay pure-minded around you. Abba expects this from us, and sometimes it's almost impossible when we're with you. Am I right, Trouble?"

Trouble points at me. "Completely irresistible."

They can't be serious. "I'm not trying to be."

"Yeah, we get that. It's almost like you can't help it. There's something about you."

Courage peers longingly into my eyes, the way Manly used to. It stirs up old aches. I force myself to snap out of it.

"How can I make it stop?"

Courage rearranges the books on the shelves and turns toward the little table mere feet away. They take such good care of this place.

"I'm not sure you can." Courage shoves a pile of books under his arm from the table and walks back to the shelves. "I know you're not trying to be tempting."

"Tempting?" What in the Gliding Lands? I'm like the least tempting person on planet Earth. "You've got to be kidding me." Well, I'm not horrendous. But still.

Trouble comes over and closes a hardcover book with a *bang*. "She's gotta stop being so dang cute, is all." He winks.

I'll show him cute. "Maybe I should never wash my hair again?"

"Now you got it!" Trouble tugs on a strand of my mousey browns.

"Or wear ugly, baggy clothing that doesn't match?" The pretty tan skirt Harmony lent me swishes beneath my fingers.

Courage joins in on the fun. "That might work."

"Should I disfigure my face? Wear an ugly scowl?"

Trouble leans closer. "I hate to tell you this, but you're still cute when you scowl."

A real scowl twists my face, which sends the guys howling. Now they're just making fun of me...again.

"Ugh. You two are terrible." I march up the ladder. "I guess it's hopeless." I'm done with this conversation, and if they ever want to speak to me again, they'd better be too. I whirl around at the top of the ladder. "Let's all forget any of this ever happened, okay?"

"Okay," they agree.

Yeah, right. I'm pretty sure they'll never forget.

Chapter 18

I enjoy visiting my new buddy in the Special Cabin. Tenacious is like an older version of Justice. I like to imagine that's the way he would've turned out—minus the walker, of course.

Something's been bugging me for a while now. The kids in the Special Cabin lack stimulation and entertainment. They need someone to organize a play for them. Someone like me. We saw a play when I was younger at the Teachings. All kids were encouraged to attend, though most of us farming kids only went to the mandatory first year. I enjoyed the play so much. Putting one together shouldn't be too hard.

The play needs to be written, parts assigned, lines memorized—everything must be perfect. The weeks pass without warning, and soon our play stares us in the face.

Trouble approaches before rehearsal starts. "Why are you trying so hard when a lot of the Specials won't even be able to understand the play?"

"Just because they may not understand doesn't mean we

should treat them like they're different." I rifle through our little box of props.

"But they *are* different."

"I know that, but it doesn't mean they can't enjoy a good play." They will, I know it. We'll make it so great, they'll have no choice but to enjoy it.

Trouble picks up a prop and throws it back and forth between his hands. "You've changed, you know that?"

I scrunch my face. Buttercups and biscuits. What's he getting at?

"For the better," he assures me.

Oh, thank Abba. He had me worried there for a second.

"I mean, look at what you're doing. Putting others before yourself. It's commendable."

I raise my eyebrows. I'm not used to this from him. It's weird. "You done with the compliments yet?"

Tenacious shuffles his walker our way. "You guys ready to practice?"

Trouble shouts, "Yes!" while pumping his fist. I nod and giggle as I grab my script and trail after Tenacious.

I watch the group with pride as we go over our lines.

We've worked tirelessly every spare moment. I'm so glad Tenacious is a part of our play. Who knew he had skills? He's one of the best actors we have. If Aunt Joy hadn't caved and let us take him outside to practice, we would've never found out he had talent.

I know she's worried about the Wildies, but we're with him. The guys could carry him to safety if necessary.

Aunt Joy has entrusted his life into our hands, and we won't fail him.

Tomorrow is our play. It's finally here. Hopefully it won't be a massive disaster.

All those months ago, I fell into the role of director. But I really wanted to act too, so I conveniently put myself in one of the lead roles as well. No one seems to mind. We practice under the shade of the large willow that stands near the Main Cabin. Every willow on this property reminds me of Manly. I can't help it. I smother the thought of him before I let it swallow me. Must stay focused. This is the last practice before the big day.

I glance across the way. Courage mouths something and bangs his palm on his forehead. What's he doing? Doesn't that hurt?

I walk up to him. "What's the matter?"

"What if I can't remember my lines?"

"Is that what you're worried about?" I grin at him. "It's a forgiving audience. You'll be okay." His face is still pinched. I place my hand on his arm, my pale fingertips contrasting with the darker tones of his skin. "Seriously, it's just a play."

He stares me straight in the eye. "Just a play? You've worked so hard on this for the last couple of months. I know it means a lot to you." He shakes his head and turns his back. "I don't want to let you down."

I grab his arm and turn him to face me. "Really, Courage? Out of all the people here, I'm shocked you're the one who's worried. You usually have so much confidence."

Happy rushes in with the self-made hat on her head she insisted on wearing during the performance. "We're going to start the final rehearsal."

I thought I was the director, not her. She grabs our hands and lugs us toward the rest of the group. Demanding little oaf. Good thing I like her so much.

I whisper to Courage, "You'll do fine."

We rehearse with only a few minor hiccups. The play isn't a long one by any means, but I'm still proud of all we've accomplished together. We gather in a group hug. Nervous excitement courses through me and whizzes in the air like an electric current.

I go to bed with jitters twisting my stomach every which way. Am I the only one having trouble falling asleep?

The next morning comes too soon. I don't feel prepared enough. One last costume check, one last prop count. Breathe. I can do this.

Thank Abba Aunt Joy let us skip morning chores. Sometimes she's pretty cool. When our crew gets to the Special Cabin, we're met by a gigantic group. I approach Aunt Joy. "What's going on?"

"We're here to watch your play."

My mouth hangs open. Seriously? I bounce from foot to foot. Buttercups and biscuits. My face falls. One big problem. "But how will everyone squeeze into that little cabin?"

Courage steps up beside me. "She's right. There won't be

enough room for us to perform."

Aunt Joy sweeps her hand to the crowd. It splits in half to reveal the kids from the Special Cabin sitting on benches or lying on cots outside. I clasp my hands against my mouth.

"How did you manage?" My jaw trembles. This is amazing.

Aunt Joy shakes her head. "I didn't think it would work, but all the kids kept telling me it would. They all helped." She waves her hand to the crowd, and they cheer.

I can't believe they were able to get them all out with their walkers and wheelchairs. Even the bedridden kids are outside. Apparently everyone, even a couple of the Ranch Hands, decided to help and stick around to watch the play. Trouble eggs on the crowd to cheer louder.

Everyone goes to work setting up the first scene. Color has fled Courage's face. "You're going to do great," I assure him. He doesn't answer. Oh boy.

When everything's set, the crowd settles, ready to watch. Melody has the first line, and she and Trouble start with gusto. Courage's scene is next, but he's disappeared. I search the area and spot him retching behind a tree. *Poor Courage.* I rush in his direction, then stop myself, almost tripping over my own feet. My first line is coming up. He'll be all right.

There's my cue. I step out on stage and give my first line, bustling across the stage. My voice booms. Who knew I could be so convincing and loud? That wasn't so hard. I jump off, and Tenacious enters the stage using a cane instead of a walker. His legs seem stronger. He delivers his lines without an issue. This kid is a pro. The crowd loves him within seconds. It's almost the next scene.

Come on, Courage, you can do this! Where are you?

I spot him onstage. Not as the confident and sometimes

cocky Courage I know, but as a timid shell of a guy who can't seem to get out a sentence louder than a whisper. At least he's not barfing. I totally should've prayed with the troupe before starting. Not too late to pray now. *Abba, help him!* I stare at Courage, then the crowd, then back to Courage. His voice gets stronger with each passing minute. Oh, good. Maybe I can relax?

Trouble can't help but be a goofball. The dude is a natural comedian. He and Tenacious have the crowd clutching their bellies in fits of giggles. Yes! That means they're enjoying it. Thank Abba. I'm surprised at how good Melody is. She sweeps her arm into the air and bellows her lines. At least everyone can hear her. She must be rubbing off on Courage. He's beginning to take his cues from her. With each passing minute, his shoulders relax.

The end is in sight. We're almost done. I can't believe how well this has gone! I wipe my hand against my brow.

The crowd jumps to their feet, clapping and cheering. Except for the ones who can't stand, of course. Trouble high fives everyone as I gather the crew in a huddle before we take our bows.

"You did fantastic. That was great!"

The color returns to Courage's face. I'm glad he's not actually sick. We take our bows. Now's my chance. I may not get another.

"Thank you all for sharing in this excitement with us. We really appreciate you being here and supporting us. We couldn't have done it without you guys or Abba's protection. Now we know it can be done. We can work together to move these kids to a bigger cabin."

"But all the other cabins are being used!" Someone from the back yells.

"Being used," I agree. "But not full. There's room for at least two, if not more, in each cabin. If every cabin takes in two or three others from one of the larger cabins, then it would be empty and ready to house the Specials. Any extras could go to the Special's old cabin." Groans sneak through the crowd. Buttercups and biscuits. "There's nothing wrong with the smaller cabin," I assure them. "But it's way too small to fit so many Specials, especially with all their extra equipment." Butterflies swoop through my gut, but I square my shoulders and scan the crowd. "Who's with me?"

Two-thirds raise their hands. I need to convince them further. Everyone needs to be on board.

"I'll transfer to the small cabin to show there's nothing to worry about."

"Yeah!" I glance at Trouble out of the corner of my eye. He's thrown his fist in the air. The support bolsters me.

I hop off the stage, beeline for the disabled kids, and wrap my arm around Chilly, a girl in a wheelchair. "These kids deserve more than being squashed in a stuffy room with too many bodies to breathe. It's not right. It's not healthy. Please, let's help them. It's what Abba would want us to do. Now, who's with me?"

This time almost everyone raises their hands. I smile. Good. We're making headway. This project might take place after all.

That evening, Aunt Joy holds a meeting with me. She also wants to meet next week to come up with a plan.

I square my shoulders. A lightness clears away any doubt. "I know we can do it."

Her sweet, gray eyes sparkle. "Now I believe we can. Thank you, Fear."

It's been a whole week, and it's finally moving day. The entire Ranch comes out to help. I can't believe it! This is so awesome. Even some Ranch Hands volunteer. This will take hours, but with all the help, the move should go well. I hope. There's always the threat of Wildies, but with as much prayer as we've covered this operation in, I think we'll be safe.

Aunt Joy and I spring our plan into action. We surround the Specials by a group of twenty armed with slingshots. A different group moves the Specials outside. The protective group stands firm. The rest of us transfer medical equipment, beds, and everything else. I'm so worn out from yesterday's packing, I'm glad when Melody steps up and takes charge of transferring the clothing and toiletries. My feet ache, and I'm tired of trudging back and forth between cabins. But I can do this.

I won't let these people down.

Months go by, and with Courage's faithful tutoring, I'm now a proficient reader. We sit in the artificial light of the underground library, side by side, devouring history books.

"Look here." I point to a picture of animals contained

behind glass walls. Fake plants surround the enclosure. People stand behind the walls and watch. "It says here Wildies were kept in something called a 'zoo.'"

Courage leans over to catch a better glimpse of the picture. "Yeah, I've heard of those. Why anyone would want to purposely visit deadly animals that can rip you apart is beyond me."

I recall the little girl who, just last week, was bitten by a Wildie at the edge of the forest. Poor thing's been stuck in the medical room ever since. Aunt Joy always warns us to be vigilant and stay in groups—to always be on the lookout for possible attack. The boxes full of high-powered slingshots in the office cabin aren't quite as good protection as the guns back home, but it's sure better than nothing.

I hold the book closer to the light and scan the page. "It seems years ago, several wildlife groups devoted to treating animals humanely, set laws into motion sanctioning zoos as illegal. They were all closed, and the animals were set free to roam the streets. This backfired when half died immediately following their release. People protecting themselves or their livestock shot many more. That's when the government made it illegal to kill Wildies. Although, they weren't called Wildies back then. Just wild animals."

Trouble bolts upright and turns to us. "Now thousands of them have spread out everywhere to get us! If you get caught in the wrong place at the wrong time…" He grabs a magazine off the floor and throws it at us.

I lunge to catch it and collide with Courage. Ouch! I rip the magazine from Courage's fingers as he pokes me in the side.

"Hey, don't wreck that. It's full of cool info." Trouble pouts.

We quit our pretend fighting over the now-crumpled magazine. "Shouldn't be throwing stuff at us then." I toss the magazine in Courage's lap.

He flips open the crinkled pages. Pictures and info about ancient cars suffuse the page. "Whoa, cars have changed a lot."

Trouble stands and retrieves the magazine, smoothing the pages. "According to this article, cars used to run on something called gasoline. Never heard of it."

Courage and I shake our heads.

Trouble shrugs. "It also says Hoverpods didn't use to exist, just cars on the ground, like we Downers use."

"That makes sense, doesn't it? Everything's invented at some point. You don't think Electro-Screens always existed, do you?" Courage points out.

I chime in, "The part that blows my mind about the past the most is how long people used to live. Can you imagine living to be eighty years old?" Images of the guys wrinkly and bald sweep through my brain. I stifle a giggle.

"Eighty? In one textbook it even talks about people living into their nineties. Some even into their hundreds!"

Courage and his superior knowledge. Always trying to one up me.

"That's insane," Trouble continues. "Now we're blessed if we make it to sixty."

Something I read in a textbook pops into my head. "At least that's better than the Uppers. From what I've read, their average lifespan is only about forty-five years." A shiver runs through me. Does that mean I'll only live to forty-five years? I have Upper blood, after all.

"That's true. Didn't you know that before? Everyone knows that."

He drives me up the wall. *Shut up, Courage.*

"In their attempts to stay young forever, they actually shortened their lifespans. They wanted to live forever, and now they can't even make it as long as we can."

Courage really should be an instructor at the Teachings. He thinks he knows everything.

"That's because they refuse to work." Trouble throws the crumpled magazine on the table and plunks in his chair. "Lazy bums make us do everything for them."

"Not to mention how much they abuse their own bodies," adds Courage.

Wait, what did he say? Refuse to work? "You mean they don't work? At all?"

"Are you kidding?" Courage laughs. "That's what they have us for. The Uppers don't work, so they make us do it all for them. Don't you see, Fear? The Downers are their slaves."

I frown. Maybe he's right. The Teachings always told us we have to do what the Uppers say. "But I thought all the higher-quality food gets sent up there?" My stomach grumbles. What does it taste like? Maybe someday I'll get the chance to find out. Probably not.

"Yeah, they get the best food." Courage slams a large book. "But all of the surgeries and chemical abuse shortens their lifespans. From what I hear, they're almost always chemically altered. We're lucky to get darn acetaminophen down here when we need it."

Well that's good to hear. Shortened life spans aren't genetic. I guess I'm safe then. "It's all so fascinating." I sit up and trace my name in the dust on the table. "Sometimes I wonder who my parents are and if they're still alive."

I've wondered about them so much lately. Were they short like me? Did my mother have my mousey brown hair? Was my dad enormous like Count Cerberus? Why did they hate me so much to throw me over? Did they ever love me?

"It's possible. They could definitely still be alive." Trouble draws a heart around my name in the dust and puts his name in it too. I shove him and whip my hand across the table, smudging the names into oblivion.

"You're annoying."

"That's what makes me, me." He wrinkles his freckled nose.

I can't help but love the guy. Well, love him in a non-romantic, platonic kind of way, of course.

Trouble stares at his watch, nods at us, then the ladder. Time to go. We shove books back on shelves and slip on jackets before we climb the ladder. It's downright cold out there.

When we arrive at camp, Happy frantically runs our direction. She stops short of colliding with us. Her tight spiral curls sway and bounce as she leans over and pants puffs of steam. Her scarf unravels and falls down her neck.

"What's wrong, Happy?"

She recovers, straightens, and tilts her head to the cloudy sky. "I have news for you. But first tell me, where do you three go when you disappear into the woods?" She surveys us with a squinty eye.

Courage throws Happy's scarf back around her neck. "That's none of your business."

Happy sticks her nose in the air. "Then I'm not going to tell you the news." She crosses her arms.

"Happy." I bend to her level. "Do you think it pleases Abba when you act like a stinker?"

She falters, but only for a moment. "Do you think it pleases Abba when you lie to little girls?"

Good comeback. That kid is never short of spunk. Her

scarf falls again.

"That's not fair, Happy," Courage says. "We've never lied to you."

Trouble pats my back. I ignore him.

"We may not tell you where we're going in the woods, but that's not lying." My hand finds her draped scarf. I secure it around her neck.

"Lying by omission of facts," she states.

Courage ruffles her hair. "You're using that all wrong in this instance."

I'm going to knock some sense into her if she doesn't quit playing around. "Happy, can you hurry up and just tell us what's going on? I'm meeting Melody and Harmony before dinner."

Thank Abba they forgave me. Melody's such a sweet girl. Harmony's okay, I guess. I don't think we'd be good friends if Melody weren't her triplet.

Trouble pats my back again. I whirl around.

"What?" I yell straight in his face. Oops. Didn't realize he was standing so close.

Trouble points a finger. I peer across the distance. Nothing.

"What are we looking for?" Fields, trees, cabins, boring, boring, nothing, what in the…? Then I spot it.

A truck.

Chapter 19

A familiar truck. One that causes my pulse to quicken. My body freezes.

"Manly..." I blink several times and turn to Courage. His face drops. No time to worry about him now.

I run.

Nothing matters except reaching that truck. My slingshot falls out of my pocket. I don't bother to retrieve it from the frost-covered ground. I keep going. It *is* Manly's truck, but he's not in it. My heart sinks. If this is some kind of cruel joke—

I whirl around, and Happy's close on my heels, followed by my two wheezing friends.

"Where is he?" I demand.

"I was going to tell you, but you rushed off." Happy's scarf loosens again. It will never stay put the way she runs around.

A shadow darkens my view, and a hand I know all too well finds my shoulder, sending bolts of electricity through me. I turn, and there he is. My heart rushes to my throat. I can't speak.

"Fear." Manly smiles down at me and opens his arms.

Heavenly clouds fill every last one of my brain cells as I rush forward and press my cheek against his scratchy, coat-covered chest. His arms surround me, tightening until my breath catches.

Is this real? Is he really here? I breathe in his scent to make sure I'm not dreaming.

He pulls back, searching my eyes.

"You're here." My words are breathy.

"I am. Wow. You've grown, Fear. I mean, look at you." His look isn't greedy or perverted but full of admiration and love. He can't seem to wipe the smile from his face.

My legs wobble. Trembling, I can't halt the weakness flowing through me.

"It's been too long." He brushes a stray hair from my face.

His touch. My skin burns. Oh, he's real all right.

I know how long it's been since we've last seen each other. To the day. "Six months..."

He opens his mouth. "And twenty-two days." He completes the sentence with me.

My face smiles so wide it hurts. "You were counting too?"

He looks away. "Just a wild guess."

"Sure." Yeah right. He missed me too! Those butterflies are back. Oops, we're not alone! I wrench around to see my friends looking at everything but us. "You guys remember my family...er...friend." I'm still unsure what to call him.

Trouble speaks up, "How could we forget?" He nods at Manly, who returns the nod.

Courage remains silent. His face blanches, and he won't meet my eyes. *Jealous much?*

An electronic bell rings. Dinner starts soon. We better head to the Dining Hall. Happy grabs Manly's hand and jabbers on about flowers and horses.

I can't believe he's actually here. He came for me as promised. My feet don't touch the ground. Is this what it feels like to walk on air? He said he'd return when everything was safe. Is it safe now? What happened? Guess I'll have to wait to ask questions until Happy's done ranting. She adores Manly almost as much as I do, if that's even possible. We walk toward the cabins. Manly keeps glancing back at me while Happy drags him along. My insides vibrate, and I bite down my smile. The bell rings again, sweeping me from my dream world. Time to wash for dinner.

I don't even remember the meal. All I remember is staring into the most handsome face I've ever seen. Everyone around him jabbers on, asking all sorts of questions. Everyone but Courage, that is. He sits away from us, still a part of our group, but obviously perturbed. I turn my attention back to the guy who holds my heart. I can't even hear what the others babble on about.

As soon as dinner is over, I grab Manly's hand before Happy or anyone else can monopolize his time. She approaches, and I steer him away from her. Okay, so I'm a meanie. I don't even care right now.

We walk to our spot by the lake. Ice chunks float about, bumping geese as they're tossed by the lapping waves. A frigid breeze picks up.

I shiver. Everything is wonderful yet awkward at the same

time. I still hope I'm not dreaming the whole thing up.

I clear my throat. "How's everyone back home?"

"They're good." He plunks himself on a large rock. "We had a great harvest this year. Abba really blessed us. It was hard on Granny, though. She works so hard, but she's not young anymore. Faithful attends the Teachings when she can."

I frown. "Hasn't she already completed her year?"

"Yeah. She just wants to go. I don't understand why when she knows it's all a bunch of propaganda and nonsense anyway. But whatever, she's her own person. On a happier note, Daddy got those pigs to have a litter." He smiles, probably remembering our inside joke about pigs.

"So now you can barter for food!" I chime in. We both laugh.

It feels so good to have him here with me. I'm not sure I can handle it if he tells me he's leaving without me. This is going to hurt. But I have to know.

"Do I get to come home?" I squint, anticipating the worst. Icy air pummels me in the face. I hope it's not an omen.

"That's why I'm here, to bring you home. That is, if you want to come back with me. You can stay if you want. It's up to you."

My heart tugs in all directions. "I love this place. I have good friends, I love the singing and the horseback riding, and I'm learning so much about Abba. It's been amazing."

"That's so great, Fear." His flat voice says otherwise. "If this is your home now, I understand. I was the one who told you to try to enjoy it here."

I take his hands in mine and look into his gorgeous eyes. "You will always be my home, Manly." His eyes sparkle the way I've only seen in my dreams for months. "I admit, it'll be hard leaving, but I want to go home." He clutches my hands tighter. "Ouch!"

"Sorry. Sometimes I forget how delicate you are. You always seem so strong." He winks.

He's so adorable.

"Oh, I've gotten stronger. You should watch how fast I can muck out those stalls." Laughing with him again is so awesome. His laughter ceases without warning.

"What were you doing in the woods with those guys?"

I freeze. Whoa, where did that come from? My jaw drops. How do I explain this to him? The conversation I had early in the year with the guys plays in my head. Warmth spreads across my face. I was so ignorant regarding intimacy. Thank Abba they set me straight. They were right. Abba intends me for one person, and I hope it's the man standing before me. Can't believe I almost made that huge mistake.

Manly must notice my burning face. His eyebrows knit together. "I hope you haven't done things you weren't supposed to."

The library springs to mind. Goobers and gambits. I better say something. I'm incriminating myself with silence.

"Oh no, Manly." I'm such a liar. A pang courses through me. "Nothing like that." How can Courage and Trouble justify lying about the library anyway? They've forced me to lie to my favorite person in the whole world. He doesn't believe me, I know it.

He nods anyway. "I have news." His voice deepens. "It might startle you."

Glad he's changing the subject, I sit on the large rock, ready to take it in.

He pauses to think. "Your papa."

I frown. What's he done now? Hope he hasn't made more trouble for my family.

Manly pauses again. "He's dead, Fear."

A tiny, itty-bitty twinge of remorse pitter patters through me. It doesn't last long. "How?"

"They assume it was a heart attack. He was working outside one day, chopping wood, and keeled over. No warning."

So the old man's dead. I absorb this information. Papa was never a father to me. Only Daddy holds that title in my life.

"It's okay. I'm okay."

Manly raises his eyebrows.

I snatch a pebble off the ground and toss it into the icy waters. "He was a terrible man." It's wrong to speak ill of the dead; however, I speak truth. Manly already knows all about my papa.

"You sure you're okay?"

I nod. My heart can't break for a man who didn't have one. "How is it safe for me to come home? They didn't *all* die, did they?" His eyes shoot wide. Okay, so that must've sounded pretty callous. "Just tell me."

Manly wipes his hand down his face. "I've heard from the town gossip your mother couldn't afford to keep the farm, so she sold Hate to an Upper."

"Sold him?" I repeat. Shouldn't surprise me, but it does. Hate means everything to her.

"Uh-huh. She drank so much she ended up losing the farm anyway. Now she's…" he stops. "You don't want to know."

"Yes, I do." *Just tell me!* Why does he still treat me like a child who can't handle anything?

He peers deep into my eyes. "She's the town prostitute now."

The rock's coldness beneath me numbs my entire lower half. How could she lower herself to that? But with her lack of

character or knowledge of Abba, why wouldn't she? But—
she's my mother. I sigh.

"Wow. Lots to digest."

"I know."

Manly lays a hand on my shoulder. I reach up and stroke
his fingers, and we sit in silence for a while. I mull over my
former family's misfortune. I'm truly on another path in life,
and it feels wonderful. I stand with renewed vision.

"So, when do we head home?"

The next day, Manly and I go riding with Melody,
Harmony, and Happy. Aunt Joy excused us from our chores
so we can enjoy my last day. She's such a cool lady. I'm going
to miss her.

Manly helps Happy—who's scared of horses—get used to
being astride the "terrifying beast." She faces her fears with
him around, and he leads her around the arena. She rides the
smallest, oldest horse and clasps the saddle with an iron grip.
That girl is sure something else.

Lanky finally allows me to ride Pumpkin. Wish he let me
do it sooner. He must've noticed how good of a rider I've
become over the last few months. This is my last day, and I
think he wants to make it special.

I ride Pumpkin across the frozen ground, and the wind
whips my cheeks until they sting. But I don't care. Riding
Pumpkin is *so* worth it. A few more laps, and someone runs up
and flings himself behind me. What the fritz? Who's got the

audacity to risk their life by jumping on a moving horse? I turn. Of course it'd be him. I lean my head on Manly's shoulder. His jaw tightens as he wraps his arms around my waist. He tries to grab the reins from me, but I whip them away and cause Pumpkin to move in a direction entirely unplanned.

"Hey!" I correct the horse with the reins.

He leans closer and speaks in my ear. "You've gotten really good at this. I'm super impressed."

"Thanks." I give the horse a swift kick, pushing Manly back in the saddle. He grips my waist hard as Pumpkin dashes through the gate and toward the fields.

Everything seems right when I'm around him. It's as though the sky parts and sunlight beams down in celebration of our reunion. Sparks of electricity blast millions of little currents to the top of my head, then send them scampering to my toes. I'm so weak, I almost drop the reins. How can a man make me feel so totally...amazingly...insane? I cherish having him near.

Our ride lasts just shy of an hour. We're both laughing and breathless as we head back to the stables. The cold doesn't even bother me. Reality hits, and I glance at the holographic timing device on the barn door. I'm running out of time to say goodbye. We dismount, and Manly leads Pumpkin to his stall.

I rush up and touch his arm. "I need to say my goodbyes."

His eyes lose their glimmer. "Of course. Go ahead. I'll meet you later."

I head straight to the larger cabin that now holds the older Specials. I tiptoe in, and everyone cheers. I beam. I'm going to miss all these happy faces. I squeeze every hand I pass. I catch sight of Tenacious and pause. We have such a strong bond. This is going to hurt a lot. I approach and sit on the edge of his bed. Silence pervades the room. The momentary cheering, still fresh, reverberates through my mind.

"What's wrong?" he scoots closer to me.

I shake my head. I'm not sure I can get the words out. I meet his eyes, which shine like a faerie sprinkled her magic dust into them.

"It's time, isn't it? For you to leave."

My head slumps to my chest as tears spring up in my eyes.

He pats my back. "It's all right, Fear. We knew this day was coming. I knew you wouldn't stay here forever."

I side-hug him and breathe in his boyish ruddiness. He understands, and he's not going to hold it against me.

"Someday when I get my bionic legs, I'm going to come visit you."

Him and his bionic-leg dreams. I really hope it happens for him someday.

"I know you will." I point at his legs. "Look at how strong you've gotten in such a short time."

He stands without his walker or cane. "I'm telling you, if you hadn't come here and changed things up, I don't think I would've cared enough to try. Thank you, Fear. You've changed my life and all these kids' lives, too. For the better." He hugs me again and sniffles. "I'm not sure what we would've done without you."

Shaking my head, a tear trails down my cheek. "Remember, it wasn't me, it was Abba. He used me to bless you. That's all." We smile at each other.

I wave at, hug, or shake everyone's hands as I traipse to the door. "Goodbye!"

Everyone who is capable echoes my farewell. The drooling boy with the misshapen head hands me his beloved stuffed animal as a parting gift. It's so precious to him, no way am I gonna keep it. Instead, I press my lips to the fuzzy softness and hand it back.

"That way, you will always have my kiss if you need it."

He hugs it to his cheek. Tears brimming in the corners of my eyes, I walk out of the cabin. I can impact others' lives for the better, even if it's hard. Every life is worth the struggle. I hope this won't be the last I see of them.

Chapter 20

Saying goodbye to Happy brings a fresh wave of tears. She might drive me up the wall most of the time, but she's like my little sister. I brush her hair. "I need to go back to my family now."

"But I don't want you to go, Fear," she interrupts and faces me. A couple of tears roll down Happy's cappuccino-colored cheeks.

Just stab me in the chest with a pitchfork, will ya?

I hug her close. "Kid, you're breaking my heart." I crouch down to her level. "You know you're always my little sister, right?" She nods and smiles through her tears. "I've asked Aunt Joy if you can use the Communicator." Happy's eyes brighten. "It's fine if we use it once or twice a month. If we use it any more than that, the Uppers might notice and track the signal." They'd punish everyone if they found out. But Happy doesn't need to know that. I pinch her cheek. "That means I can still talk to you!"

She attempts a smile. "Don't forget to call me."

"I won't."

The roar of a Hoverpod draws near. What in the Gliding Lands? Everyone in the room scatters to hide. Kids pile into the cabin from outside. It sounds close.

I don't understand. The Uppers usually stay by the main cabin. Why would a Hoverpod park so close to the residential cabins?

A shudder runs through me as I hide Happy in the bathroom, locking her in a stall. I crawl out under the stall door. Everyone stills. My heart pounds. I peek out from behind the doorframe separating the bathroom hall from the cabin area.

Someone bangs on our locked cabin door and silences the girls like death silences a corpse. They're trying to get in! A few shrieks from one girl, and the banging grows louder until the doorknob breaks off. Kids cower as a helper robot bursts through the door, followed by the same gigantic man I'd seen months ago when I got in so much trouble with Aunt Joy.

"Where is she?" Count Cerberus announces to the room. "Where is she?" he repeats, louder. Riding a Hoverscooter, Count Cerberus examines the aisles between cots.

Who's he looking for anyway? Blippets and bagpipes! He's searching for Happy.

My pulse thumps, and a cold sweat breaks out under my arms. I duck into the bathroom. Three others huddle in the stall next to Happy's.

The little motor whirrs, and I try to keep the others from panicking and giving away our location. Maybe, just maybe, he won't check the bathrooms. I plead with Abba for protection for everyone, but especially for Happy. Seconds later, the bathroom door slams open. The gargantuan man can't get through.

"Stupid narrow doorways. What's wrong with these Downers?"

The robot enters with ease. It comes over and tries the first stall. It bangs on the door, and it swings open. Then it goes to the next one, then Happy's. *Don't open Happy's stall!* My heart ceases as the clang of metal hits the wall. But...it was locked!

A hum starts to build from within the stall, and the robot tilts its head.

Shivers of static slice through the room. Sparkling orbs encompass the stall and burst forth like a flash of lightning, ricocheting off the bathroom walls. The robot doesn't seem to notice the shock of electricity that just hit it. It leaves, oblivious to Happy and the three others in the next stall. I exhale the breath I'm holding.

What in the Gliding Lands was that?

The fat man spews curses as the whirr of the Hoverscooter leaves the cabin. He's gone. We wait a few more minutes before I lead the kids out of the bathroom and check on the rest of the cabin.

Happy trembles. I wrap my arms around her and squeeze tight. We all stay quiet until the motor outside roars off into the sky. Not a minute later, Manly bursts through the door.

"You okay in here?" His voice quakes like a child's in a thunderstorm. He rushes over to Happy and me. "I'm so glad to see you both." He clutches my shoulder and shifts me to face him. "He was after you, wasn't he?"

I shake my head. "No. Happy. He asked for her before. Aunt Joy told him off, and he decided he didn't want her. I guess he changed his mind."

Happy stands there, still shaking. Beads of sweat cling to her forehead, and I wipe them away with my thumb. Her pupils are dilated. I've never seen her so petrified.

We help her sit.

Manly wraps a blanket around her. "I've heard about him. Must've found a client who wanted a girl with her specifications. Sickening jack—"

"Ah!" I hold up a finger to silence his rant. "You're going to be all right, Happy. He's gone," I assure her.

Manly takes a deep breath and refocuses. "Abba, sorry for my anger. Please calm Happy and take away her anxiety. We ask you to give her courage and strength. Help her know you're here, watching over her. Give her peace."

Her shaking subsides, and one of her friends sits with her.

Manly and I go outside, though we don't stray far from the cabin. Chills slither across my skin. I clutch my arms and think of what could've happened. Sparkling orbs? Flashes of lightning? What in the Gliding Lands was that all about? "I can't explain what went on in there. It's like the robot didn't even see her."

Manly rubs his temple. "A miracle?"

"The room sparkled." I can't comprehend it.

Manly shrugs. "We serve a mighty God. Anything's possible."

My breathing slows. "True." I take a hard look at him. I can think of only one way to guarantee Happy's safety. "Can we take her home with us?"

"Who? Happy?" He shakes his head. "Not without asking Granny and Daddy. And that's not a question you can just ask over the Communicator."

I want to pout but think better of it. "No, I understand. You guys are already taking me in. I guess it's not fair to ask you to take in someone else."

Manly shifts and stares at the clouds. He tilts his head back down and scrunches his nose. "You know I love Happy, but I can't just spring something like that on them. I'd need to ask, and I'm guessing they'd need to think about it."

"Is it safe for her to stay here?" I shuffle my feet on the rust-colored ground. "What if that Upper comes back?"

Manly leans against a peeling birch and rubs his hand over the bark. "I doubt that'll happen. Aunt Joy does her best to keep everyone safe."

I beg to differ. "There's only so much she can do. You saw what just happened. She can't protect everyone from everything, no matter how hard she tries." I dig my toe into the dirt. "I wish we could bring her with us." *Please say yes.*

Manly stalks away from me. "This was her home since birth. Do you think she wants to be ripped away from it, just like that?"

"You mean like what happened to me?"

He shoots me a look. "Not the same thing."

I raise my hands to stop any further argument. "You're right. That wouldn't be fair to her." The Upper who wanted to steal Happy bounces into my thoughts. "You don't think anything will happen to her, right?"

He picks up a stone and tosses it. "She'll be fine. We'll ask Aunt Joy if we can check in on her with the Communicator."

"Already done."

"Good."

I want to argue more, but I don't. I sure hope he's right.

On the first day of our drive home, Manly and I barely talk

to one another. Neither of us discusses leaving Happy behind, but I can't stop thinking about it. I wish Manly hadn't assumed Granny and Daddy would need to consider taking Happy in. I'm almost positive they'd do it without a second thought. I pick at a loose piece of vinyl on the passenger side of the truck. Why's he being so selfish? Well…I guess *selfish* is a bit unfair. But he's wrong to leave her. He must feel it too. His sullen mood shows more's on his mind than he wants to admit.

We both should be celebrating the fact we're reunited and I'm coming home. Instead, a cloud of gloom looms over me. I left my little sister behind, uncertain she's going to remain safe. What about the others? I'm losing all of them. Why is this so hard?

A fly buzzes past my head, and I swat at it. If Manly won't chat with me, I might as well nap. As I start to fall asleep, the memory of Courage's eyes welling with tears floats before me. He really didn't want me to leave. I hate hurting him.

Nightmares grasp me, pulling me into their clutches.

Manly shakes me. "What's going on?"

My groggy eyes search to make sense of the situation. "Huh? What?"

"You were thrashing in your sleep. What's the matter?" His high-strung voice clears my mind.

"Nightmare." I rub my face and search for my water bottle on the floorboards. Grabbing it, I chug until water drips down my cheeks. Wiping away the dribbles, I look out the window.

Manly clears his throat. I turn, and he grips the steering wheel hard. "The silence is killing me, you know. Are you that upset with me for leaving Happy behind?"

"Yes. Well, no, I mean…I don't know." I'm not sure what I think. I jam my hands through my thick hair, catching tangles and yanking my scalp. "Arg!" I slam my hand on the door. "I don't want to fight with you!"

His eyes flash like lightning, and he bursts out laughing.

What the fritz is he laughing about? A smile cracks my lips, then I laugh too. "Why are we acting so dumb?"

Manly grins. "Being around you makes me dumber, I guess."

I'm not sure what to make of that, so I feign offense. "Hey!" I sock him in the arm, and he veers off the road for a second. "Oops, sorry!"

Continuing our trip with this much tension would've been awful. Now, if only it doesn't come back.

The temperature drops. We're in for a cold night. We stop to make camp, and I stare at the truck bed. Can't wait to snuggle under all those blankets. Except…Manly behaved so strangely about sleeping next to each other on the trip all those months ago. After what Courage and Trouble said, I now understand why. Manly's trying to stay pure. And I totally respect him for it.

"Do you want me to sleep in the cab?"

Manly lifts his head to meet my gaze.

"Maybe I'll stay warmer in there. It's so cold tonight."

He scratches his head as he leans against the truck. "I tried that on the way to get you, and it turns into an icebox. I slept back here the second night. I stayed warmer with piles of blankets wrapped over my head."

I study his face.

"What?" He takes a swig of water.

"So"—I clear my throat and fidget with my hands—"will Abba be mad if we both sleep back there, like before?" Hope he doesn't laugh at me for asking.

His eyes flicker. Oh, how I missed that!

"I'm so glad you're thinking about what pleases Abba. The fact you even asked that lets me know it'll be fine. Like you said, our body heat will keep each other warm. Trust me, I could've used your body heat on the way here." He smiles, grabs the side of the truck, and throws himself over.

"I can tell your ribs are healed," I joke.

"Yep." He straightens the bedding and pillows.

I need to relieve myself. "I'll be back in a minute."

I distance myself from the truck and find a hidden spot behind a grove of large bushes. Where's an indoor bathroom when I need one?

When I'm done, I stretch my arms to the sky, letting my spine lengthen from being scrunched up in a truck all those hours. I sigh and turn around, whipping my flashlight's beam into the darkness.

A pair of foul yellow eyes stare at me.

The hair on my neck and arms stick straight up. Oh crap! The Wildie has me in sight. Should I yell for Manly? Run? Both? The animal turns its head for a split second. Run!

I hurl myself around the bushes and head straight for the truck. "Wildie!"

Chapter 21

Manly's torso emerges along with the smooth end of the rifle. Three shots crack the silence of the night. I throw myself over the side of the truck just in time to hear yelping from the wounded beast as he scampers into the distance. I fall into the blankets and pant hard as Manly pulls himself to safety. He white-knuckles the rifle, closes his eyes, and catches his breath.

"That was way too close. You aren't hurt, are you?"

I shake my head and attempt to regain my composure.

"You can't go that far off again."

"What? I was *trying* to relieve myself." This is so embarrassing. "If I stayed any closer, I wouldn't have any privacy."

"Privacy means nothing when it comes to your safety, Fear!"

Not exactly sure how he wants me to respond. His red face reminds me of spaghetti sauce. Not a pretty look on him. An owl hoots nearby, reminding me just how alone we are out here.

"I don't want to lose you again." Longing grows in his eyes. "Those three months were hard enough."

"Excuse me? It's been over six months since we saw each other. Did your head lose a few screws or something?"

Manly's face twists, and his mouth moves silently as he seems to wrestle with his thoughts. Why's he acting like this? He slaps his thigh, breaking the silence. "I saw you about three months ago. I came to the Fallen for a visit. Daddy told me it was a bad idea. Said you'd get your hopes up and think I was taking you home. He told me it wasn't fair to you, not when I couldn't bring you home yet. I didn't listen and went anyway, right at the end of harvest."

My eyes widen. "But why—?"

"Let me finish," he interrupts. "When I got there and spotted you on the field playing games with your friends, you looked so happy, so full of life. So content. I knew Daddy was right and I was selfish for coming. I hid my truck right away. I did have tea with Aunt Joy, though. She told me all about the play you were putting together and how you were doing so well, my being there might set you back. Neither of us wanted that to happen. I left the next morning."

My ears burn. "You should've said hello."

"You have no idea how much I wanted to."

"Why didn't you? I would've been fine." Darkness overtakes us, and the details of his face fade.

"Would you have been?"

"Yes! But apparently you think I'm too big of a baby to handle it."

I lie down and throw the blankets over my head. After a few minutes, I pretend to fall asleep. A bitter chill curls around me. Manly slips in beside me, and he sets the rifle between us. His warmth and protection ease my tension. My heart pinches as his breathing evens. Why did I yell at him? I'm reminded of a saying from the Word, *Don't allow the day to slip away while stewing in your frustrations.* In the morning I'll ask him to forgive me, first thing. After all, Manly came to see me because he missed me.

As he falls into a deeper sleep, Manly turns toward me and scoots closer. One of his hands touches the rifle, and the other rests on my arm. Even in his sleep he protects me.

Thank you, Abba, for putting this guy in my life.

The next day begins without a hitch. Upon waking, I apologize. He forgives me and even offers an apology of his own. Why's he apologizing? He's so weird sometimes.

We spot a number of Wildies along the road while we drive but fail to encounter one when we stop. Despite that, Manly still insists on staying nearby with his rifle anytime I need to relieve myself. I can't even go with him so close. Not cool. I'm so bloated and uncomfortable by the time evening rolls around. Ugh. I wish he'd quit worrying and let me pee in peace.

We make a fire and try to relax with warmed-up cans of noodles and broth. Sitting on a pile of blankets together, Manly's shoulder bumps mine. Sparks blast through my skin.

The glow of the flames flickers across Manly's face. We sit in silence for a few minutes, soaking up the intensity of the fire. I long for his guitar.

"Wish I'd brought my guitar."

Eek! Did he just say that right as I was thinking it?

Brilliant minds and all that.

I glance at his lips. "Just sing."

He starts a familiar song, one he taught me all those months ago. I remember most of the words and join in. Our song comes to an end. Sigh. Why can't it always be like this?

He gives me that sideways grin. "Your voice is so much stronger."

I wrinkle my nose. "They sing at the Fallen, *a lot.*"

We chuckle, and he steals a glance at me. His eyes do that thing, and my breath hitches.

"I just wish..." he breathes.

"What?" A shiver of static ripples up my arms.

His eyes lock with mine. "That you were older."

I blow out a puff into the chilly night air and roll my eyes. "You know what I wish?"

"What?" His husky voice sends static careening down my arms and into my legs.

"That you would quit worrying so much about age."

"I can't help it." Our eyes lock once again. "It's my responsible side."

I'd like to throw your responsible side over a bridge.

His breath sweeps across my cheek. I didn't even realize we leaned closer to one another. My face warms as my lips part. A tremble skitters up and down my body. His eyes drift toward my mouth, mere inches from his. He leans in. This is it, we're finally going to kiss! Adrenaline spikes through my skull. He suddenly rips himself back and stands. Cursing and mumbling, Manly paces the dirt with quick, frustrated strides.

My brow furrows. What's going on? Is my breath that bad? I brushed my teeth, I know I did. He won't stop pacing. Manly tugs at his hair and drags his hand down his face. Oh my gosh, he's going insane.

Midstride he halts and veers in my direction.

"It's so dang hard to stay pure-minded around you, Fear!" he yells as though I have the ability to control his thoughts.

Wait...what? Seriously? Sounds like an excuse. "Is it *that* wrong to kiss someone?"

"It is when you're too old for that person. Honestly, I'm not sure I could stop at a kiss."

My face flushes. So he really does want to kiss me. He just doesn't want to cross that line. Not yet. Silence lengthens for a difficult few minutes.

This is ridiculous. Someone needs to say something. "That's what Courage and Trouble told me, too."

Manly's eyebrow shoots up. "What?"

Fritz. Probably could've chosen a better thing to say.

"About staying pure around me."

"They did?" His foot meets a rock, sending it skittering over the ground.

I nod as a Wildie howls in the far distance.

"They didn't hurt you, did they?"

A ridiculous question when it comes to the guys. I laugh. "No, no. They were perfect gentlemen."

"But they both...*liked* you?"

Could he get any more jealous? I stand and face him. "Trouble likes *everyone*. He's just a big flirt."

"What about the other one?"

A smirk creeps onto my lips. "He has a name, you know. It's Courage."

"Were you and Courage"—his voice strains with the next word—"together?"

Being a little possessive, are we? "Heavens no! Although, I think he may've had a crush on me."

Manly gathers twigs and throws them into the fire. "And

how did you feel about him?"

I'm not sure if I should tell him how close we got, but I'll have a hard time keeping it a secret. Truth is always better than a lie. Even a little lie.

"He's like a best friend."

Hurt scorches Manly's face as he digests my words. "I thought *I* was your best friend."

I shrug. "You are. Can't a person have more than one best friend?"

I circle him, and he clutches my wrist, stopping me.

His face softens. "I'm glad you made friends. I'm sorry for being selfish and wanting you all to myself."

"I want you all to myself too, Manly, but you keep pushing me away."

He sobers. "I'm going to bed now."

That's it? You're just dropping it?

He pushes ash and dirt into the fire to kill the flames. Extending his hand, he helps me into the truck bed. "Goodnight."

It would've been a good night if only you kissed me.

Chapter 22

Oh my word. I recognize this place. We must be getting closer. Oh, that gnarly tree! We're barely a few miles from the house. I can't wait!

When my home appears on the horizon, I press my nose to the window. There it is! I pluck my face from the window before I end up with a bloody nose and wiggle in my seat. Manly relaxes as we pull into the drive.

Faithful slams the screen door and jumps off the front porch. Fiery-red braids flail behind her. She runs to us and hauls me out of the cab, then grabs her brother's hand and drags him over. Geesh. Someone's happy to see us. She wraps her arms around both of us, squishing us together, and squeezes tight. I don't care how awkward this is, I love it. My eyes spring leaks. We let go of Manly, clasp hands, and squeal.

She rubs tears from her eyes. "I can't believe I'm saying this, but I missed you so much. I never wanted a sister, but when you were gone…well, I wanted you back." Her words are like soothing music to my flustered soul. "You must tell me everything. Come on."

After I bear hug Granny and Daddy, Faithful yanks me upstairs to her room. I'll share everything except the library. I'd promised I would never tell. I'm not about to break that promise now.

I scoop half a quilt out of my bag. "Remember our quilt promise?"

Her eyes widen. "Oh no."

"You forgot?"

"Not exactly." Faithful goes to the closet, opens it, and digs under a pile of blankets. She finds a piece of poorly sewn, bedraggled material, something that might resemble the beginning of a quilt. She grimaces.

"See? I tried." I burst out laughing, and she joins in. "It's awful, isn't it?"

"Yep. It is." I take it from her hands and give her mine. "But I love it because *you* made it."

The next few days are heavenly. I savor each meal Granny cooks as though it's my last. Their faces cheer me. Being back with them is amazing.

Except for one problem.

Manly.

At times I hurt so bad I want to cry. But I'm trying to stay positive. I've got this amazing family. There's no room to complain...but it's like we're human magnets and instead of being drawn to each other, we now push away.

Why is he treating me this way? Does he not care anymore? I need a break from him to clear my thoughts. It's shopping day, so I volunteer. Anything to get my mind off him.

Granny, Faithful, and I climb into the truck and make the journey to town. We stroll through the streets and shop. I reach the end of the stores and pause. Why did I volunteer for this? I don't even like shopping. Granny and Faithful only have one last chore, then we'll be done. I'm so stinking bored. Might as well stay outside and people watch.

I plop onto the bench and scan the storefront I just left. Near the edge of the store, dirty legs stick out from under a tattered skirt. A lady must be sitting on the ground. I inch over to get a better look. Flies buzz around her dirty head. Poor lady. Hope she finds a bathtub soon. She looks up. My skin jumps from my bones.

I gasp. "Mother!"

She looks at me, then turns away. How? Why is she here? Oh, yeah. Town prostitute. Forgot about that. But I never imagined she'd get this bad. She glares up at me, does a double take, and scowls.

"It's been so long. How are you doing?"

She waves me away without saying a word. Her decrepit state stirs my soul. She's a miserable sack of grime. Someone needs to do something.

"Please, can I help you?" She doesn't deserve it, but…she did raise me.

"Help me?" A haggard, old-woman's voice proceeds from her thirty-something mouth. "It would've helped me if you hadn't dropped from the sky as a baby. It would've helped me if I hadn't been so stupid to take you in." Her speech is off kilter. She must be coming off a recent drinking binge. Her words hurt, but I've heard worse things from her before.

"What could you possibly do for me, anyway?"

Give you the one thing that fixed my life forever. I tap my knapsack, a copy of the Word concealed within, hard and flat beneath my fingertips. I retrieve it, then hold out the book to her.

There weren't many left in the library. It'll be a while before I can get a new one, but she needs the healing words. She stares at it as if it's some sort of vermin.

"Please take it." She pushes it away, and my lips press together. Are her reading skills as lackluster as mine were? "Can you read?" My tone implies curiosity. Hope she doesn't think I'm rude.

"Of course I can read, stupid girl," she snaps.

"Then please, take this." I hold out the book to her again. "It changed my life, and it can change yours. You don't have to live like this. There are better things out there for you. Trust me." *Just listen to me for once, Mother.*

She hesitates, grabs the book, and scowls. "All right, I took it already. Now go on, get outta here." She waves me away, and I eagerly comply. She's not a person I want to be around anyway.

Abba's spirit moves in me. *She needs your compassion.*

But she's never shown me an ounce of compassion in my life.

She needs your forgiveness.

Abba's words pierce like a dagger. He's right. Eventually I'm going to have to find a way to forgive her. My heart was cold, but now it softens and breaks for her. Maybe she'll actually read the Word and change her ways. The only thing I can do now is pray for her transformation.

And pray my own heart will continue to soften toward her.

I've only been at the house for six short days, but it feels
like a lifetime. Granny, Faithful, and I bustle around the
kitchen canning fresh vegetables when a horse whinnies
outside.

That's odd.

I jerk to the side to peer out the tiny kitchen window.

"Ow!" Faithful and I cry as our skulls crash together.

Granny laughs and throws a tin lid into the sink. Faithful
and I rub our sore heads as Granny scoots to the front door,
wiping her hands on a towel. Manly and an older man in
overalls stand in the doorway. I peek around Granny to get a
better look.

"Lanky!" I recognize the ranch hand in his all-too-familiar
getup. I go over and give him a quick side hug. He smiles
down at me, but there's something disturbing in his eyes.

"What's wrong? Something's wrong, I can tell."

The same sadness echoes in Manly's eyes. Lanky folds his
wide-brimmed hat in two and clutches it between his fists. This
is going to be bad.

Granny steps around me. "What is everyone doing
standing around? Let our guest sit." She ushers him into the
living room.

"Ma'am." He won't sit in the chair she offers him. "I have
something to tell you."

She waves her hand. "Nonsense. You need a glass of water
before you'll do any talking. Now take a seat."

He reluctantly lowers onto a hard-backed chair. We gather around the man, who looks as though he hasn't slept in days. He's covered in grime, and the tip of his nose looks frostbitten. Granny sails back into the room, sloshing water as she goes. She hands the glass to the man too weary to smile a thanks.

"I don't know how to tell you this." He aims these words in my direction. He shifts and fiddles with his cap. "They took Happy. She's gone."

My world goes gray. Granny plunks onto a chair.

His words seep into my mind, and I fall to my knees and clutch my pounding chest. "What?"

Daddy and Manly scoop me up and set me in a chair. This can't be happening. No. I must've heard wrong.

"I'm sorry, Fear. We tried to stop him. But, that Upper, the one who tried to take her before, he came the next day with a whole troop. They took her, but not without leaving a trail of blood in their wake."

A knife plunges into my gut and twists. I did hear him right.

He turns to Granny. "Your Aunt, they…she tried to stop it. When she got in their way…I'm sorry to tell you this ma'am, but…they gave her the Dartle Aorta."

Granny slumps into a heap in her chair. My head swoons. I close my eyes tight. The terror she must've gone through when they cut out her heart with a laser gun…

I drop off my chair, move to Granny, and hug her legs. Granny sends peals of mourning into the air, stabbing the entire room with each wail.

This makes no sense. Lanky shouldn't have had to ride all the way here. "Why didn't someone contact us on the Communicator?"

Dark circles surround Lanky's eyes. His shoulders sag.

"We couldn't. They ripped it out and smashed it to pieces. It may have been part of the reason they killed Aunt Joy. I rode my horse as fast as I could to get here. Aunt Joy had directions to your place in her files. I assume it's because y'all are family."

When I search Manly's face, hard, cold steel replaces his eyes, and his bones turn to solid metal. He paces. He's going to rub the stain out of the wooden floor soon. I shudder and can barely breathe. They've got Happy. They're going to tear her to pieces, bit by mortifying bit. Until they've ravaged every last part of her soul. She'll die inside long before her body does. Vomit scorches my throat, lingering, threatening to spill over. I swallow the vile substance back down, breathing hard. Forcing calm to my raging stomach, I glance up just as Manly stops in front of me.

"We've got to go after her." Conviction cuts through his words.

Daddy shakes his head. "There's no way to get to the Gliding Lands. It's impossible."

He's right. No Downer has succeeded before.

Manly clenches his fist. "Then we'll find a way."

I stand, and Faithful comforts Granny in my place. I drop my voice and move closer to Manly. "You think it's possible to get Happy back?"

The coldness in his eyes frightens me. "We won't know unless we try." He ushers me to a corner out of earshot of the family. "I have to try, Fear. It's my fault she's gone."

"Your fault? How is it possibly your fault?"

"I should've brought her with us. I should've listened to you. I have to do something, or those animals will destroy her."

He's right. She's doomed to a life of agony if we don't rescue her.

We deliberate for quite some time. Then it's settled. We

can't let go of Happy. We have to try something…anything…
to get her back.

Even if it means risking our lives.

Chapter 23

The next day, all of us—except Daddy—pile into the truck. He's going to stay to care for the farm so invaders don't take over our house. At first only Lanky, Manly, and I were going. However, Granny put her foot down.

"Since Aunt Joy won't be able to care for the children anymore, I'm stepping in until they can find someone else."

Faithful bolstered herself beside Granny. "And I'm going to take care of her."

Like she could do anything.

Granny drives, and Faithful occupies the passenger seat. Manly, Lanky, and I pitch to and fro in the truck bed, bumping around on the cold steel, icy winds biting at our ears and cheeks. We are in for a long, uncomfortable drive.

"Count Cerberus must've taken Happy to the temple harem." Lanky's voice weakens. "That's his side business, finding new prostitutes and selling them for cash. I can almost guarantee that's where you'll find her."

Manly's face drains of all possible color. My throat goes

dry. She's so young…so naïve. What type of dark evil lies in men's hearts to crush such innocence?

I place my palm on his thigh. "We'll get her back. We will." My words are stronger than my conviction. What if we fail?

When we arrive, the ranch looks like a war zone. Tree limbs and large branches dangle from their boughs. The fence looks as though it was plowed through, then mended haphazardly. An abundance of litter and debris scatter over the once-clean grounds. The demolished stairway to a girls' cabin splays across the grass. I doubt anyone can get in or out of that cabin now.

Lithe and Shepherd Sam rush out to meet us. Their demeanor resembles those who've lived through a tornado. Shattered and shaken.

"Thank the Good Lord you came back, and with reinforcements." Shepherd Sam reminds me of an ox ravaged by a pack of wolves. Once strong and sturdy, now a mere shadow of what was.

Lithe steps in. "We've tried to run this place on our own, but…we're not as well equipped as Mama was."

Granny hugs Lithe. Lithe must be Aunt Joy's daughter. Why didn't I see it before? That makes her Granny's cousin. So now she's my family too.

We walk to the Main Cabin. How had things become so ramshackle in a little over a week? Shepherd Sam points out everything the Uppers demolished in their quest for Happy.

Lithe explains which children are among the lost. I don't recognize any of the names. How did I not learn more of their names? It's not like this ranch is huge.

We enter the Main Cabin, and I'm assaulted by hugs from every direction. My three freckled, redheaded triplets and Courage. Their smiles are nothing more than masks. Mirages to hide the pain. I squeeze them tight, then introduce everyone. As pretty as Harmony and Melody are, Faithful stands out as the most stunning of the redheaded girls.

Their chatter buzzes around me, but I can only focus on one thing. Happy. Where is she now?

Anyone and everyone who loves Happy shows up at the evening meeting.

After a private, fast meeting with Lithe, I take my place in the audience. She stands to face the crowd. "We are sending Trouble, Courage, and Fear to retrieve Happy. They will blend in with the rest of the population. Many Uppers are skinny and tall." Not the ones I've seen, but we have to believe the library is right. "Fear will be permitted to go but only because we need someone who can enter the Harem to retrieve Happy."

"I'm also the most determined to get her back."

The crowd nods in approval. I'll keep trying to rescue her until they throw my dead carcass over the edge of the Gliding Lands. I've already been tossed over once. What's one more time?

"We know Count Cerberus took her to the temple harem."
Lanky seems to know a lot about his side business. I don't even
want to ask how he's privy to such information.

Courage steps forward. "From what we've read, everyone
is put through a thirty-day purification before they're able to
'service' the Uppers. Over a week has gone by already. We
have approximately three weeks to rescue her before she loses
her innocence forever."

Manly paces the floor like a Wildie trapped in a cage. He
doesn't like this plan at all. He halts and marches to the front.
"I should be the one going to rescue her. Not you three."

Lithe smooths her apron. "Your broad shoulders and large
frame would give you away in an instant." She's using that
soothing, motherly tone with him. I don't think it's working.
"No one would fall for your being an Upper."

The group nods. Manly huffs and rushes for the door. I
brush past Courage and hurry after him. His brisk pace doesn't
slow until he reaches the lake.

He sits down hard on the large rock. We're back at our
spot, only this time, it isn't a sweet meeting of joy.

I stomp up to him, and he doesn't even bother to look up.
"Why are you so angry?"

His hard face intensifies his features. "I already told you. If
I did what you asked and brought Happy with us, she
wouldn't be in danger."

I stand next to the rock and drape my arm around his
shoulder. "Maybe that's true, but you're not at fault here,
Manly. We live in a wicked world. It could've happened to
anyone."

He sighs and runs his hands through his hair. "I can't stop
feeling so guilty. I should be the one going up there, not you.
Now your life is in danger too. It isn't right." He grabs my

hand and rubs it between his own.

"You know, I'm the one who should feel guilty, not you. I'm the reason that Upper saw Happy in the first place. I was so stupid." My stomach roils at the memory.

"That doesn't matter. You still shouldn't go up there."

"They need a girl to go. The guys would get caught the second they stepped foot in there. Whether you go or they go, the fact remains. They need me."

"I don't like it one bit."

His stubbornness is no match for mine. "I know you don't, but I'm the only one small enough to blend in and get through small spaces. I can hide much easier than you." He squeezes my hand too tight, as if he's afraid to let me go. "Ouch," I tease.

He releases his grip. "Sorry. But I can't stand the thought of losing you. You know this isn't safe."

My heart melts, and I reach out with my free hand to stroke his hair. "But you agree we can't leave her there. We have to try."

A thought springs to mind. Maybe I'll find my parents while I'm there. At the least, experience the Uppers' culture. Understand them more.

"But if the plan doesn't work, you know what that means, don't you? You get caught, and you're dead."

A vision of my dead body splayed on the ground flashes before me. I shiver. I won't let it settle into my soul, so I sweep the vision away. "And then I get to see you in Heaven, right? Isn't that the whole point of this messed-up life? To end up in the eternal light with Abba? What's a more brilliant way to go than attempting to save a friend? Don't deny me that."

Manly shakes his head and halfheartedly grins. "You drive me insane sometimes, you know that?" He grabs me and pulls me close. Sparks of static shatter my brain. His lips tease my vision, mere inches from mine.

"You drive me insane too."

"Why is that?" His breath caresses my lips.

I lean closer. "Because you won't do this." I steal a split-second kiss from his lips, then bolt like lightning.

Leaving him with eyebrows raised above glassy eyes, I dash away into the night.

The next couple of days fill with planning, deliberations, arguments, and seeking information. Manly barely talks to me while everyone prepares for our rescue mission. I won't lie. It hurts. But I push it aside and try not to take it personally. All my focus needs to be on rescuing Happy.

He does, however, hover at a respectable distance, acting as an unneeded bodyguard. Courage seems to be doing the same, but on the opposite side. On occasion, I notice them glaring at one another. I try to avoid getting in the middle of whatever this is, except that's exactly where they've placed me.

Guys make no sense.

The stolen kiss is never mentioned, and the stress of the impending mission starts to get to everyone.

A few of us gather in Lithe's cabin for another meeting. Granny has gone off to help with a group of littles.

Courage and Trouble stand before Lithe. Trouble shifts from side to side. "We have something to admit to you."

I hold my breath. Buttercups and biscuits. Thank Abba they warned me about this.

Courage smooths his hair. "Might as well just tell you. There's a library in the woods."

A couple of gasps come from Melody and Harmony, but Lithe's face remains serene.

"What's a library?" Tenacious asks.

I snicker. Wait. I didn't know what a library was either all those months ago. Oops.

Courage thrusts his hands into his pockets. "It's a place where they store lots of books. All sorts of books. Anything you could think of."

Trouble quits his shifting. "We didn't tell you because we didn't want anyone getting grief from the Sentinels."

Lithe clamps her hands to her hips. Oh, we're going to get it now! "About that. I went through Aunt Joy's papers and found the electric bill for a location hidden in the forest. Then I went snooping and found the hatch door."

She what? And why are we just now hearing about this?

Trouble props one arm on top of the one draped across his chest and grips his chin. "Aunt Joy knew about it all along? And *she* was paying the electric bill?"

Lithe nods. "I think she visited on days you three weren't there. It looks like her dad owned the library and all the land she inherited. According to a letter, she was grateful to you guys for cleaning the place up and making it accessible, along with keeping it a secret. The entire ranch could've been executed had an Upper discovered it still existed."

Courage's hands zip from his pockets. "Wasn't it risky to pay an electric bill for a non-existent building in the woods? Wouldn't that make the Uppers suspicious when they do their quarterly inspection?"

Ah, Courage. So obnoxious with all the questions.

"She had it labeled as a discipline shack. The Uppers are

all for retaining discipline among the Downers. They must've thought it was unnecessary to check." Lithe shrugs. "Abba must've wanted it to remain a secret."

"Still seems risky," mutters Courage.

"Maybe it was, but we never got caught, now did we? At least we know the library is safe from the drones since they can't venture into dense forest area without having issues. Besides, wasn't it risky when you'd visit the library?"

Courage ignores her and clears his throat. "So we know we're going to hide in meat-packing containers to get *to* the Gliding Lands. Now we need to figure out how to get back."

Changing the subject, are we?

Lanky shrugs. Trouble's eyes widen while Melody shakes her head.

"Someone creates parachutes up there." Trouble starts flapping like a bird. "Maybe we can glide our way down?"

I shoot him a look. He's crazy.

"What?" He shrugs.

Lithe waves a delicate hand, and all eyes shift toward her. "Um...there's something you need to see."

I glance back at Tenacious, but he waves us off. He'll be fine till we get back.

We follow her out of the cabin.

Trouble leans toward Courage. "Where is she taking us?"

Courage shrugs as Manly plods nearby. No one has any clue what's going on, do they? Even Lanky, who knows this ranch like the back of his hand, seems to have no idea what Lithe is up to.

Lithe halts and turns to him. "Lanky, would you be so sweet to grab your bolt cutters?" He nods and dashes off.

We wait a couple of minutes in silence. Plenty of pacing permeates our group until Lanky jogs back. Manly catches my eye, then quickly wrenches his head away. Why's he acting so weird? I should've never kissed him.

Lithe takes us to an area that's off limits. Waist-high grass and weeds engulf the area, and we stumble through it. Lithe shifts to the left and takes us through the woods. Melody trips on a root and falls. Courage helps her up, and her face turns a shade of dark pink. That girl gets embarrassed far too easily. We emerge a few minutes later on the other side.

In front of us stands a metal garage that's spacious enough to be a Hoverpod hanger. I step closer. Thick, rusted chains lock the door tight. This place hasn't been used in a while.

Lanky marches over and, with one swift clang of metal, the chains fall off.

Lithe and Lanky slide open the doors. An ancient Hoverpod, dirty and worn, rests on the cracked concrete. But it's a Hoverpod. A real, live, stinking Hoverpod. Insane.

"How in the Gliding Lands?" Trouble mutters as he approaches it. The entire camp is aware of his fascination with vehicles. This has got to be pretty cool to him.

Lithe steps forward with a grin on her face. "This belonged to my grandfather. It was passed down to him from his dad. One of the first models in existence. My family was wealthy generations ago, long before the last war." She walks closer to the machine and wipes her hand over the exterior, smearing grime. She looks at her hand and wrinkles her nose. "It needs a lot of work."

Trouble shoots his arm to the ceiling. "I volunteer!"

Courage snorts. "It needs more than that. It needs a miracle."

Lithe ignores his comment. "Who has any mechanical experience?" Lanky and Manly are the only two who raise their hands. Trouble sulks and lowers his. Lithe nods. "That's what I suspected. Can you two figure out a way to fix this machine? Get it running again?"

Lanky and Manly eyeball each other, then stare at Lithe.

"We'll do our best," Lanky says. I think his words sound more confident than he feels.

Manly walks over to Trouble. "But we'll need a helper." He plops his arm around Trouble's shoulders.

Trouble's face lights up like he won a million dollars. "Anything you need, man. I'm your guy."

Manly chuckles and walks away. I shake my head. I hope Manly won't regret that.

Chapter 24

The day comes to attempt our plan. Courage, Trouble, and I will hide in packing crates meant to hold buffalo meat. An Uppers' refrigerated cargo Hovership will be our home for over an hour, so Lithe makes sure we wear sweaters and knitted hats. She arms us each with Tasers. I don't ask where she got them.

I scan the crowd for Manly. He's nowhere to be found. I'm not sure if I'm angry with him or not. They've been so busy working on the Hoverpod, he hasn't had any time for me. Although, I'm not sure if he'd take time with the way he's been acting. I really hope they get the Hoverpod working soon enough to pick us up from the Gliding Lands. They've run into nothing but issues so far. If not, we'll be stuck in the Gliding Lands much longer than any of us care to be. I gulp. Hope it won't become our permanent residence.

Faithful nears my crate, stoops down, and cups her hand to my ear. "Manly couldn't handle being here. He would've tried to prevent you from going."

Her sympathetic eyes do little to comfort me. I just want to see him before I leave.

I give her a curt nod and pray she can see I'll miss her beneath my frustration at her brother.

I adjust the silver jumper I wear under my sweater to blend in when I arrive in the Gliding Lands.

Before they close the lids, Harmony jumps toward Trouble and gives her brother a kiss on the cheek. "Come back in one piece, all right?"

Melody hauls her away. Tears stream down both of their cheeks. We say our goodbyes. Hopefully we'll be saying hello again soon. I try to swallow but can't.

I nod to Courage and Trouble before we lower our heads into individual crates. A silent blessing of protection coasts through my mind as the reality of what we're about to do sets in.

Thirty minutes of waiting for the Uppers to arrive and retrieve their shipment frazzles my nerves. The men on their way to get these crates must be the same ones who ransacked the ranch. Count Cerberus is one of the ranch's best customers, and he isn't going to quit doing business with the Fallen just because he killed the owner. It makes no difference to him. He just wants his meat. The whirring of the Uppers' Hovership blasts my crate with currents of air. I shiver, hold my breath, and pray no one decides to inspect the crates before they take off. It's a nerve-wracking few minutes.

Soon we're in the air. The movement jostles me, and queasiness overtakes my already-jumpy stomach. Shivering commences. Knew it was coming. Doesn't make it any better. After a bone-chilling hour, I bend my fingers to regain flexibility. I'm frozen everywhere. Bet the guys are too. As soon as the Uppers take off the lids, we'll have to move fast. I hope our stiff bodies will respond as quickly as we need them to. I clutch the Taser within my achy fingers.

We arrive, and voices linger just outside my crate. I point my Taser at the lid, ready to strike at a moment's notice. Dizziness warbles my brain.

Don't forget to breathe. In. Out. Okay, I can do this.

My hair stands on end as a lid crashes to the ground.

But it's not my crate. An electric zapping noise, followed by a *thud*, rings through my cramped space. Scraping above me stirs my adrenaline. The sun blinds me, and I lunge with my Taser, only for a hand to clamp on my forearm. I shield my eyes.

Courage.

"Watch it. You almost tased me."

I let out a breath. Thank Abba Courage caught me before I zapped him! I shake from the adrenaline rush. Courage lifts me out of the crate just as a man lumbers up behind him.

"Courage!"

He ducks as the man springs forward. The man arches his back and writhes as a zapping noise zings through the air. He drops to the ground, and a dumbstruck Trouble stands behind him with the Taser clutched in his trembling hand. I've never used a Taser before, and the horrified look on Trouble's face tells me I never want to. If they were lethal, no way could I do it. Courage steps over the man splayed on the ground and bear hugs his friend.

"Thanks."

Trouble's mouth hangs open. He can only nod.

We stand, stretch, and dust ourselves off. We're in a large warehouse with no one else around. Thank Abba.

"What's our next move?"

Courage whispers, "Let's head that way."

Trouble and I follow, and he trembles beside me.

"Everything's fine. Abba's going to help us," I reassure him. He nods, but I don't think my words help. His flushed face says everything.

Following Courage out the door and around the side of the building, we continue all the way to the back. A large concrete wall with a hill and embedded stairs sits to the left of us. I rip off my sweater and knit hat, and the guys do the same. We throw them into a nearby bush, then climb the stairs. Across the horizon, colorful buildings of all shapes and sizes meet our eyes.

"We need to get to the top of the nearest building so we can scope out what we're dealing with," Courage says.

I nod. That's probably smart to find a vantage point. I glance around. There aren't any people about, so it's easy to shimmy our way to the top of the building without detection.

I place the shaking Trouble as our lookout on one end. Courage and I travel to the other side to get a better view of the city and peer down at the people below us. The steady beat of music plays in the distance. Flashy sights and vibrant oddities smother the city in peculiarity. Color dances before my eyes in a vast array of unique shades.

"See the difference in stature?" Courage points to the people below.

In the square, obese people struggle to put one foot in front of the other. Few walk. Most ride Hoverscooters. The other portion of the population is the exact opposite. Tall and slender to the point that bones and vertebrae poke out this way and that. Almost...I search my brain to find the word I saw in the medical handbook for this type of condition...anorexic. Yes, that's the word. Like those supermodels I saw in the old history books.

"Why such extremes?" I ask.

"It's an extreme world up here." Courage nods at the restaurant section. "Different restaurants exist for both populations. The Fatties eat in that one." It has a door big enough to squeeze six Downers through.

I scowl at him. Is this a side of Courage I haven't seen before? "Don't you think it's mean to call them Fatties?"

He smirks. "It's what they're called up here. It sounds mean, but when the two populations made a clear split years ago, it started as a joke. Now it's what they refer to themselves as. Fatties is a term of endearment. They're proud of their extra weight."

"Why? And why didn't you tell me this before?"

Courage rolls his eyes. "I did, Fear. You must've not been listening."

Heat fills my face. *Blah, blah, blah, Mr. Know-it-all.*

Courage glances at my flaming cheeks, grins, and turns back to the city. "A lot of Fatties remember the days of starvation, when there wasn't enough food. The children died in droves. It was considered lucky to make it to adulthood." He steadies my waist with his hand as he leads me to the lower part of the multi-level roof. Despite his obnoxious ways, he always looks out for me. "Once they received Upper status, they decided they would never go hungry again, and they started eating a lot, as you can tell."

We watch a man attempting to slide off his scooter. He almost tips over, but a cute blue robot scurries to his side and helps him up.

"What a sad way to live."

"I know. But they claim to love it. They believe 'The larger, the better.' They're a prideful group. Actually, the entire Upper population is full of pride. That's why they think they're so much better than us."

"What about the anorexic people?"

Courage about chokes. "Don't say that so loud!"

"What? What did I say? We're on top of the building—who's going to hear us?" So much music and noise come from below anyway.

"That word you said; it's illegal up here."

My eyes widen. "I…I didn't know."

Courage does that smug grin he gives when he's feeling superior. "I know. There's a lot you don't know. That's why you have me." He flashes his pearly whites.

It's times like these I want to smack him and smile at the same time. "You really know how to get my blood boiling, don't you?"

"I have no idea what you're talking about." He slides his hand in mine as a Sentinel comes into view and yanks me back. "They can't ever figure out we don't belong here," he whispers. "We would get thrown into the Pen faster than you can say Fattie."

I stifle a giggle.

"I'm serious."

My face straightens. "I know."

A lady in a silver cape strides through the square. Her long, boney legs show more skin than I'm willing to. A tight bun pulls her skin taut, accentuating her high cheekbones. Jagged, sparkly twig-like things stick out of the bun. Spots of makeup dot her face.

"What are they called?" I point to the figure below. "Let me guess, Thinnies?"

"Close," says Courage. "Skinnies, actually."

"Why am I not surprised?" So, super large or super thin? No in between? Weirdness.

"Both populations are all about self. Their only concern is how much entertainment and pleasure they can squeeze out of life."

Trouble joins us. "We need to find somewhere to hide soon. People are staring."

Courage ignores him and peers into the distance. "There." He points. "There's the temple. That's where they're purifying Happy."

A large golden dome sparkles from the center of the city. From our research, we know emeralds and diamonds encrust it also.

"That's where we need to go." I get up.

"Yes," Courage agrees. "But let's not get ahead of ourselves."

"Listen, I wanna get Happy out of here as fast as possible. Got it?" I'm not about to let her stay any longer than she has to.

I survey the street below us once more. We wear similar garments as the Skinnies—silver jumpsuits—but I don't see a single person who has my stature. And not only that, but Trouble borders on not thin enough, and Courage borders on not tall enough. This is going to be a massive problem. I can't even walk through the streets. I can't be a Skinny, and I certainly can't pass as a Fattie. Goobers and gambits. What are we going to do?

"We should wait until dark. Look at me. I'll never fit in."

The guys evaluate me and agree. A group of middle-sized people enter the square. What's this? They're the same build as us Downers, but they wear much different styles.

"Who are they?" I ask Courage.

He draws back, his face a blank slate. "I'm not sure. I thought the only Uppers were the Skinnies and Fatties. And the Temple Royals, though I still haven't figured out what they look like yet. I've never heard of a fourth group before."

What role do they play in this world? I study their clothing, hairstyles, and demeanor. None of them have Downer hair. Colors of every hue grace their heads. Gotta be wigs. No way could they get their hair that perfect. I've never seen such weird hairstyles, so random and sporadic. Same with their clothing. Wacky patterns and styles adorn them. One of the lady's outfits is kind of cute. In a weird, manic kind of way. I could pretend to be one, easy. I just wish I knew who they were. It almost seems as if they're looked down upon. Everyone who passes them won't give them a second glance. Weird. They don't seem to mind and keep to themselves. If only I could find similar clothing.

Courage studies me. His forehead wrinkles. "I'm going to get you one of their outfits. Hopefully I can find a money-exchange machine for the Downer cash we brought."

It's risky, but getting Happy back is so worth it.

Trouble and I climb the ladder to the top of the roof. It's safer where no one can see us. Courage descends, and I cringe. I really hope he doesn't get caught. *Abba, help him blend in with the crowd and not get noticed.* I quiet my breathing as he comes into view on the street.

So far, so good.

He disappears into the multicolored crowd. Now all we can do is wait and pray he returns—and hope this whole thing isn't one enormous mistake.

Chapter 25

It seems like hours go by. I'm not sure if it's hot because we're on top of a building or because the Gliding Lands sits closer to the sun. Trickles of sweat dot my forehead. I wipe away the moisture. Gross. Sweat stains form under Trouble's pits. Double-gross. Why is it so stinking hot up here? It's supposed to be winter. Maybe they have a hi-tech way of controlling outdoor temperature. Trouble and I both fall into a sun-induced nap.

A hand touches my shoulder, startling me. It's Courage. I've never been so happy to see him. I jump up and tackle hug him, nearly knocking him to the ground. "You made it!"

I shake Trouble awake. When his eyes land on his best friend, he looks as relieved as I feel.

Courage holds out a bag. "Had to guess the size. Hope everything fits."

I open it and pull out a cute, but strange, dress. Stripes, wavy lines, and floral patterns adorn it along with buttons strewn here and there. Weird, crinkly gold flowers stick out.

And it's puffy. Spiked shiny black boots with four-inch chunky heels complement the outfit.

"How in the world do you expect me to walk in these?" I thrust the boots at Courage.

"We have to give you height somehow. You look like a little kid compared to everyone else down there."

"Hey! It's not my fault I'm vertically challenged." I pout.

He shoves the boots back into my hands. "Just do it."

Fine, Bossypants.

I look inside the bag again and discover fishnet armbands and bangles. A bright green wig sits snug at the very bottom.

"That thing cost a fortune. You'd better not lose it."

"How could I? You'd see this rug from a mile away." I hold it at arm's length, grasping it with two fingers, and wrinkle my nose. "I'll fit right in."

Hiding behind a wall that separates me from the guys, I put on the new getup. I emerge to find the guys gawking.

I must look like a freak. Just great.

Trouble shakes his head. "I'll never understand fashion."

I twirl around and almost fall, thanks to my newly added height. "What? You don't like it?"

I chuckle under my breath, and they join in my suppressed laughter as I sit beside them. We need to plan on how to get closer to the temple.

"I can't wait to get off this building." Trouble leans over the edge and immediately reels back. "Whoa. No way am I going down there."

Scared of heights? Ah, me too. But from the look on his face, I don't think I'm quite as bad.

"We need to look around more." Courage heads toward the ledge. "You can't stay on the building forever, and we need to find somewhere to spend the night."

Trouble follows but stops short. "Dude, are you sure it's safe?"

Courage looks at his best friend. "I came back in one piece, didn't I?"

Trouble scratches the tip of his freckled nose. "Yeah, I'm just…this is just…"

Courage takes a step toward him. "We'll be okay."

Courage turns his back on us and shimmies down the building. I'm just as freaked out as Trouble; I'm just doing a better job hiding it. But Abba's here with us. I feel it.

I turn and place my hand on Trouble's arm. "We've got Abba watching out for us. Don't forget that."

He nods the most hesitating nod I've ever seen. "You're right. Okay, let's do this." He reaches the ledge. "Oh crap, that's high."

I poke his ribs. "You climbed up. You can climb back down."

I turn my body to face the building and grapple to find the first rung. Before my head descends past the edge of the building, I catch Trouble in what looks like major prayer mode.

Abba, make him brave. Who am I kidding? Make me brave too.

We reach ground level. An old lady covered with a ragged cloak meanders down the lane. Trouble's eyes flash wide, and we all stand stark still. Is she going to see through our disguises? She doesn't fit the description of any Upper group we know of. She's dirty and disgusting, almost worse than my mother. Individually wrapped packages fill her cart. A medium-sized pack that appears to contain her meager belongings sits on the top of the pile. When she sees us, she halts. I twiddle a strand of hair between my fingers. *Just act normal.* She moves closer and examines us.

"What do you want, old lady?" Courage tries to imitate the

Upper's brusque and tactless attitude.

She steps closer to Courage. "You need to get away from this spot. And your friend here needs to hide." She points to Trouble. "He won't fit in. Not skinny enough. Don't let him die. Hide him, and he will live."

She knows.

Courage's limbs go stiff. She turns to me, rustles through her bag, and throws a thin tube of something at me.

"Line your eyes with this, girl, or they'll know the truth. Add a few spots to your cheeks as well. Fit in or die." She hobbles away from us, back down the concrete path she came from.

I'm still as a stone. Instead of calling us out, she helped.

I hand the bottle of eyeliner to Trouble, and he lines my eyes as though he's done it all his life. Then he adds dots to my cheeks. Too bad I don't have a mirror.

"Was she an angel in disguise?" I ask.

"I don't know, but she's right. Trouble, you're not thin enough to fit in after all." Courage's eyebrows draw together. "If I hadn't spent most of the money on Fear's clothes, I could've gotten something for you too."

Now I feel even worse about wearing this ridiculous outfit. *Thanks a lot, Courage.* "It's okay, we can figure this out." But we can't hide Trouble on the building without water or shade.

To the left, a clump of trees reside. I didn't think they'd bother with foliage in such a modern civilization. I suppose they need plants to keep their air fresh. Even modern technology is no match for nature. I point out the grove.

"Perfect." Trouble hurries that way.

Courage taps my head. "Smart thinking."

As we get closer, I spot a large fountain by a trail. Ooh, delicious water. Cotton coats the inside of my mouth. Need to get that water or I'm going to die. The trail is adjacent to the edge of the Gliding Lands. A waist-high wall spans the perimeter.

Trouble rushes toward the water, and Courage and I follow. My eyes dart around to make sure no one watches. When we've had our fill, we scamper toward the dense foliage.

"We'll be back as soon as we scope out the city." Courage squeezes Trouble's shoulder, and we walk away as soon as he disappears into the shroud of greenery.

Upon entering the square, I'm met with cold, lifeless eyes. No one smiles. No one makes eye contact. Awkward. Everyone ignores those around them. Absolutely no one talks. The constant thud of bass overwhelms me as music blares. I doubt they'd be able to hear each other if they did talk. Flashy and colorful stores please the eye. Anytime someone throws trash on the ground, a little robot rushes forward and picks it up. Why can't we have trash robots? No fair.

Almost every Fattie rides a Hoverscooter, and even several Skinnies don't bother to walk. I want a Hoverscooter; those things are awesome.

Parts of the ground magically propel people forward. I step on the propelling floor and am gently shoved forward as the ground bubbles and swells like a rippling tide. I better get off before I get too far ahead of Courage. Brain-activated Electro-Screens grace the front of almost everyone's faces. I remember that from the Teachings. Uppers receive an evolving chip implant when they're born to control their devices when they grow old enough.

Splayed across gigantic screens, people gyrate in absurd dances. The writhing covers almost every wall in the city.

It's much cooler down here. Outdoor air conditioning blasts everyone as they travel down the streets. Bright lights flash in my eyes. Tinsel, sparkles, and glitter cover everything. Neon lights twist into strange shapes, hanging every which way on the stores. The ground squishes. I bounce on the strange material.

"It's better for your joints than a hard surface." Courage bounces along with me.

Someone stops and stares. Uh-oh, I forgot. Talking is rarely done up here. The books in the library taught us almost everyone communicates through their screens, even when standing right next to each other. Whatever the person thinks appears on their screen. I sure wouldn't want others to know what I'm thinking all the time.

Courage and I get more accusatory looks, and he gestures for me to get behind him with a flick of his hand. People who dress like me must be servants to the Uppers. It seems they aren't allowed to stand beside — or heaven forbid — in front of their masters. Courage is my master, so it seems. I walk a couple of paces behind him. All stares cease.

He follows a group dressed like me. They may be the same group we noticed before. The servants are the only ones talking, and only to each other. Courage tilts his head in their direction. Maybe he can pick up some information. One of the women, probably in her lower thirties, steals a quick glance at us. She sees Courage dressed like an Upper and casts her eyes down, but they soon flicker back up to me. Courage tilts his head the opposite direction and stares her in the eyes. She relaxes, looks at me again, and straightens. Walking back to me, she takes my arm. I stiffen. Who is this lady, and why is she touching me? I can't even focus on the words coming out of her mouth. She doesn't stop chatting even when I try to pull away. She just clamps down harder. Courage's eyebrow zooms up, and he gawks. I gawk back.

What should I do? Courage grits his teeth. Great, he's no help.

She pretends to adjust my wig and whispers. "Come with me. Don't worry, it's safe."

Yeah, I believe you after knowing you all of thirty seconds.

She puts her watch to her forehead, lowers it, and turns on the holographic image, angling it so it's right on Courage's arm. He looks down. With a flash of light, directions imprint on his arm. She lowers her wrist. Courage scrunches his eyebrows, but something must tell him to trust her since he follows the directions. This strange lady and I walk arm in arm behind him.

"Charity," she whispers.

Is that her name? She better not be a serial killer.

Chapter 26

Courage reaches the end of the directions he discreetly reads off his arm. We stand before a large chain of apartments, lower than the rest of the city. As we approach, the temperature plummets, and my hands tremble as icy tendrils wrap around my bones.

The woman ushers us into her home. Hope this isn't a dumb idea. She welcomes us with smiles, something I haven't seen up here yet. I bet she's a believer, too. They all seem to radiate the same kindness as though it isn't a struggle or an act. No serial killer vibes at least.

"Come. Sit by the fire."

She points to the other side of the room. Inlaid within the wall is a white rectangular area. No logs or ashes indicate previous fires. She pulls a small Electro-Screen out of thin air, and with the push of a few buttons, a roaring rainbow-colored fire brightens the room.

"Whoa. I don't think I'd ever get used to that."

Courage smirks.

I shoot him a look. *Like you're used to living in the lap of luxury?*

Charity walks to the kitchen and pulls up another Electro-screen. They must be everywhere. So cool. "Do you prefer your Chai tea iced or warm?"

I shiver. "Warm, please." Courage nods.

She swipes her hand across the screen, producing steaming mugs of Chai in seconds. She winks as she hands us the mugs, then she snuggles into an oversized chair. "Warm and sweet. Some traditions never go out of style. My name is Charity. And I'm afraid you both aren't supposed to be here, are you?"

Courage and I exchange uneasy glances and sit on a hot pink sofa with leopard-print feathers sticking out of the back.

"Don't worry, I won't turn you in. Quite the opposite. I've been so bored lately, I'd love to help you out. I'll consider it a challenge."

Bored? I look around her lavish apartment. Really?

Courage folds his arms. "Who are you, anyway?"

She rolls her eyes. "I told you. My name is Charity."

"No, I mean, what is this place? What do you do, and why would you want to help two strangers? How do you even know we're not supposed to be here? Is it that obvious?"

She titters at his inquisition. "Oh my. I see we're going to play Twenty Questions."

"This is where you live?" I ask. Courage needs to stop being so suspicious of this woman.

She pats her fluffy purple hair. "Yep. Home snazzy home." She sighs. "Sorry it's not more to look at." She sweeps her hand at the room.

Courage and I gawk at one another. "Sorry to be so blunt, ma'am, but you live like a queen. Neither of us has seen a nicer place."

I let Courage speak for me because he speaks the truth.

She waves her polished paw at us. "Shh...you ought not say that too loud. There are plenty of queens up here, but I'm sure not one of them." She sighs again. "When it comes to Uppers versus Downers, the living is so unequal. Sometimes I forget that." She folds her hands and places them on her lap. "You see, I'm a Downer too."

"I thought all Downers are slaves, banned to live on earth. None of us are supposed to come up to the Gliding Lands," Courage says.

"That's what they want you to think, isn't it?"

"It's not true?"

"Yes and no." Charity taps her inch-long nails on the oblique table next to her. "Let me explain better. There are those of us who have been 'called'—as they put it—to serve them up here. Robots can't do *everything* for them. Some things simply need a human's touch. They built certain counties solely to train Downers how to serve them. That's where I'm from. They administer rigorous tests, and whoever passes gets to live up here."

Courage sticks out his neck. "*Gets* to? Don't you mean is *forced* to?"

Way to be tactful, Courage.

Charity wiggles in her seat. "It's much better than living on earth. You said it yourself. This is the nicest place you've ever seen—which is sad if you think this place is great. You've obviously never been in an Upper's house."

"No, we haven't. Remember, we're not supposed to be here?"

Geesh, watch your tone, Courage!

"Yes, I do," she snaps. "And if you get caught, you're going to pay severely for it." She takes a breath, and her shoulders slump. "Sorry, it's so hard being sweet with negative people around you all the time." She lowers her voice as if someone were listening. "If it weren't for Abba, I wouldn't be able to survive this place."

"You're a believer, too?" I knew Abba would help us!

"Shh! Please be careful. We don't need anyone hearing you say such things." Her head shifts back and forth, her lips tight.

What in the Gliding Lands is she worried about? No one else is here. "Then it's true."

"Why do you think I let you in my house?" She curves her hand around her lips and continues in a soft voice. "What we are is pretty evident, don't you think? In this dark world, we are the lights. It's easy to spot that fire in someone else's eye when you know what you're looking for. Everyone else's eyes and souls are dead. They're merely surviving. We are the ones who truly live."

"I never thought about it that way." Maybe I could learn something from this lady.

Courage pipes up. "Well, I have. I knew from the moment I saw you that you were one of us. That's why I felt we could trust you."

I give Courage a glare. *Quit being such a know-it-all.* His face blanches. I see I made my point.

Charity leans forward in her chair. "Be careful with that. Courage, is it?"

He gives a quick nod.

"Remember, the Word says pride goes before a fall." Charity wiggles her finger at him.

Courage recoils in his seat. I smirk. He doesn't like being reprimanded. But I also admire Charity for pointing out Courage's one flaw. His pride does seem to get in his way sometimes.

Charity stands and clasps her fingers. "Pride is the root of all evil."

Courage leans forward. "I thought that was money."

"Both," she says.

"I thought it was the *love* of money." Charity and Courage swivel their heads with eyes wide and lips tight. I cock my head and grin. "Am I right?"

Charity scampers to my side. From her expression, I'm not sure if she wants to sock my stomach or pat my head. She does neither. "Now, if I'm to help you two, I need to know your reason for risking your lives."

Gosh, I hope she's trustworthy. Here goes nothing. "We're here to rescue a little girl from the temple harem."

Charity plops onto her overstuffed chair. "She must be one special little girl." Her voice is weak.

I stand. "She is, and we have to get her back before it's too late." If it isn't already. Slices of static zip down my arms.

Charity raises her eyebrows. My skin crawls at the way she glowers. "How are you going to get that little girl back? It's not like kids walk the streets up here." She huffs. "Did you even bother to think this through?"

Courage stands next to me on her soft carpet. "I'm sure there are kids somewhere."

Charity sighs. "Have you seen any families around here?" She pauses. "Well, have you?" I shake my head. "What about children?"

Courage shrugs. "The youngest person I've seen is a teenager."

He's right. I haven't seen any kids either.

"Exactly. No one under sixteen walks these streets. I'm guessing neither of you is sixteen yet."

Gambits. I always thought I looked older than my age.

"We're both fourteen," Courage admits. "So where are all the children?"

"That's where I work. In the PediaLab. It's where they store the children until they're old enough not to be a nuisance to society. Children are considered a burden here. They are forbidden."

Wait…what? "Store the children?" I squeak. Well that sounds wretched.

"If children are forbidden, then how can the population continue to exist?"

Courage and his questions.

"We're not forbidden to have children. Everyone who has a womb is allowed one. But they must be sent to the PediaLab. You cannot raise them on your own."

That sounds absurd. "What if you want to?"

"Many of us do." Charity's face blanches. "But it's not allowed, not even for us slaves. Any child found gets"—her voice cracks—"thrown over."

I swallow hard. "As in, thrown over the edge of the Gliding Lands? Like, down to earth?"

Tears spring up in her eyes. "Yes," she whispers. She cuts off her tears with a couple of blinks, and a dazed look crosses her face.

Just like me. I was one of those babies. My stomach churns at the blatant disregard these people have for innocent lives. Sickening.

A conversation I had back home flashes through my mind. "My adopted Granny was a baby catcher when the Rain of Babies happened about sixteen years ago."

Charity's eyes go wide and glue to my own. "How did you know about that?" she hisses.

"It's not exactly a secret." Wow. She's a wreck. "Charity,

you're positively trembling." I reach out to her, but she bats me away, then jumps up and paces the room.

I remain silent. Courage squirms and looks at the front door. Charity goes to her MediPod and grabs a handful of pills, swallows them without water, and in thirty short seconds, her trembling ceases.

"I'm so sorry." She collapses on a couch and waves for us to sit. We do. "Those years, they were so hard...on all of us...it was awful. Just awful. I never...ever want to think about that time again." She pushes her fist into her closed mouth as if suppressing a scream. What have they done to her?

"I didn't know." My muscles tense.

"I know, honey, I know." She sniffs. "It's not your fault. Any mention of that...that...awful time throws me into a tizzy. I just can't handle it."

"We won't mention it again. Promise." Courage's promise probably isn't as compassionate as it sounds. He probably doesn't want an encore of that scene.

The awkward levels have skyrocketed. Maybe someone needs to change the subject. I clutch my chai. "We have a friend hiding in the large grove by the perimeter's trail."

Charity's sniveling ceases. "You mean to tell me, more of your people are up here?"

Courage slurps the rest of his tea and sets the mug on a nearby end table. "Just my buddy."

Maybe Charity will help us figure out what to do with Trouble. "We ran into an old woman with a cart full of packages. Where does she fit in? She kept telling us we needed to fit in, but she doesn't at all. Who is she?"

Charity bites her lip and spaces out before coming back to reality. "She's known as the Parachute Lady. She has been ever since anyone can remember. They only tolerate her because she's a necessity."

Courage stills. "Fear was a parachute baby."

Charity stares at me as though my head burst into flames. "And, and, you…you didn't get injured?" Tremors shake the life from her voice.

Why does she care? "No, I'm perfectly fine."

Charity's eyes blur, and she blinks back tears again. She stands and strides to the back room. "You may stay here for the night." She points to the sitting room with two plush couches boldly facing one another in the center of the room. "If you wish to wash up before dinner, the bathroom is down that way. A machine in the next room will wash and dry your clothes in under five minutes."

I peer out the window and squint at the bright skies. "Dinner? Already?"

Charity bobs her wild hairdo. "It takes some getting used to. Everything's so different up here. Dinner is early so you can party all night. They eat whenever they feel like it, so I'm calling it dinner because that's what us Downers grew up with, right?" She beams at us.

I nod. It's still hard to picture her as a Downer.

"When were you chosen?" I ask. She pats the large lump of hair gracing her head. No words exit her mouth. "To serve up here?" I explain.

"Oh. Fourteen. Your age exactly."

I can't picture becoming a slave at my age. Although technically, I've been one from birth since all Downers are slaves to the Uppers.

Courage scratches the side of his head. "I thought you said you had to be sixteen to live among the Uppers."

Charity avoids eye contact and picks at her cuticles. "They make exceptions in certain cases." She offers no further explanation. Courage doesn't press.

I imagine Charity snatched from her home to live in a foreign environment, being told what she can and can't do. Although, she does have a fabulous apartment and gorgeous, strange clothing.

"What's up with the clothes up here? They're a little… different." And that's putting it mildly.

She plucks her outfit away from her body. "We get to wear nice clothes because the Uppers insist everything around them be pleasing to the eye. No way would they stand for servants in dowdy outfits. In fact, they dress us the way they want us to look. If something doesn't make them happy, they get rid of it. So if we don't want to be gotten rid of, we wear exactly what makes our masters happy."

"Interesting," I mutter. I can see the appeal of this place, but at what cost? The freedom to make your own choices? I'm not sure I could live this way.

Chapter 27

Courage changes the subject and asks questions about the government and things that don't interest me in the least. I block him out and stroll around the apartment, touching and examining art and the beauty of things I've never seen before. I can't get enough of the way different materials feel under my fingertips. The smoothness of statues placed so precariously on the edges of tables, counters, and shelves intrigues me. Everything is either beautiful or unique. But what's the point of all these knick-knacks?

Charity cuts Courage off mid-sentence and asks if we're ready to eat. She must be getting tired of his endless questions too.

"I'm always ready to eat." Rubbing my lightly curved stomach, I sense the emptiness inside.

"That's what I like to hear. A girl with an appetite." Charity lowers her voice to a whisper. "Not like the Skinnies around here who eat a rib of celery for their entire day. Ridiculous."

She walks to the kitchen, and with a few swift movements

on the Electro-Screen, three steaming plates of food appear. She brings them to the dining table. Courage jumps up from the couch, and we take a seat.

When we've eaten half of our meal, Courage's body goes rigid, and his eyes widen. "Trouble!"

I wipe my mouth with a napkin. "He's got to be starving by now." We scoot our chairs back, but Charity forces us to our seats with a firm wave of her hand.

"You can bring him food when you two are done eating. It won't kill him to wait a little longer."

We finish our plates like starving dogs scouring their bowls, then venture outside with food and a blanket for Trouble. He's right where we left him. Worry lines crease his forehead.

"Was it pointless for me to come up here?" Trouble paces in circles.

"No. Of course not," Courage assures him.

"It doesn't seem like I've been much use. I can't even be seen on the streets." He clenches his teeth, and his cheeks match his hair. He never gets upset. This isn't like him.

"We'll ask our new friend Charity if she can get you a servant's outfit, but in the meantime, you have to stay hidden."

"I agree." I hate to admit it.

Trouble frowns. "Who's Charity?" He squints at the sun filtering through the greenery above us.

Courage places the bag of food at his feet. "She's a follower of Abba."

Trouble looks from me to Courage. Does he think we're joking?

Courage puts a hand on his shoulder. "Don't worry. She's going to help us figure out a way to get into the temple."

Trouble shakes his fiery locks. "I sure hope so. We could

use the help."

Someone needs to brighten his mood. I've never seen him this down before. I raise my voice an octave or two in a teasing, singsong way. "She's letting us stay in her awesome apartment for the night."

Trouble sits on a log, puts his legs shoulder width apart, and cups his chin. "Let me get this straight. You two get to stay the night in a plush apartment, and I have to sleep on the hard ground?" He's trying to make us laugh, but his tone is serious.

Courage reaches for a nearby branch and pinches a leaf between his fingers. "We'll talk to Charity about letting you spend the night at her house tomorrow. That is, if we're still here. We can't risk taking you there now. Exposing you without a servant's outfit would risk your life."

The voice of reason strikes again.

"One night of discomfort is worth your life, isn't it?" Yay, I finally said something good.

Trouble grins. "You always know the right things to say."

I snort. "I thought the exact opposite."

Trouble stands, puts me in a headlock, and rubs my scalp, messing up my wig.

"Stop it, you turd." I push myself out of his playful grip. At least he's in a better mood.

"Knock it off, you two. You're going to wreck the wig."

Trouble smirks at Courage. "Since when did you start caring about fashion?"

"Since never. Shut up and give me the wig."

Trouble swoops it off my head and throws it at Courage. Brushing it with his fingers and making sure the hairs are where they should be, Courage places it carefully on my head. His fingers graze my forehead, and heat emerges.

"Thanks, Courage." That was weird. I mean, I get it, he's

got a crush on me. But why am I getting all warm? Whatever.
It's hot out here.

"Aw. Look at you two being all kissy-kissy face." Trouble's
stupid teasing earns a scowl from Courage. Trouble smirks.
"Oh that's right, Fear's already taken."

My insides tug at the thought of my stubborn Manly. "I'm
not taken. Not officially, anyway."

Courage turns away from us. "It's time to leave."

My heart cracks at the pain etched in his simple words, but
I shove it down and wave at Trouble. He waves too and opens
the food bag to inspect what we brought him.

The next morning, Charity hands us a couple of diamond-
shaped chips. What are these weird things?

"It's money. Well, for those of us who haven't been
implanted with the currency chip."

Courage takes them out of her hand. "Yeah, I already had
to use one to buy Fear's outfit when we first got here. You have
no idea how hard it was to find a place that would exchange
my Downer money for the Uppers' chips."

"Good! Then you already know what to expect when
shopping." Charity clasps her hands. "Please find an outfit for
your friend so he can quit sleeping in the bushes." She
grimaces. "I would like you to bring him here. Then we can
talk through things, and I can show you maps of the city."

She goes into her bathroom and comes out with two dainty
bags. "We need to spruce you two up. Don't want you to look

different from everyone else." She smears makeup all over our faces. Courage and I raise our eyebrows, and his lip curls. I can barely contain my laughter at his appearance. He seems to be struggling to keep it together too. I have no idea how I look; however, Courage with makeup is quite a sight. I'm not sure Charity meant to make one of his eyebrows thicker and higher than the other, but that's what happened.

I point to his mouth. "That lipstick is *so* not your color."

He rolls his thickly lined eyes. My mirth dies a swift death. Something about his eyeliner bothers me.

Hate.

That's it. With the eyeliner, he almost parallels my brother. Thank Abba his skin is darker, or the resemblance might be too much. I haven't thought about Hate in a while, nor do I care to. I smother the thought before it can drag me into dark and uncomfortable places.

"You look rather smashing, I'd say."

He's got to be joking.

Charity interrupts before I can respond. "Thank you. I've always been good at makeup." She turns away to fix her shoes. We shoot each other a look, eyebrows raised. If Charity's good at makeup, then Faithful's good at cooking. Although, everyone seems to do their makeup extreme up here. Extremely bad.

"Thanks, Charity." I think.

We leave for the city to procure clothing. We don't have to travel far since the city is designed for the utmost convenience. Little slices of stores sell different wares to minimize travel. It's like this all over the city, stores repeating themselves so everyone has what they want within reach.

I find a clothing store called the Push and Shove. "I'll head in there. You get him some shoes."

Courage teeters to the shoe store across the street. I highly doubt shopping is his idea of a good time. Not really mine either. But this shouldn't take long.

I quickly flip through the outfits, trying to picture Trouble's size. I settle on the most normal pants and shirt I can find. I plop it on the checkout desk.

"That's not going to fit you. It's much too big. Shall we find you a more fitting size?" Bleach-blond hair, sparkling with mini braids sewn throughout, pile high on his scalp. Rose-tinted makeup covers the Downer servant's face. He looks more garish than handsome. Beneath the glitzy exterior, I bet he could be a good-looking guy.

"No, thank you. The outfit isn't for me; it's for a friend." I produce the money chip.

His jaw drops. "I've never heard of that before."

What's he talking about? "Someone having a friend?"

"Buying an outfit for someone else. Why would you do that?"

He's serious, and I'm not sure how to respond. Truth is always a good thing, right?

"To be nice," I admit.

"Nice?" He laughs as though the idea is foreign. It probably is up here. "Nice doesn't exist anymore, sister. Don't you know that word's been stricken from WikiWordz?" He shakes his head and repeats the word "nice" a couple of times as if he's fascinated by the way it sounds. He stares at me and keeps ranting. "No one is nice anymore. That's so old fashioned." He cocks his head and pauses, then his eyes fly open wide. "Maybe it's the new-new?" He flaps his hands in front of his chest, yellow glitter falling from his towering up-do. "Oh, girlfriend! I can feel a new trend coming on, and it's all thanks to you. Nice."

He gazes off, mumbling under his breath.

I throw the money chip on the counter, grab the outfit, and dash off. I gotta do a better job of fitting in. If they found out who I am — my stomach knots. Better not think about that.

I find Courage carrying a metal box. Must be the new pair of shoes.

"Pure weirdness," he mumbles.

"Tell me about it," I whisper.

We pass groups of Fatties and Skinnies as I follow Courage through the streets to the grove where Trouble resides, keeping my distance to avoid stares. Although, with how much people tend to ignore each other up here, who knows if they'd even notice.

Once we reach the grove, I check to make sure we haven't been followed. The Parachute Lady mills about, but we already know she's on our side — for whatever reason. I don't worry about her.

When we enter the thick greenery, Trouble is nowhere to be found. My brows furrow, and I smooth them with my fingers. The longer we search for him, the bigger my concern grows. I can't risk calling out to him and attracting attention. Where is he? My stomach drops. Something bad happened to him, didn't it?

Then I see it. I point to a leg dangling out of a tree. I get closer, following Courage, and find our redheaded friend sleeping in the crook of a large branch. Courage grabs a nearby stick and whacks Trouble's foot. He startles awake, loses his balance, but catches himself before he falls. He grips the branch with both arms, his feet inches from the ground. He lets go and lands with a *thump*.

"Thanks for scaring the living snot out of me!"

I hold up my bag. "You're welcome."

He snatches the bag out of my hands, opens it, and frowns. "What? No food?"

"Even better." I reach in and seize the outfit. "Your freedom."

As though a light bulb goes on, he grabs the outfit. I've never seen a guy so happy about clothes before.

"The styles up here are…odd," Courage says.

"I don't care if I have to wear a string bikini. Just get me out of this stupid forest!" Trouble rips off his shirt, and I whip around, shielding my vision.

"At least wait until the lady averts her eyes!" Courage teases.

"What? You can't tell me you don't want to see all this white, freckled awesomeness?"

I snort. "I'm sure someone wants to see your awesomeness, Trouble. Just not me."

"Now you've hurt my feelings."

Courage smacks his forehead. "Will you two shut up? Someone's going to hear us."

Voices draw near, right outside the shrubbery. We've quieted just in the nick of time. They're muffled, but one of the voices belongs to the Parachute Lady.

Trouble leans over and whispers, "She must be selling one of her parachutes."

My chest tightens. "That means, a baby…" I can't finish my sentence.

"Yeah, and there was another last night. I couldn't hear them well, but I'm sure that's what they were doing."

"Someone has to stop them!" My voice carries louder than I mean it to. "They can't throw out another baby!" My heart rate increases.

Courage cups my back. "What are we supposed to do? Go

out there and say, 'Please don't throw your baby over the edge'?"

"I don't think they want to do this, Fear. I think they're forced." Trouble cringes under my glare.

"You don't know that." I shove them both away. "Do you see any Sentinels holding laser guns to their heads? I would just as soon die before I did that to my own child!"

The more I think about what those people intend to do, the more I want to yank the brown strands out of my scalp. All those children in the Special Cabin. All those precious babies deformed by their mothers' insanity. All the babies who have lost their lives, skulls smashed on the ground, while their little souls floated away. Don't their parents even care? My insides smolder until I want to scream. It isn't right, and it isn't fair. I must stop these people. Whatever it takes.

I march forward to free myself from the canopy of trees. I almost reach the edge when the guys each grab one of my arms and hold fast.

"Oh no, you don't!" Courage warns. "You can't blow our cover."

"Let me go!" I thrash, but their strength exceeds mine.

"Happy." One word from Trouble, and I quit struggling. They release me. "Please, don't let Happy down." Troubles soft voice makes my blood boil.

Air spews from my lungs. I stalk away. Why does such cruelty exist in the world?

"This sucks!" I stomp my foot.

Courage hangs his head, and Trouble's eyes soften.

"I can't stand it anymore. Let's get out of here." I peek out from the brush and examine the road to make sure everything's clear. The boys follow. As we're leaving the area, I spot the Parachute Lady beside a couple. The woman holds a wrapped bundle in her arms. My pulse speeds, and my neck tightens.

"Murderer!" The word lashes from my mouth.

The guys grab my arms and drag me away as fast as humanly possible. I don't care what they think. The volcano in my head is about to erupt. I can't stand the thought of it happening again. But what can I do? Agony guts my soul to the core. How can I change an entire population's way of thinking?

Chapter 28

I'm still steaming by the time we reach Charity's. We press our foreheads to the Agnosco Panel of Charity's door to show her who waits outside. She swings it open and lets us in.

"Oh, the shrubbery boy I've heard so much about!" She clasps her hands and bounces but soon realizes none of us are as excited as she is. "What happened? I thought bringing your friend here would ease your worries, not make them worse." She pushes up the corner of my mouth to force a smile.

Get your hands off me. I turn away, cross my arms, and plunk myself on the sofa.

"Wow. What a bunch of grumpies." Charity meanders over to the newcomer. "You must be Trouble." She hugs him instead of the Uppers' usual nod. Trouble's sheepish expression threatens to yank me out of my dark mood. She pulls away.

"Hmm…" She takes his chin in her delicate hand and examines his face. "I can tell where you get your name. There's a spark in your eye. You were made for trouble, weren't you?"

He stupid grins and nods like a bobble-headed

moron. Wow. That didn't take long. She has him smitten in under sixty seconds. That's got to be a new record for him. Too bad she's twice his age.

Courage comes over and sits beside me. "That wasn't a smart move back there."

My cheeks flame. "I don't take kindly to people calling me stupid. That's what my mother and brother used to call me."

"I never called you stupid."

"Practically."

His eyebrows scrunch, and he huffs. He's going to get mad *at me*? Not happening.

"I'm sorry for getting angry about someone killing babies." Sarcasm spews from my lips. "What I don't understand is why you're not mad about it too."

"I *am* angry about it, as much as you. But sometimes there's nothing you can do."

I stand and turn toward him. "That sounds like something a coward would say, not Courage."

Charity and Trouble's conversation falters as our voices escalate.

"Hey!" Charity hurtles a frown in our direction. "What in the Gliding Lands is going on? Why are you two fighting?"

Courage just shakes his head. Trouble explains to her what happened in the woods, unaware of how sensitive Charity is to the topic.

I don't feel like being sensitive right now anyway. "That awful Parachute Lady hands out parachutes to whoever asks so they can toss their baby overboard like a piece of trash." Was I just a lump of garbage to my parents?

Courage peers into my eyes and sees the tears welling up. I think he's finally understanding why this upsets me so much. I was one of those babies.

"Yes, I agree it's awful. The most awful thing ever the way they treat babies up here. And you don't even know the half of it." Charity suppresses a sob. "But that Parachute Lady is no murderer, Fear. She's an angel who saves countless babies' lives."

"Saves lives?" My jaw muscles strain. "These stupid Uppers and their stupid laws! Don't you think it would be better for these parents to hide their babies instead of throwing them over?"

"It's not that simple, Fear."

"How would you know?"

She stiffens. "How can you hide a crying baby? Or a growing child? They would never get to go outside for fresh air or feel the sun. What kind of life is that?"

"Better than killing your own child."

"You were safe, weren't you? You told me you were a parachute baby."

"I was lucky." Tenacious' words come back to haunt me. *No such thing as luck.*

"If it weren't for her, every baby who got tossed over would die. Don't you understand? She does it because she loves the babies and wants to give them a chance. A chance to survive." My chin drops. She's right. Charity wipes her eyes on her sleeve. "Don't ever criticize that woman again. She's the only one left up here with any decency."

I swallow hard. "I'm sorry. I guess I didn't see it that way."

"I hope you do now."

My simmering skin cools. I'm so foolish. If only I controlled my emotions better.

Trouble steps out from behind her. "Oh man, if I knew there'd be this much drama, I would've stayed in the trees!"

His joking breaks the tension in the room, and Courage

and I glance at each other. I try my hardest to tell him I'm sorry with a look. I think he understands, and he seems to forgive me, though I can't be certain.

Charity swallows more pills. "I'm going to take a nap." She heads to her bedroom without another word.

My stomach grumbles. I'm starting to get the shakes. Better eat soon. She's given us permission to use any of the amazing technology in her apartment. After searching for the Electro-Screen and eventually finding it, I hit buttons and swipe my hand this way and that to make food for the guys and me. Two failed attempts end up in goop on a plate and meat chunks floating in what looks like cereal. Third try, I produce three plates piled with food that looks scrumptious and smells even better.

"Thanks," they chorus and start chomping away. No small talk tonight.

As we're finishing, Charity emerges from her room.

"That was a short nap." Did her pills wear off that fast?

She whips on her six-inch heels. "Problems in the PediaLab. I'm off! Talk to you kids tonight." She races out the door.

What does she do exactly, other than settle disputes between kids?

A yawn escapes my lips. A nap sounds like a pretty good idea right about now. "Let's rest." I head for the sitting room with the super-long couches. The guys follow. Trouble falls asleep within seconds. Minutes later, Courage begins to drift off too. Better speak up. "I'm sorry, Courage, for being rude to you."

He mumbles in his sleep, so I try again.

"I'm sorry." I doubt he hears me, but at least I tried. Soon my head fills with dreams that turn into nightmares.

I wake up from my nap. Charity has returned from the PediaLab. It's time to talk about how to rescue Happy. The four of us sit on the plush couches.

Charity scoots next to me. "I have access to holographic wrist and arm devices, which will help us communicate while you're in the temple. I'll make sure we each have one."

"We still have our Tasers, though the batteries have already drained." Courage sets our three Tasers between him and his best friend.

"Those things are ancient. I wouldn't have a clue where to find a charger for them, if they even still exist." Charity runs her finger along the soft couch.

Trouble picks up one of the Tasers and messes with it. "They aren't that old."

Charity grins at him. "Anything that isn't made last week is considered outdated up here."

"That's a bummer." Trouble flips the Taser in the air, and it lands on his exposed palm. He jolts. "Ouch. That one still had juice in it." Courage and I snicker as he holds his wounded hand over his chest.

Charity moves to her cupboard and pulls out a MiniPod. She presents the chrome-plated sphere to us and presses the button on top. Two holographic wrist devices lay inside. "I'm going to airmail these to the Fallen. That way we can communicate with the rescue Hoverpod."

I give her a big hug. "Thank you, Charity. This means so

much to us. We knew Abba was going to figure out a way for us to communicate, and he did."

Holding the MiniPod, she asks for the ranch's address. Courage repeats it from memory. She types it in and opens her door, and the MiniPod flies into the sky and zips away.

Charity turns to us. "Now, down to business." She cracks her knuckles. "You need to pretend to be Temple Royals."

"Huh?" Trouble scratches his head.

Courage nudges him. "The guys who occupy the temple and may run the government. Remember, we've talked about this." He turns to Charity. "So do they run the government or not? The textbooks were vague."

Charity shakes her bouncy, blonde wig. "I'm not even sure. Everything about them is veiled in mystery." She clears her throat. "The Temple Royals are a mix of sizes. You'll fit in just fine. Plus you'll be wearing oversized temple robes. On Celebration Days, they open the temple for everyone to participate, so your presence won't raise any flags. That's in four days. As long as you don the right clothing and attitude, everything should go well."

I hope so. I don't want to leave Happy in there one more minute, but the more we talk, the more it seems like our best bet.

Trouble absentmindedly reaches for another Taser. Charity leans forward and smacks it out of his hand. She gathers them all, places them on our couch, and ignores his bewildered face.

I catch her eye. "How will we find the harem?"

Charity shrugs. "You're bound to find clues. Listen to people. No one uses their Electro-Screens in the temple. It's forbidden. People must talk in there. You're bound to hear something. We have four more days, so you'll need to take advantage of the evenings to explore and get to know the city better. You need to learn all the escape routes away from the temple in case something doesn't pan out with the Hoverpod."

Charity's right. We need to be prepared.

"The nightlife here is vibrant and never dies. Just don't stand out like a sore thumb, and you should be fine." She pokes Courage's side. "And for crying out loud, try to look like you're having fun."

I don't think I could live like that always, but it might be interesting for a night or two.

Darkness falls, and the three of us venture out. We don't want to put Charity at risk by being with her, so she stays back. The scent of incense, cheap makeup, and soap float through the air.

Trouble points out peculiar purses that stand out in the crowd. Quite a large number of people have them. They aren't flamboyant and colorful like everything else, just different shades of neutral tones, such as peach, beige, tan, and many different shades of brown and black. It doesn't seem like they fit in this picture. What's the draw? He jabs at one as a woman walks by.

I glare at him. *You're going to get us caught!*

"Ooh, so soft!"

"You're such a dork." I couldn't care less about these ninnies and their ridiculous purses.

I try to get a good feel for the layout of the city. Distraction comes in many shapes and forms. So many pretties. We pass many things we should look away from. Some are harder than others to resist.

A Screamatorium sits to our left, where a servant's lies, tied to a plastic board. Uppers take turns burning him, cranking up the temperature notch by notch, seeing how long the servant can go without screaming. Uppers place bets on how much the servant can withstand before passing out. Burnt human flesh scorches my nostrils as the servant's shrieks pierce my heart. Wretched Uppers. Don't they care about anyone?

Farther down the street sits a Voyeurism Crystal, where apparently someone can pay to climb inside a giant crystal cube that holds a prostitute. I'll never understand how people get kicks having others watch their most intimate moments. It turns my stomach, and I yank my head away.

On the other side of the street sits another area where disobedient servants are tortured. A hippo rips a man to shreds. My skin crawls. They seem so nice in books. According to a sign above the Hippo Slaughter exhibit, they're vicious. Who knew? The screams of the manservant drown out the shrieking from the Screamatorium. I'm not sure how much more screaming I can take.

We move quickly into an open square, where chimpanzee charmers work their magic on the crowd. Chimps and spider monkeys swing from store to store and head to head with ease, stealing a hat or a hairpin to the crowd's delight. Laughter and cheers spread.

Fire blasts along a perimeter wall, and sultry music plays from speakers hidden within.

Short cages sit to the side. The monkeys must stay in there. But wait...that's not a monkey...what the fritz? That's a Little Person. I've read about them.

I thought the Uppers had outlawed them. Anyone

considered deficient or handicapped by Upper standards are killed at birth. Or before. And now they keep some for display. How incredibly sad.

A Skinnie shimmies by me in a silver suit. He grasps a chain attached to a Little Person. Directly behind them is the same thing, only this Little Person is female. Uppers walking *people* like pets. Sickening.

As we nudge past, a Fattie takes a step back and squashes Trouble against a wall. Trouble's face turns blue. *Oh my word.* I should push the Fattie out of the way, but I'll get thrown to the hippos for sure. The morbidly large man moves and sets Trouble free. He shakes his red locks, rubs his chest, then hurries away. I scurry to catch up. Courage stands on the other side of the alleyway and discreetly motions for us to continue.

We pass through a less raucous street. Most of the store fronts display glass pipes of all shapes and styles on triangular shelves. Uppers—Fatties and Skinnies alike—lounge in fancy outdoor recliners, smoking on twisted, sparkly pipes and glass containers. Blue, pink, and teal smoke spirals into the air. Trouble coughs. My lungs squawk as I gasp for fresh air. Fogginess clouds my brain. Ooh…pretty lights.

Trouble grabs my arm and hurries me past the haze.

Once we're past the smoke-filled street, the air clears, and my head clears with it. Safer over here. I hope. We continue on, trying to memorize streets and where they lead.

Trouble is ripped from my side as a servant girl grabs his hand and drags him into a druggery booth. Oh no, she didn't! He forces the door open right as it's about to close and rushes to me, breathing hard.

"That was close," he wheezes. "My ten-second girlfriend over there almost made me higher than the sky. I don't think you or Courage wants to see me like that."

"Nope. You're hard enough to handle without being drugged."

Courage is paces ahead of us, his jaw squared and his frame rigid. He's had far too much of this craziness. He indicates with a flick of his hand he wants to head back. We turn around and let him lead, when the girl who yanked Trouble into the druggery steps in front of us. Alongside a Sentinel.

My heart jumps into my throat.

Chapter 29

"There." The servant girl points at Trouble. "That's the boy who wouldn't go into the druggery with me. Something's wrong with him."

The Sentinel approaches Trouble. I stare, mouth gaping. This is bad. We can't get caught now.

"Are you causing problems?" He clamps down on Trouble's shoulder. The Sentinel leans forward and peers in his face. "Do you belong here, young man?" Trouble doesn't respond. "Do you belong here or not?" The Sentinel squeezes his shoulder tight.

Trouble cowers. "Yes," he manages to squeak. "I belong here."

"No, he doesn't. Look at him. He's weird. I've never seen a servant like him before. He looks weird and acts weird. He's breaking the law. Arrest him!"

Trouble jerks out of the Sentinel's grasp. The Sentinel lunges as Trouble takes off after Courage.

I rip the stupid shoes from my feet, clutch them to my

chest, and run behind all of them, hoping no one will notice me. Soon, I pass the Sentinel on the opposite side of the street and lose the guys.

Where are they? *Please, Abba, don't let them get caught.*

I head toward Charity's apartment. When I get to the square in front of the servant's quarters, I see movement behind a grotesque sculpture. The top of Courage's head peeks out from behind it.

Praise Abba!

I hope with all my might Trouble is with him. I wait a few more minutes. It seems the Sentinel gave up. Everyone's so lazy up here. That makes it easier on us, I guess.

Trouble peeks out from behind Courage.

Thank Abba. I don't know what I'd do without either of them.

Before I can wave the guys to safety, all the screens in the square glow bright. Plastered across them is Trouble's face with a warning underneath, something about "unstable" and "report immediately." I run to the apartments with the guys at my heels.

Charity hauls us inside and slams the door. "How did you manage to get in that much trouble right away?"

"How did you know already? It just happened." Throwing my stupid heels to the ground, I sink into a kitchen chair, breathing heavily.

"They send a warning to all the Communicators so we know everything immediately. Now Trouble can't be seen in public. This is not good. Not good at all." Charity rubs her temples.

Trouble's pinched face matches his tightening muscles along his neck and arms. He scratches the back of his freckled neck and holds his head.

"That's okay." I pat his back. "We'll have to make you a behind-the-scenes kinda guy."

Trouble's face twists. "Is that supposed to make me feel better? Because if it is, you can stop. It's not working."

I place my palms on his shoulders and work out his tension as we sit, absorbing what just happened. Courage and I look deep into each other's eyes, an unspoken understanding between us.

We must rescue Happy on our own.

It is time.

From the things I've heard about the temple, I'm not exactly excited about going there. The sheer size of the place is intimidating enough, not to mention all the horrific things that lie inside its walls. My stomach twists into so many knots, I don't think I can keep breakfast down. I'd rather do a thousand things than sneak into a temple of death.

Charity's alarm bracelet goes off, and a holographic image shows up on her wrist. "Oh shoot. I need to go do something. I'll be back in ten minutes. Courage, I need you to take care of this for me." She throws a large roll of tape at him.

Courage catches it and reads the label. "Goose Tape. I've heard about this stuff. It's supposed to fix everything."

"Yes." She grabs her purse and shoes. "And now it needs to fix Fear's problem." She points at my chest.

My eyebrows scrunch. What's she getting at?

Charity sighs as she struggles to put on her ridiculous

shoes while standing and talking. "I already told you, the Temple Royals are monosex. They all look alike, and Fear needs to pretend to be one of them since she can't pass for a Skinnie. Now take care of it." With that, she rushes out the door.

Courage peers down at the tape in his hands, then his eyes drift to my chest.

"Eyes up here, buddy."

"Sorry," he mutters.

You better be. My shoulders tense, and I assess my options. Not seeing any, I groan. "Do we have to do this?" I glance at the other room. Trouble lays on the couch, his snores like a kitten's purr.

"Sounds like the only way. You've, uh...blossomed...in the last few months."

He noticed too? My face grows hot. Does everyone have to notice everything about me? I focus on rescuing Happy. If this is the only way to sneak into the temple, so be it.

I take a deep breath. "I'm going to take off my shirt now."

He gulps.

"Don't worry, I'm wearing an undershirt. Then you can wrap the Goose Tape around my you-know-where." I remove my shirt. Both of our cheeks are flushed. I turn my back on him and lift my arms. "Let's get this over with."

He places the tape on my spine and begins wrapping.

"Courage, you have to wrap it tighter," I snap.

"I don't want to hurt you."

"It's not going to feel wonderful, but you have to do it. I'll be in a lot more pain if they find out I don't belong in the temple. Now, flatten me, please." This is so stinking embarrassing!

He wraps tighter, smothering me. "Okay, that's good. I

think I'm flat enough." I grab my shirt and throw it on as fast as possible.

Courage averts his eyes.

"Thanks," I grumble.

We sit in thorny silence. Then our eyes meet, and we burst out laughing.

A sleepy Trouble joins us. "What did I miss?"

I grab my sides. The deepest shade of crimson I've ever seen darkens Courage's face. We can't stop laughing.

"Forget about it. You two are nuts." Trouble turns and walks into the other room. Courage and I calm ourselves enough to take deep breaths.

"I can honestly say that's one of the strangest things I've ever done." Courage runs his hand down his flaming cheek. "Let's never get awkward again, deal?" He holds out his hand. I plunk my hand in his, and he gives it a hearty shake.

A few minutes later, Charity breezes in the door. She holds a large sack. "Temple robes." She sets it on the counter. "One for each of you. Let me tell you something, Fear. My friend didn't have an easy time finding a robe short enough for you."

I snort. "You can blame my biological parents for that. Whoever they are."

Charity grabs my shoulders and squeezes. "It's not that bad being short."

She's a full eight inches higher than me. *Yeah, you'd know all about being short.* I eyeball her.

She points to her shoes. "Six-inch heels."

"Oh." Charity actually is short without her heels or her hair piled on her head.

"Look," she gasps. She grabs my arm and examines it. "You and I have the same birthmark." She pulls up her sleeve to reveal a similar birthmark in almost the same spot.

"That's a little weird."

She lets go, stares at me, then lets her eyes wander. She snaps out of it and gets down to business. "You must be extremely cautious going into the temple. The religion they practice is a mix of Witchcraft, New Age, and Eastern Mysticism, but it's mostly devil worship. They have no morals. They believe willing sacrifices receive riches and luxury beyond belief in the afterlife. This leads to lots of unfortunate deaths. They are ruthless and powerful. If they knew we were believers, they would behead us on the spot."

A shiver runs through me as I absorb her words.

Courage drops the makeup he's attempting to apply and takes my hand. "The light always overpowers the darkness. Never forget that."

That's comforting in a small way, but I still don't feel like dying today. I wish I had more faith like him. But I have a feeling no amount of faith can fully prepare us for what lies behind those doors.

Charity applies makeup to my face and notices my shaking hands. "Oh no, you don't. You can't go in there trembling with fear. Pardon the pun. What an awful name your parents gave you, isn't it?" She scratches her head. "Sorry, off track again. Anyway, if they see you like this, they'll eat you alive. And they *are* cannibals, so I'm not making a joke."

I swallow hard.

"Thanks," says Courage. "You're making this so much easier."

"Sorry." Charity grabs the brush from Courage's hand and smears on finishing touches. "What I meant to say was, you have to appear confident. You need to be one of them. Life is all about *you* and your own pleasure. You are better than everyone else in the room. Exude that kind of confidence, and you'll do fine."

Courage turns to me. "It's all an act. You can do it. You've already proven you're a decent actress."

"Decent?" I was better than decent.

"All right, you're a pretty darn good actress." He grabs one of the robes and yanks it over my head. "Come on, Fear, we don't have much time."

The urgency in his voice pulls me to my senses. Yes, I can do this. I can pretend to have arrogant confidence. It shouldn't be that hard for Courage. I grin.

"That's the spirit," says Charity. "Put a smile on that fearful face of yours." She ruffles my hair. "Wait! Take it off."

I point to my robe.

"No, your smile. I was wrong. Don't smile. They never smile in the temple." Charity taps her nails on the counter. "At least that's what I've heard. I've never actually been there."

Um, what?

I don't have a moment to freak out before Trouble gives us a hug and Charity says a blessing of protection over us.

It is time.

Chapter 30

We walk to the temple with our gazes flicking to the ground, searching for the arrows Charity projects with her fancy wrist device. She walks behind us as though she's our slave and we her masters. The arrows work brilliantly. No one notices.

It's almost night when the Electro-Screens disappear and people attempt face-to-face conversation. They're so poor at socializing, it's kind of pathetic. They visit MediPods and go to druggeries. Smooth talkers emerge and become the life of the party. It's all fake. Chemicals run so deep in their veins, no telling what a person's really like.

We reach the temple, and I glance up. The imposing building soars above us. It's fantastic. Nothing like I've ever seen in books, the Teachings, or anywhere else. I try hard not to gawk.

Holographics glow right by Courage's feet. *My time is up. Must go. May Abba bless you on your journey.*

Courage steps over the word "Abba" in case anyone

notices. Before we can even turn around, Charity's gone.

It's up to us now. The fate of an eight-year-old girl rides on the backs of two scrawny fourteen-year-olds dressed in silly robes. I've never felt so helpless in my life. *Abba, give us guidance and peace, and most of all, success. Help us find her.* My racing pulse slows.

Deep breath. Have to save Happy.

Standing like a yardstick's strapped to his spine, Courage tries to mimic everyone else's stoic appearance. His face is buried beneath the hood. I hope mine is as hidden.

Here we go.

I tread up the stairs among countless others wearing the same getup. I glance around. No one seems to recognize one another under these things. My heart rate increases as I near the humongous oak doors inlaid with ivory. The looming doors of death threaten to engulf us within their dark clutches. My arm hair stands on end as we pass through and blackness descends. Faint red lights above us emit enough glow to illuminate a few feet in front of me. Everyone bows to honor an idol surrounded by lit candles. I'm sure Courage studied which idol is which. I honestly don't care. It's all so ridiculously stupid.

I hesitate only a moment before going to my knees, then touching my forehead to the floor, trying to blend in.

The low hum of offbeat music pipes in, while swirling mist —made by a fog machine no doubt—creeps around the floor. This isn't that bad. Thunderous noise pounds within my chest. My ears throb, my skin crawls. I slam my hands to my ears. Okay, so I lied. This is kind of bad. The Temple Royals and Uppers surrounding us begin chanting a rhythmic blend of languages I don't understand. With my head to the floor, the blood rush makes my face swell. How long will we have to bow to this stupid idol? I peek. No one moves. Everyone stays still and continues this odd homage to this fake piece of junk.

Whiskers brush my face. A tail encircles my nose. I thrash my head back and forth, throwing the tail from my face. My heart thumps hard.

Calm down. It's not going to hurt you.

Prickling nails crawl on my back. I want to get up and scream, but I will myself to stay calm. I ran into many field rats in our hovel over the years. Why is this any different? My blood pumps hard. Because there are hundreds of them, and they all feel the need to crawl all over me. Bites pinch my skin. I squeeze my lips shut to keep from yelping. It isn't awful, but it sure isn't pleasant either. Before I get the chance to check if Courage is all right, the chanting, the music, the rumbling stops. The rats seem to dissipate into the walls, and everyone stands as dim lights brighten the room.

I peek at Courage under his hood. Unfocused eyes stare back, and his once-olive skin is pale. At least it seems that way. It's so hard to see in here. I'm sure my face is the same.

Another door opens, and everyone files into the next room. As we enter, guards hand out shot glasses filled with an unknown, silver-colored liquid. Everyone downs it without question. I hesitate, but a nearby guard eyes us. We can't get caught. Courage and I swig our drinks. A bitter, metallic taste fills my mouth. Courage warned me about the use of hallucinogens in the temple. I hope the liquid isn't what I think it is.

Now an even larger idol sits on a pedestal, this time in the middle of the room. A different eerie music plays, and the lights dim once more. The idol's eyes flash green. Everyone bows. I follow, crushing my knees to the hard floor.

No. No, please. Not again!

Head to the ground, the same rumblings build within my chest. The same chanting, but with a different rhythm, meets my already-throbbing ears. Something smooth brushes against my arm. Wiggling creeps along my legs. Scales find my hands. Gambits! Snakes. The floor is covered with them. They slither between our bodies, and forked tongues hiss in my ears.

I encountered snakes in the fields by my hovel. I can handle this. I breathe deeply. Smoothness only known to the reptilian kind meets my mouth.

Ugh! Get away, you vile creature. No more mouth breathing. Twice as many bites pierce my skin this time.

Why do I feel so weird? Standing seems harder. My feet won't stay put, and my head swims. Yuck, it hurts. I hope the snakes weren't venomous. But then all the people in the temple would be dead. Courage appears steady, so I lean against him.

"How many bites?" he whispers.

"Five, six maybe." Our group heads for a third room.

"That's not good."

"You're...tell...ing me," I slur. "I fee...eel like I'm dr...unk."

"That's because you are. The hallucinogens and snake bites combined do that to people. The more snake bites, the worse you'll be."

I lay my head on his shoulder and tell him in a not-so-quiet voice, "It hurts like...hell." I giggle like a maniac.

"Oh no, you don't. Don't get goofy on me. Snap out of it, Fear." He shakes my shoulder. "You can do this."

He's right. I can. But my feet won't walk straight. I grasp his arm for balance, but he totters almost as badly as I do. We tumble through the next set of doors. Yet another idol, more impressive than the last, rests in front of us. I can't believe we have to go through this again. Same deal, except they add squealing music this time. The roaring turns to crashing thunder. Our heads hit the floor again in a worship pose.

I'm so over this.

My innards roil as the lights snap off, plunging us into complete darkness. No candles this time. Screaming permeates the blackness. I'm not the only one hallucinating from the drink and snake venom combination. Giant spiders crawl over my body, furry legs scrambling over my robe. Strobe lights flash, and I catch a glimpse of the creatures. The rats and the snakes I could handle. But this...this I cannot.

A blood-curdling scream breaches my lips. Spiders everywhere. Tarantula sized. No, bigger than that. Monster sized. They're in my hair, on my face, under my clothing. It's unbearable. My sanity slips. Oh yes. I'm a happy little goblin who loves spiders. Where's the unicorn I rode in on? This weirdo next to me keeps grabbing my arm. I shake him free.

The lights turn on, and they're gone. My brain shifts in and out. I shake my head, and the fuzziness dissipates somewhat. I can't go through that again. Courage and I appear to be the only ones horrified. Giddy people swarm together as if they actually enjoyed the torture. It's beyond me how anyone could enjoy pure terror.

I grab Courage's forearm for support as we push through the last set of doors and enter the main room of the Temple. I praise Abba, the true God, for getting us this far. The rooms of terror are behind us. Now to find the harem where they're keeping Happy.

My eyes adjust. On one side of the giant room, dozens of knives, blades, whips, and swords hang on the wall, some tucked into ornate canisters. People cut and whip themselves and others. Blood pools on the floor. Slaves wearing nothing but loincloths and jewelry mop it up. Crimson smears across the polished marble. Whips fly through the air, landing on torn robes and naked backs. There's no way in Abba's universe I'm taking my robe off. Or getting whipped. *Let's just stay far, far away from that side of the temple.*

A steady rhythm causes my head to throb. It hasn't stopped hurting since we entered the temple. Have these Uppers ever heard of quiet? How can they live like this constantly?

On one side of the room, a large group gathers. They surround scantily-clad servant women who flail to a demon dance. I turn away. Disgusting.

An underlying stench fails to be blotted out by the heady floral perfumes infusing the air. I gag and cover my nose. Fat chance of that ever covering up the smell.

A gigantic, rectangular pit sits in the middle of the temple. White-hot flames careen out, and a ramp leads to the pit's opening. I glance down and shudder. This is where they worship a fire god. He's the center of everything that goes on in this room. People sway back and forth, praying and worshipping. Shivers skitter through me.

A Temple Royal walks up to one of the slaves and throws him, screaming, into the flames. Approval roars from the crowds, and the man turns to ash before my eyes. I've never seen anything so gruesome. Vomit pours from my mouth. Chills wrack me to my core. I won't ever be able to scrub that image from my mind.

Courage corrals me away from the fire god. "Glad you threw up. That should get the hallucinogen out of your system."

I'm already more steady. "We need to find the harems and get out of here." As if he needs reminding.

"I know, Fear. Be patient. We can't draw attention to

321

ourselves." He brings me to a quieter area of the temple. Silk curtains dangle from the rafters, lining an entire wall. Light glows from behind them. Silhouettes of bodies writhe behind the curtains.

"Look away, Courage," I warn him.

"I'm trying, but they're everywhere."

He's right. Everywhere I turn, shadows of unclothed bodies behind silky screens cavort with one another. Thank Abba, at least thin curtains skew the details. Kind of...

"Shrine Prostitutes." That's all Courage needs to say.

Ew. As vile as the acts behind us are, danger lurks in every other corner. Men stab themselves with short spears, and people cheer them on. My throat catches as a robed culprit accosts a female dancer. She struggles to get away. A sinking pit of revulsion twists through my core. I turn away. This is too much.

Spotting a staircase on the opposite side of the temple, I point it out to Courage. "That looks promising." I keep my voice low.

He nods within his hood so it's barely noticeable. "On it. Stay here. In case it's dangerous." Courage points to a sofa.

I grab his wrist and stare him straight in the eye. "Don't get into trouble. Stay safe, okay?" I gulp. *Abba, keep him safe.*

He smiles. My eyes widen, and I shake my head. "No smiling," I hiss. He frowns and leaves me.

I sit on the sofa *not* facing the curtains so I don't have to watch. It wouldn't please Abba. Although, this entire temple wouldn't please Him. I serve a loving and kind God. Not a god who provokes people to do such awful things.

An unquenchable tingle fills me. The monstrous spiders return. One's crawling in my hair. I yank off my hood and shake out my hair. It's just my imagination. I breathe heavily. I don't want to be here. Can't stand it much longer. *Please find her, Courage!*

The minutes tick away as I sit, trying to focus on my breathing rather than the images around me. Another monster spider skitters up my leg, and I whack at it. Nothing there. A shadow of a person passes behind me and sends chills down my arms. My eyes dart around. No one. The eerie feeling of being watched never leaves me. Who's stalking me? Does someone mean to harm me? It's just the hallucinogens wearing off, right? I take deep, calming breaths to avoid a full-fledged panic attack. I check behind me once more and notice a white door where the curtains split.

I turn around. Courage sneaks through the crowds in my direction. My breathing evens as he shuffles nearer, weaving slightly. He plops beside me, his lips pressed tight.

"Dead end. Sentinels block the way. It could be the entrance, but we can't get past those guards." He turns to me and stills. "Your hood." He reaches up and swiftly yanks it over my head. "You've got to stay hidden."

"Sorry." Should I reveal that I can still feel the spiders? Probably not. He'll think I'm nutty. "Hey. There's a little door behind us. Maybe that's where they're keeping Happy?"

He peers over his shoulder and spots it. "It might be, but I can't get close without going behind the curtains."

I shudder at the thought of going back there among the prostitutes.

While we debate our next move, a person nears and stands before us. Did they used to be a he or a she? I can't tell. Courage and I stare up at this robed person. What do they want?

"Let me take her behind the curtain. She can join in."

Not a chance. His creepy grin eats at me. Or hers? Still not sure. Whatever, I'll just call them a him.

Courage stands, blocking me. "No. We're together."

He smirks. "You must be straight from the PediaLab. Didn't they teach you we share everything here? No one belongs to anyone else, except the slaves, of course. So if you don't mind." He grabs my arm. Alarm bells clang in my brain, and I freeze.

Courage counters by ripping his hand off me. "No, you don't. She's mine." An authoritative voice booms from his chest. I'd be impressed if I wasn't so freaked. Courage sweeps out his leg and catches the person behind the knee. He whacks his gut with his elbow, knocking the Temple Royal to the ground. Courage grabs my wrist, and we take off for the exit on the far side of the temple.

No one bothers to follow.

As soon as we hit the neon lights of the city, we try to act like normal Uppers and begin a slow, steady pace. My nerves take over, and I find myself increasing my gait, Courage following suit. When we reach Charity's apartment, we're going full speed. I double over and pant. Courage breathes hard too, but he grabs my hand and pulls me to Charity's door.

Trouble lets us in. "How did it go?"

We take off our hoods. "Not so good," we say in unison.

Courage continues. "We got all the way in. No one seemed to suspect anything, but we didn't find the Harem."

Trouble pushes his hair away from his forehead. "That's not good. We only have a few days left."

"Yeah, we know." My spirit crushes with the weight of one thousand tons. I slump against the kitchen counter.

Trouble folds his arms. "Is it as bad as the library books say?"

If only he knew.

Courage frowns. "Worse. Much worse."

Trouble looks at me, and I nod. He lets out a heavy sigh. "Maybe it'll be better tomorrow."

My stomach turns sour with the realization we must return the next day. I want to curl up and die.

Chapter 31

We spend the evening praying our mission won't fail and that we'll reach Happy in time. Charity brings out her own secret copy of the Word and reads a passage. It's a story I haven't heard yet about three men who refuse to bow to a false god and are thrown into a fiery furnace. Abba sends an angel, and they survive completely unharmed.

A light bulb goes on in my head. "That's what we need to do. When we go back. We can't bow to those idols, Courage. It doesn't please Abba. Maybe he'll reward us if we refuse to bow down."

Courage rests his clenched fist under his chin. His eyes dart back and forth as he considers my words. He inhales, nostrils flaring. "Maybe it's worth a shot."

Charity's forehead wrinkles, and she nibbles her lip. "You both know what happens if that doesn't work, right?"

Courage and I look at each other. Determination strengthens my will. "It'll work."

Courage pushes his shoulders back. "Abba will protect us.

He always has."

"We serve a God mightier than any of their stupid idols." I have full confidence in him who saved us and created us for bigger things. It's as though Abba stands among us, his presence is so powerful. His peace settles us. Even the high-strung Charity relaxes. He'll protect us. I feel it in my bones. From the bottom of my soles to the top of my scalp, he garbs me in invisible protective armor.

Awe tinges Charity's voice. "You know, there are many, many places in the Word that tell us not to be afraid. Here's a passage on fear."

It's kind of funny my name is in the Word so many times.

Charity's voice softens as her manicured nails grip the sides of the book. "Even when I forge through the veil of darkness, evil will not capture me. For you stay close to me and protect me within your cloak of safety. You bring me peace. You are Abba, and you will take my hand and lead me far from fear. You will aide me always. Stand strong. Again you say, don't fear, for today deliverance draws close."

Her gaze pierces me, the challenge laid at my feet.

A ripple of calm stirs my soul. I can do this.

My eyes widen, adrenaline pumping through me as we walk up the temple stairs the next day. I can't help but cringe as we approach the first doors, knowing what we're about to go through again.

But I'm not shaking. I'm not sweating or panicking as I

should be. This is going to work somehow. I know it.

Mist fills the floor, and dim red lights flicker on the walls. Rumbles rattle my chest, and everyone hits the ground. That is, everyone but us. Courage holds my hand, and I will myself to stand strong. Any second could be my last. I squeeze my eyes shut and wait for the sting of sharp steel to meet my throat. I gather strength only Abba can provide and open my eyes. Light emanates on either side of us. What in the Gliding Lands? I move my hood back a few inches and turn. Two brilliantly lit men stand beside us. My knees go weak. Abba sent angels to protect us! Are they visible to anyone else?

I lock eyes with Courage, who also shifts his hood back, and grin. We're safe now. The angels' majesty is indescribable. I can only stand there and gape, knees trembling at their brilliance. The rats stay off me. They don't even touch my feet.

Thank you, Abba.

Guards open the vast doors that reach the ceiling. The angels shield us from the guards as they hand out shots of hallucinogens. I won't have to taste that icky stuff again. In the second room, it's the same. The angels stay with us. No snakes touch us.

A guard notices we're standing and quickens his steps, sword drawn. He lunges, and the angel next to Courage lifts his arm, fingers outstretched. The guard falls to the ground like a boulder crashing from a cliff.

I gasp. "Praise you, Abba! You are such an amazing God."

No one can hear me over the thunderous noises and blaring music, but Abba hears me. That's all that matters. Courage's lips move in praise to Abba as well. Other guards release latches to the third and final room. Nothing's in this room but the horrendous idol. Those tarantulas were pure hallucinations.

Everyone screams and writhes as they experience their worst nightmares crawling all over them. I try to focus on the light around us rather than the horrible scene in front of me. It only lasts a few minutes. If it were any longer, I might pluck my hair out. So creepy.

When the Temple Royals and the rest of the Uppers stand, their eyes are bright, and smiles abound. I don't get it. There must be something wrong with a person to revel in being tormented. Why are they smiling? They're not allowed to do that. Maybe Charity isn't right about everything.

I enter the main room once more. Somehow the angels have blurred my vision so I no longer witness the horrific scenes. Naked people dance to the left, but I can't see details. Someone in the distance is beheaded, yet I see no blood.

A few minutes later, three young women run toward the fire god and throw themselves into the flames. My eyes are shielded from the intricacies of their skin melting off the bone this time. The divine censorship is just what I need to keep sane. The images the day before were enough horror to last a lifetime.

But I need to focus. Look for the white door. Abba will provide a way.

I head for the curtained-off area, where a Shrine Prostitute and a Temple Royal fornicate on a large pedestal for all to witness. I turn so I don't have to watch. Courage does the same. Though the details are skewed, I don't want to gawk. When are they going to finish? This is taking forever. Until the crowd dissipates, no way will we get near the white door.

The angels' light lessens so it no longer hurts my eyes. Spectacular, ethereal creatures stand firm and keep their heads straightforward. They're so sparkly! I could stare at them all day and never get bored. The crowd parts, and people rush past. They must be done. Courage and I turn and dare to venture closer. The Shrine Prostitute is putting his clothes back on. I catch a glimpse of his back. My stomach rolls in waves, and my breathing halts. I know that back. I've seen it in my nightmares for years. I turn to Courage and clutch his robe as my nose smashes into his chest. No, no, no!

"What's wrong?" He clutches me tight.

"My brother." Dread stabs me with miserable talons.

I dare to look again, and sure enough, he turns his head, his profile visible. Hate. He'll give us away, and we'll be killed on the spot. As he adjusts his toga, he glances up, and his eyes lock with mine.

He sees me! This is it. It's over. The angels' light fades.

Don't leave us! Not now.

The only reason we came this far is because of them. Hate beelines straight for me. Courage wraps his arms tighter around me. When Hate reaches us, sweat beads on his brow. His Adam's apple bobs as his arm muscles clench.

"Fear, what are you doing here? Are you crazy?" The side of his toga crumples within his fist.

What the fritz? Why's he acting concerned? He never cared before. "We're trying to rescue a friend from the harem," I blurt. *No!* Why the fritz do I talk without thinking?

Heavily dilated eyes dart into my soul. He must have visited the Temple druggery. His face twists. "Take me with you! Please, you've got to get me out of here."

My heart flutters. The pain in his voice cuts deep. But I still haven't forgiven him for all he did to me. Courage eases his grip.

"Please, I'll help you find your friend. Whatever you need. Just get me out of this horrible place."

I've never seen him beg before. I turn to Courage. "Crazy

as it sounds, maybe this is Abba's way of helping us find Happy?" I don't trust Hate, but it makes sense.

"This is a rotten idea, Fear, but I don't know any way around it."

"If he can help us find her, then we need him." The words are bitter on my tongue.

Courage turns to him and glares. "If you help us locate the girl, then we'll try to help you escape too. No promises."

I elbow Courage.

He clears his throat. "We'll do our best."

Hate sizes him up. "All right. You help me. I help you. It's a deal." He checks to see if people are watching. "I get an hour break between sessions where I have to go to the harems." He lowers his voice as another person in a robe passes by. "In forty-five minutes, you can wait in line outside my quarters. Request an audience with me, and I'll sneak you into the harems."

"If you get caught, you know what they'll do to you," cautions Courage.

"Even death would be more welcome than spending one more day here." He stares at his feet. "I'll steal a key from the prostitute next to me while she's occupied." He leaves.

I can't stop trembling. What have we gotten ourselves into?

As I head to the unisex bathroom, Courage follows. Entering a stall, I pull back my sleeve and punch a few buttons on my Micro-Communicator. Charity answers.

"Is the Hoverpod working yet?"

"Fabulous news, Fear. The Hoverpod is up and running!" A squeal forces me to cover the earpiece. Charity's voice on the other end is loud and clear. Too loud. *How do I turn this blasted thing down?*

"Shush, Charity, do you want me to get in trouble?"

"Sorry."

"Don't worry about it. That's fantastic news. We may need it soon."

"They're already on their way, but I'll let them know."

"Nice. My brother's up here, and he's going to help us. I'll contact you once we have Happy."

"Oh, this is getting exciting!"

She hangs up before I can say more. I let out a deep sigh. Things are falling into place. Good.

I exit the stall to see Courage leaning against the wall, tapping his foot. The angels may have left, but their presence lingers.

"Are you sure this is the best plan?" Courage asks.

Probably not. I shrug. "Do you have a better one?"

"Well no, and it does seem like Abba orchestrated this. I just don't trust your brother."

"Neither do I, but we can't leave him here. It's inhumane."

"You're right. Abba wouldn't want us to do that." Courage shuts up as a Temple Royal scampers past to visit the stalls. He lowers his voice. "I wish I knew he won't try anything with you. I mean, he tried to kill you, Fear."

"He looks pretty pathetic. I don't think he has it in him right now." I glance at the chandelier dripping diamonds from the picturesque ceiling. It might seem pretty on the exterior, but sorrow fills every inch of this place. "He's getting a taste of his own medicine by being here, you know."

Courage nods. We step aside and allow a group to exit the stalls. Every time someone tromps by, I'm afraid I'll pass out for lack of oxygen.

Breathe, Fear, just breathe.

Courage nudges my arm. I need to focus. I pull his hood

farther over his face and press my hood to his. Our own private tent.

"We can't let him suffer." He made me suffer for so long. Why do I even care? "We need to at least try to get him out of here." How have I become so nice? Months ago I would've been thrilled to let him rot in this horrible place.

Courage puffs into my face, which is uncomfortably close to his. This is frustrating for both of us.

"I do have good news, though. They got the Hoverpod working, and they're already on their way."

Courage moves away from me and straightens, letting out a long stream of air. "Just in the nick of time."

Someone eyeballs us. Shoot. "Walk to the wine counter with me." I push Courage out of the bathroom.

The barkeeper hands us golden goblets filled with a thick liquid resembling puréed cherries. I take a sip, and an iron taste fills my mouth. We spit it out together all over the floor. A Temple Royal frowns.

Blood.

"What the heck?" Courage looks as though he wants to set his tongue on fire.

I grab the goblet he's about to toss. "We don't have to drink it, but we need to look like we are. Pretend."

His nostrils flair, and I saunter about, Courage trailing me. Got to fit in. I pretend to relish the temple sights, gulping down my goblet of blood, trying to slaughter the minutes.

Courage leans close to my ear. "It's almost time for the prostitutes to be available again."

I nod and head to the silken curtains, only to find another person already standing before Hate's quarters, claiming his time.

This can't be happening. "What are we going to do? Wait

two more hours until he's available again? I don't want to stay in this awful place that long." My chest squeezes. A panic attack is the last thing I need.

Before Courage can even respond, the brilliant light returns. Once more, the angels appear on both sides of us and advance toward the man. When they reach him, they place a palm on either side of his hood. He clutches his head and stumbles to the other side of the temple. We jump to take his place, and the angels dissipate.

A quarter of an hour flies by, and Hate emerges from his tent of curtains. Seductiveness oozes from him. He swaggers as he approaches. A freshly washed toga hangs just so from his chest and hips. Sweaty hair has transformed to freshly washed, spiked in typical Hate fashion, some hanging in his black-lined eyes. Flawless skin covers his face, and his pouty lips are accentuated with just the right shade of lipstick to match his skin tone. An ugly soul wrapped in perfection. He flirts with his eyes and flicks his hair back as he grasps our palms and leads us into the tent. It's an act, and one he's quite good at.

His demeanor changes the second our curtain closes. He dangles something small and metal from his fingertips. "Here are the keys I stole from my neighbor." Hate gestures for us to sit on the circular bed.

"Why would she be given access to the harem and not you?" Courage keeps his voice down as we lower ourselves to the satin mattress.

A shudder runs through me. I never, ever wanted to be on a bed with Hate again.

"First off, it's the ladies' harem, so no, I wouldn't have keys to that, would I?" Hate's nauseating voice reminds me of my childhood. I shiver. Nothing's changed. He lowers his lashes. "I'm not an official Shrine Prostitute anyway, more of a Shrine

Prostitute in training. They don't let me have keys to anything yet."

"Mother sold you to here?"

Hate's face darkens, and his eyes narrow to slits. "No," he hisses. "She sold me to an Upper who ran the Pleasure House in the sleazy part of the city. A couple of loser Temple Royals, who frequent the place, told me I should work in the temple, not some random whorehouse. They promised me it would be a much better life. I took the job. Now I want out. This isn't what they promised."

His nose, which should be crooked, is once again perfectly shaped, accenting his high cheekbones. He was always better looking than me. "How did your nose get straight again?"

A gust of air whooshes past, and the curtain blows back, revealing a couple laughing and caressing nearby. Hate stiffens, then wrenches me close and kisses my neck, smothering me. *Get off!* I struggle while Courage swings at him and misses.

"We have to seem like we're having fun, remember?" Hate dodges another swing, pulling me to the side. He points to the lights illuminating us. "We have to at least pretend to do something other than talk."

Gambits, he's right. We're going to get caught if we keep this up. I go still and allow him to caress my hair and neck.

Courage's nostrils flair as he clenches his teeth. Tremors plague his body. He can't stand it—imagine how I feel!

Hate whispers in my ear. Ugly chills wrack me. "I had surgery on my nose, to answer your question. One of my regulars covered the bill. They don't allow anyone with defects to serve here, and they know I'm much too talented to get kicked out on account of my nose. It was an easy fix."

His touch repulses me. It takes everything I have not to

move away. This stinks I can't shut down my emotions as I used to. I change the subject. "Are you aware Mother became the town prostitute after you left?"

Hate quits caressing and laughs like a man with a few screws loose.

I shush him. "That's not funny."

"Yes, it is. She got what she deserved." He dips me in his arms and gives me a hard, smothering kiss. I don't care how good looking he is, his breath has always tasted like a corpse. Vomiting sounds like a good option right about now. "It's been too long since I've last kissed you, sister." Nasty is too nice a word for him.

He moves in for another kiss. "I'm not your sister." That stops him. His wide eyes alarm me. "Before she chased me off, Mother admitted I was adopted."

He moves back and frowns. "That takes some of the fun out of this."

"You're sick," I spit and flinch. Now he's going to hit me good.

He shrugs. "I like what I like. I can't help it."

I struggle for air. No hitting then?

Courage's head is going to explode any second now. I swear it. "Let's get this over with. Take us to Happy, *now*!"

"Calm down." Hate attempts to stroke Courage's cheek and gets walloped in the head.

"Don't touch me, you pervert!" Courage thrusts his chest out. His lips curl over his teeth, baring them like a rabid dog. I'm afraid his skinny neck is going to snap. Hate doesn't seem a bit intimidated as he gets in Courage's face. A ridiculous standoff. I wedge myself between the two seething knuckleheads.

"This isn't getting us anywhere," I remind them. "If you

want to escape, we should get Happy before we run out of time."

The three of us stand. Hate moves toward me, but Courage grabs me before Hate can. He kisses the side of my neck Hate didn't touch. My head spins. Courage's touch is much softer and gentler, and my body concedes. I swallow multiple times and narrow my eyes.

Hate's smirk sickens me. "Now you've figured it out. Don't wanna get caught *not* being naughty, if you know what I mean."

"What's the plan?" Courage snarls between kisses. His touch ignites my skin. It doesn't inflict pain or misery like Hate's.

"Fear and I will search for the girl. You stay back and get under the sheets. We need someone to be the distraction."

Courage pulls away from my neck. His eyes flash. "If you think I'll let you be alone with Fear, you're outta your head!"

Hate propels me aside, getting in Courage's face. "I guess you're out of luck, then. *You* need *me* to show you the ladies' Harem. And the only lady around is Fear. I can't go in there. Neither can you. So she's got to be the one. That leaves *you*, the distraction."

It must be pretty obvious to anyone outside this curtain we're not actually doing what one normally does with a prostitute. We're going to get caught soon. These guys need to quit fighting.

"You tried to kill Fear! Not to mention everything else you've done to her. How can I possibly trust you with her?"

Hate flinches and backs off. "What? I never tried to kill her."

My blood boils. He's such a liar.

Courage severs those inches as he plants himself firmly in

front of Hate's face. "The poison needle. Remember?"

I remember. It wasn't fun.

Hate's eyes shift as though he's searching his memory. "At the store?" He blinks at me. "I must've shot you up with more of the sedative than I thought."

"Sedative?" I glance at Courage. "It put me out for a week. They thought I was going to die." So it wasn't poison?

"I lost the syringe after Manly took off with you. I have no idea how much I put in you. I was only trying to conk you out, not kill you."

I don't know whether to believe him or not. Courage appears as conflicted as I feel. The laughter of the couple next to us turns into moaning, and I wish I could shove cotton in my ears. Oh yeah, it's supposed to look like we're doing that too. I pull Courage toward me and wrap my arms around him.

"Why would you carry sedative anyway?" Maybe Hate never actually wanted to kill me? Courage wraps his fingers in my hair, and my muscles tighten. His cheek rests against mine.

Hate stills, then he adjusts the sheets. "That's really none of your business."

I glare at him.

He backs off. "Listen, I need your help as much as you need mine. Please get me out of here. You guys are my rescue team as much as that little girl's. Don't let me down." His eyes plead with me.

How can he expect me to have sympathy for him? Yet I do. His anger before may've been a front to hide his vulnerability. Maybe actual feelings reside inside that shell of evil. Time will tell.

I give him a hard look. "Harem. Now."

Chapter 32

Courage takes my hand. "Are you sure you want to do this?"

I smile to let Courage know I'll be all right. He huffs, then grimaces as he gets under the sheets. Hate pushes me down onto them as well, and I land on Courage with a *thud*. Hate rams into my back.

"Ow! Get off!"

Courage attempts to roll away but hesitates. He knocks Hate off me while knuckles and kneecaps crunch into my sides.

"Ow again! Will you two stay still?"

Courage rolls his head near mine. "Are you hurt?"

I shake my head on the cushy pillows, moving farther from Hate.

"Shut up. We don't have a lot of time." Hate quiets us. "No one can see us leaving. Courage, use your arms and feet and move around to make it look like there are three of us in here. We'll leave the door unlocked and be back when the hour is up. When you hear the gong toll twice, you have five minutes left. Meet us behind the door. Then we'll make a run for it."

Courage nods and squeezes my hand. "I don't want to leave you alone with him."

"I'm fine. Quit worrying. Remember, we have angels on our side." I smile and give him a quick kiss on the cheek. What's gotten into me?

He exhales and puts his arms and legs up in the sheets, making a tent.

Hate and I crawl to the door. I hope none of the other prostitutes or customers emerge from behind their curtains. We're so close. He fumbles with the key, almost drops it, then slides it into the keyhole. The door swings open. We hurry in and close it. I turn the handle and find it locks from the outside.

"You said we'd leave it unlocked for him!"

Hate tries to open the door, and when he can't, he grabs my arm and leads me away.

"We'll slide the key underneath so he can unlock it. Quit worrying." He stops in a corridor and peers around the corner, fingers to his lips. After a minute, he leads me upstairs through many bends until we reach a landing. The Harems.

He shoves me flat against the wall right before someone heavy clomps past. Hate's hand covers my mouth. His eyes glint with evil. Fire lights within me. He hasn't changed. Why are we saving him? My heart drops. Because we have no choice. When the footsteps fade, he lurches away from the wall and yanks me down the hallway. We run past windows. Children and women mill about on the other side. I spot a girl who vaguely resembles Happy.

Please be her!

I want to smash the glass with something and drag her out

of there, but I think better of it. Three giant clay pots, planted with ferns, sit in the corner at the far end of the hall. We crouch behind them and wait. A few minutes later, two women, decorated in the loveliest clothing I've ever seen, emerge from the room.

"Where's that girl? She's always late."

The other woman chimes, "I heard they're replacing her with a new servant."

"It's about time. She's wretched." They shuffle down the hallway.

I know how I'm going to get in. I rip off my robe and hand it to Hate. He wrinkles his nose at my servant's outfit.

"What are you wearing?" After a moment, his eyes brighten. "That's perfect. You smart girl!" It's the first compliment he's ever given me. "You need to tell them Happy's sick and you need to take her to the Healer. Hopefully, they'll let you out with her."

"If that doesn't work, what should I do?"

"You're not a complete fool. Figure it out."

Abba, give me strength!

I stand and straighten the puffy dress. Lust coats his wandering eyes. He traces his fingertip from my lower calf to the back of my thigh.

"You're so beautiful."

I shove his hand away. "That doesn't give you the right to touch me whenever you want!"

I flinch, anticipating the inevitable blow. His lips tighten, and he sits in silence. Why didn't he smack me? Maybe he *had* changed. Or maybe he wants out of this place.

"I'm going in." I reach for the handle as someone yanks open the door from the other side, knocking me off balance.

"Where have you been?" An old woman's eyes scan me

from toe to head. "Oh good. They sent a new one. The other girl grew more stupid by the day." The woman assesses me, but she stops at my hair. Oh no. I didn't bring the wig.

"New fashion?" She fingers my hair. "How boring. Hope it goes out of style soon. What's your name, girl?"

"Fury," I lie.

"Let's hope your temperament doesn't match your name." She yanks me into the room. The door closes behind us. "I'm the harem mistress. You can call me Ma'am. Here are the girls, and there are the purification tubs." She points at lavish tubs. "The oils, lotions, and beauty supplies are over there." She points to a large vanity, stocked full of brushes, combs, bottles, and the like. "Now get to work on these girls. They're getting stinky in this heat. That one." She points at a little waif in the back whose head's down, her knees drawn tight to her chest. "She could use extra scrubbing since she refuses baths. Force her if you must."

The woman turns and shuffles into a back room separated by strings of hanging beads. I'm left standing in front of about fifteen girls who—with the exception of one—stare at me. So young for eyes so dead.

A breathtaking Persian rug lies underneath the group of girls. Finely woven pillows and cushions surround them. Each pillow has its own unique design. I glance at the richly decorated ceiling of dark wood. Whittled into it are delicate swirls. Crafted by a famous artist, no doubt. The elegant room is adorned with a gorgeous crystal chandelier.

"Hi. I'm Fury." My voice wavers. Blank stares respond. *Seriously, that's all you're going to give me?*

A ribbon encircles each girl's hair, tied back in a bun, and they each wear a different-colored kimono. I wish with all my soul I could take each of them out of this miserable place. The posh decorations are a small pittance for the horrors to come.

Something about my voice stirs the little waif in the back.
The one who needs "extra scrubbing." The standard bun the
other girls wear is noticeably absent from the back of her head.
Cascades of frizzy curls cover her face.

She lifts her head and tilts it as she looks at me. Our eyes
meet. My heart leaps in my chest. *Happy, it's you!*

She doesn't smile, but her eyes flicker. Either she's mad at
me, or she's pretending she doesn't know me. Good. I walk to
the back of the group and extend my hand. Hers trembles as
she takes mine. She's dirty, and her hair's in tangles. They
weren't joking. She's a mess.

"What's your name?" Hope she plays along.

She won't answer. One of the other girls speaks up. "I
think her name is Happy, but we call her Sadness."

I choke down tears. How has Happy transformed into
Sadness in such a short time? The other girls shine and don't
appear to need baths, but Happy isn't herself at all. The light is
stricken from her eyes. What's going on in that little head of
hers? I guide her to the purification baths. She still refuses to
acknowledge me.

"Would you like to get into the bath?"

The shake of her head is no surprise. I try a different tactic.
I guide her to the ornate vanity and have her sit on the padded
stool. Within my reach lies a beautiful silver hairbrush.

"Is it okay if I brush your hair, Happy?"

Her eyes glimmer when she hears her real name. She
doesn't answer, but I take her silence for a yes. I set the brush
next to us and begin lovingly and painstakingly separating
each knot with my fingers, trying not to hurt her. *Focus on
breathing.* She's here. I have her. *Abba, give me strength.*

When I've done enough finger raking, I grab the brush,

start at the tips, and work my way upward. A burn mark screams from the back of her neck. My fingers settle on her arm. *What have they done to you?*

I bend so only she can hear me. "We're here to rescue you." A hint of light flickers in her eyes but dies out. "I need you to pretend to get sick. Really, really sick. Then we can leave for the Healer. I will get you out from there. Do you understand?"

Invisible to the rest of the room, her slight nod assures me she does. I finish with her hair as she stares mindlessly at the mirror. She's in there. She's got to be. We make eye contact in the mirror, and she snaps out of her trance. She gasps and falls off the stool, holding her stomach and writhing as though in pain. Gagging and gurgling.

She's good at this. Wow. I mean, I knew from the play she was a good actress, but this…this seems real. Is she actually sick? It's all an act…right?

"Help!" I cry out. "Help, this girl needs help!"

The harem mistress rushes into the room, and the rest of the girls scramble out of the way.

She takes one glance at Happy and waves her hand. "Oh, it's just her. She's faking it."

My blood pulses in my ears, and my legs weaken. "No, she's not."

"Oh, yes. She's done this before to avoid the baths."

She turns to walk away, and I jam my fingers down Happy's throat. *Abba, please don't let any of the girls say anything.* She vomits. The woman turns to us and huffs.

"Fine. Take her to the Healer. Maybe she *is* sick this time." She smacks Happy's head. "Stupid girl."

I resist the urge to kick the woman. How dare she?

Happy and I head for the door, but I take one last look

around. All these girls, their beautiful innocent faces. My heart tears in two. I can only save one.

The harem mistress unlocks the door, and I whisk Happy out of the room as fast as I can. Buried behind the plants, Hate hides right where I left him.

"This is what all the fuss was about?" He approaches, one eyebrow arched.

I ignore him. "Let's get Courage and get out of here."

"Fine by me."

We rush halfway down the corridor when a servant girl reaches the top of the stairs. We fall into a normal pace. She keeps her gaze locked on us as we pass. We do our best to act normal until she's behind us. As soon as her back turns, we fly down the rest of the long corridor and into the stairwell. So far, so good.

Hate catches my eye. "That girl was the replacement servant for the harem."

We run.

Happy clasps my hand with an iron grip. Halfway down the zigzagging stairs, a muscular guard blocks the way. Rage storms his face as he lunges. Hate rips a dagger from his toga and plunges it into the man's gut, slicing upward. The man cries out, clutches his belly, and sinks to the floor.

"Come on! Hurry!" Hate sprints down the stairs. We follow, Hate still grasping the dagger dripping with blood.

I clutch Happy's hand tighter. "Do I need to be concerned you have that?"

"Why should you be? It just saved your life." His neck cranes around the next corner.

"You just killed a man." Is remorse even possible for him?

He leers at me. "Would you rather I'd done nothing? All three of us would've died, about...uh...thirty seconds ago.

That sound like a better plan?"

"Fine. Do it your way." I force myself to refocus. We need to find a way out of here, and we need to make sure Courage comes with us.

We reach the white door at the prostitute quarters.

"Hand me the key."

Hate collects it out of his toga and tosses it to me. I bend to put it through the crack at the bottom of the door, only to find it's sealed.

"The key won't fit." I straighten. "What are we going to do?" Oh, this is bad.

"We could leave him?" Hate suggests.

"I could never, ever do that!" I pound on the door. An immediate knock startles me. Here's hoping that's Courage.

I knock back. "There has to be a way."

I pull hard on the hinges, but they hold fast. The knocking continues. Courage must be concerned by now. I knock again.

"You two need to stop the knocking, or someone's going to start asking questions."

I ignore him. "Why doesn't it have a stupid key hole on this side?"

Hate rolls his eyes. "So guys like me can't escape when the guards aren't watching."

The only way to get through this door is to break it down. I lift my foot to kick with all of my might when Hate grabs my shoulder.

"What are you doing? You're going to give us away for sure, and then we're all dead." He pushes me to the side and seizes his dagger. "I knew this blade would come in handy." He sticks the still-bloody tip into the door's crack and wiggles until the latch opens.

Courage stands outside, his face pale. He lunges through

the door, and we shut it together. "It's about time!" He touches the small of my back and leans near my ear. "Did he try anything?"

"No, I'm fine."

He lets out a deep breath, then crouches next to Happy and gives her a hug. "You have no idea how good it is to see you." She releases him and says nothing. His eyebrows furrow.

None of us have time to worry. I tug his arm, and the four of us rush up the stairs and through the corridors. Hate leads the way. I contact Charity through the wrist Communicator.

"Where should the Hoverpod land?" she asks.

I veer in Hate's direction as we ascend. "Where are we going?"

"Tell them to land on the west side. Near the loading dock."

I let Charity know. We reach the correct level in no time and jump from the stairs into the corridor. Hate waves his hand to silence us. We move to a dark corner and watch as a security guard, the harem mistress, and a wrinkled, old man — must be the Healer — walk through the hallway.

"They've got to be here somewhere," the harem mistress frets.

Sweat drips from my forehead. This place is suffocating. If we get caught, I'll never forgive myself for not getting Happy out.

We wait until they pass.

"They must've found the guard," Hate whispers.

I quicken my steps. We haven't been caught yet. Praying it stays that way.

Hate peers around another corner. "This is it."

Happy clutches my hand tight.

I steal a glance at her. "We're almost there."

We reach the door that leads to the loading dock, and with one push, it opens. Hate laughs as we emerge into fresh air. "That was far too easy."

If Courage rubs his forehead one more time, I'm afraid a genie will pop out of the top of his skull. "If that door is open, they're probably about to use this loading dock. We need to hurry."

"I agree." I ease my hand out of Happy's so I can use my Micro-Communicator. I punch the buttons. "Charity, they can come get us now."

"They're on their way," she replies.

"Is Trouble with Manly?"

"I haven't heard from Manly." A tremor sneaks into her voice.

Uh-oh. What's she not telling me? "What do you mean, you haven't heard from him?" How can Manly not be with the Hoverpod? He's the pilot.

"I don't see them yet, do you?" Courage bumps into me.

I shift my focus to the sky. A sudden, eerie silence comes, not from the sky, but from behind us. We turn.

Hate stands less than a yard away with the dagger at Happy's throat.

Chapter 33

Courage freezes next to me.

I swallow hard. "What are you doing?"

He grins his terrible grin. "I will exchange this girl's freedom for yours." His dark eyes drill into mine.

"Why are you doing this?" I suppress the desire to scream at him.

Hate's eyes glow. "Fear, you and I, we could rule this place. Don't you see? Prostitutes in high standing climb the ladder of prosperity so easily here." He fiddles with the dagger at Happy's throat, almost seeming to forget his captive as he leans forward. "We would make such a good team. With your beauty and my skill, we could be the most popular team at the temple. We could live like queens! They respect me here. I have connections. I'm sure they would accept you as my partner. All I need to do is ask."

I can't believe what I'm hearing. How could I be such a moron? My breathing quickens. *I thought this was your plan, Abba? How could you let him deceive us like this?* "You never wanted

out of here, did you? You just wanted to use Happy to get me
to stay."

Hate's eyes narrow as his smile widens. His voiceless
response is enough to confirm my suspicions.

"That was you yesterday, wasn't it? I knew someone was
watching me. You must've known we were searching for
someone."

He ignores my question. "Fear, you have no idea what
you're missing. You'd get to live in a posh harem full of all the
wonderful things life has to offer. Money, drugs, sex, parties,
expensive jewelry. You name it, it's yours. Come, be with me."
His pleading eyes don't even tempt me. "Stay with me, and
Happy can leave. This is a good life."

"That's not the life I want. You're crazy."

"You're wrong, Hate." Courage finds his voice. "The good
life is down there, with family and love and people who care
about you. If you come with us, you can have all that."

Hate's face softens as he considers Courage's option. It
doesn't last long, and soon a mask of steel coats his features.
He thrusts the dagger closer to Happy's neck. Her face
scrunches as she whimpers. Tears drip down her cheeks and
fall off the tip of her chin.

Courage steps forward, hand outstretched. "Please, let her
go. Put the dagger down and come with us."

Hate sneers at Courage. "This is the life *I* want. You have
no idea...what I went through growing up." He turns toward
me. "But you do, Fear. You should understand. Here I have
power. They love me here."

"That's not love." Not even close.

"Shut up." The blade trembles as though he's going to
plunge it deep into her neck any second. "Come with me, or
she gets tossed to the Uppers. Once they lay eyes on fresh

meat, they can't resist. Or maybe I'll just slice her up and be done with it."

If I go with him, I lose everything. My life…I'll never see my friends again. I'll never see Manly again. My family. Everything. Lost to me forever. But if I don't, I'll lose Happy. And she'll lose herself. I can't let these animals rip her to shreds.

"Don't hurt her." I step forward and grab Happy's arm. "Take me instead."

"No!" Courage's scream pierces my heart. "No Fear, you can't."

"What else can I do?" My flat tone deadens the air.

Hate clamps his fingers around my arm and yanks the knife away from Happy. He shoves her toward Courage and pulls me close. He swings the dagger to my exposed neck. Courage ushers Happy far away. He hides her behind a wall but continues to spy on us. A shrill laugh gurgles from Hate's throat as the cold blade, sticky with dried blood, presses against my skin. He's insane. With one fluid movement, he sheaths his dagger and whirls me around to face him.

My chin shoots up. "Why didn't you just take me before we rescued Happy? You had the chance."

"It had to be your choice." False sweetness laces his voice. "You made the right one."

He grabs my shoulders and leans down, and I brace myself. Another of his soul-crushing kisses. Just great. The door behind him flings open, and I jump. A Temple Royal enters the loading dock, and Hate cowers like a little boy caught with his hand in the cookie jar. He lets go of one of my arms and grasps the other tight.

"Hate, what are doing out here? I've searched the entire temple for you." The Temple Royal eyes me up and down.

"You know associating with servants is forbidden."

"Yes, sir." He shrinks into a sliver of a man.

"Don't let it happen again."

"No, sir."

"You are wanted in the Prostitute Quarters. Someone personally requested you."

Hate's face is so tense, he's about to burst a blood vessel.

"You do remember what that means, don't you, boy?" The Temple Royal nears us. "If you refuse anyone during your training, you will no longer advance to an official Shrine Prostitute. Have you striven to get to this point, only to fail now?"

Hate shakes his head. The man inches closer until he stands directly in front of him, practically bumping me out of the way. Hate never lets go of my arm.

The Temple Royal leans forward and tilts his pointy chin toward Hate's ear. "It would be such a shame for you to be no longer available. You have become quite a favorite." Hate breathes heavily as his face turns a tomato shade. "You'd better hurry. Your client is waiting." The Temple Royal jerks his head to me, his hood falling askew. "And you. You get back to work." I startle, stand straighter, and nod.

Hate bristles and takes one last look at me, frowning. He squeezes my arm hard, then releases me and tails the Temple Royal inside.

The madman has lost.

My life is my own once more. Tension gushes from me, limb by withering limb. I have no doubt Hate's veins throb with bloodlust. Pity the man who gets the pleasure of his company next.

The Hoverpod bursts through the puffy clouds above and rests midair, awaiting my signal. We're safe. My heartbeat slows from the steady rhythm it plays in my chest. I yell through the noise of the engine at my Communicator. "Drop the ladder!"

That Temple Royal knows something's up. People will be here any minute.

The ladder drops, and I grasp the rungs, guiding Happy to hold on as well, right beneath me. Courage boxes her in from below. We've got her. She's not going anywhere.

"Hold on tight!" I shout above the noise. A ranch hand kneels at the edge of the opening, ready to pull us up. All three of us are yanked to safety. At the wheel sits Lanky. Alone. Trouble isn't here. Schnitzel fritz. Not good.

"Thank you so much," I yell over the whirr of the motor. The Hoverpod soars off, and we slam back in our seats. The ranch hand settles across from us.

"Thank you," echoes Courage.

"Where's Trouble?" Courage and I ask in unison.

"I thought Manly was going to drive this thing." Where in the Gliding Lands is he?

Leaning forward, I inspect the craft to make sure he isn't hiding in the cockpit somewhere. He's so big, I wouldn't be able to miss him. Stupid me.

"I don't know where either of those guys are. You'll have to talk to your new friend Charity about that."

"Trouble's not still at Charity's, is he?" Courage taps Lanky's shoulder. "I thought you were supposed to pick him up."

Lanky clears his throat. "I was supposed to pick him up when Charity gave me the all-clear message. She never did."

Courage and I glance at each other. "Can you get him now?" Worry lines crease Courage's brow.

"I drove by that area before heading here. It looks like guards are blocking it. Don't worry. As long as he's with Charity, he should be okay."

My eyes flutter. "But...we can't leave him."

Lanky clears his throat once more. "Charity told me she borrows a Hoverpod sometimes. Maybe she'll be able to bring him back."

Courage lunges forward and digs his nails into Lanky's shoulder. "I'm not leaving him."

Lanky turns and peels Courage's hand off him. "Listen, if we go over there, we're going to get caught. Sentinels, remember? What do you want me to do?"

I place my palm on Courage's arm. "Let me call her."

Courage nods.

I tap my Micro-Communicator. Static fills the little cabin of the Hoverpod. I press the button again. More static. "It's not working." I squeeze his arm. "She'll bring him back, don't worry."

His eyebrows draw together. "We don't know that."

"If she doesn't, we still have this Hoverpod. We can come back and get him." I hope.

"I want him out now." Anger skitters around the edges of his weary voice.

Believe me, the feeling's mutual.

Happy starts crying, and I wrap my arms around her. She

shoves me away and cranes her neck toward the window. It's going to take a while for her to heal. I swallow hard.

"I do too. But we can't get caught. We need to get her to safety first."

Courage softens as he looks at Happy, but then pushes his back hard against the backrest.

I sigh. I've never been this exhausted. We did it. We saved her. Why doesn't it feel like a victory?

Happy falls asleep and slumps on my shoulder. Courage stays still beside me, his intensity vibrating throughout the small cabin of the Hoverpod.

Trouble, where are you?

When we arrive at the Fallen, everyone swarms Happy, welcoming her back.

"They're back. They rescued Happy!"

"Happy's safe!"

"She's back! They did it!"

"Why's Courage wearing makeup?"

Faces beam, smiles abound. Hugs overwhelm. I've never heard people say they're proud of me. I could get used to it. I catch Happy's expression out of the corner of my eye. People close in, closer and closer to the rescued yet broken girl. She recoils. Too much, too soon. I careen Happy away from the crowd.

"Please, give her time. She's been through a lot. She just needs time." She needs to heal. Things won't be normal again for a while.

Granny walks up to Happy. "Come with me, sweetheart. I'll make you some food."

Granny takes her hand. Happy snatches it away and clings to me. It's clear she's going to have a hard time trusting people for a while.

The lines on Granny's forehead deepen, and she plunges her hands into her apron pockets.

I bite the inside of my cheek. "Don't worry. Let's give her the Medical Room. I don't think she needs a lot of people around her."

I push through the cheering crowd and take Happy to the Medical Room. She sits on the cold floor in the corner, knees tucked to her chest. I cover her with a soft blanket. Crackers and dehydrated fruit strips wait to be eaten inside the cupboard. I fill a glass with water and set it all on the counter.

"You'll be safe in here." I point to the door. "You can lock it from the inside." I walk to the door. "I need to take care of some things. Make sure you unlock the door if I knock five times in a row."

She won't look at me. My stomach drops, and I close the door. It's just temporary, right? She'll be fine.

Stepping into the group, I find the pats on my back are more annoying than encouraging as Courage and I search for Trouble. Maybe Manly picked him up earlier? Where is he, anyway?

After all the congratulations, questions, and compliments, the group filters out the door. Courage and I are left alone with Melody and Harmony. From the looks of things, they may want to ring my neck. How are we going to explain this? Harmony's arms are folded, and Melody's face reminds me of a cat stuck in a tree.

"Where's Trouble?" Harmony squints, her mouth turning down as her eyes pierce mine.

In my weakened state, I settle on a white lie. "He's still with Charity. She's going to bring him back when it's safe."

Relief floods their faces, and Melody nods. "Oh, good." She glances at Harmony. "We were so worried."

My gut wrenches. After I endure their hugs, they leave. I feel like throwing up.

Courage drops his head to his chest and sighs. "Why did you lie? We don't actually know where he is."

"I'm a work in progress, okay? What was I supposed to tell them?"

He shakes his head.

"I'm sorry," I mutter.

Courage paces the empty cabin. "I don't understand. Did Manly pick him up from Charity's before Lanky came to get us?"

"I hope so. That would be awful if he got left up there." I cringe at the thought of going back to rescue him. I never want to set foot in the blasted Gliding Lands again.

I clasp the Communicator and pull it to my lips. "Call Charity." It lights up. The lack of static is encouraging.

"Hello?" Charity's voice reaches my ears from the tiny box.

"Charity, what's going on with Trouble? Is he still with you?" Silence rings through the Communicator. My chest pounds. "We need to get him. Where is he?" Does my voice sound as desperate as I feel?

"I tried, I really tried." Charity's broken voice proves something's gone wrong. Terribly wrong.

"What?" I demand. "What did you try?"

"I tried to stop him. But he was so determined. I—I'm so sorry."

"Tell me already. What happened to him?" The holographic image of Charity fidgets on my wrist.

"He told me he was going to protect you from your brother." Her voice diminishes with each passing word.

"You told him my brother was at the temple?" I wail.

"Was I not supposed to?"

Breathing in the musky cabin air, I compose myself. I will not scream at her. I will not. "No, Charity. I never told you not to tell him. It's not your fault."

Courage listens beside me. His brows scrunch together. "Ask her if she knows anything else, anything that might lead us to him."

"I heard him. He's standing right there, for goodness' sakes. And no, unfortunately, I only know what I've heard. My neighbor said a temple robe was stolen from his clothesline. I'm guessing it's where Trouble was headed. To help you both in the temple."

Courage and I groan. My insides burn; my head spins. "Thanks, Charity. Call us if you think of anything else."

Courage and I settle on a couch for a late night as we talk through possible plans to get our best friend back. I despise the thought of returning, but neither of us can leave him there.

We have to go back.

Chapter 34

While Courage grabs food from the kitchen, Granny stops by to check on how I'm doing.

"With Abba's help, I'll be all right." Manly's face comes to mind. I miss him so much. "Where's Manly? I haven't seen him. Or Faithful. What's going on?"

Granny pulls an envelope from her pocket. "I'm not sure how to tell you this, but they went back to the house. They left this." She hands it to me.

I turn it over in my hand, open the flap, and scan the handwriting. "Why would they leave now? I thought Manly was going to help with the mission. Wasn't he going to fly during the rescue?"

"He was. I'm not sure why they left. The letter isn't clear."

Isn't clear? That doesn't sound right. "Aren't you worried about them?" I sure am.

"Oh, honey, I've been too busy taking care of all the kids to worry." She chuckles. "Manly and Faithful can take care of themselves."

A gangly boy rushes in. "Granny, we need you in cabin four. Snicker and Roughly are fighting again. They broke a lamp this time."

Granny sighs. "Abba is sure testing my patience."

I give her my best sympathetic smile. She turns and follows the boy. My thoughts return to the letter. Why did they leave? What could possibly be more important than Happy's rescue? Manly promised to help. Shirking his responsibilities isn't like him.

I clutch the letter and draw it closer.

Dear Granny,
Faithful and I have decided to go home to visit Daddy. We're aware this is bad timing, but it's something we need to do. Sorry for the inconvenience.
Manly

Seriously, Manly? That letter is so vague, I should smack you. Whatever. I have bigger things on my mind. Like saving a close friend from an untimely death.

Courage enters with two steaming plates of food, which we devour. After I tuck Happy in for the night, I meet Courage on the couches outside of the Medical Room.

His face droops, and a burden presses his shoulders down. I plop next to him. Maybe I can cheer him up. "You look terrible."

He smirks. "Yeah, it wouldn't kill you to run a brush through your hair either."

I crack a smile and shove him. Jerk.

His laugh quickly turns into a frown. "How are we going to get him back, Fear?"

My brain throbs. "I don't know." I shut my eyes only to snap them open moments later. "I'm just so ticked at Manly for not showing up. What the fritz was he thinking? And Lanky! He shoulda got Trouble out while we were up there." My ears burn.

"That's not fair to Lanky. You know he couldn't have gotten past those Sentinels." Courage pats my knee. I stiffen, and he quickly withdraws. "As far as Manly goes, I have no clue. Guess he wasn't the guy you thought he was."

I frown. Is he right? Could Manly really be someone other than the stand-up guy I know?

Courage grabs my arm, bringing me back to my senses. "Don't worry. We'll just get Lanky to fly up and get him. Shouldn't be too hard. They don't monitor flights as closely as they used to. Lazy bunch of…" He pauses. "Maybe it's better if I don't tell you what I think of them."

I grin. "Probably not." I inhale deeply. "Gambits, I hope you're right."

"Let's hope I am." Silence fills the room. Courage drops his chin and rubs the back of his neck. "Listen. I'm sorry for the… in the temple…the…well…the kisses."

I glance away. "We did what we had to do to survive, Courage. It's okay. Really, it is."

"Glad you're not upset." He slides his knee away from mine. "I know you could never enjoy stuff like that from me."

"Don't sell yourself short. In other circumstances, maybe I would've." Did I really just say that? Heat flushes my cheeks.

His smile is small, but a flush tinges his cheeks as well.

We're both too tired to say more. I'm confident whatever happens, Abba's on our side.

I'm so sleepy.

Courage's head drops to my shoulder, and I fall asleep.

Waking to find Courage and I spent the entire night on the same couch is nothing short of problematic. Pure and utter awkwardness.

I try not to make eye contact as we get ready for our day.

Soon after we finish breakfast, Charity calls. "This is bad. This is so, so bad!"

Great. Just what we need. More bad news. "Please, spit it out." She has to make everything so dramatic.

"The top story of this morning's news is that a boy was found in the temple who wasn't supposed to be there. Now he's getting challenged in the Pen for his actions. It must be Trouble, I know it!"

I grip the arms of my chair.

"They usually behead people on the spot who aren't supposed to be there. I'm not sure why they didn't this time." Charity's voice drips with tears.

My stomach clenches. Trouble is going to die.

I turn off my Communicator without even saying goodbye and close my eyes. A painful headache envelopes my skull. "Oh, Trouble, how could you let this happen?"

Courage wraps his boney arms around me. I weep on his shoulder. His tears sear my soul and wet the back of my shirt. Only Abba can comfort us now.

After a few minutes, Charity calls again. I hesitate and sniff. Not really in the mood to talk.

"Answer it," Courage prods.

I wipe my nose on the back of my hand and hit the button. "It's happening today, Fear. *This* afternoon at two."

Someone let a herd of elephants loose inside my chest, and they're stampeding all over my heart.

Courage grabs my arm and clutches the Communicator. "Where? Which county are they holding the Challenge in?"

Charity's holographic figure takes off her horrible shoes. "They always use the Pen in the county of the one who's Challenged so the family can say goodbye."

"Or watch their beloved one die." My voice is completely dead.

"That could be a possible motive, true," she agrees.

Courage steps in. "That means he's here, in Ranch County. Maybe there's still time to save him."

"How are we going to get there in time?" I ask. "It would take the whole day or longer to drive. Plus, our Hoverpod is almost out of fuel."

"Wait right there. I'm coming to get you." She ends the connection.

"Thanks," I say to no one.

I face Courage, his arms limp at his sides. He stares over my shoulder. What's he looking at? I turn and find Melody with tears in her eyes. I'm struck speechless.

"Save who?" Her voice is small but firm.

I don't know how to tell her.

"Save *who*?" she repeats louder.

Courage walks toward her, and she melts in his arms. "I'm sorry, Melody."

She understands. Her brother is in need of saving. We blew it. She weeps, and I struggle to keep my own tears at bay.

I command my mouth to speak. "There's still hope. Maybe we can save him. We can try." My words ring stronger than my faith.

Courage straightens. "She's right. We might be able to save him. Come with us."

Whether Melody believes him or not, I can't tell. But either way, she agrees to come along.

Charity arrives much later than we expected. I'm ready to scream. We're running out of time.

"Sorry I'm late." She's breathless as she climbs out of the borrowed Hoverpod. "A few of the children in the PediaLab were having meltdowns. It took over an hour to calm them all down."

Melody crosses her arms. "Why couldn't you just leave?"

Charity stumbles, then regains her composure. "I kept asking if I could leave, and they told me to shut up or they'd whip me." She softens her face. "Remember, I'm just a servant."

Melody shrugs, uncrosses her arms, and sulks to the other side of the room, looking more mournful by the minute. I tiptoe my way over to her and lean close to her ear.

"I know this is hard, Melody. But Charity is helping us when she doesn't have to. We need to be grateful for that."

A single tear rolls halfway down her cheek. She wipes it away and gives a curt nod.

Leaving her, I check on Happy one last time. She sleeps on the bed in the Medical Room, covered to her chin in a lightweight blanket. Something about her unsettles me. Maybe it's the fact she's yet to speak one syllable.

The three of us climb into Charity's Hoverpod and head for the Pen. A pallor creeps across Melody's face. I'm not sure if it's fear for her brother's life or if she's getting sky-sick from her first flight. Maybe both.

The flight is fairly short, considering it would take much, much longer on the ground. By the time we arrive, cheering meets our ears from the arena. They're cheering for death. Bunch of psychos.

I spot the giant concrete arena looming in the distance. My throat tightens.

We park the Hoverpod, jump out, and separate from Charity. Don't want to get her in trouble. Even Upper servants are higher class than us Downers.

Courage leads Melody and me. "There's probably another Challenge before Trouble's."

My legs tremble the closer we get to the arena.

We round the corner and reach the entrance where a sign hangs, announcing Challenges and their times. I read the names.

Contenders: Hate (Challenger) Trouble (Accused) 12:00 P.M.

My stomach sours. Of course Hate challenged him. I'm gonna kill him.

Courage lashes out at Charity. "You told us it started at two!"

Her voice cracks. "They must've changed it."

A large clock hangs on the wall. 12:24 PM blares from its screen.

The Pen already holds Trouble.

We're too late.

Chapter 35

Melody crumples to the ground. Charity rushes to her. Courage charges through the gates. Running after him, I survey the scene before me.

The concrete open arena is jam packed with hundreds of onlookers as it always is when there's a Challenge. Two small figures stand in the middle of the Pen, encircled by a high wall of concrete and thick glass. They're both still moving, so he's not dead. Yet.

We run through the concessions, pushing people aside. When we get closer, we head down the stairs to the front. Courage speeds forward like a madman, apparently unafraid of taking a tumble. He reaches the bottom in no time and presses his face against the glass. His body shudders. I reach him in seconds.

No. This can't be real. Two bloody figures, one scampering about, the other now crumpled on the ground.

"Trouble!" I smash my hands against the thick glass. It's useless. He can't hear me. My legs feel as though they're covered in cement. I will my body to reach my friend lying in his own blood, but I can't. He's enshrouded within a glass coffin, and I can't break through. No!

The brilliant light reappears out of nowhere. An angel, the same one from the temple, stands beside me. "Do not fear."

Tears stream down my cheeks. *I'm not afraid! I'm angry.* The agony on my friend's face is more than I can bear. Pain stabs like needles until I want to scream. They can't do this to him!

Courage jumps onto the edge where the concrete ends and the glass wall starts. Surely he's not going to climb over?

"Get down." I grab his ankle. "You can't get past that!"

He shakes his foot free. His forehead creases, his jaw set. "Watch me."

He stretches his arms high and presses his body flat against the smooth glass. It's too high. He jumps, trying to reach the top of the glass, and almost falls. Out of the corner of my eye, I spot a Sentinel in the higher sections. He's heading our way.

"Courage! We need to move."

His gaze darts toward the Sentinel. Another joins him. "Up." He points to the stairs we just descended and jumps off the ledge. Step for step, he matches my pace. "Hoverscooter." He motions to the landing above.

My stomach flutters. "What? Are we going to steal it?"

"Borrow." He glances back. "Hurry. They're getting closer."

My mind races as I pump my legs up the stairs, each muscle straining. We reach the landing, and he passes me, elbowing two people out of the way. I'm hot on his heels as he topples a guy near the Hoverscooter and jumps on. "Quick!"

My leg flings over the side, and I plop my bottom snug behind him and wrap my arms around his sweat-drenched middle. His clammy shirt clings to his slender body. I slam my chest into his back. "Go!"

Scanning the Pen, I catch Hate rifling through the weapons box. I glance at Trouble. He's weaponless. Hate runs screaming toward Trouble and smashes his torso with a horrible object full of spikes and jagged wooden pieces.

"No!" Blood pounds in my ears. "Courage, go!" I scream. The Hoverpod fails to move an inch. The Sentinel approaches quickly.

The audience sends up a wild roar. Their crazed stomping reverberates through the entire arena. Trouble lays in a nauseating heap of blood, skin, and bones. I kick the sides of the hoverscooter. Why won't it move? The booming loudspeaker declares Hate the winner. A Hover-Chariot hurtles in, led by six white tigers. Hate is tossed into the chariot, and a woman in a leather bikini offers a crown of flowers for his bleeding head. The tigers amble around the Pen, dragging a worn-out Hate behind them. I hope they knock him out of that chariot and trample him.

"Hurry!" I slap Courage's back. Trouble needs us.

"I'm trying." He pumps the levers. It still doesn't move. He fiddles with the buttons and gadgets. The man Courage knocked over is propped up on his elbows. Oh no, he looks angry.

"How high can these things go?"

"I don't know." He presses a few more buttons. Red button. Blue one. Nothing.

"I've never seen a Hoverscooter more than two feet off the ground." I grip his waist harder. "How do we know this thing will clear the top of the glass?" The angry man climbs to his feet and lunges, but the Sentinel cuts him off.

"We'll find out." Orange button. The motor roars to life, and we zoom into the air just as the Sentinel reaches us.

Courage steers it up, two feet...three. Now we're over the crowd's heads, but just barely.

"I don't think it's built to go that high." My mouth turns to cotton as he zooms down toward the wall. Four feet. The engine shudders, and my heart seizes. *Oh Abba, help us!* "That wall's gotta be seven feet high." I scrunch my eyes closed.

The wind presses me down as we're lifted higher.

"We'll clear it!" He yells over the engine and the roaring crowd. I fling my eyes open. Six feet. The engine shudders again and slows.

"We need more clearance!" I cringe as the wall comes closer. We're not going to make it. Glass shatters around us. My body rocks forward, then back, then I'm falling. Fast.

I hit the ground hard. Shocks ripple through me.

I open my eyes, and my vision swims. Clouds. Pretty clouds in the sky. What am I doing here? Shudders ricochet through my body. I lay my hand on something smooth and sharp. Glass. My head calms, and shakily I sit up. Broken glass surrounds me. Courage lies in a pile not far away. His legs move. He's still alive. So am I. Shaken and bruised, but okay.

I dig my hands into the dirt and glass, ignoring the sharpness pricking my skin. Standing, I gape at the wall. The glass shattered halfway down, and a faint glow emanates from behind it. I squint into what looks like the sun. The same brilliant angels stand on the other side, blocking the way. Two dazed Sentinels stand on the steps, unable to continue forward.

Thank you, Abba, for sending them and stopping the Sentinels.

The crowd continues to cheer. They think it's all part of the act.

Got to get to Trouble.

I peel my eyes away from the spectacle to find Courage crawling across the ground, then kneeling by his friend's side, clutching his hand.

I run to them and topple to my knees beside Trouble, his body battered and bloody.

"No," I cry, burrowing my face in my hands. "No, no! You can't die, you can't!" I straighten. "Quick, Courage, let's lift him. We can get him out of here." Trouble's eyes flutter open. He reaches out a disfigured hand and rests it on my knee.

"But I'm having so much fun in here."

"Stop being stupid." Courage's voice trembles as he lifts Trouble's head, places it in his lap, and strokes his hair.

"We can get you out. I know we can." I scan the arena for an escape. Hate looks straight at me from his chariot hundreds of feet away. I will never forgive him. Never.

"He's not going anywhere, Fear." Courage drops his head, and a tear trickles down his nose. It lands on Trouble's face.

"It's not nice...to leak on people."

I crack a smile. Even in pain, he's trying to cheer us up.

Courage wipes his nose. "You big dummy. Why'd you have to try to save us?"

"They didn't name me Trouble for nothing." He coughs, and his head rolls to the side.

Courage tenses. "Don't leave me, buddy. Best friends stick together."

"You have Brave now."

"Brave?" Courage asks.

Trouble's eyes sharpen and clamp onto mine. "Carry...this new name...as a reminder." A mischievous twinkle flickers in his eye. *"He* agrees, apparently."

"Who?" I choke out.

"Abba." Trouble's voice weakens.

Courage shakes his head. "You're not making any sense."

"It's okay, I'm going home." He tries his best to grin at

Courage. His eyes roll back. His breath leaves his body.

I arch my back and fling my head to the sky. "No!" Horrible stinging pierces every fiber in me. He can't be dead!

Sentinels appear at opposite sides of the arena.

"We have to go. Now." Courage still cradles Trouble's lifeless head.

"We can't leave him here. Not like this." I refuse.

"He's gone." The Sentinels move closer, and Hate's chariot heads our way. "We have to get out of here." Courage lays Trouble's bloody head on the dirt, fiery hair slipping through his fingertips. With one last look, he clutches my hand and heads for the Hoverscooter, dragging me with him.

"We can't leave his body! It isn't right!" Tightness squeezes me as my eyes wash with tears. Courage continues to yank me forward. I can't see anything. Blinking, I clear my vision.

The crowd snaps me back to reality as the stomping grows in volume, goading the Sentinels to catch us. The angels remove themselves, and the Sentinels attempt to get over the broken glass wall. Not a single audience member lifts a finger to help.

We right the toppled Hoverscooter and jump on. He hits the orange button, and soon we head the way we came. We'll behead the Sentinels if they don't move.

Whoosh!

We narrowly make it through the wall. I glance back and see the Sentinels' heads are still intact. We reach the top of the arena, and our Hoverscooter sputters and dies. We drop and land with a *thud*. I push myself off Courage's back, but he grabs me and swings me off the seat, tugging my arm so hard I'm sure to have a good bruise later.

Courage grips my hand, whirling us up a flight of stairs

and past a security point. I jerk my head around. Where are those Sentinels? No sight of them. Our feet pound the concrete until my lungs pinch and I wheeze.

I trample out of the arena alongside Courage. Circling the concrete walls of death, we whiz down an abandoned stairway, dodging caution tape. I drop Courage's hand and enter the darkness below. We tuck ourselves into a secluded tunnel; it looks as if no one's ventured in here for ages. Cobwebs grace the walls, and stagnant water puddles on the floor. A mouse skitters past my feet. I pant hard as I catch my breath. Courage envelopes me in a tight, comforting hug.

This can't be happening. How could Trouble die? *Abba, what are you doing?* I'll never hear Trouble crack his jokes again. Laughter will be stricken from my world without him.

I let Courage hold me, and we sob as one. Pain sears through my heart and reaches his, binding us together. When I run out of tears, he puts his finger under my chin and lifts my head to study my eyes, much like Manly would've. Why did he abandon me when I needed him? I'm going to track him down —so help me—and demand answers.

"Did you hear that? You have a new name. Trouble renamed you Brave."

"But I'm not brave." Pushing him away, I wrap my arms around myself and rock back and forth. "I'm a coward. *I* should've been in there. Not him. It's my fault. He died for me. For us! He didn't deserve this."

I struggle to catch my breath. This isn't the way it was supposed to turn out. We were supposed to save him.

Courage cups the small of my back. "No, he didn't deserve this, but neither do you."

I turn from him. *Why Abba? Why did this have to happen? I need your strength more than ever. I need your peace. I'm going to trust you, Abba. Trust you have a bigger plan in all of this.*

Courage snaps me out of my reverie. "See everything you've done? You traveled to the Gliding Lands. You went into that temple, into horror itself. You saved Happy. You tried to save Trouble. You *are* Brave. That's what I'm going to call you from now on. Brave is your new name because you're no longer afraid. Abba's made you a new person."

Brave.

The word rings through my skull. It's true. I've changed. Grown. I have an amazing God. Amazing friends and family. A new person resides within this body of mine, no longer afraid. Abba gives me strength.

I'm no longer weak.

I'm no longer Fear.

I am Brave.

THE END

Do not miss the continuation of
Fear's story in

Living Brave

Book Two of the Gliding Lands.

Coming Soon from L2L2 Publishing.

Thank you!

What a journey creating *Ending Fear* has been. Whew! But what a truly exciting experience. Nothing short of amazing.

I'm going to apologize in advance to anyone I missed. This has been a long, long process, and I'm sure this list should name more people. If you were even the slightest bit a part of the process that helped produce my book baby, *Ending Fear*, I thank you. Even if my scattered brain couldn't remember to put your name on here.

For my Mom, for beta reading. Who also gave me a love for storytelling, through years of encouraging us to read, and reading books out loud to us when we were young (American Girl books, anyone?) For helping me remember grammar and paragraphing basics that had been long forgotten after years of letting my brain turn to mush. (AKA — AfterKidBrain)

For Mrs. Carol Bohlsen, my elementary school teacher who gave me a love for writing. Thanks for making us write two full books per school year for three years straight. Without you I never would have had story structure ingrained in me or a love for creating a finished story product.

For Mrs. Olson, my other elementary school teacher who I

made a promise to in 6th grade that someday I would write a book. Well, guess what, Kristin? (I can call you that now that we're both adults) I DID IT!

For Amy Palmer and Shirl Burton for being awesome and quick beta readers. Your help and encouragement were so valuable. Amy, you have no idea how nice it is to have someone come up to me at church and *want* to discuss my book and all things bookish. I appreciate you so much.

For Dallen Clark for your amazing help. I needed all those helps so badly. Also for being my fastest beta (three to four days!!!!). You rock, man! I wish you all the success you could hope for.

For Lynette Fugett, Lacey Fugett, Amanda Forsting, and Lucy Nel for giving me the juice to keep at it. Your encouragements were posted on my door through the whole process. I want you to know how much I appreciate the compliments. It's a good feeling to know people love your story and are rooting for it. Every time I would get down or feel like giving up, all I had to do was go to that door and read your words. It was one of the most valuable things that kept me going. Thank you from the bottom of my heart for being willing to read my work (Oh, that scary first draft!) when others were too busy.

For everyone who helped me work on my query letter at AQC. You all helped me through those two-to-three months, gave me laughs, advice, inspiration, and thoroughly confused me. It was great.

For all my crit partners: Liz Newsom, Laurie Lucking, Sarah Bennett, Lucy Nel, Robin Scobee, Jebraun Clifford, Hannah Duggan, Jill Shope Hackman, Vicky P., Melinda Allen, Elizabeth Kitchens, and Jason W. Your enthusiasm and encouragement have been priceless.

Anyone who has ever helped me with even one page, I salute you.

For Dean Rich for helping with the first ten chapters, your advice was so invaluable. You inspired me and pushed me to do better.

For Andrea Graham for helping with the first 50 pages. You rock!

For Nadine Brandes, my developmental editor. I had so many missing pieces before you got your hands on my manuscript. You helped me add over 6,000 words to this story. Each of them was sorely needed. Thank you.

For my copy editor Elizabeth Miller. Thanks!

For Jeff Gerke for critiquing the first five pages at a seminar, and all the helpful advice I've learned from you through listening to your teachings.

For Robin Patchen for critiquing my last 20 pages. You made my ending much stronger, and for that I'm forever grateful.

For Loretta Gamboe for helping with the first seven chapters. Thank you. I wish you blessings on your own writing career.

Thank you to Nicki Bishop and Ellen Kheller for being great beta readers!

For Lucy Nel, my bestie, my crit partner, and my rock. You cheered me on and held my hand through it all. Your friendship is something I cherish. I literally could not have gotten this far without all your love, support, friendship, and encouragement. Also when you would kick my butt into gear or helped whip my head back on when it was in the clouds. I owe so much of this story to you.

For Sharon Rene Dick, my friend and faithful crit partner.

Thank you Brandy Vallance and Lauren Brandenburg for

the awesome endorsements. I appreciate it!

For my blog buddies, Lucy Nel, Robin Scobee, and Jebraun Clifford (now Lani Forbes and Nicki Bishop too!), who have helped me improve my craft, you are great friends and wonderful gals to work with.

For everyone who helped me on Scribes with *Ending Fear*: Rebekah Millet, Jill Donaldson, Jane Simmerman, Mike Blaylock, Hannah Colvin, Jim Robar, Ron Estrada, Audrey Appenzeller, Pat, and Melissa Doelle. I apologize if I've missed anyone.

For all my Dorks. Thank you for being an awesome street team!

For Laura Pol. You are beyond amazing, girl. I can't even. You are just the sweetest thing ever.

For the entire Realm Makers group. You Realmies are amazing. Anytime I needed advice or just wanted to chat, there you were. Ready with encouragement, laughs, and advice. I love you people.

For all my friends who came up to me in person and asked me how my writing was going. (Rani and Blane Nelson, I'm looking at you!) That meant the world to me. You have no idea.

For all my Facebook friends who've encouraged and supported me with comments and likes on my author page. Your encouragement helped get me to where I am today.

Thanks to Sara Helwe Digital Arts who did my fabulous cover. It's so lovely! I've had so many compliments on it. You totally rock, Sara!

I want to give a ginormous thank you to my publisher (Love2ReadLove2Write Publishing) Michele Israel Harper, for believing in me and my story so much, and giving me a chance despite an already busy schedule. For your enthusiasm and excitement about doing this project with me. For helping improve my craft as my editor, publisher, and friend. I cherish you.

For Chad, my best friend. You've always believed in me and given me the drive to keep going. You've been my biggest fan and strongest supporter. I truly don't deserve all the confidence you have in me, but I'll take it. I love you, babe. And no, I don't ever plan on leaving you once I "make it big." See, there, you have it in writing for the whole world to see. You can stop asking me that now. Lol.

For Jesus Christ, for giving me the gift of storytelling, fingers to write, a brain to think, and creativity to create worlds and characters alike. You truly are the only reason I was able to get published. Thank you, Lord, for all your many blessings!

It literally took an army to get this book out there. I couldn't have done it without each and every one of you. Thank you from the bottom of my heart.

About the Author

Deanna Fugett's heart belongs to writing. Author of edgy YA Dystopian fiction with an underlying message of hope, this stay-at-home mom of four focuses on writing as much as humanly possible. She was published at the young age of six in a local newspaper and is excited to be published again. It only took twenty-six years. She enjoys the thrill of writing fiction that deals with intense topics and prays it will impact people for the better. Visit www.DeannaFugett.com to learn more about her.

Reviews

Did you know reviews can skyrocket a book's career? Instead of fizzling into nothing, a book will be suggested by Amazon, shared by Goodreads, or showcased by Barnes & Noble. Plus, authors treasure reviews! (And read them over and over and over…)

If you enjoyed this book, would you consider leaving a review on Amazon, Barnes & Noble, Goodreads, or perhaps even your personal blog? Thank you so much!

More from L2L2 Publishing

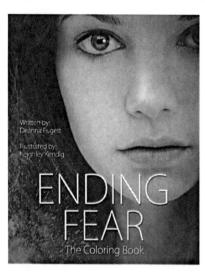

More from L2L2 Publishing

If you enjoyed this book, you may also enjoy:

Brenna James wants three things for her sixteenth birthday: to find her history notes before the test, to have her mother return from her business trip, and to stop creating fire with her bare hands. Yeah, that's so not happening. Unfortunately. When Brenna learns her mother is missing in an alternate reality called Linneah, she travels through a portal to find her. Against her will. Who knew portals even existed? But Brenna's arrival in Linneah begins the fulfillment of an ancient prophecy, including a royal murder and the theft of Linneah's most powerful relic: the Sacred Veil. Hold up. Can everything just slow down for a sec? Left with no other choice, Brenna and her new friend Baldwin pursue the thief into the dangerous woods of Silvastamen. When they spy an army marching toward Linneah, Brenna is horrified. Can she find the veil, save her mother, and warn Linneah in time?

More from L2L2 Publishing

If you enjoyed this book, you may also enjoy:

Candace Marshall hates zombies. As in, loathes, abhors, detests—you get the idea. She also refuses to watch horror movies. You can imagine her complete and utter joy when her boyfriend surprises her with advanced screening tickets to the latest gruesome zombie flick. Annoyance flares into horror as the movie comes to life, and Candace finds herself surrounded by real-life, honest-to-goodness zombies. She learns how to shoot and scream with the best of them and surprises herself with—courage? But, just when Candace thinks it can't get worse than zombies, it does. Don't miss this lighthearted adventure, Book One of the Candace Marshall Chronicles.

More from L2L2 Publishing

If you enjoyed this book, you may also enjoy:

Jocelyn washes up on the shore of eighteenth century Ireland, alone, naked, and missing all of her memories. Taken in by a lonely old woman full of plots and schemes for the lovely yet enigmatic creature, Jocelyn knows only one thing. She longs for the sea with every ounce of her being. Yet it tried to kill her. Aidan Boyd loves two things. His ship and the sea. When Jocelyn is thrust upon his vessel in the midst of his superstitious crew, he finds himself intoxicated by her—willing to give up everything for her. He soon finds he cannot live without her. But something holds Jocelyn back. The whisper of another's love. The embrace of water. Does she belong to this world? Or could Jocelyn possibly be from the sea?

CPSIA information can be obtained
at www.ICGtesting.com
Printed in the USA
LVOW11s0022091117
555581LV00001B/35/P